THE POISON CUP

BY
M. G. DAVIS

"There is a way that seems right to a man,
but the end thereof is death."
Proverbs 14:12 KJV

xulon PRESS

To my Savior Who gives me abundant life,
And to Spencer, my husband and best friend, who multiplies all my blessings times two.

Chapter One

He could have shot Farley that day. The scene played through his mind for the millionth time, his haughty, sanctimonious uncle striding up the front steps of the Turner farmhouse on the day of the funeral. Then, when he saw Pete pointing the rifle at him, his mask slipped. His expression turned from pride to abject fear. With precious satisfaction Pete watched Farley beg for his life. The shot rang out and he saw the monster crumple to the ground like a deflating punch toy.

He could have shot Farley that day, just like he imagined it, but if he'd gone to prison for killing him, that would have been one more win for injustice. He couldn't allow Farley to have the last laugh from the grave.

The irony of this present imprisonment did not escape him.

A week ago a cop found him sleeping under some trees, and the deputy threw him in the slammer for vagrancy. He remembered it was October tenth because it was Mary Kate's birthday. The humiliation was more than he could bear. Instead of signing his name, Pete Turner, he'd scratched an "X" and mumbled incoherently, hoping the sheriff might take him for a harmless halfwit and release him. The sheriff of Grimly jail showed no pity. Apparently, he enjoyed lording it over his helpless victims.

Pete ran his hand through his matted hair and beard. It was hard to believe he'd worn a military haircut once as a sailor in the U.S. Navy. Now he looked the part of a halfwit, a victim of the world's injustice. While Farley remained free as a bird, he'd probably rot forever in this remote corner of hell where the guards laughingly referred to him as Prisoner X. How much lower could he fall?

What if he dropped the ruse and demanded his one phone call? No doubt his brother thought he was dead. This was 1955. He'd been out of touch ten years, running from his guilt, his anger, and his hate, but those demons stuck closer than a brother! He laughed at his corruption of the Biblical phrase. If there was a God, He certainly favored rich men like Farley.

Three days of torrential rain and high winds throughout much of the state of Georgia had filled roadways with broken limbs and debris. In Grimly, the sheriff drew upon the occupants of his jail to clean up the mess. He referred to them as a work crew because chain gangs were now illegal in the United States. However, in reality, that was the best way to describe how prisoners were used in Grimly. Eighteen men were divided into two crews. One crew worked the main road in town, a collection of wooden buildings to include a post office, a jail, one hotel, and a general store. Two saloons were still boarded up since the days of Prohibition, which had been repealed nationally, but not in the state of Georgia and certain Southern counties. A steeple church, a school and a row of white frame houses completed the scene. Beyond, small farms dotted the distant landscape.

Prisoner X had been assigned to the second work crew. Those in this group rode on a covered truck to outlying parts where several downed trees and mounds of debris blocked the road out of town. At what would have been sunrise had the sun ever broken through the dull clouds that morning, nine convicts jumped from the truck. They wore horizontal black and white striped prison garb and leg shackles. The guards wore forest green uniforms with the State of Georgia seal sewn on the shoulders and pockets. As each prisoner hit the ground, one of the guards hitched him to a common chain. A heavy iron bowling-size ball was attached between each pair of men for them to drag along as they worked. "Get a move on. Come on. Hurry up," the chief guard said, a massive fellow with hate-filled eyes. He used his rifle as a prod, ordering the men to line up side by side across the muddy road. Another guard released two German Shepherds out of their cages and tied them to a tree, a reminder to the convicts that if somehow any of them managed to get free of his chains and try to run, the dogs would track him down and tear him apart. The rattle and clunk of the iron fetters and the barking of the dogs accompanied the men as they shuffled into place.

Two prisoners were violent criminals. Number 5130 stood about six feet tall, a hefty fellow with small, staring eyes. Number 4850, a slight brown man, wore a black patch over an empty eye socket where the eyeball had been gouged out. These two had committed heinous murders and were carefully watched by the guards. The next eight men were incarcerated for petty robberies with the exception of number 5960, whom the guards designated as Prisoner X. His only crime was having had his money stolen.

The line of nine men continued moving down the road, gathering the detritus, and tossing it into the two dump trucks. Whenever they came to a downed tree, the chief ordered the guards to unhitch X and one of the other less violent prisoners to carry the obstruction out of the way.

Each time he was freed from the common chain, he considered his chances of escape. With the leg shackles he couldn't run very fast. He wouldn't get far before he was shot in the back, just one less for the guards to bother about. Besides, there were the dogs. He considered hiding in one of the trucks under the debris. When the driver took it away to dispose of the load, he could escape. Wishful thinking. The dogs would sniff him out, and there was hardly a moment the guards weren't watching. It was a hopeless situation. He would rot in Grimly. No one back home believed he was still was alive. There was no one to miss him and to try to find him.

Mid-morning, the chief of the guards motioned for one of his men to remove Prisoner X from the longer chain and take him two hundred feet off to the side of the road down close to a copse of trees.

"Hey, Stupid," the guard said to him, thrusting a shovel at him. "Know what to do with this? Can you dig?"

Prisoner X nodded he could. The guard led him down the hill. When they reached the bottom, he was ordered to dig a trench four feet long and three feet wide for a latrine. Under the grey threatening sky, he pulled out the wet ground cover and began to dig.

Before long his shovel struck a wooden object, something in the way. He sighed. Like his life, one problem had followed another since his daddy's death, the day that changed his whole life. Nothing was ever the same after that.

He thrust the edge of the shovel against the piece. He'd have to dig out.

If his daddy hadn't died, Farley would never have gotten the upper hand and taken over the running of the farm, but his mother was weak. Farley was her brother, and with Rusty gone, she let him have his way. Pete would never forgive her.

The thing in the way of his shovel appeared to be a wooden handle. He tried to grab the object and wrench it out of the muck, but the end of it was buried deep.

No, there was no justice in this world for him. At his last job he had argued with his boss over his wages because he'd been shorted. The owner of the garage called him a trouble maker and fired him on the spot. It was their loss. He could always find work. He was an expert mechanic. So, instead of beating the guy's face in, he'd packed up his stuff and hitched a ride up the Tallapoosa River on a fishing boat. Late in the day when he heard the fishermen say they were passing the town of Grimly, he jumped off and swam to shore. After spending that night in the only hotel, he awakened the next morning to find somebody had stolen all his money. He was always able to get more money, but Grimly was an odd town where they didn't cotton to strangers. He found no one to hire him.

Then, his shovel hit something iron. That aroused his interest. With much effort he dug around it before he removed enough mud to extract it. His heart raced when he saw the thing was a sledge hammer.

He eyed the guard who was enjoying a smoke. This was his chance to strike the guard in the head with the mallet, bust the chain connecting his shackles, and run for it. However, a second, watchful guard patrolled from the top of the hill. He'd put the dogs on him. Bending down, he pulled it from the muck and quickly heaved it into some bushes. It thumped when it hit the ground almost as loud as the pounding of his heart. He looked again at his captor. With the rattling of his shackles, the guard didn't hear it.

The guard finished his smoke and threw the butt in the mud. He eyed his prisoner suspiciously. "You finished or you just standing there dreaming? Whatcha dreaming 'bout?" he sneered, coming closer. "What goes on in the head of a halfwit, I wonder." He prodded him with the rifle. "Get a move on. We ain't got all day."

The other guard came down the hill. "What's the hold up?"

"Stupid here is slow. That's what."

The second guard came forward and slammed the butt end of his rifle into the prisoner's back. "Get moving," he said.

His blisters burned under the tight leg bands. He'd heard of men getting gangrene if infection set in. While he finished his digging, the sledge hammer lay in the bushes, taunting him with his inability to put it to use. Afterwards the guard brought him back to the top of the hill and shackled him again to the others.

At mid-day the prisoners were marched back to the truck and given a fifteen minute break for gruel and water. Here they were unofficially allowed to talk to one another. The man with the patch muttered, "You call this food?"

Number 5130 next to him said, "You better get used to it. Nobody leaves Grimly jail. You be buried here less you got some big connections which I bet you ain't got. The sheriff, he never heard of no 'due process.' Likes his nips too." They continued to grumble under their breaths about the food and to fanaticize about seeing family, or getting laid, or getting drunk if they ever got free.

During this break time, each man was called out and accompanied by a guard to take his turn at the latrine. Prisoner X took his turn, and shuffled down toward the trees. His eyes bore into the brush and he could see that the hammer was exactly where he'd thrown it, but how was he to have time to retrieve it and break his leg irons before getting caught? He watched the man with the rifle light up a cigarette. He was the older and the more seasoned of the two subordinate guards, one who didn't take any chances. Standing three feet away, his eyes never left his charge while Prisoner X relieved himself. He realized his chance to escape would not likely come today.

His life had spiraled down to this, a vagrant and a convict on a chain gang. He could rot in a Grimly jail on the back side of nowhere and never be missed. One man's sneering face had driven him from home ten years ago. He had tried to outrun the pain in his chest, and each time he thought he'd beat it, there it was again like a recurring bad dream. Farley was still winning, still disgracing the Turner name. He trudged back to the truck with the guard ambling close behind him. Setting his jaw, he vowed if he ever got free again, he would find a way to get revenge. No more wandering. He'd been a coward long enough. *If* he ever got free...

After the meager food, hardly enough to sustain grown men, the chief guard blew his whistle, signaling for all the prisoners to get back to work. "Pick up that chain. Come on. Get a move on," he bellowed. Back on the road, they lined up again side by side and continued gathering armloads of debris and depositing it in the dump trucks.

By the end of the day, before dusk could begin to settle across the already grey landscape, a drizzle of rain began to fall. The guards, anxious to avoid getting soaked, started rounding up the men, herding them to the covered truck. The first two in line, numbers 5130 and 4850, climbed on, clanging their leg irons. The rest followed in succession. Prisoner X stood at the end of the line. He watched the prisoners ahead of him get on the truck. The dogs were already loaded in their cages. It was his turn to climb up. His mind recoiled with the thought that once on board, it was back to the sheriff's jail. In his mind's eye he could see the hammer lying inaccessible in the bushes where he had tossed it, but of no use to him locked away in the jail. On impulse he motioned to the guard and pointed downhill, "Latrine! Now!"

"Well, I guess you can talk after all. Too late," he was told with a shove.

He doubled over and began to groan. "Now, now," he cried. "Can't wait."

"I said it's too late. Stop your crying." The guard prodded him with the rifle. "Shut up I said and get in the truck."

Alerted by the commotion, the older guard walked over. He considered the situation briefly before he said to his younger subordinate, "You, unlock him. Don't want no accident and no smells in the truck if he messes himself and I gotta ride with him."

The younger guard gave a frustrated grunt, stood his rifle on end and bent down to unhitch the groaning prisoner's shackles from the chain. Cursing him and the rain, he followed him down to the latrine. Prisoner X continued his charade, bent over double and moaning. He staggered down the hill. The rain began to pelt.

"Hurry up, you. Do your business and be quick about it or I might just shoot you and have done with you." The guard reached in his pocket for a cigarette. He had to bend his head and cup his hand to shield the match from the rain. A gust of wind blew it out. He cursed and fumbled for another.

The heavens opened in a downpour. Prisoner X saw his opportunity and lunged at the guard, knocking him down so that his face went smack into the hole the men had used to relieve themselves. While the guard sputtered and cursed, X grabbed the rifle and slammed him in the head with the end of it until he was out cold.

From the top of the ridge, he heard the chief of the guards yelling, "What's taking so long. We're gonna leave the both of you. Get back up here now."

X pulled the hammer from the bushes and sat down in the wet mud. He had only to break the chain connecting the ankle shackles. With all his force, he brought the hammer back and slammed it forward against the connecting chain. He thought it would snap into, but to his dismay, it held together. He hit it again, but without breaking it. Metal clanged upon metal. Glancing up through the curtain of rain, he could see the other guard coming down the hill to investigate. "I'm done for," he muttered. His hands shook from frustration while the pelting rain soaked and chilled him to the bone. If they caught him trying to escape, he'd never see the light of day again. Desperately, he struck the chain. The hammer clanged against it, ringing like an alarm bell, piercing through the sound of the water beating against the ground and the noise of his heart pounding in his ears. He'd been able to take the first guard by surprise while he was intent on lighting a cigarette, but this one coming down the hill was already wary. The chain was mangled, but it held. Maybe the guard would like nothing better than an excuse to shoot him. Again and again he struck the metal links, and again, and again. It was no use. Farley had won. He always won. Bitterly, for good measure he exerted one more desperate swing of the hammer against the chain, and…incredibly…he heard it snap!

He began to run. The rain was coming down in sheets, providing cover for him. By the time the guard reached the one on the ground, even if he yelled for the dogs, the pounding rain would drown out his call. No one would hear the cry for alarm until the guard climbed back up the hill and got to the trucks. By then, Prisoner X would be in the river.

He stumbled his way across a field of stubble, dragging the pain burning into his flesh from the metal bands. The Tallapoosa was just beyond. With every stride, he repeated one angry word reverberating in his heart—and that word was *revenge*.

Chapter Two

In the narrow backroom kitchen of the Crossroads Diner, Charlie Ross guffawed. In his rural southern drawl he was telling Jimmy Garner, the new boy he'd hired, that ole Sheriff Money always insisted on his barbecue with "no fat." Charlie toweled the sweat and tears from his pleasant face and dark hair. Flipping his towel under the metal sink, he moved his short, wiry frame from the sink to the cabinet that was wedged between the range and a chest style freezer. A rotating fan on top of the cabinet whirred in the background. Jimmy propped open the swinging door between the kitchen and the serving area and leaned against the door frame. He glanced back now and then to see if any Monday lunch customers had come in through the front.

The diner, named for its location at the junction of U.S. Highways 21 and 421, had become a popular stopping place for locals and anyone passing through. Charlie served truckers, field hands, and travelers coming from up north as far away as Pennsylvania and New York and from down south as far as Georgia and Florida. He sold Esso gas at the pumps out front, but it was his fresh made barbecue and sweetened ice tea that drew the local customers back time and again. If you weren't a fan of barbecue, you could get burgers and fries and ice cream sundaes. Despite the variety of traffic, with Charlie's good humor and the smallness of the place, a sense of personal, friendly intimacy encouraged a free exchange of local news and gossip.

Charlie lifted hot pads from a hook on the side of the cabinet and pulled a pan of fresh cooked ham from the oven. He set it down on a scorched Formica table. "Money, he comes from over Wilkes County." Charlie paused to slap his side and laugh again. "About six weeks ago he come in and seen me through that door there take a ham like this 'un outa the oven and he calls to me. He says, 'Kin you make me a sandwich outa that? Don't want *no fat*.'"

"No fat? Sure, I can do that. I cut off a slab of that there pure fat about yea thick." He measured a half inch with his thumb and forefinger. "I slapped that slice of fat on the grill, browned it real good and doused it with barbecue sauce. Fixed it on a bun with plenty of slaw and a thick slice of tomato and served it up to the sheriff. He flat wolfed it down, licked his lips and said it was the best dad-burned sandwich he'd ever had. 'No fat,' he says," and Charlie laughed some more.

The dancing light in his eyes reflected the fun in his joke, just part of the long-standing game of one-upmanship between the local lawmen and the likes of Charlie. Growing up in the Appalachian foothills of Wilkes County, he was part of a clannish breed of family and their neighbors who achieved notoriety as moonshiners and bootleggers. Moonshine, as everyone in the mountains of North Carolina knew, was the illegal, untaxed whiskey distilled "under the light of the moon" away from the prying eyes of the government revenuers. Those who produced it became known as "moonshiners." "Bootleggers" were those who hauled it to the customers or distributers. The term "bootlegger" is said to have originated when laws against selling alcohol to the Indians caused the traders to hide flasks of liquor in their boots to avoid detection.

When there was a lull in the diner, as there was now after the breakfast customers had left and before the lunch scene got hectic, Charlie loved to entertain anyone who would listen to his stories of his former days in the whiskey business. "In '42, I was married and with three young ones," he said, "but I did my duty and enlisted in the Second World War. It was just luck I reckon I had the opportunity to go to cooking school. After the War ended, I opened the diner 'instead of going back to the whiskey business, but I still proudly identify with my Scotch-Irish ancestors and that fiercely independent spirit of theirs. Their long history of home-brewing and their special whiskey recipes made it possible to survive through generations." Charlie paused to wipe his hands on a towel and then proceeded to bone the ham. "Way back in the 1700's the British government started claiming that the only legal whiskey carried the English seal. They slapped a tax on the homemade brew and them Scotch-Irish ancestors of mine fled to America. They spread to Pennsylvania and New York and from there to states that later become Virginia, North Carolina, Tennessee, Georgia and Kentucky. When my ancestors was settling in the foothills of western North Carolina, their farms was small and the red clay hard."

He looked up to make sure Jimmy was paying attention. "Now contrary to what you might be thinking, those great southern plantations were never a part of the scene, not where my ancestors settled. And it was the Indians that taught them how to grow corn and how it could thrive in the rocky red clay soils. But, think about it. The corn had to be hauled down from the mountains in bulky sacks to be sold. When they learned they could take a bushel of corn worth fifty cents at the market and distill it into the three gallons of corn liquor, easier to tote and worth an unbelievable two dollars apiece, well any idiot could see that was the better way. Distilling corn into whiskey made sense to their practical minds. Distilled liquid corn became the perfect solution to their impoverished lives."

Charlie began chopping the ham and scraping it from the chopping board into a pan. "From that time on those folks believed God intended them to make whiskey. The way they saw it, God made the corn that grew on the slopes of the hills, the wood to fire the stills and the tumbling streams of cold mountain water to cool them coils to condense the alcohol into a liquid. Like their ancestors before them, my people and their neighbors considered moonshine nothing more than an extension of their agriculture, and bootlegging was simply delivery of their farm product to market."

He stood up, and after covering the pan of chopped ham with foil, he put it in the refrigerator. Then he continued chopping and sorting the scraps, separating the good from the gristle. "If you learned your southern history, Jimmy, you'd know that the economic depression that came after the Civil War killed the South. I remember my grandpa telling me it felt like when you were already knocked down and gasping for breath, then that there Great Depression just came rolling over you to finish you off. You can understand, can't you, how southerners compared that Federal Government up North and its laws to some foreign nation trying to interfere with their way of life? They especially despised them reviving a 1794 tax on whiskey to pay off government war debts and inventing the Internal Revenue Service to collect it. They believed they had a God-given right to survive in the ways they knew how. And that hasn't changed any. They don't cotton to government interfering." Charlie grinned with pride. "My great uncle Elmo made his moonshine in those hills and hollows of the misty green lands and rocky slopes that reminded him of his Irish homeland. He was mad that his side lost the war and said he wasn't payin' no tax to 'that furin government' that was tryin' to profit off his hard labor. He vowed never to pay a cent of tax on it. He used a telescope to keep an eye out for tax collectors and federal agents that were always showing up at his farm trying to find his stills."

Charlie pulled up the edge of his apron and wiped his face. "Despite the end of national prohibition more than twenty years ago, bootleggers are still prospering in Wilkes County. Before Sheriff Money came on the scene, local law enforcement mostly looked the other way because they couldn't with clear conscience arrest their own family and neighbors. The federal agents were not so easily put off, though. And now a man'll still go to prison if an agent catches him hauling unlicensed liquor or if they find him with his stills. The challenge for those agents is finding the stills and catching the bootleggers." He grinned. "Fortunately for the "shiners" there aren't many federal agents around. The local people won't help the Feds because they dislike and distrust them, and usually the local sheriffs resent government agents coming on their territory. Sheriff Money, however, ran his election campaign on the claim that he would crack down on the moonshiners. Like a lot of campaign promises, though, this one's fallen through the cracks because Money and his deputies have found it harder to catch those shiners than they figured on. Even though they boast of having better cars with two-way radios, they find the surviving bootleggers challenging because the shiners still have the fastest cars. Besides the shiners know these rough country roads like the back of their hand, and law enforcers usually end up confused and lost. I still see it as a game of foxhunting." Charlie laughed. "Trying to outrun and outsmart the law is a tradition ingrained in us present and former bootleggers from our heritage. It's about the wily foxes outsmarting the sniffing dogs."

He told Jimmy, "I reckon everybody within a fifty-mile radius of Wilkes was in the whiskey business at one time or another. Those sheriffs would try to run us down. It was a race, but we had the best cars by far. The revenuers would try to catch a bootlegger in a curve and bump him at an angle, so he'd spin out, but we learned how to slow down just a bit, wait for the revenuer to get close, then we'd gun it, sending him spinning off the road."

By now Charlie had forgotten the ham. His eyes glowed with nostalgia. "We got hot rod parts from California for our cars. They took to putting cowcatchers on their bumpers to hook onto ours when we were carrying a full load, climbing uphill, and going slow. That way they could put on the brakes and slow us down so they could get us, but we came up with putting our back bumpers on with coat hangers. When they'd run up and grab on, we give it the gas and the bumper would tear loose and roll up under their cars. By the time they got loose, we were gone. Another thing they did, they'd shoot holes in our radiators. When the water leaked out and it overheated, we'd have to stop and they could confiscate our liquor. Then they'd get the car and tow it to the courthouse and sell it. The sheriff got a bunch of money when the bootleg cars sold. After that, we got to sending another car to follow the one with the load of moonshine. Then when the sheriff came, the second car would block him, run him in the ditch, bump him, whatever he needed to do so the car with the liquor could get away."

The front screen door to the dining area slammed and a voice called out, "Anybody here?"

Charlie blinked and grinned. "Speak of the devil." He moved from the kitchen to turn on the grill. The grill space was separated from the serving area by a lunch counter lined with eight wooden bar stools with seats covered in red plastic. Between the counter and the screen door at the front entrance, several square tables with four chairs each filled the space. Red-checkered vinyl "cloths" covered the tables. Charlie nodded for young Jimmy to serve Sheriff Curtis Money and Deputy Lance Ward where they were sitting down at the counter. The sheriff, six feet tall and well-fed, seemed imposing even when seated, despite his rounded, slouching shoulders. He had curly, dark hair he kept short and neatly groomed. It was his bushy eyebrows with a naturally exaggerated arch that gave him a sinister look. Deputy Ward was a thin, blond fellow, who seemed to recede into nothingness next to the sheriff.

Jimmy passed menus to the two lawmen and greeted the next customers coming in the door. The first was tall, but bent Walter "Hud" Hudspeth. Behind him came Bennie Farnes, a mill worker considered one of the local dirt track heroes. He was followed by one of the local farmers, Johnny Purdue, wearing bib overalls.

The sheriff put down the menu. "Kin Charley make me one of them pork sandwiches? He knows how I like it."

Charley said without turning around, "Sure thing, Curtis. How about you, Lance? You want the same?"

"No, I'll have a burger and fries and some of that ice tea," Lance said.

Charlie slapped a sizzle of the pork fat on the grill. "I'll have it right up, Curtis," he said, giving Jimmy a wink.

Soon the place filled up with the buzz of voices, the smell of frying food, and the smoke rising in clouds from Hud puffing his cigarettes and drinking his coffee. Jimmy waited tables. Charlie turned from the grill long enough to see a tall fellow about thirty with a brown, cow licked flattop, facial stubble and intense, brooding eyes take the last stool at the counter. Stooping to grab a stack of frozen burgers from a cooler under the counter, he recognized him as the son of an old family friend. So, this was the Pete Turner he'd been hearing was winning races at the dirt tracks all around the Piedmont. It had been at least ten years since he'd seen him, but the resemblance was unmistakable. Standing to momentarily face the younger man, he said, "You Pete Turner, Rusty Turner's boy?" He turned back around to slap a beef patty onto the sizzling grill.

"Was."

Charlie made no comment while he dished up Hud's barbecue sandwich. Many from around here remembered Rusty Turner as a prosperous bootlegger who died over fourteen years before in '42. With the revenuers on his tail, he'd been running a trunk load of his famous Turner

22

moonshine when his whiskey car spun out of control and rolled down the side of Brushy Mountain.

Charlie's family had been the Turner's closest neighbor with their farms a mile apart. Rusty Turner and Bill Ross went way back and were probably related by marriage somewhere down the line. During the good times, Pete and his brothers hauled their daddy's moonshine out of the mountains and down Highway 421 to make deliveries to the speakeasies in Charlotte, Winston, Greensboro, and even into Virginia. Charlie and his brothers often were running the same roads to haul their corn liquor.

It had been nine months since Pete's escape from Grimly. Running for his life in the pouring rain, he had hidden out in a farmer's barn. When the sun came out the next morning, he observed the wife hanging out her wash on a clothesline. As soon as she went inside, he grabbed a pair of trousers and a shirt to change out of the prison stripes. The waist was too big and the legs too short, but he had had to make do with them until got out of the state of Georgia. At the first opportunity, he obtained scissors and a razor to cut his hair and shave his beard. When the sheriff at Grimly sent deputies out to recapture him, they found no one who could say they had seen a halfwit in prison stripes.

From the outskirts of Grimly he'd hitched rides to Rome, Georgia and from there to Spartanburg, South Carolina where he found work as a mechanic in a local garage. Talking to guys hanging out around there, he heard names of bootleggers he knew of from around Wilkes who were winning on the dirt tracks. Some were even making themselves heroes at Daytona and some of the larger speedways. He was told that with the boom in new car sales since the War, you could get a '39 or '40 Ford body for fifty dollars. With another fifty you could get an engine. Intrigued, Pete bought a junk car and rebuilt the motor. On his off time he began hanging around the dirt tracks and soon took up a challenge to compete. He couldn't believe how easily he could win. The prize money wasn't much, but he thrilled to the speed. It reminded him of earlier times when he and his brother Johnny hauled liquor for his daddy. Everybody was saying the bootleggers learned to drive running from the revenue agents. Their fear of prison or losing their load made them heedless of any other danger.

Nonetheless, for Pete Turner, racing was merely a side interest. When he left Grimly in October, he meant to acquire a few dollars to live on, enough to make his way home, where he intended to do some investigating. There must be those around Wilkes County who knew that Farley Oaks wasn't all he appeared to be. If he could persuade them to talk, he'd expose Farley for what he was. It would be the best day of his life to see his uncle stripped of his arrogance and sitting behind bars. Wonder how *he'd* like prison stripes. Pete smirked with satisfaction just imagining it.

Lance asked, "So you're Rusty Turner's boy. How long you been back?"

"I reckon about two months since I crossed the state line," Pete said without looking up.

"So you the Pete Turner that beat out everybody last night at Billy Hinton's cow pasture?" Charlie said. "The breakfast crowd was talking 'bout it this morning. Had no idea it could be you. People around here been assuming you was dead."

Lance picked at a hang nail on the side of his thumb. "Rusty's other boy, your brother, Robert, he's an attorney in Wilkes. You're the younger one ain't you?"

Pete nodded.

"So, you been making a name for yourself racing at the dirt tracks. Don't remember ever hearing you was racing before, except drag racing maybe, but then them dirt tracks sprung up ever where since the War." Lance paused to bite off the hang nail. "You didn't stick around here long after you come back from the War. You musta been running from something seems to me." He turned to look at Pete. "Maybe you robbed or killed somebody. Else why would a boy leave like that and not even let his family know of his whereabouts?" He looked back at his nails. "Well mark my words. Evil deeds 'will catch up with ya."

Pete concentrated on the menu and tuned out Lance, whose ruminations reminded him of an old cow and were equally boring.

Lance continued, looking satisfied that he had the attention of the eavesdroppers if not Pete's. "You just disappeared like Charlie said, and nobody ain't heard from you in years, not even your ma. It was generally concluded you was dead. Ain't nobody with a conscience don't let their ma know and wouldn't even come to her funeral if she died."

Between coughs Hud said, "We sure didn't know you were *that* Pete Turner, Rusty's boy."

"So, racing what brought you back here?" Lance asked.

Pete kept his head down. He'd already memorized the menu.

Deputy Lance touched his arm to address him. "Hey, Turner, you still with us?"

Pete looked up, annoyed.

"I asked you is racing what brings you back here?"

Pete got up from the stool and stood to his feet, showing his back to Lance, ignoring his question.

Sheriff Money turned to Pete, his eyes full of concern. "Don't you be trying to foller in your daddy's outlawing ways. You keep in the bounds of the law and strive to be an upstanding citizen like your Uncle Farley."

Pete tightened his jaw. It might have been a mistake to come in here, but he needed to get the lay of the land. He should have expected that his return would create something of a sensation, like he'd come back from the dead.

Sheriff Money continued his lecture. "You ain't planning to come back here and haul no illegal likker are you, boy? 'Cause I'll catch you if you do. I'll catch you and lock you up. I don't care how fast you think you are. We've cleaned up most of them illegal stills around here. People gone to work at honest jobs in the mills." The sheriff took a big bite of his sandwich and chewed with a look of satisfaction. He washed it down with a gulp of tea.

Pete said to Charlie, "How about fixing me a chopped barbecue sandwich and some ice tea." He slipped to a table in the back corner. The sheriff shook his head in disgust at Pete's dismissiveness while the conversation at the counter continued.

"Not so, Sheriff," Hud said from behind the counter where he was helping himself to a coffee refill. "They've gone to work in the mill because somebody's forcing them to sell." The comment sent Hud into a coughing spell. He reached in his pocket for another cigarette. When he got his voice back, he said, "Who you reckon is putting the pressure on the farmers?"

"Chris Riley told us it was some feller out of Charlotte, big textile manufacturer there, was the one behind it," Jimmy said.

Sheriff Money took another bite. "Well, I don't reckon I know there's any pressure other than economics," he said, chewing and gulping another swig of tea. "With the price of sugar they can't make no money and it's just as well cause what they're doing is illegal. Makes my job upholding the law easier. What's left over I have to clean up. That's all. And I know there's some been making that whiskey a long time and they're at it big as ever, but we'll get 'em."

"Some folks is saying you putting the bootleggers out of business so as Farley Oaks can buy 'em up," said Johnny Purdue.

Deputy Ward replied, "You know, Johnny, my momma always said, 'Believe half of whatcha see and none of whatcha hear.'"

Bennie Farnes spoke up, "Well now I reckon Mr. Oaks don't need to get his hands dirty with breaking the law. He's plenty rich and he done a lot of good for the people around here."

Johnny said, "Lot of folks 'round here don't remember like I do that them Oaks was dirt poor. Their daddy was an alcoholic, but Farley, he run off to Georgia and some say he made his money in bootlegging whiskey and other ill-gotten gain."

"Don't be spreading rumors, Johnny," Bennie said. "I don't believe Mr. Oaks was ever doing any of that illegal stuff, but irregardless of his past, now he's the most successful and upstanding citizen we got around here. We're lucky to have him. Mr. Oaks has got his fingers in a lot of pies, all legit, I might add. Besides his Ford dealership, he owns several gas stations, and no telling what other successful enterprises because he don't flaunt his success. Now take this race track I hear he's going to build, the biggest in the state, and it's going to be located right here in our county near Wilkesboro."

"Yeah. I've heard the rumor," Johnny agreed, "but we ain't seen nothing happen yet."

The front screened door opened and a scruffy, wiry little fellow came in with a child about ten. Her simple pink dress was soiled and her face was streaked with dirt. She attracted Pete's notice because although she appeared grubby and unkempt, underneath the dirt, she was pretty with her pale ivory skin and long blonde hair. She seemed a strange companion for the ferret-faced man she was with. Surely she wasn't his child. The man wore grey pants and a grey cotton shirt with "Wooten Plumbing" stitched over the pocket. Pete caught a glimpse of the girl's blue eyes, though she kept them cast down. It wasn't his business, but he couldn't help but stare at her.

The strange pair sat down across from Pete at the only remaining vacant table. Something about the man was repulsive. His shifty eyes gave Pete a creepy feeling but it was the child that held Pete's attention. For several minutes he couldn't take his eyes off her. Because of how she kept her head down and made no eye contact with anyone, Pete sensed she was afraid. Jimmy approached them with two menus. The man picked up one, glanced over it quickly, and then ordered for himself and the child, who so far had not spoken. Pete wondered if she had a speech problem and couldn't talk, like maybe she was deaf and dumb, yet she made no attempt at sign language or in any other way to communicate with the man accompanying her.

Jimmy, wiping off their table, made an effort to engage her in conversation. "What's your name?" he asked. When she made no reply, he said, "You got pretty hair. I got a niece probably same age as you. How old are you?" She didn't speak. Jimmy asked the man, "You from around here? She your daughter?"

"Naw. My sister's kid. Well, she *was* my sister's. Terrible wreck. He put his hand over his heart as if to show the depth of his pain. "Her mama and daddy's both dead. Naw, she's not mine. I'm taking her to live with my older sister in Virginia. This sister, she ain't got any kids and she loves this one. She does love this one. The least I can do. Take her to my sister where she can get lots of love and care."

When Pete heard the man's explanation, he decided he'd judge him wrongly. He expected the worst of people and usually wasn't disappointed. Apparently, the man didn't know anything about children. He was at least doing his duty as the kid's uncle.

Jimmy finished taking down their order and left it near the grill for Charlie. Then he went about his work wiping off tables and taking customers' payments at the register.

Pete soon lost interest in the man and his charge, paying no attention when Jimmy took a carry-out bag to him or when Hud went out front to pump gas for the man's truck. Pete barely glimpsed through the open door to notice the black paneled truck drive away. Only later in another place he would see it again and remember.

Jimmy brought Pete's sandwich and tea. Pete anticipated eating uninterrupted, chewing his food slowly, and wondering about how his brother would react if he stopped by his law office to see him. He was certain Robert thought he was dead like everybody else. Thirty miles away in Wilkesboro, he probably hadn't heard anything about Pete's victories at the rural dirt tracks. Pete was really curious to know what was happening at the Turner farm, what it was like after ten years, but he wanted to avoid seeing his mother. *I will never forgive her because she welcomed that snake of a brother to the farm when Rusty had never permitted it. Daddy didn't explain why because he didn't gossip or talk bad about people, but we knew he had his good reasons.* Pete hoped he could glean some information about the farm from Robert. He was lost in these thoughts when Bennie Farnes, with his Elvis style side burns and wavy, slicked back hair, sat down at his table. Pete looked up with an expression of annoyance. He didn't want company.

"You're Pete Turner."

"Who wants to know?"

Short, slender and greasy, the man held out his hand. "Bennie Farnes." Pete ignored the hand and Bennie, looking undeterred, leaned forward and put his elbows on the table. In his mid-twenties, he was a few years younger than Pete. "So, Farley Oaks is your uncle. It's a pleasure to meet a relative of Mr. Oaks. I wish I could thank the great man in person. I had a talk with him once. I bought my first car, '51 Ford, from his dealership in Wilkesboro. He happened to be in there at the time and struck up a conversation with me. He won't tryin' to sell me or nothing since I already signed the papers and all. I told him 'bout working at the textile mill down at Winston and that I just come from a funeral that morning for my sister's husband. He worked at the mill same as me. Had a heart attack and died. Only thirty-two years old. Her and her little Susie, they were about to be put outa their trailer and didn't have no place to go." Bennie wiped a tear from his eyes. "That fine man offered to put her and her little girl in one of his rental apartments and said she didn't have to pay nothin' until she could. He didn't have to do that. And he was true to his word. I helped them move in. She coulda stayed as long as she needed to. I never could figure out why she just up and left after three weeks." He scratched his head. "Don't know why when Mr. Oaks said she could stay as long as she needed to. Don't know why she did that." He shook his head. "Maybe she was too proud to take his charity. But Farley Oaks is a nice man. He's a local hero if you ask me."

Pete narrowed his eyes, "You got a right to your opinion, I reckon," he muttered. He picked up his sandwich, hoping this pesky fellow would get the hint.

Farnes spoke with increased animation, "Did you hear he's givin' land for a new school? It'll be named in his honor, Farley Oaks Elementary. Got a ring to it, don't it?"

Pete said irritably, "Do you mind if I eat in peace?"

Bennie seemed taken aback. His eyes zeroed in on Pete. "Say, what's...what's eatin' you? Farley Oaks is a great man. You oughta be proud and honored that he's your uncle."

Pete decided he'd heard just about all the adulation of Farley Oaks his stomach could stand. With the blood rushing to his face, he stood up and grabbed the short man by the shirt collar, knocking over a chair. It clattered to the floor as he shoved Bennie up against the wall. Speaking through clenched teeth he said, "Farley Oaks is no hero. He's dirt. He's scum. He's a slime ball. And that's a fact. And you," he shouted, pointing to the sheriff, "you claim to be cleaning up around here. If you weren't after the decent people who just want to make a living, you might not be letting the scum go free."

The place was still as death. Pete turned on his heels and walked to the register. The sheriff got up and moved toward Pete. "You walking a thin line," he said in a lowered voice, placing his hand on Pete's shoulder in a fatherly gesture. "Don't you even think about comin' back here and causin' trouble. Your daddy was no hot head. But you…What ails you, son?"

Pete knocked the sheriff's hand from his shoulder. "What do you know about my daddy? And I'm not your son," he said with a sneer. "If you're going to arrest me, then arrest me, but otherwise, keep your hands off me."

"Everybody knew your daddy," the sheriff said in a soft tone that implied he was using his utmost patience. "He got a lot of respect. Even my father-in-law, the sheriff back when your daddy was alive, respected him for the good man he was. He disapproved of his whiskey business and had to send him to jail a time or two when he confiscated his load, but he liked him. I heard him say more than once, 'That Rusty Turner minds his own business and don't say nothing mean about nobody.'"

Pete continued to smirk in defiance. "*Tried* to send my daddy to jail, you mean. He never could find his stills. It was my brother, Tad he sent to jail."

For a moment the sheriff's eyes narrowed and he fingered the handcuffs hanging from his belt, but he let his hand slide away. "I'm trying to help you," he said with a stern look, "but you want trouble, we can give it to you."

Taking his wallet from his back pocket, Pete threw two one dollar bills next to the register and pushed past the sheriff. He walked toward the door, aware all eyes were on him, even as everyone in the place had more or less resumed eating.

"Don't reckon he's ever gonna forgive Farley Oakes," Lance said to the sheriff. "Still thinks Farley was trying to take his daddy's place when all he was doing was helping his ma, Eugenia, run that big farm."

Pushing the screened door open, about to step outside in the bright sun, Pete came face to face with a slender young woman a head shorter then he, coming in the diner. Caught by the sunlight, her untamed mass of red hair seemed to Pete like tongues of wildfire that licked her shoulders and flickered about her oval face. He almost expected the collar of her blouse to burst into flame from the brush of her hair. "Excuse me?" she said with a quizzical smile, her green unflinching eyes holding him captive. Then he realized he was blocking her way in. Mumbling an apology, he let her pass.

"Hi Charlie," she said as she floated to the counter. "It's Monday so I came to pick up Daddy's pound of chopped barbecue. He expects me to bring it on Mondays, you know."

"Myra Claire," Charlie said, with a welcoming smile.

"*Myra Claire.*" The name echoed in Pete's head. *Who's her daddy* he wondered.

He walked out the door and around the back of the diner. He was still contemplating the beautiful green eyes and flaming red hair when he noticed a stranger leaning up against the hood of his '39 Ford. Short and dark, the man looked very Italian. Then Pete remembered him and a shadow crossed his face. "Salvino Pezzo," he said.

Chapter Three

Salvino Pezzo was born in the interior of Sicily in a poor hillside village. All his old man ever talked about was his dream of coming to America. He saved every penny he could, put the money in a box he kept under the bed, and lived for the day he had enough to pay the steamship fare to the place where the streets were paved with gold. Every April, when the boat sailed from Palermo without the Pezzos, Antonio felt remorse that another year was lost to them. They were missing out on the golden opportunities that awaited them in a rich, new land across the sea.

In 1910 his brother agreed to lend him the money to make up what he needed for the fare, and on April 22, 1912, when Salvino was eight years old, the family sailed from Palermo in the crowded section of a creaky ship to a world alien beyond their imaginations. His father found the streets were not paved with gold in the Lower East Side of New York City, but tar and concrete. From their quiet, sparsely populated Sicilian village, they had arrived in a place crowded, noisy, strange, and terrifying. They had no knowledge of the language, customs, values, or behaviors. They had exchanged their familiar poverty for a meaner one. Hoping his children would benefit from the free education, and having no money to return to Sicily, Antonio endured the cultural shock of the new land. Salvino's lack of interest in school and repeated truancies became a great disappointment to Antonio.

The neighborhood was filled with immigrant boys who had quit school because they didn't know the language. They were restless for better than what they saw their parents had. They watched their fathers work long hours, come home exhausted, and make hardly enough money to keep the family in food and shelter. Salvino scrounged for money any way he could get it. He carried packages for a local hat maker, a grocer, or anybody who needed an errand boy. However, he soon learned there were easier ways: He joined his contemporaries in the street gangs, robbing stores and grabbing handbags from old ladies, while he dreamed of riches, of someday making a big score. Antonio kept saying every kid in the neighborhood was growing up to be a crook. They were surrounded by crooks, many of them people who were supposed to be legit, like the cops on the beat, the politicians, the shopkeepers and the landlords.

The real pros that Salvino and his friends envied were the rich Dons from the old country who drove around in their big black cars. Their mothers and fathers were scared to death of them, but the kids took note that they were rich, and rich was what counted because the rich got away with anything. Salvino realized quickly that some people had money and some didn't. He made up his mind he would be one of the haves.

There was a significant occasion when he and members of his gang got picked up by a cop because one of them had stolen a leather jacket. Salvino had nothing to do with it, but as he put it, "his old man beat the crap outa him right there in the police station." Sicilian fathers were the law in their own homes and their morality was unbending. Antonio would tolerate no shame brought on the family by a son being arrested, even if he were guilty only by association. After that, the rift between father and son deepened, and Salvino spent less and less time at home, getting ever deeper into crime.

He began delivering drugs for the neighborhood narcotics dealer, hiding them in the hat boxes or grocery packages he delivered. Each week he earned a handful of bills, as much as a hundred dollars some weeks, far more than he earned delivering hats and groceries. In 1923 at the age of nineteen, he got caught and did time in jail for a year. After that he stayed clear of the narcotics business.

Instead, he fell in with some of the local racketeers. These were men like Charles "Lucky" Lucania, Frank Costello, and big Mafia bosses, Joe Masseria and Salvatore Maranzano, Ciro Terranova, and others who were getting rich beyond anyone's wildest imagination bootlegging illegal whiskey. For early in 1919, a new world of crime had suddenly opened up to them when on January 16, the ratification of the Eighteenth Amendment to the Constitution of the United States banned the general manufacture, sale and transportation of intoxicating liquors and beers. However, millions of Americans were not going to stop drinking, thereby opening up a lucrative market to New York gangsters.

In the pay of the rich gangster, the young Salvino found his most profitable work ever, hijacking whiskey deliveries that came off the boats from Cuba and Canada. There was fierce competition among the northern bootleggers during their heyday. Hijacking could accomplish two purposes: getting the liquor to fill an order and at the same time seriously damaging a competitor.

When Prohibition ended, the gangsters and racketeers turned to well-planned loft and warehouse robberies, stealing anything that could be fenced, while they controlled all the gambling as well as other illegal businesses with the help of cops on the take. Salvino continued to work as an underling for the rich bosses, while he planned to one day be a leader instead of a follower. He hated being on the outside looking in while the ones he worked for grew richer and richer.

In 1931during the Castellammarese War between Masseria and Maranzano, guns became a really big business. At that time Salvino came into contact with Angelo Correlli, a New York gun dealer, who found his business exploding by supplying guns to the Mafia bosses. Salvino often came into the gun shop to order or to pick up an order from Angelo for his employer. With business expanding like it was, "Angel" as everyone called him, brought Salvino on to work for him, delivering his merchandize to the warring Mafia factions in and around New York City. In time, Angel promoted him to purchase guns on the black market and introduced him to his contacts up and down the east coast, eventually making him his right hand man. However, Salvino was still discontent that he was working for a rich man rather than becoming one.

It was during the early spring of 1956 that Pete came into contact with Salvino. Having followed the dirt tracks as far north as the state of New York, he caught the attention of the rich Italian gun shop owner. Angel became fascinated with Pete's fearlessness, his skill in handling a car and the chip on his shoulder that seemed to drive him. He sought him out. "I like you, boy," he'd said. "I like watching you. Never saw such hell-bent fearlessness. I want to give you some money, help you make it to the big time in the up and coming NASCAR circuit." He invited Pete to come to his gun shop, where he took him down in the basement to show off his stash of thousands of guns and assault weapons, most of them illegal. When Angel had to take a call upstairs, he left Pete in the company of Salvino, whose glib manner immediately made Pete wary. When he touched Pete's shoulder to direct him toward a particular display, Pete took it as a familiarity that was both condescending and repugnant to him. He would have decked him if Angel had not returned just in time. It was not likely that Salvino meant to offend Angel's newest pet, but simply to ingratiate himself. Besides, the younger man might have gotten the best of him. Salvino wasn't in the fighting shape of his younger days. Since coming to work for Angel and conducting business in suits and silk shirts, he'd fattened up.

Pete was eager to make his exit. He thanked Angel for his offer and said that he'd stick with the dirt tracks, that NASCAR had too many rules and regulations. "Racing's just a hobby," he said. "I like the speed and all, but I'm going home to Wilkes County, North Carolina to my daddy's farm to produce the moonshine that made the Turner name famous with his customers."

"And notorious with the government agents, yes?"

Pete nodded in the affirmative.

"You're sure that's all you've got in mind?" Angel asked. "When I look into your eyes, I see pain and anger."

Pete flinched.

Angel scrutinized him with a sly look. "You know, if you ever need anybody eliminated, somebody that's causing you grief, I got connections."

Pete averted Angel's gaze. "Been away from home too long. Just want to get back and make my daddy's whiskey."

"If you change your mind, you know where to find me," Angel said with a grin. "Remember that and may Lady Luck smile on you."

Glad Angel graciously accepted his refusal, Pete left the meeting in the gun shop, shrugging off Angel's offer like an unwanted coat. For sure he didn't care to be sponsored. He was his own man and he preferred to keep it that way. Furthermore, he was leery of Angel's ties to the Mafia. He had no wish to get entangled in those tentacles. There had to be another way to get his revenge. Even so, Angel left the offer on the table. If that proved the last resort, well, as Angel said, Pete knew where to find him.

Just days after Pete left New York, Angel got wind that Salvino was stealing from him and working some deals on his own. One day he sent two thugs into the shop to remove Salvino with this message: "You ungrateful bastard. After all I've done for you. If I ever see your face again, I'll have it rearranged for you. And if you ever try to move in on my customers again, I will kill you." Then they beat Salvino senseless and threw him in a dumpster. He lived, but his period of recuperation was slow and painful. It was a month before he could walk with a cane.

After he could walk, afraid to show himself anywhere within miles of New York City, he left to go to Florida to try his luck there. However, he needed money. He'd lived fast and loose without ever considering a rainy day. Then he remembered Pete Turner. It didn't take long to pick up his trail from the race tracks and catch up with him in the outskirts of Winston Salem in the tiny place called Brooks Crossroads.

Outside Charlie's diner Pete stood facing Salvino in the July sun. He said, "I have no business with you, Salvino." He opened the door or the Ford. "Get out of my way or I'll knock you out."

"Still full of vinegar, I see. Angel had you pegged. He said one of these days you were going to boil over and explode."

Pete tightened his jaw and turned toward the Italian. "What brings you to Brooks Crossroads, Salvino? Aren't you a long way from home?"

"Business, but since I was coming this way," Salvino lied, "Angel said to check on you. Last time I saw you in the gun shop you said you were headed home somewhere around Wilkes County, North Carolina. I see you made it and I hear you're still tearing up those dirt tracks. Are you producing that famous Turner moonshine yet?"

"That's no business of yours," Pete said with contempt.

I'd like to watch you race some time, see if you're as impressive as Angel says. You got a race coming up?"

Rubbing his chin, Pete studied the broad Sicilian face with suspicion. He'd almost forgotten how much he disliked this man with his penetrating dark eyes and expensive clothes. He wasn't one for trusting anybody, but this Salvino Pezzo had sent up red flags from the first time he'd met him.

"Yeah, I've got a race coming up," Pete said, "but you wouldn't care for it. You'd get your nice clothes dirty. There's a lot of red dust that gets in your lungs, and the crowds are boisterous and too uncouth for your taste."

"You seem to think you know a lot about me," Salvino said, forcing a smile that didn't match the intense, calculating look in his eyes. "I'm guessing it's that Farley Oaks who has you spewing all over the place. He's your uncle, eh?" Sweat ran down the man's neck and dripped from his chin onto his expensive silk shirt.

Pete's eyes narrowed. "What do you know about Farley Oaks?" he demanded.

"Somebody up the road said Charlie's Crossroads Diner was a good place to eat. I walked in just in time to witness your little temper tantrum, whipping up on that fellow smaller than you. There's no subtlety in you Turner. You wear your feelings on your sleeve. Easy to figure why you didn't see me. It's this Farley Oaks that has you boiling over."

"My business with Farley Oaks is none of yours," Pete said.

With pudgy fingers Salvino pulled a silk handkerchief out of his back pocket to blot the droplets of sweat seeping under his gold necklace and glistening on his dark, curly chest hairs. "Why don't you save your antagonism for your enemies? Remember what Angel told you. If you ever needed anybody eliminated, Angel is the man to talk to."

Pete said, "Angel told me *he* had connections, that *he* knew the right people. He didn't say anything about you."

"You have somebody in mind to do the job?" Salvino said.

"You're assuming there is a job. I told you there isn't. I'm not a killer."

"Of course not. Killing is for professionals when there's a need, and here I am at your service with all the connections."

"You're mistaken, Pezzo. I have no business with Angel and none with you. Now get lost."

"Hey it's a free country. It's a little backward compared to the big city, but it has a certain charm, and I'm only passing through. Why don't you be reasonable? Angel likes you. He wants to help you like he said."

"If I want Angel's help, I'll let him know."

"That's not how he does business. He goes through me. He sent me to negotiate. Besides he's out of the country for at least a month. He's in Italy for his ninety-year-old mother's birthday. You couldn't talk to him if you wanted to, but you can talk to me."

Pete put one leg in the Ford. "What's in this for you, Pezzo? Does Angel even know you're here? I told him I wasn't interested in his services. I believe Angel would respect my decision. If you're looking to negotiate with me, I don't have any money. I'm a drifter."

"You're a bootlegger. You can get it. We can do business."

"I'm not a bootlegger any more. Anyway, I don't need your help or Angel's."

"Looks to me like you do. That Sheriff Money in there," Salvino nodded toward the diner, "wasn't he threatening you?"

"Only if I haul liquor," Pete said. "Get out of the way of my door, Salvino."

Stepping aside, Salvino placed a cigarette between his lips and flipped open a gold lighter. Pete bent down and lowered himself into the driver's seat. Once again thoughts of defeat assailed him. His narrow escape from the Georgia chain gang had shocked him into realizing how low the son of Rusty Turner had sunk. He had tried for ten years to outrun his pain. Speed on the dirt tracks had been his only escape, but at the end of the race, the pain was there, waiting like a buzzard hovering over road kill. He needed a permanent solution; he needed to perform his duty. So, what was the going price for a hit man, a real professional like Angel could set him up with? Probably five thousand or even more. He didn't have that kind of money. Right now he was hardly more than a bum, but if he should consider a hit man, it wouldn't come through this sleazy fellow.

Salvino blew smoke from his nostrils. "That Farley Oaks sounds like a powerful man, and maybe he's got that sheriff working for him, like one of those men in the diner said. Better watch your back."

Pete said, "I can take care of my own business."

"I'll be back in a few days," Salvino offered. "Think it over. Give me your final answer then. We can do business."

Pete cranked the engine. Salvino moved aside as Pete spun away, throwing up gravel in his wake. The more Pete thought about Pezzo, the more he convinced himself he should not trust him. Somehow he smelled a rat in that fellow. No, he'd take care of Farley. All he needed to do was ask some discrete questions. Somebody had information they'd be willing to share, unless they were all brainwashed like that fellow Bennie Farnes. Before he did anything, he'd talk to Robert.

Chapter Four

Pete's black '39 Ford was not distinctive on the streets of Wilkesboro, the seat of Wilkes County, where he drove through downtown on this humid Monday afternoon. These automobiles were in common use with many of the area bootleggers and dirt track racers, often one and the same. Here was a venue he'd not seen in ten years, and his emotions surged bittersweet. He parked the Ford on a side street around the corner from the Wilkes County Courthouse, a stately, white neoclassical building covering most of the city block. Behind it was the old red brick jail. Across from that was the new jail where, according to what Charlie had told him, the sheriff's office was located. Pete wanted no encounter with Sheriff Money. He hurried past to find his brother's office.

Pete needed information, mainly about his uncle and the Turner farm. He'd have to be discreet when it came to questions about Farley. He couldn't let Robert know his real motive.

Would his brother even be pleased to see him...or would he yell at him for not letting anyone know his whereabouts for ten years. He wondered if Robert was married. Did he have kids? He couldn't explain why he'd never contacted his only living sibling. The past held him hostage with painful memories, with visions that were never far from his thoughts. The awful knowledge he carried with him cut into his heart.

He'd run away, had passed through states from the east coast to the west, all the time with him thinking he could leave the memories behind. They had haunted him relentlessly. Now he was back.

He passed Spencer's Drugstore and Baumgartner's clothing shop where he'd bought his first suit, the one he wore to his daddy's funeral. After his daddy's accident, his uncle's intrusion into their family was enough cause for four-teen year old Pete to resent him, especially when he believed the sun rose and set over his daddy. With Rusty out of the way, it seemed to Pete this outsider had walked in and taken over like he owned the place. Once entrenched, Farley's arrogance and condescending remarks about his daddy in Pete's hearing further enraged the boy. It convinced him that his uncle had long felt the sting of Rusty's snub. Pete winced at the remem-brance, and yet he could wish this had been his only reason to despise his uncle. No, there were worse things, and Eugenia had put up no resistance!

Well, Farley got his pound of flesh, didn't he?

Pete left the farm soon after his uncle started coming around. He'd begged his mother to let him quit school and run the farm and whiskey business. He'd always helped his daddy and knew his ways of doing things, but Eugenia said "no," declaring that Pete had to go to school. Really, it was Farley who said "no." He made it clear who was in control. So, Pete moved in with his daddy's younger brother, Pete's Uncle Jake, until he finished high school. He avoided the farm and Farley and Farley's skinny, devious brother, Freddie, the idiot Farley set up to directly oversee the farm and liquor stills. Even then, his uncle was careful not to get his own hands dirty. He stayed behind the scenes so that he could appear to be the irreproachable, exemplary citizen.

Oh, how it all came back in a rush…and it rankled. It still rankled. If Pete had only swallowed his pride and stayed at the farm. If he'd been there, he would have seen…he should have prevented the dishonor, the suffering. Instead, at seventeen, he joined the navy. When the War ended, he came home to the shock of discovering that Mary Kate was barely skin and bones, his fault. *If only…*Pete thought. Oh, the many times he had he been around this mental circle, and he always came back to the same place. It was his fault.

Pausing at the next intersection, he stared at the traffic rumbling by on Main Street and pondered his present state of affairs. Farley, for all his pretenses, was still a snake under all the guises of benefactor and fine, upstanding citizen. Pete had no doubt of that, and his foremost mission in seeing his brother was to get enough information to begin his spying. Did Farley come around the farm these days to see Eugenia? Where did he live? Where was he most often seen around town? Charlie didn't know, but his brother would. He might know how much Sheriff Money danced to Farley's tune. If he played his cards right, his brother might even reveal what he knew about that, and most important, who were Farley's other victims? Who could tell him that? Robert would most likely not approve of Pete spying on his uncle, but if Pete was going to expose his uncle's true character, then this was the first step in his plan. It felt good to be finally facing his problem and doing something about it. According to Charlie's directions, Robert's office should be a couple of blocks away.

Pete would have his revenge. Then he would kick Freddie off the Turner land, and he would run everything just like Rusty, just like he'd always intended. He even had his daddy's special recipes and customer list. That serpent had tried to get them, tried to bribe, then threaten Pete for them, but Pete hid them where he was certain Farley would never have them.

The light changed and he crossed Main, hurrying past two-story brick storefronts, a hotel, and then some smaller shops. A worry continued to flit across his mind. Would Pete's interest in Farley's whereabouts and activities arouse Robert's suspicion, even anger him? Maybe he, like everyone else who knew the family well, would assume Pete was still carrying a fourteen year old boy's resentment. He came to the one-story wood frame building with draperied windows on the front. "Robert E. Turner" was painted in black letters on the door. Pete's heart raced as he pushed open the door.

He stepped into a reception area. It was cooled by a window air conditioner in one of two, small, undressed windows above the front windows. The cooling change to his sweating face and back felt pleasant. Before him was a counter and beyond it, surrounded by a wall of black filing cabinets, a matronly woman with grey hair sat behind a desk covered with papers. She was talking on the phone. She put her hand over the receiver and said she'd be with him momentarily. According to the nameplate on her desk, she was Gladys Purdue.

So, this was his brother's law office. His daddy's dream had been for his sons to get out of the whiskey business, go to college and find a safe, legal line of work, instead of always having to look over their shoulders for the feds, to always be one misstep away from prison. Rusty would have been pleased to see Robert now.

When Pete joined the Navy in 1944, Robert was still in undergraduate school. That was fine for him, but Pete loved the challenge of the whiskey business. He always meant to follow in his daddy's footsteps and operate the Turner farm just like his daddy had. It was all he'd ever wanted to do. He knew he was good at it, having learned from the best. He could handle a car better than Rusty or any of his brothers. He'd been driving since he was eleven. He knew how to build one, how to tear it down, and what made it tick. He savored the agents' pursuit because he could outrun them. It was the same confidence he experienced on the race track.

Two days after he came home from the navy, his little sister's death shook him to the core. He tried college for two years. When he got into an argument with a professor and almost struck him, Pete ran before things got worse. He'd been running ever since.

Pete took a step forward and surveyed the small, simply decorated reception area. To his left was the counter that separated the reception area from the secretary's office. Across from him there was a door that he assumed led to the offices where Robert carried on his practice. It was closed, so he couldn't see beyond it. To the right beside the door were two maroon tub chairs with a lamp table between. Against the adjacent wall was a Chippendale sofa where he chose to sit in order to see when the door opened. His brother might walk out any time. Would he be surprised? Would he recognize him? Pete cracked his knuckles and stared at the wild duck prints over the tub chairs. Then he heard a voice summoning his attention.

"Yes?" The woman from the desk was standing at the counter. "Can I help you?"

"I'm here to see Robert."

"Mr. Turner," she said pursing her lips, "is not available at the moment." She raised her eyebrows and with a smug look that indicated she knew perfectly well the answer to her question, she asked, "Did you have an appointment?" Gladys managed the office efficiently and she prided herself in knowing her boss's schedule better than he did. She also knew who had an appointment and who did not.

Pete shuffled his feet. Never having dealt with lawyers, he was suddenly uncomfortable with the formality. "No appointment. I'm his brother."

She clasped her hands and bounced them against her upper lip, her eyes shooting darts of distrust. "We," she said, "were unaware Mr. Turner had any living siblings."

Pete looked again at the closed door and realized this woman was going to guard it like it was the entrance to Fort Knox. He could ignore her and go on back, but Robert might have a client and he didn't want to make a scene. The phone rang. "You'll have to come back," she said, "when you have an appointment." She moved briskly toward the desk to pick up the phone, while keeping Pete in her scope. "Robert Turner's office," she said. "Yes, this is Gladys."

Pete didn't want to come back. If he could get past this Cerberus, he wouldn't have to. Gladys pushed aside papers and picked up her appointment book. Unable to read through the pages and keep an eye on Pete, she glanced away at the book. At that unguarded moment, he opened the door into the hallway and slipped in. His impatience to see Robert overtook his concern about interrupting him with a client. He would just have to excuse himself if Robert was with someone, but he would at least let his brother know he was waiting. Now to figure out which office was Robert's. He passed the first door. It was open. He looked in and saw a young woman with long brown hair sitting behind a desk. Her fingers were flying over the keys of the typewriter in front of her as she typed each line and pushed the carriage back with a snap. He passed on. Other doors were closed. Looking down the hall, he figured Robert's office would be the one at the end. He went back to the open door where the brown haired typist continued at her work. "Excuse me, ma'am. Did Gladys say Mr. Turner's office was the one at the end of the hall?"

The girl paused and stood up. Pete looked at her approvingly. She was slender, about twenty-something, and dressed in a silky, long sleeved white blouse with a ruffle at the neck and a straight navy skirt just below her knees. She came to the doorway. "Didn't Gladys tell you Mr. Turner is in Charlotte?"

Before Pete could register his dismay, he heard Gladys's sharp voice call to him. "Young man, what do you mean by this impertinence? Leave now or I will call the police."

Pete demanded, "When will my brother be back?"

Gladys turned on her heel. "I'm calling the police."

"Wait! I'll go. Just tell me when my brother will return," he shouted to Gladys's back as she flew through the hall door to get to her phone.

For the moment, trapped in Robert's office with the likes of Gladys and having no desire to get tangled up with Sheriff Money or one of his stupid deputies, he knew his best bet was to run for it. He hurried to find an office with a window. The first door that he tried opened into a room occupied by a young woman sitting at an oval conference table piled with law books. Though her intense expression revealed she was deep in thought about what she was researching, her red head jerked up at the intrusion. Pete brushed past her. "Excuse me, ma'am. I just want to open the window." There were two. He rushed to the one without the humming air conditioner, raised it, unhooked the screen, and leaped out onto the pavement. His feet hit the ground running. On the way to the Ford, a thought struck him. He would swear the red head that he'd just passed sitting with the pile of books was the same girl he'd seen coming into Charlie's diner at lunch time. *Charlie had called her Myra Claire.*

Chapter Five

It was Tuesday morning just before daybreak, the day after Pete's frustrated attempt to see his brother, when he turned off Highway 421 onto a narrow county road. He'd started out early before the sun came up in order to arrive unde-tected, hopeful that he might snoop around and find out what Freddie Oaks had been up to, and if that scum Farley had been around. He drove another five miles and veered onto a private gravel drive. It wound through green woods of pin oaks and leafy maples that arched overhead, creating a shady passageway that would later provide a pleasant canopy from the hot July sun.

Several times before he had tried catching Charlie for a private conversation to learn if he knew anything about the latest happenings at the Turner place, but Charlie was either busy at the diner or at home sleeping. Charlie's wife seemed to be the one who managed the motor court where Pete was staying, but he didn't really know her. So, impatient to get some answers, even against his better judgment, he had come on his own to scout out the premises.

He dreaded any contact with his momma. He no longer had any tender feelings for her, and seeing her would be uncomfortable at best. It might be more than he could do to refrain from saying things a man should not say to his momma. He could not forgive her because she didn't deserve to be forgiven. She had closed her eyes to things she must have seen and known. As for his intentions toward Farley and Freddie Oaks, it was too soon to reveal his hand. Despite the episode at the diner on Monday, the word of his return may not have reached Wilkes County. Most people who would remember him apparently thought him dead, and the dead were soon forgotten.

When the white two-story farmhouse came into view, Pete pulled the Ford out of sight into the surrounding woods and walked the rest of the way. In the half-light of the early morning, he slipped around the back to the bungalow, which he assumed was still home to Freddie Oaks. He peered in a side window. There were some overalls and beer cans scattered around on the floor and an unmade bunk bed, but no sign of Freddie. He didn't remember Freddie being an early riser. He moved towards the barn. He did not go inside, but watched and listened for any indication of activity in there. Nothing. He walked back to the house and looked in the kitchen window. There were no lights on the inside that he could see. Chipping paint on the exterior of the house and knee high grass in the yard suggested neglect. After a quick glance behind him, he stole around front and went up the steps to the porch. He tried the door. It was locked. That was surprising because the Turners had never kept their doors locked. He rubbed his chin. This was a puzzle. It appeared no one had been here for a least several days. Maybe his momma had gone to Edenton to see her sister. If Mabel were ill, Eugenia would have gone to nurse her back to health. He had to admit she was quick to go to the sick and help however she could. She knew all kinds of potions and remedies for whatever ailed a person. As a boy, he could remember running when she came after him with her bottle of grey chill tonic. He could still taste that awful, grainy stuff. He tried never to sneeze in his mother's presence for fear of that bottle.

Other than the absolute quiet and the signs of general neglect, everything was just as he remembered it on the day of Mary Kate's funeral. His heart squeezed into his throat. That sanctimonious Farley had the audacity to stand beside Eugenia, like he had a right to stand in that place, and to play the part of the aggrieved uncle to friends and family offering their condolences.

Pete spat on the ground the way he had wanted to spit in Farley's face that day and to announce to all the people present what he knew, but even then, they would have thought it was boyish resentment toward Farley for seeming to try to take his daddy's place. They simply would not have believed him. That was the obstacle he had yet to overcome. What evidence could he uncover to prove Farley Oaks was scum and not what he presented himself to be? *What if he has reformed? He still has to pay. I don't care if he's a saint now. I can't forget what he did. I won't.*

Satisfied that no one was around the house or the bungalow, he hurried back to the barn and stables. In the glory days of Turner moonshine production, the pack mules were kept here. Because they could go where no car or truck could travel, they were used to haul bags of sugar up the slopes to the hidden stills and to transport the gallons of whiskey down for loading into the whiskey cars for deliveries.

The barn door squeaked when Pete pushed on it. Breathing heavily, he waited, then opened it just enough for him to squeeze inside. The barn was cool and musty. A field mouse scurried into a crack. When it appeared he was alone, he walked over to a wooden platform. It was empty of the bags of grain for feeding the mules. A shovel leaned against a wall in one corner where it had always been, but where were the bags of grain and the mules? Something wasn't right. He grabbed the shovel to pry loose two of the platform boards, being careful not to rip the wood. Then he dug down two feet until he hit the metal box. He'd placed it there soon after Farley had taken over. Pete's chest rose and fell like the undulating waves of the sea before they break on the shore. Then a pent-up breath heaved from his lungs. With trembling hands he pulled out the box and dusted off the dirt. He opened it, daring to hope the coveted papers were there. To his great relief, he found Rusty's recipes and customer list. It had not been disturbed for fourteen years. He ran his hands gently over the yellowed pages, touching them like the treasured pieces of the past that they were. He brushed his arm across his eyes to wipe away a tear that leaked out before he caught it. It was the first he'd shed in many years. Then, carefully placing the papers back inside the box, he closed the lid and set the box aside while he shoveled the dirt back in the hole and replaced the boards. Next he picked up the box and found a temporary hiding place for it outside in some bushes. He planned to take it with him, but he had one more trek to make first.

Following a wide stream, he climbed with speed and agility up a rocky slope through the tangle of roots and vegetation. At intervals, he stopped to catch his breath and to wipe away the sweat from his face and head with his shirttail as the sun was now fully up. At one point he threw himself on the ground and splashed the cool water from the stream on his upper body. Afterwards he removed his shirt and soaked it in the water before putting it back on. When he felt rejuvenated, he continued his journey. If he followed this main stream a mile or more, there was a crystal waterfall tumbling down into a ravine where he and his brothers swam on humid days like this one. However, he didn't follow the main stream, but soon detoured to track along a narrow secondary branch that fed from the wider one. There was no trail. One simply followed the narrow, bubbling stream. He could almost smell the mountain laurel with its purple flowers, now past its blooming season. He expected to turn and see his daddy, ready to give him and his brothers the familiar instructions. "Unload the

sugar bags from the mules. Check the mash. See if it's done."
He could feel Rusty's and Robert's...and Johnny's presence.
Johnny was the brother between Robert and Pete. Five years
before Rusty's death when Johnny was only fourteen, he was
killed in a knife fight outside the Bloody Bucket, a thinly dis-
guised tavern or speakeasy off Highway 421 where brawls
were frequent. Johnny just happened to be there with a buddy
when he found himself in the middle of a drunken altercation over a woman he didn't even know. He was dead before
ever learning what it was all about. Pete remembered it was
Hugh Green who came to the farm on his motorcycle to bring
the news.

Johnny was Eugenia's favorite. He was so much like her,
affable and outgoing, but strong-willed and impulsive underneath his laughing, devil-may-care charm. After they put
Johnny in the ground, Eugenia fell into a deep depression. Her
hair turned prematurely grey and her entire demeanor changed.
Even after a year she refused to put off wearing black or to
unloose her hair from the tight knot she took to wearing it in. To
make matters worse, she got religion. She would go to a tiny log
church up in the mountains where rumor had it that these zealots
handled snakes. The last Pete had heard, the preacher who led
the group died from a rattlesnake bite. Some said Eugenia
began preaching up there after that, even though in these parts
most people thought it was blasphemy for a woman to preach.
Her turning to this weird obsession caused Rusty much grief.
He wasn't opposed to religion. He told Pete he believed in a
good God, not the one of fire and brimstone and condemnation
for the moonshiners that some of preachers railed about. He had
no use for them and said he would worship God his own way.
Pete shook his head at the thought. God had never done anything for him. He let his daddy get killed and he let Mary Kate...
He swallowed the bile that rose up in his throat, the ache in his
chest, and pushed the thought away. No, he had no interest in
religion. God had never done any good for him.

He trudged another half mile up the steep ridge, following the lively flowing stream. After a while he thought he smelled mash cooking. He didn't want to encounter Freddie. His intent was to see without being seen. Trudging on, he grew more certain he smelled mash. He would know that odor anywhere. The basic recipe for southern moonshine referred to two steps: cook the juice of the rotted corn and capture the potent steam. Being careful to make as little sound as possible, he tromped through the bushes following the scent until he came to a familiar shed. He went inside and was not surprise when he discovered a batch of corn soaking in water. In a few days when the kernels germinated and sprouted, the malt would be ground and soaked again. Pete saw that everything was clean and in order, but where was the mash he smelled?

He slipped back out of the shed. With caution, he listened for voices. All he heard were birds chirping in the tall trees high above him. He looked up into the green leafy branches where patches of blue sky and sunlight broke through in places. He half expected to catch a glimpse of Freddie or one of his lazy underlings sitting on a low branch watching him through a gun sight. If they were there, he couldn't spot them. So, where was that usurper? Freddie might shoot him without hesitation if he found him spying on his operation.

Then Pete thought he spied a glint of metal, burnished copper that indicated a whiskey still. Working his way toward it, he pulled apart the bushes and saw one, two, three large stills. They were not his daddy's, though similar to those Pete remembered. Well, after ten years things needed replacing he guessed. These vats sat on propane-fueled furnaces. His daddy had used wood. Judging from the pungent odor, the sugar and yeast had already been added to begin the fermentation process. This was the mash he'd been smelling.

The entire apparatus was made of copper except the oak barrel that received the end product. The stills and pipes and coils were all constructed of copper because it was a good conductor of heat and didn't leech into the alcohol, affecting the taste. Before long, the mash would be finished fermenting. Then it would be heated, and the pressure from the alcohol steam produced by the heated still would force its way through the cap arm, a pipe that led from the top of the still into the worm. The worm was a coiled length of pipe that wound down into the worm box, which was filled with cold water diverted by a pipe from the mountain stream that Pete had been following for the last hour. This water was constantly circulated to keep the coils cool. The cold water would condense the alcohol to a liquid that would then flow from a hose at the end of the worm through a filter and into the great oak barrels. What went into those barrels was clear moonshine ready to be put into plastic gallon containers and taken to market. Pete checked all the connections and found them to be fitted to his satisfaction.

He was so taken with examining the stills that he did not notice the slight crunch of twigs behind him. It was the rifle in his back and the voice that demanded, "Don't move or I'll shoot and ask questions later," that caused him to freeze. "Now put your hands in the air and get down on the ground."

Chapter Six

P ete was vaguely aware of the sun glistening through the branches of the trees from where a bird tweeted a cheerful song that seemed to mock his present dilemma. An intermittent breeze caressed the leaves that murmured in response. He heard the stream's ripple beside him and clenched his teeth.

There had never been anything but mutual hate between him and Freddie Oaks. If this younger nephew of Farley's thought the prodigal son had returned to take back his land, he didn't doubt Freddie would shoot him and let the buzzards pick his bones. There was no reason to hope he wouldn't recognize Pete. Folks often said he showed a strong resemblance to his daddy, especially about the mouth and chin, although he'd inherited Eugenia's brown hair and brown eyes rather than Rusty's red hair and green eyes. He couldn't say if Freddie Oaks ever saw Rusty while he was alive. No doubt, though, he'd seen pictures of Rusty and all the boys in the main house. At the moment he'd better think fast and come up with a convincing story as to why he was up here examining these stills. Otherwise, he was certain Freddie would kill him. It would be a hard sell to say he was wandering and got lost, especially if Freddie recognized him. Every Turner knew these hills like the back of his hand. If he said Robert and some others were on the way to join him, that wouldn't keep Freddie from disposing of him and swearing he never saw Pete. All this raced through his mind while one of the two men poked the gun in his back. The other proceeded to pat him down and remove the pistol he carried strapped to his ankle. Too bad he hadn't been smart enough to have it ready. Hindsight. Why was he always a day late and a dollar short?

After they confiscated his weapon, the one with the gun said, "Okay. Stand up, turn around, but keep your hands in the air. You move one inch and I'll put a hole in you."

The funny thing was, it dawned on Pete that the voice sounded very familiar and it wasn't Freddie Oaks. Pete turned slowly. His fear of taking a bullet and having his body disposed of in an unmarked grave turned to surprise and relief at the sight of his captor. About the time he shouted, "Jennings?" the rifle dropped to that man's side.

"Pete? Pete Turner? No! It can't be unless you're a ghost." Jennings planted a hand firmly on Pete's shoulder in a show of warm affection while his eyes gave Pete the once over.

Although Pete was not given to levity or a show of affection, he allowed himself half a smile when he said, "I promise I'm not a ghost, but if you'd been Freddie Oaks, I was figuring I'd soon be one."

"Not likely to be Freddie Oaks. He's doing some time right now." Getting his wits about him Jennings said, "Oh, this is Mack Johnson, a friend of mine."

Pete nodded.

"Howdy," Mack said. "I'll be in the shed, if you need me Paul."

When Mack walked away, Pete turned to Jennings. "What was it you said about Freddie Oaks? He's in prison?"

"Almost two years or maybe it *has* been two years," Jennings responded. "I reckon he'll be gettin' out any time now."

Pete couldn't hide his amusement, nor his surprise. With a satisfied grin, he shook his head and asked, "What happened?"

"An unhappy snitch, somebody that worked for Freddie for a while, said he tried to cheat him. Feds caught Freddie at the edge of the woods behind your ma's house with crates full of gallon jugs of moonshine ready for distribution. They arrested him and hauled his butt off to prison. Farley done his best to try to get Freddie released, but he don't have so much clout with the Feds. There wasn't nothing he could do."

"And Farley now?" Pete asked.

"Don't know nothing. Except for all the buzz 'bout him planning to build a big racetrack somewhere in the county, I don't know nothing."

"I'll bet Robert will know. Being a lawyer, he's bound to keep up with business news and all. Yesterday he was in Charlotte, but I'm hoping he's back today."

"Sorry I can't tell you nothing more. Farley ain't no concern of mine. I don't think anybody's seen him around lately."

"Maybe one of his enemies came out of the cracks and did him in and disposed of his sorry carcass," Pete said with a smirk.

"You're still carrying a grudge for him, ain't you? Things change; people change. Whatever happened was a long time ago."

"Don't be fooled by Farley's image. It's all show."

"Maybe so," Jennings allowed. "There's been rumors from time to time, whispers about him I wouldn't want to repeat, but nobody's really accused him openly of anything. Maybe they're afraid to. Maybe some folks are jealous of his success and just want to put him in a bad light, plant suspicion. Some old fogies like to bring up the criminal life he led in Georgia. It grinds their guts to think of him getting rich doing things they wish they'd done, if they'd had the brains and the energy Farley's got. The truth is, Farley's used his money to quietly buy people's good opinion of him. Lot of folks give him credit for bringing jobs to this here community, and he gives to a bunch to charities. Don't know how many stories I've heard 'bout him helping folks down on their luck, and there's been a lot of interest 'bout this race track he reckons to build. Kinda surprises me you still got it in for him. You been gone ten years. Maybe Farley's changed and you should consider that whatever he done so long ago is just water under the bridge."

Pete looked away. "So whose stills are these?" he asked.

"Your uncle Jakes. He's operating some on his own property, but knowing no one would think about anybody making whiskey up here on Rusty's land, with Freddie in prison, your ma gone, and you gone, Jake decided there ain't no reason to let this land go to waste. He figured this would be the perfect place to set up a secret operation. Me and Mack oversee this production." Jennings walked over to check the cooking mash and Pete followed him, inhaling and savoring the smell. What a relief to see the buddy he'd grown up with, had dragged raced with over every road in the county, had hauled whiskey with.

Jennings, whose first name was Paul, knew Pete better than anybody alive. For one thing, he'd known Pete all his life and was related to him by marriage through his Aunt Isabelle, Uncle Jake's wife. Although Jennings was two years younger, he and Pete had played together as boys and had been close all through school until Pete joined the navy. Both were farmer's sons who grew up doing farm work and helping in the whiskey business. Back in those days before Rusty's crash, Jennings had known Pete as a carefree boy, exuberant, fun-loving, and full of pranks and laughter.

Jennings turned to Pete and said, "The last time I saw you was at Mary Kate's funeral, almost ten years ago. Farley was next to your ma, standing in for Rusty."

"I got my shotgun and ordered him off the property."

"I remember that. You created a scene that people 'round here talked 'bout for a long time," Jennings said. "You didn't stick around. Then after that you did two years of college somewhere in Florida, but you dropped out."

"Yes, I dropped out. The next eight years I bounced around the country."

"And news of you became more and more scarce. Then somebody said you got yourself killed in a fight just like your brother Johnny."

"Who said that?"

"Don't remember. I just heard it. I know you didn't have no time to grieve for your daddy before you had to deal with Farley taking charge of the farm, which I could understand you woulda resented."

"You think like everybody else, that I resented him because I was jealous of him taking my daddy's place. For sure he could never fill my daddy's shoes, but I resented him because I respected my daddy's judgment."

Jennings said, "Rusty was a quiet, deep-thinking, hard-working man that minded his own business. All the same, if he didn't like something or someone, he kept his distance and didn't feel no need to explain or make apologies for his actions."

Pete said, "From early in his marriage to my momma, so I've been told, daddy let it be known that Farley was not welcome at the Turner farm. No one knew his reasons, not even Eugenia, but once daddy made his decision known, he didn't talk about it or explain it, and needless to say, Farley Oaks never darkened our door. Daddy made it plain he didn't expect my momma to shut herself off from her entire family, but she'd have to be the one to go to them. He didn't really care for any of them except for her Aunt Louise who raised her. Louise, however, lived in Virginia. She was rarely able to visit momma after her marriage to Rusty, especially when Louise's health got bad."

"And because your daddy didn't want Farley around, you took on the same opinion not to like him just because your daddy didn't like him."

Pete kicked at a tree root. "My daddy's opinion was good enough for me. He refused to let Farley set foot on the Turner farm because he wanted to protect his family. Yet, before the gravediggers threw the last shovel full of dirt on Rusty's grave, Farley was on the scene. By all rights the farm was Eugenia's, and there was nothing I could do short of putting a hole in him. Believe you me, it was a tempting thought many times after she welcomed him in with open arms and let him take control."

"What stopped you, even at Mary Kate's funeral?"

"What do you think? I didn't want to go to jail and give Farley that satisfaction." Pete kicked the root again. "The problem was Eugenia had no interest in managing the farm. After the death of my brother, Johnny, she got involved in some strange religion up in the mountains and attended less and less to matters at home. It got to be a source of great misery to Rusty, but the woman seemed possessed. Nothing he said got through to her."

"I remember," Jennings said, "how she didn't take off them black dresses after Johnny's death and was always quotin' the Good Book and preaching hell fire and damnation to everybody. I was almost scared to come in the house when she was around."

"Or she was silent and depressed," Pete added. "When daddy tried to talk to her about her responsibilities, she often gave a strange laugh and had a vague, empty look in her eyes. Sometime her talk was plain craziness. Certainly, Johnny's death affected her real bad. Sometimes I felt sorry for her, but her giving in to her grief and not doing her duty for her family, the burden it put on Daddy was unfair; it made me hot. Then if it wasn't bad enough to dishonor my daddy when he was alive, her allowing Farley into our home after he died, after he had expressly forbidden it, for that I could make no allow-ances. Farley told Eugenia he was going to oversee the busi-ness end of maintaining the farm and manage her finances. He recognized the weakness in her, and with Rusty gone, he stepped right in to take advantage."

"But Farley didn't actually live at the farm."

"No, Pete said. "For a while he continued living in Atlanta rather than the farm, but he came and went as often as he pleased, leaving that stupid brother Freddie to manage everything. It's no wonder he got caught with the moonshine. He wasn't capable of running my daddy's business."

"So Rusty never let on what he had against Farley?" Jennings asked.

"He never told me what it was. Daddy understood people. He could read them, but with Farley, he didn't have any proof, and it wasn't his way to accuse a man without evidence. Just the same, he had every right to protect his family. No, he never said what he had against Farley. I wish he had told me. Maybe I wouldn't have been so blind, but I know now for a fact what Rusty only knew in his gut. I know now, and it's way too late."

"So what was it?" Jennings asked.

Pete hacked at the tree root with the heel of his shoe and said nothing.

"You're gonna bust your foot," Jennings said.

Pete stopped, leaned against the tree and popped his knuckles.

"So," Jennings continued, "when you realized you couldn't do nothing to get rid of Farley, that's when you moved in with Jake and Isabelle."

"Yes, until I finished high school. When I turned seventeen, I joined the War effort and enlisted in the navy, the only branch of the service that accepted men earlier than eighteen. Three years later after the War ended, I came home. By then Farley had moved from Georgia back to Wilkes County. He still didn't live at the farm, but he came around a lot."

"Two days after your homecoming, you had another tragedy."

"Mary Kate'd just turned fourteen. We'd kept in touch writing letters while I was away, but mail delivery was not regular. Her letters attempted to be cheerful, but I could tell something wasn't right. In between the lines there was a sadness. I assumed like everyone else she was grieving over our daddy's death and from the changes we all suffered as a result of losing him."

"You're saying that wasn't it? Wasn't why she killed herself?"

Pete gazed off into the distance. "I was completely unprepared for how much she was suffering when I saw her. At first I thought surely she was ill with some disease she'd been keeping from me. She was thin as a broom handle. Those sad eyes broke my heart. I'll tell you she was nothing like the joyful young girl I remembered. She had always been so full of life. You know how she loved music and nature and was always writing her own songs about everyday adventures on the farm. Then two days after I came home, she was gone. If I'd never left the home place, I would have seen...I would have seen..."

"What?"

Pete leaned his head against the tree in despair. "Let's leave it at that. I was too busy hating Farley to see anything else."

"My sister, Betty Anne noticed at school how Mary Kate was looking ill and letting her grades fall. She told Ma, and Ma told Betty Anne to talk to Mary Kate and try to help her. Betty Ann did try, but she said Mary Kate just clammed up, shut her out. Like you said, we thought losing her daddy, then you leaving the farm, and her mother going nutty, was too much for her."

"It was a lot for her to handle, but Mary Kate would never have taken her own life...never!"

"And you blame Farley for that. Why?"

"That's what I came back to prove. If he didn't kill her with his own hands, he caused her death. As sure as I'm standing here, he caused it."

"How you gonna prove that? After ten years?"

"I don't know yet, but I'm working on it. I'm wanting to talk to Robert, see what he knows about Farley and where he keeps himself these days. I think I can trust Robert to be discrete. I don't want it to get around that I'm asking questions."

Jennings and Pete sat down on the ground on a patch of grass while Mack tended to the mash. "So, if Freddie's been in prison, who's been keeping up the farm?" Pete asked.

"Jake. He ain't been farming your daddy's land, but when he has time, he sees the grass is kept cut."

"He must have been busy lately. Grass is long. Paint is peeling, but I'm gonna fix all that one of these days very soon."

"So, when did you get here and what're you gonna do next?" Jennings said.

"You think Jake would let me haul some of his shine?"

"Man! I can just about guarantee it. He needs somebody like you that's fast behind the wheel, somebody he can trust, especially now that Sheriff Money is trying to crack down on shiners. At least he's ordered his boys to crack down. The sheriff has big plans, but he's too lazy to overly exert hisself. Some people are saying the glory days of the bootlegger is past. For sure, I'm ready to get out. Them cops and Feds they got two-way radios now, and faster cars." Jennings laughed, "Even so, they can't find our stills and they don't know these county roads like us trippers do."

"You think Sheriff Money's working for Farley so Farley can get control of the whiskey business in the county?"

"If he is, it ain't because your uncle ain't rich enough already. It's the mill owners that's wanting the shiners shut

64

down. They don't like their people coming to work under the influence because then they ain't productive and they're more likely to cause accidents."

"You racing any?" Pete asked.

"Sure thing. I'm aiming to get good enough for them new tracks they're calling NASCAR. How 'bout you?" Then understanding crossed Jennings's face. He jumped up and slapped his side. "Wait a minute!" He grabbed Pete's shoulder and pulled him to his feet. "You're the Pete Turner's been winning like crazy, in Kernersville, Greensboro, Wilson." He shook his head. "I never considered it was you, since the Pete Turner we knew was dead and all." Jennings laughed. "I'll be durned." He took a few steps in one direction, turned around and stood in front of Pete. "Can't believe I'm standing here talking to you. Just never expected to ever lay eyes on you again. Even though you ain't been around since you left for the navy, you ain't changed much. You still look 'bout the same, except maybe you a little thicker in the chest and arms. So why you want to haul shine, you being a college boy like your daddy wanted."

"I need some quick money. Eventually, I want to run the farm and make good quality whiskey just like Rusty. It's the only way to make sure nobody related to Farley Oaks will ever set foot on it again."

"With Farley involved in other enterprises and Freddie gone to prison, it looks to me the way is clear."

"Well, there is the fact that my momma owns it which means Farley's still in control and...I don't want to have to see her."

Jennings looked puzzled. "You don't know?"

"Don't know what?"

"By Jiminy Cricket! Nobody's told you yet."

"Don't know what?" Pete asked, insistent.

"I'm real sorry, Pete, but your ma passed away about a little over a year ago. I think it was around the first of May."

Pete waited a moment to let that sink in. "Then she's not at her sisters in Edenton. That's what Lance Ward meant. None of his business." Pete was surprised at his reaction. He felt an unexpected shock and a sadness. He allowed his emotions to linger a moment. Then he shook himself. "Well, I guess the way is clear."

"Ain't nobody but you and Robert for the Turner land to go to."

"There's just one obstacle to remove."

"What's that?" Jennings asked.

"Look," Pete said, standing up, "I need to go."

"Okay," Jennings said. "I didn't mean to shock you about your ma."

"It's okay," Pete said.

"You sure?"

"Yeah. I'm sure. I gotta go. Put in a word with Jake for me, will you?"

Jennings grinned. "First I'll let him know you're alive."

Pete nodded and turned to go.

"I'll be over at Billy Hinton's track this afternoon working on my car. Gonna race her on Sunday. You wanna help?" Jennings said.

"Can't. Not this afternoon. I'm going to see Robert, but I'll see you around," Pete said, and took off running back toward the farm. He felt in his pocket to make sure he had the number for Robert's office.

Chapter Seven

With a satisfying burp, Sheriff Money finished the corn on the cob, biscuits, and molasses the wife Lucille had packed for his lunch. He sucked on a chicken bone to extract any leftover shreds of meat. When it was stripped clean, he stuffed down the big piece of chocolate layer cake with pecans in the icing. Raring back in his swivel chair, he rested his feet on his desk and considered how he was blessed with a wife who cooked from scratch and not like those women who were using the newfangled cake mixes. The scarred wooden desk and creaky chair had come from his office in the old jail. He supposed the powers-that-be thought new furniture as well as a new jail would look extravagant to the taxpayers. A fan rotated on the desk, blowing directly on him, and the shades were down on all the windows to keep out as much July sun as possible. Yet, the dimly lit room could hardly be considered cool.

A door behind and to the left of Money opened into a narrow hall off of which were smaller offices the deputies used. At the end of it were some stairs leading down to the cells where the prisoners, usually drunks and petty thieves, were locked up. With his secretary gone to lunch, the door to his office stood open so he could see whoever came in. So far, only Deputy Oliver Garner had come in to leave some mail for the postman. He gave his boss a salute and hurried out to back up Lance on a call. The sheriff licked his fingers. With his napkin, he wiped away the giblets of food and grease from around his mouth and down the front of his khaki shirt. He yawned and closed his eyes so his food could digest. Soon he dreamed of lazing by a mountain lake where the fish jumped silver in the sun.

A block away, Salvino parked his Cadillac on the street and walked toward the jail, hoping to catch Sheriff Money in his office so he could pick his brain. Heat and acrid smells emanated from the street. It was a hot, muggy day and his short sleeve silk shirt clung to his back. His feet were perspiring in his silk socks and custom made leather shoes that made no sound on the pavement, an indication of the quality of the craftsmanship. Salvino had grown accustomed to nice things and he intended that his change in fortune was only temporary. The cacophony of noontime traffic seemed lazy compared to the noise of the Big Apple. He crossed in front of the stately courthouse, thinking it rather impressive for a small southern county like Wilkes. A tall slender man crossed the street a hundred feet ahead of him. For a moment he thought it could be Turner, but it wasn't. He'd get back to Turner when the time was favorable.

So far Turner wasn't cooperating. He would come around though. It was obvious even the mention of this Oaks fellow made him crazy. If he hated his uncle when he was miles away, now that he was home and close to whatever happened to burn him with this man, he'd be running to ole Sal before long. Salvino meant to find out where this Farley Oaks lived and what places he frequented. Then he could figure where he could get the best killing shot when Turner was ready to deal. Turner would not know Salvino planned to be the hit man. The Italian was still a competent marksman, although he didn't move as fast since he'd put on a few extra pounds.

He intended to get all the payoff himself. Anyway, he was blacklisted from being a middle man with any of Angel's contacts. None of this was information he planned to share with Turner. Salvino learned long ago that it was best when the left hand did not know what the right hand was doing and vice versa. Let Turner believe Salvino was the middle man. When the time came, he'd tell him where to take the blood money to the "contact." Salvino laughed at his own ingenuity. *What happens to the fool after that, I haven't decided.*

Even so, having been unsuccessful in pushing Pete Turner to action, Salvino believed there was more than one way to skin a cat when exploitation was the name of the game. If Turner wasn't ready to play, maybe his enemies were. For instance, that Bennie Farnes. It was true Farnes didn't have any money, not the numbers Salvino required, but when men are fools, you can never tell what they will manage to come up with. On the other hand, if Sheriff Money was in cahoots with Oaks, he might just be the linchpin in Salvino's little scheme, especially if he could convince him Turner was plotting against his secret source of income. Now there might be a real gold mine. What would Mr. Oaks pay for valuable information? This Italian was an expert at playing both ends against the middle. The worse slip up he'd ever made was underestimating Angel. Here in this place, though, he was dealing with a bunch of unsophisticated country bumpkins in a boiling pot that Salvino could surely make use of. He found the red brick jail and hurried in the front to find the sheriff's office.

Money vaguely heard the door creak and opened his eyes. The visitor was short, pudgy and looked very Italian. For a moment, the sheriff thought he was dreaming. He leaned forward.

Salvino, seeing the secretary's desk abandoned, stood for a moment adjusting his eyes, having come out of the bright sun light.

"Yeah, what can I do for you?" Money said.

Salvino hurried forward to shake hands, but the sheriff, not desiring to change his relaxed position, indicated the visitor should drop the formalities and pointed to a chair. After seating himself, Salvino explained he was a one-man real estate operation from upper state New York. He had come to Wilkes County to evaluate the area for a client who thought he might want to invest in opening a furniture manufacturing plant. Salvino produced a certificate of incorporation, just in case the sheriff did any checking. "My client has money he's looking to invest. Likes the idea of a small town, a place to raise his family."

"We in Wilkes County welcome investment in our fine community if your client is a law abiding person who intends to open a legitimate business."

"I understand you are a tough law and order man," Salvino said, laying on the flattery. *This fellow would be putty in his hands.* "That would be a plus for my client."

"You got it," Money said. "That's my mission. Law and order. When I took this job I said I was going to clean up them bootleggers. That's about the only real criminal element we have around here, and they're successful only because the people protect them. Now, my wife's daddy, he was sheriff before me, he'd got kind of complacent, if you know what I mean. Didn't like to offend his friends. As long as the status quo didn't create no major problems, he let things be, but I want to improve on that, and I've set out to make it happen, although it's tough when the citizens are often working against you." He reared back, locking his hands behind his head. "Law and order. That's my credo."

"I admire you, Sheriff. Any retaliation?"

"Oh, I've got a couple of death threats from disgruntled folks, but that goes with the job." Money leaned forward and looked Salvino in the eye. "You say you're from New York. You look like one of them New York Italians. You ain't representing none of them Mafia people are you? We don't want no Mafia here in Wilkes County."

"No," Salvino said, raising an eyebrow and returning the sheriff's stern look as if the idea of representing the Mafia were an unthinkable idea. "My client is a legitimate businessman who wants no connection to the Mafia and for that reason wants to get away from the big city."

"Good for him," Money said leaning back in his chair. "So, what is it you think I kin tell you?"

"Who is this Farley Oaks? I keep hearing his name."

"Oh, now Mr. Farley Oaks, he's our most respected citizen, a local businessman and entrepreneur." Money scratched behind his ear. "Now, I have heard stories he was born into a very poor family, that his daddy was an alcoholic. When he weren't more than a boy, tall for his age they said, he ran off to someplace outside of Atlanta. Got in with a big time bootlegger down there, was tripping for him. 'Tripping means delivering the booze if you didn't know."

Salvino moved his head back and forth to indicate he was taking in the sheriff's instruction as though bootlegging were a mystery to him.

"Then, he acquired his own stills and got very rich in the illegal liquor business, and other illegal operations some say, but whatever his past, the man runs legitimate businesses now, and he's done a lot to bring jobs and revenue into this community. A lot of people here see him as a local son that's done well and come back to his roots. Lives up close to Trap Hill. Built a big house up there, so I been told. Ain't seen it myself. Don't know why he needs a big house, though. Nobody's ever lived there but him and his wife 'til she died 'bout two years ago. He's got plenty of family here and there that he's put in charge of his businesses, but none live up in the big house with him. Guess these rich guys need a status symbol. That's all I can figure."

"You say you've never seen the house?"

"Never had a need to bother Mr. Oaks. I hear it's impressive, a big white house built like a southern cotton plantation. People that's seen it say it's got six columns and two porches, an upper and a lower that extend across the front. As I said, he's a law abiding, respected citizen. No need to bother him."

"Wonder if you could introduce me to him," Salvino said.

The sheriff rubbed his chin. "He's actually become a sort of recluse these days. Only place I ever hear of anybody seeing him is at the race tracks, the larger paved ones. If there's money to be made, Oaks has a nose for it. Seems his newest enterprise might be building race tracks similar to what that France fellow's doing with his NASCAR."

"I sure would like to meet Mr. Oaks. My client might want to talk to him."

"Good luck with that. He travels a lot. One fellow said he heard Oaks was in California. Then somebody said Mexico. He used to be more visible. Often had his picture in the paper. Just lately, he's stayed out of the public eye. Don't suppose anyone ever really knows where he is except maybe his house boy and he sometimes takes him with him when he travels. When the good man is in town, the house boy picks up his mail every day or so at the post office."

It occurred to Salvino that if Oaks was a recluse, it may be days before anyone would noticed if he should go missing. "That Pete Turner doesn't have any use for him."

"How do you know that?" Money asked, scrutinizing Salvino.

"I saw him get in a fight yesterday at the Crossroads Diner because that other fellow complimented Mr. Oaks."

"You saw that did you? Yeah. That Turner's a hot head. Gonna get himself in trouble if he don't watch that temper."

"Maybe Mr. Oaks could be in danger from him. If I hear anything, I'll let you know."

"You acquainted with Turner?"

"Never saw him before yesterday. What's he got against Farley Oaks? What did Oaks do to him to make him so full of venom?"

"That you'll have to ask Mr. Turner. I don't know what these questions have to do with anything that would be of interest to your client."

"Just curious. I also hear, Sheriff, you are working for Oaks." Salvino scrutinized him, expecting to see some reaction to this direct approach, that it surprised him or made him uncomfortable.

The sheriff merely smiled. "Believe half of whatcha you see and none of whatcha hear."

"And people are saying you're closing down the small bootleggers under the guise of law and order for Farley Oaks to get control of the illegal whiskey business in this county. It's very lucrative I understand. People like the product and the price is much lower than the government approved whiskey they have to get in other counties."

"You've done your homework, Mr. Pezzo, but the part about me working for Farley Oaks couldn't be nothing further from the truth. I've heard the rumors, pure speculation and gossip. I work for the people of Wilkes County. They elected me and I work for them."

Salvino was unconvinced the sheriff was leveling with him. "So this Mr. Oaks is living like a recluse in a big house up around someplace called Trap Hill. You got an address?"

"There's one road to Trap Hill. Take Highway 18 from here and turn off when you see the sign. Then you got about a ten mile drive. But you won't get close to the mansion. There's a stone wall around the estate and it's gated. And beware of the dogs."

For now, Salvino had learned what he needed. He thanked the sheriff and said he'd be on his way, with one last note of flattery. "Law and order, now that's a high calling and must keep you a busy man. I'll leave you to your business."

Without getting up, Money pushed back his chair and dropped his feet to the floor. "Thanks for coming in, Mr. Pezzo. Your client will find our town progressive and prosperous. If he's what you describe, he'll find himself welcome here."

Salvino hurried out to find Farley's mansion, with malice aforethought toward whomever he could apply it.

Chapter Eight

Salvino considered himself a sleuth of sorts. The truth was his natural curiosity, like his greed, drove him to find satisfaction in getting answers to questions that might benefit him. Having tracked Pete Turner all the way from New York City to the end of nowhere in rural North Carolina, he thought how he had certainly discovered much to look into.

Wasting no time after he left the sheriff, he drove the Caddy along Trap Hill Road until he saw up ahead what had to be Farley Oakes's estate. The big plantation style house enclosed with a high stone wall sat at the top of an incline just as the sheriff had described it. He turned off the road onto a winding drive that passed through a thin buffer of woods. A quarter of a mile from the estate wall he pulled into a field of grasses and blue Bachelor Buttons and parked within a copse of maples. He sat behind the wheel to study the lay of the land before him. There was no sign of life, no vehicles coming or going from the estate. Except for the bees buzzing about the flowers, all was quiet. Satisfied the Caddy could not easily be seen, he wiped sweat from his brow and gathered a knapsack from the trunk of the car. His knapsack contained climbing gear, lock picking equipment, a telescope and meat seasoned with a sleeping aid for the dogs that the sheriff had warned him about. Slinging it over his shoulder, he walked toward the stone wall a good distance away from the gated entrance. Salvino had broken into houses larger and more protected than this one when he worked for New York gangsters. Today, his main objective was to work on Plan A, that being drug the dogs, get inside the wall, scope out the place, and plan how he would eliminate Farley Oaks when Turner came across with the money. At this point, he was still considering his options. He could take Turner's money and run for it without incurring the risk involved in eliminating a prominent citizen, but Turner was no fool. If he insisted on half the money before the hit and the rest when the job was complete, Salvino would have to actually do the job. There was still the possibility Salvino could work his deal with Oaks and double cross Turner. For that reason and more, he didn't want to be seen prowling about the Oaks estate. He had to figure what he could do to induce the rich man to pay without Salvino seeming to cross any legal or moral lines. That was a problem. Salvino was not used to having to keep within the law. In New York he had plenty of protection from crooked cops as well as the backup from the gangsters who wielded the power with the cops and politicians.

In the pit area in the middle of the red clay track, Pete finished checking the springs and shocks of Jennings' supercharged '38 Ford. In his grease-stained overalls, his slender, six-foot frame, shirtless and tanned, came out from under it. He had worked several hours on Jennings' car by boring and stroking the engine, adding cubic inches and an extra carburetor to increase the horsepower. The black two-seater coupe had formerly been the whiskey car of a bootlegger in Galax, Virginia, with the trunk often carrying a hundred and fifty gallons of moonshine. When the owner got caught and the car was confiscated, Jake bought it from the local sheriff at the auction on the courthouse steps. Later, he sold it to Jennings who hadn't made it yet to the high-banked, longer paved oval tracks where the real money was made and where only new "stock" cars, not beat up old jalopies, ran the circuit. He'd learned this history of Jennings car just a few hours before when he talked to Jake about hauling his moonshine for him.

Facing the brunt of the hot July sun, he swiped his arm across his sweaty forehead and shielded his eyes from the flashes of sunlight glinting off the crude grey wooden bleachers. On Sunday, eager racing fans would sit there or stand around the wire fence. Here in the area designated "the pit," the drivers would wait to roll onto the track, their revved up coupes would seem like anxious, snorting horses, impatient for the sound of the gun.

Pete looked out over the dirt track. He could remember when this place was nothing but a cow pasture. After the war, when Henry Ford's fast, gas-powered automobiles became affordable to the general public, small local dirt tracks like this one began springing up all over the south. The marriage between the automobile and the illegal whiskey business was producing quite a phenomenon in the sports world.

After World War II, the new car boom freed the southern mountain man, who heretofore had rarely traveled more than a mile or so from his place of birth. He developed a fearless love of speed while outrunning the revenue agents who tried to catch him hauling his trunk loads of illegal whiskey. As he sped over rough county roads to get his processed corn to market, he knew he had to be the fastest driver and have the fastest car if he was to keep out of jail. For the bootleggers who'd argued all week about who had the fastest car, these dirt tracks became the proving grounds. A farmer could easily turn a pasture into a race track with a tractor and some wire fencing. They began with one-half mile circles for racing their souped-up junk cars. At first, maybe a few people saw the dust cloud and came to see what caused it. The next time a hundred would show up. Soon they raced every Saturday or Sunday, but usually Sunday because farm work went on until dusk on Saturday. At night they might be hauling liquor in the same car.

Sweat mixed with grease rolled down Pete's face and neck. "She's talking good to me today," he said to Jennings who was leaning against a fence post. He wiped his hands on an old tee shirt Jennings handed him. "I'm taking her for a trial run,"

"You ain't told me why you showed up here this afternoon," Jennings said, "after you left in such a hurry this morning, like you had a yeller jacket stinging your butt."

"Yeah, I had planned to see my brother, but it didn't work out," Pete said, frowning and handing the shirt back to Jennings. "So, I got nothing better to do than help you get this car of yours ready to whip that Bennie Farnes."

"You know Bennie Farnes?"

"We've met," Pete said with a smirk. He slung open the door of the Ford.

Jennings cocked his head, giving Pete a quizzical look, wanting further explanation. When Pete ignored him, Jennings said, "I take it there's more to this than you're saying."

Pete popped his knuckles and looked toward the track.

"Bennie don't race on this track," Jennings said. "It's not big enough for his ego. He races Sunday on the dirt track in Hillsboro, but he talks of nothing but NASCAR. Thinks he's gonna be good enough to go for the big time."

"More power to him," Pete said, "if he wants to bother with all the rules and regulations imposed on those drivers racing on the larger paved tracks. Besides, if a tire blows, you could hit the wall at 190 to 200 miles per hour. It takes more than skill. It takes pure luck. You hear of them crashing, cars cut and broken in two. Imagine a motor gets thrown out at 200 miles per hour. You don't want to be in its path. I prefer to depend on my skill, not luck, and if you can't make money in dirt track racing, well, there's still bootlegging," Pete told him.

"And you think that's safer?"

"Yeah. All you gotta do is be smarter and a better driver than some pesky federal agent. Easy."

Pete bent over and sat sideways on the seat, then swung his legs around and folded himself in behind the steering wheel the size of a washtub. He turned the ignition and the engine thundered to life, vibrating and tugging to be let loose. He drove the car onto the track and pushed down the gas pedal. Loving the sensation of speed and the sense of control that he experienced nowhere in his life but behind the wheel, he watched the gage go up, up, up, and the Ford zoomed ahead. Soon the pit, the wire fence, the stands, the woods flashed by his periphery vision, faster and faster, until the whole scene became a blur of color. *Just keep the pedal down and lean left. That's all there is to it. Even with all the red dust getting in your mouth and lungs, there's nothing like it.*

With no competitors to beat or agents to outrun, he settled into the sensation of the speed, his mind wandering to his earlier frustration that he'd been trying to put aside. He was attempting to keep his impatience in check, even though he was like a hunting dog wanting to go after the bird.

After he left Jennings at the Turner farm, he had no other thought but to learn whether Robert had returned from Charlotte. He had hurried to the first gas station to find a pay phone booth. He dreaded tangling with Gladys again because he knew he would get no information from that bulldog, especially if she had any notion he was the man she had called the law on. So, he decided he would ask for Myra Claire. He didn't even know if the red head he'd seen was in fact the one Charlie called Myra Claire at the diner, but it was worth a try. It was the only name he knew that might get him through to anyone but Gladys. Biting his lower lip, he dialed the number on the card. The phone rang several times before the voice answered, "Robert Turner's office." It was not Gladys. Pete breathed a sigh of relief. "I'd like to speak to Myra Claire," he's said.

"She doesn't come in on Tuesdays. She's only here Wednesdays and Thursdays. This is Arlene. Is there something I can help you with?"

Pete said, "I need to speak to an attorney pronto. A friend of Myra's said I should talk to Robert Turner. Is he in?"

"No, he's in Atlanta the rest of this week. He won't be back in the office until Monday or Tuesday of next week."

In his disappointment Pete almost dropped the receiver. He leaned his head against the glass of the booth. It was warm in there. He opened the door.

"Sir," came the voice over the receiver. "Sir, are you there?"

Pete swallowed. "I'll call next week," he said and slammed the receiver into the holder. Pete felt he would choke. It seemed once he'd made up his mind to come home and get his life back on track by carrying out what he'd thought about every hour of every day for ten years, he'd met nothing but road blocks. His heart fell into his stomach. He went back to the motor court and paced in his room for fifteen minutes before he decided the only thing he could do to pass the time was to see Jake about hauling his liquor.

After Jake got over the shock of seeing Pete, he led him inside to the parlor of his two story farmhouse, very similar to the one Pete's daddy built. They sat down and over a glass of sarsaparilla tea, Jake asked him, "So what's on your mind?" When Pete told him, Jake frowned. "I'm sure your daddy would turn over in his grave if he was to know you was bootlegging again. He would've given anything to get an education liked you've got, but he didn't have time. Now for myself, the good Lord didn't bless me with the keen mind your daddy had. I never entertained the notion of going to college like he did. He was determined his boys would go. Stilling whiskey is hard, dangerous work and you have to always be looking over your shoulder. Revenue agents, rival "shiners," local snitches are all a threat to the life and livelihood of the bootlegger, but I don't have to tell you that."

"I can handle it," Pete said. "I hauled moonshine for my daddy from the time I was old enough to reach the gas pedal."

Jake shook his head. "Your daddy wanted better for you. He wouldn't like me getting you into this business again." With a look of concern, he drummed his fingers on the arm of the vinyl covered sofa. Finally he looked at Pete straight on and said, "But you're a man now and you make your own decisions. Ain't no question 'bout the fact that I could sure use you."

Pete nodded in appreciation. "Thanks, Jake," he said quietly.

"Are you ready to make a run to Winston tonight and to Greensboro on Saturday night?"

"Well, I wouldn't want to be putting Jennings out of any business."

"I've got other runs for Jennings. You won't be takin' nothing from him."

And that had settled it. Next thing Pete knew, he was driving over to see Jennings at Billy Hinton's cow pasture.

Pete came out of his reverie. After several times around the track, he was satisfied the Ford met his expectations. "Yeah, girl," he said, "you're humming." He let off the gas and rolled back to the pit.

Jennings leaned against the fence. "How'd she do?" he asked.

"Ninety."

"Jiminy Cricket! Nobody 'round here's gonna beat that except maybe Bennie Farnes." Giving Pete an approving grin, he walked over and touched his hand to the hot metal of the Ford hood.

"Think you can handle that kind of speed?" Pete asked him.

"You wanna race her Sunday, Pete?"

"No. My Ford will do ninety or better. I can beat you and Bennie Farnes both."

"Then race in Hillsboro on Sunday afternoon. I'll come to watch. It would be durn satisfying to see you beat that smug ass Bennie Farnes. He's made hisself a celebrity around here. It would be too much fun watchin' you whup up on his reputation. You will beat him, won't you, Pete? I warn you though, he's a dirty racer. He'll do anything to win."

"Maybe. According to the word circulating back at Charlie's, he's been telling everybody he was going to whip my butt. He's still sore because I threw him up against the wall at Charlie's." Pete scowled.

"That have something to do with how you met?" Jennings said with a grin.

"Some folks just don't know when to mind their own business and you have to teach them a lesson. Anyway, I can't see Robert before next week, and nobody seems to know anything about my fine upstanding uncle's whereabouts. Might as well pass the time beating Bennie Farnes in Hillsboro."

"There's a funny story about Charlie and Bennie's brother, Rufus. It was during the gas wars and Rufus pulled up to the gas pump out at Charlie's and the sign out front said 19.9 cents a gallon for gas. Charlie goes out and Rufus says, 'How come your gas is 19.9 cents a gallon and Tommy's across the street is 17.9?'

"And Charlie he says, 'If you don't like my price, why don't you get your gas at Tommy's?'

"'Well, I would,' Rufus says, 'but Tommy is closed.'

"And Charlie he says, 'Well, when I'm closed, I sell mine for 15.9 cents a gallon.'"

Jennings burst out laughing and slapped his side. "Ole Rufus he didn't know whether to laugh or cuss."

"Ole Charlie's a good guy," Pete said with a half-smile.

"Sounds like you been hanging around Charlie's a lot."

"I eat there most of the time since I'm staying at the motor court. If I could get hold of Robert, I might could find out where Farley's lurking these days. If he'd not likely to come around the farm, I'd stay in the bungalow, now that Freddie's in jail."

"You could stay in the house."

"I'm not ready for that yet."

By this time it was late afternoon and Pete turned his ear to the sound of a motor, one he'd heard before, one maybe he'd tuned up some time ago. He looked up to see Salvino's Cadillac pull onto the gravel outside the wire fence. *I recognize that Caddy now. It used to be Angel's.* He said to Jennings, "This is somebody you don't want to know. Let me go over and find out what he wants."

Salvino emerged from the Cadillac. He looked around for the closest shade tree and walked over to stand out of the sun. He watched Pete stroll through the gate. The message he conveyed in his body language was that he was in no hurry to meet with the Italian. Salvino dabbed his head and neck with his silk handkerchief and muttered, "Turner thinks he's too good to do business with me. A little humility's what he needs. Funny how eager these local hillbillies are to talk to me. They're so curious to find out the business of the stranger with the big black Cadillac from the big city. Then I tell them I represent a client who wants to leave New York to improve his life by settling among them and investing in their community, and it's amusing how much they want to do the talking."

But he hadn't learned the one thing he had tried most to discover. What was the reason Pete Turner hated Farley Oaks? What had Oaks done to fuel such fury, such explosive hate that burned just beneath the surface, which waited for the igniting match?

Salvino wanted to find that match and set off the explosion. That's how he was forced to survive right now, exploiting passions. Most of the old-timers he'd talked with said young Pete resented Farley trying to take his daddy's place. Salvino didn't buy that. Turner would have outgrown that by now. It didn't explain the hate he had nurtured and carried for ten years, the hate that had brought him home to get revenge. Revenge had to be what drove him. Salvino understood people's evil desires and the need to get revenge was what was driving Turner.

At the diner, he couldn't get anything out of Charlie. Walter Hudspeth said it was rumored Farley set up Rusty Turner's accident because he wanted the Turner land. Now why would Farley need to eliminate Turner to get his farm and liquor business? He had apparently acquired a great deal of wealth before he ever left Atlanta. According to the sheriff, Oaks left home at barely fourteen, followed an ex-con to Georgia, and worked for him until he could set up his own stills. Then he got into other illegal enterprises as well. Many of his poor relations he brought to Georgia to run his thriving liquor business. Later, when Farley needed to "get out of Dodge" just before the law caught up with him, he came back to Wilkes County and set up several legitimate businesses to include the Ford dealership in Wilkesboro. So far as anyone knew, Farley Oaks had not been involved in anything illegal since he came back to North Carolina and presented himself as a model citizen. Why would he need to set up Rusty's Turner's crash to get his farm and liquor business when he could have bought ten farms around Wilkes County? It didn't add up. Oaks didn't need money. What he needed was the good reputation he had been working so hard at earning. Turner's crash had been an accident. According to Sheriff Money, there was no evidence it had been anything but that.

One person he talked to, Johnny Purdue, hinted it had something to do with a younger sister. In a whisper he said her death was never really explained. There were rumors that although Farley Oaks appeared to be very kind to the girl, some dared to suggest that Farley had her murdered. From what Salvino learned, he found suicide, what the death certificate indicated, to be more believable. People remembered that after Rusty's fatal crash both the mother and the girl went kind of crazy. Purdue said the girl had been a beautiful, vivacious, straight-A student, but after Rusty's death she began to fail in school, became withdrawn and quiet, became depressed like her mother.

"Seems to me Farley Oaks did well by them to help out. That's what most people around here apparently believe," Salvino murmured.

Salvino also talked to Bennie Farnes and met his brother, Rufus. It was no surprise that while Bennie had looked to impress a relative of Farley Oaks, now he wanted to kill Pete. Not only had Pete humiliated him in Charlie's diner, but Bennie wanted no competition from Turner showing him up on the track. Bennie had a hero's status to defend, but in Salvino's estimation, Bennie Farnes struck him as a coward at heart. Despite the Farnes brothers' fury at Turner, which Salvino might be able to channel to his purposes, they didn't have two nickels between them to rub together, a decided disadvantage since money was the reason Salvino had come to these backwoods.

Salvino folded his arms. "I'm growing very impatient with you, Turner," he said under his breath as Pete sauntered toward him. "I'm sick of this heat, sick of this hick town and its small-minded people, and sick of you. Farley Oaks is probably the most intelligent and interesting resident of this entire county. I'd rather work a deal with him than you, Turner, or better still, work both ends against the middle, but it does not appear Oaks is real sociable."

Pete stepped up to Salvino and with an unwelcome scowl he said, "You still around? You keep turning up like a bad penny."

Salvino gave a shrug. "Then I don't guess you'd be interested in my information. It's about your uncle."

"Yeah? How much is it going cost me?"

"This is for free, just a favor for a friend." Salvino winked and Pete narrowed his eyes. He didn't trust this big city Italian.

"Your uncle lives up around Trap Hill."

Pete nodded, his tanned face glistening with sweat. "I know the area."

"He's built a big white house with a gated high stone wall. Then there's an inner metal fence. He lives there with a very small staff of hired help and lately he almost never goes out or receives visitors."

Pete drew a circle in the gravel with the toe of his shoe. He heard about the big house. If Farley didn't go out, it would be difficult to catch him in any uncompromising activities, especially if he stayed holed up in a fortress. "How do you know all this? Have you seen the place?"

"I know this because it's what I do; I check people out." Salvino gave a leering grin. "Angel never did business with a man until he knew his secrets, something he could use as leverage. Everybody has secrets, you know."

"Have you seen the place?" Pete repeated.

"As a matter of fact, I have. And one more thing, he has dogs, pit bulls that don't like strangers. Guess that's the reason for the metal fence. From what I saw, they could tear a man to shreds, and would, too." Salvino mopped his face and head again. He did not actually see any dogs. He didn't actually see anybody. When he got inside, he found the whole place deserted. "So, this job of knocking off your uncle could be more difficult. That means the price has gone up. It's a job way out of your league in case you had ideas of doing him in yourself. It will take a professional who can silence the dogs and get inside the house, or find a way to lure Farley Oaks out in the open into the sights of a long range shooter with a high powered rifle."

Pete scowled at Salvino. "I told you I'm not a killer."

"So you've said. Money should be no problem for you, seeing as how you can haul moonshine for your Uncle Jake."

Salvino had no way of knowing of Pete's deal with Jake, he was merely probing, based on the sheriff's warning to Pete in Charlie's diner on Monday. Despite Pete's attempt at deadpan, Salvino saw the involuntary squint of his eyes, the flicker of surprise they registered that said, *how does he know?* Salvino laughed, "I told you finding out about people is what I do. I learn their secrets. If you want your uncle removed, you need to let me handle it. Just give me the word and the money. I'll make the contact to set it up. I know the same people Angel knows, people who can do the job efficiently. It will never be connected to you."

Pete narrowed his eyes and frowned, "There has to be another way." He glared at Salvino, "I told you I don't want your help. You got that?" He turned his back and began to walk away.

"You will," Salvino called after him. "You will," he said, folding his handkerchief into a damp square and rubbing it over the top of his head.

Chapter Nine

Salvino had witnessed Turner humiliate Bennie Farnes in the diner. Soon after, he'd made it his business to introduce himself to the little fellow. Now that Salvino himself was smarting from Turner's rebuff, with growing impatience he began to consider how he could use the Farnes brothers to his advantage. Tuesday evening at dusk, he cautiously drove the Cadillac over the rutted, littered ground and overgrown brush of the trailer park where they lived. He preferred to work alone because involving others could get messy and keeping them in line could prove to be a bother. However, with Turner hesitating, Salvino saw no alternative but to force his hand. *What happened ten years ago that made Turner run? What made him come back? Revenge. I can smell it. It comes off Turner like steam from a boiling pot. All he needs is a little push. So, why didn't he take my offer? Does he have his own plan? That could open up a whole new possibility—blackmail.*

He found the Farnes brothers drinking beer and lounging in lawn chairs by the steps of their small trailer. When he strolled up to them, they eyed him with distrust, evidently wondering what business this flashy Italian would have with them. "Pezzo's the name," he said without offering his hand.

"We remember," Bennie said with a scowl.

But when Salvino mentioned he had a proposal and there might be money in it for them, their wary expressions changed at once to wide-eyed interest. With little prompting, Salvino found Bennie and brother Rufus readily agreeable to the idea of giving Turner his payback. "My little brother and me, we ain't got no use for Turner," Rufus said, crushing his empty beer can. "When he disrespected Bennie, he disrespected me."

"You'll need some help," Salvino told Rufus, the bigger one of the brothers. "Bennie here doesn't look like he can offer much in a fight. Turner's no wimp. As you've seen, he's got a short fuse, and when you mention Farley Oaks, that will really set him off."

"What's the reason for sayin' anythin' about Farley Oaks?" Bennie asked.

Because that's the trigger that will make Turner do what I want him to do, Salvino thought. To Bennie he said, "Do you want to let him get by with so publically slandering your benefactor?"

"My benefactor?"

"Sure he's been your benefactor. He helped your sister when she was down and out and you bought your first car from him. He was friendly to you, showed an interest in you. A big man like that, he didn't have to do that, but he did."

"Yeah." Bennie pondered Salvino's speech for a minute and then said, "You know, I still can't figure why my sister just up and left from that apartment he put her in. Kind of embarrassing, her being so ungrateful and all."

"That's even more reason to make Turner pay, to make it up to Mr. Oaks."

"How do we do that?" Rufus asked, pulling out his container of chewing tobacco.

"Find an opportunity to jump him. Tell him it's payback for insulting Farley Oaks' good name."

"How about my good name?" Bennie said.

"Your good name don't mean a hill o' beans to Turner," Rufus rebutted.

"Right," Salvino said, "We want him to think his esteemed uncle is out to get him."

"But Mr. Oaks probably don't know nothin' about that tussle at the diner," Bennie said.

"It's your job to convince Turner that Farley Oaks does know and that he intends to run Turner out of town for slandering his good name."

"I don't know," Bennie said with a frown. "Farley Oaks ain't a violent man."

"Of course he isn't, but Turner obviously hates him, and what he believes about his uncle isn't your concern. You'll be doing an upstanding citizen a service to get rid of that troublemaker before people get to wondering if there's something to what Turner says. Besides, you'll be doing yourself a favor as well. Turner's got the fastest car around and a reputation for winning. Do you want that kind of competition?"

Bennie's eyes narrowed. "When you put it that a way," he said.

"And spread the rumor that Farley Oaks is helping the sheriff close down the moonshine stills and that he's got Turner in his sights," Salvino added.

"What's that got to do with Turner?" Bennie asked.

"Turner is hauling moonshine for his Uncle Jake."

"How you know?" Rufus asked.

"I know," Salvino said, rubbing his chin. "I have it on good authority," he continued, *ad libbing* as ideas came to him, "that Turner got mixed up with some really bad people before he showed up here. He needs money, big money, like he can only get hauling moonshine."

"What kind of bad people?" Bennie asked.

Salvino put on his most distressed countenance as he recalled his conversation with Sheriff Money. "Mafia people."

"Mafia," Rufus said, wide-eyed and with another string of expletives.

"Turner came back here to haul liquor for his uncle Jake because he owes these people money. They don't take your excuses too long before you just disappear from off the face of the earth. So, unless you guys discourage him, he'll get his money, pay off the Mafia, and stay. Salvino noted he'd gotten both brothers undivided attention. "Turner left home before because he and his uncle didn't get along. He'll leave again if he thinks Farley Oaks is making things too uncomfortable for him. He's a runner. That's what he does when things don't go his way."

"Then he don't get the money to pay off them Mafia people," Rufus said.

"So he has to keep running," Salvino said, getting impatient. He wanted to take these two dummies and bang their heads together, but he held himself in check. "That's all you care about, that he doesn't come back here to stay."

"But what's in it for you? What you got against Turner?" Bennie demanded.

"That's my business. Yours is to make Turner believe his uncle's out to get him and keep our agreement mum. That's all you need to know."

"When you said there was some bread in it for us, how much we talking about? We ain't doin' your dirty work for chicken feed," Rufus said.

"How does a thousand sound?"

Rufus took a deep breath. "A thousand smackaroos? Just for roughing up Turner and spreadin' some rumors?" The brothers lit up like Christmas trees. Bennie whistled and Rufus expressed his joy with a profusion of profanities.

"You've got to earn it first. Harass him and make sure he's convinced his uncle is behind it. That's important," Salvino said. "You get rid of Turner, Bennie keeps his number one status at the tracks." Inwardly he was laughing at the thought of these clowns with a thousand bucks.

"It will be a pleasure to teach that Turner a lesson, won't it Bennie?" Rufus said, adding a few more expletives, as he spit brown juice into a dirty Mason jar.

"When do we get the money?" Bennie asked.

When Hell freezes over. "When I say so. That's when you get your money."

"How long's this gonna take?" Bennie asked.

"You saw how he exploded at Charlie's. He's close to the edge. We just have to give him a little push. That's all. Once you beat him up good and make him believe his uncle is behind it, we'll see what he does."

"So we rough him up. Then where do we find you to get our money?" Bennie asked.

Salvino thought a minute. He didn't want to be seen any-where near the Farnes brothers, but he needed to keep them on task until Turner caved. "Where can I find you that's a public place but still out of the way, where no one would necessarily connect my being there to see you?"

"Why you don't wanna be seen with us?" Rufus said, cocking his head back accusingly.

"Because if you fellows screw up...

"We ain't gonna screw up," Rufus said. "You kin find us at the Bloody Bucket just 'bout any time after dark. It's ten miles from here on Highway 421. You can't miss it because you'll see all them pick-up trucks and racing cars parked 'round it. Ain't no sign. Don't be lookin' for no signs."

"Yeah," Bennie chuckled. "They don't advertise."

Salvino had heard about the notorious speakeasy. It was a typical redneck joint where fights and knifings occurred on a regular basis. Sheriff Money had told him about it and said he wanted to shut it down, but so far he'd been unable to get any hard evidence to do so. The customers who frequented the place were mighty closed-mouthed. Salvino wasn't too sure he liked the idea of meeting there. He could protect himself if he needed to. He carried a gun and a knife on his person, but he didn't plan to use them. The wrong kind of attention, especially from the sheriff, would not work to his advantage. Better to keep his hands clean and let these idiots do the dirty work. Furthermore, he preferred not to spoil his silk shirt or scuff his genuine alligator skin shoes. "Is that the only place we can meet?"

"Don't know nowhere else. It's where we hang out," Rufus said.

"All right," Salvino agreed reluctantly. "After you do this job on Turner, be on the lookout for me at the Bloody Bucket at dark. We will touch base there."

"We have to find him alone, Rufus said. "Where do we do that?"

"You'll find a way if you want your money," Salvino said.

When he satisfied himself that the Farnes brothers had fully latched onto the plan, he left as quietly as he had come, confident in his ability to manipulate. He congratulated himself that he excelled in taking a spark of discontent and fanning it to his advantage.

Chapter Ten

Pete made his first deliveries in Winston-Salem on
Tuesday evening. He stopped at several speakeasies
across the railroad tracks in the poorer end of town, but to
his surprise there were other customers on his list who were
owners of popular restaurants. They didn't advertise moonshine since it was illegal to sell it, but discreetly provided it
to customers in-the-know who preferred Jake's moonshine
to the government's certified brew. Since he couldn't see his
brother before Monday, Pete channeled his impatience into
work, helping Jennings and Mack at the stills. On Saturday
night he traveled to Greensboro to make similar deliveries,
all without incident.

He also had a growing urge to get back on the track and he
considered entering Sunday's race at Hillsborough. Despite
Jennings's constant questions about whether he planned to
take on Bennie Farnes, Pete kept his thoughts to himself.
Customers at Charlie's also urged him to challenge Bennie.
It was obvious Farnes had been boasting that he was going
to win. Pete let them laugh and speculate, intending to keep
the element of surprise to his advantage if he decided to do it.

After making his moonshine deliveries on Saturday
night and getting in early Sunday morning, he slept little.
The Hillsborough race was that afternoon and his indecision
about entering was driving him crazy. His gut told him to

forgo this one because this rivalry with Bennie Farnes could only lead to trouble. On the other hand, he convinced himself that rivalries were a necessary part of the racing scene, motivating drivers to strive for their utmost performance and that none need last beyond the parking lot. Nonetheless, a goading voice in his head that superseded every argument was Bennie's praise of Farley, and the outrage he felt was eating a hole in his heart. He could think of nothing to shut down that voice except the satisfaction of showing up Bennie at the track. Humiliating Bennie would be like killing a part of Farley. Both were lumped together in his churning anger. Finally, he made the inevitable decision. When he called Jennings to tell him, his friend elected to skip racing at the Hinton track and meet Pete in Hillsborough. "I'd much rather see you beat Bennie Farnes," he said.

"Maybe I won't. Maybe he's better than me," Pete said.

The arrow on a red Coca Cola sign pointed to the turn off for Sparky's Race Track. The gates had opened at noon, although the main event wouldn't start before 4:00 p.m. Midday on this hot July Sunday, Pete's '39 Ford bumped along a dirt path that circled a wide open field, crowned in the distance by a tiara of hazy mountains under a cloudless blue sky. He trailed a string of modified Fords and Chevys. Here, the '39 and '40 Fords were the most popular vehicles among the racers. For obvious reasons most were painted black because the majority of the racers were trippers and their vehicles were never flashy. Except for a large white number painted with shoe polish on both doors, there were no distinctive paint jobs, or chrome pipes, or loud mufflers. On the highway, when their trunks were loaded with their jars and jugs of the white lightening, they wanted to blend into the mainstream of traffic without drawing the attention from the law. They intended that their distinction at the tracks would be in the speed and the skill that their lives often depended on when they were hauling.

Pete parked in a row of vehicles and got out. Gravel crunched under the soles of his Converse tennis shoes. He was already tasting the red dirt mixed with the odor of gasoline. The drivers, nervous and smoking their cigarettes, revved their engines or gathered in loose huddles, swapping stories and arguing over bragging rights. There would be brawls and fist fights with drivers and fans alike once they had several beers in their bellies. It was all part of the afternoon's entertainment.

Beyond where he stood, he saw a wire fence that separated the parking area from the spectator stands and the track below. Pete walked up to the ticket booth, a wooden structure about the size of an outhouse. A middle-aged bouffant blonde wearing too-tight jeans and a blouse about to pop its buttons took his two dollars and gave him a ticket and a big smile. In her rural southern drawl she welcomed him to Sparky's Speedway. "We ain't seen you here before," she said, fluttering her long Maybelline eyelashes. She was old enough to be his mother. He took his ticket and moved on. Most places he'd raced were only half-mile tracks or less and the prize money was pocket change. The farmer who owned the land just put out an old football helmet and hoped the fans would throw in a coin or two. A ten dollar prize wasn't much when it cost two to enter, proving this was not about money but the thrill of the competition.

The wire fence enclosed a space where tuffs of grass cushioned the hard red dirt where fans and families of the drivers sat around in folding lawn chairs and opened up picnic baskets and coolers of beer. A crowd had gathered and there was loud laughter and excited conversation. Pete walked past them to get a look at the layout.

The stands were wooden bleachers sitting on top of an incline that banked the spectator side of the red dirt track below. A high fence stretched across the top of the bank further separating the fans from the track, a security measure Pete had not observed at the smaller circle tracks with which he was most familiar. He knew of a recent situation where one of the racing cars threw a tire that flew into the stands and killed a man. A fence like this one might have protected him.

He walked to the fence and looked down on a red clay track ringed with advertising signs for RC Cola, Lucky Strike cigarettes, the Bank of Hillsborough and some other local businesses. To keep the dust down, workers were on the track now, dumping water onto it from a tank on the back of a pickup. This helped initially, but a time or two around the oval track with the cars throwing up the red dirt, it drifted through the air and into the stands, finding its way into all body crevices. Nothing could keep the dust out of the nose and throat. In some places Pete had seen drivers wearing goggles to protect their eyes from the dust. He'd also seen old football helmets worn because crashes were plentiful, but around here, trippers considered these extras as "sissy."

On the far side at the left end, he saw the grassy space that served as the pit. A road led outside from the pit area through a buffer of trees to the place where the drivers would wait for their turn to line up and go onto the track.

Pete hadn't seen Jennings yet, who had said he'd watch the race from the pit and lend a hand changing a tire, adding gasoline, or helping to trouble shoot a problem. Pete left the stands to walk among the spectators and look for him. Stepping around kids and blankets, he moved between clusters of people enjoying the warm afternoon.

"Young man," he heard a female voice behind him. It floated in his direction amid the sounds of male laughter and the kids yelling and chasing about. He didn't know anyone so he kept moving. "Young man," the voice became more insistent. He turned around. A plump, matronly woman was smiling at him. Her greying hair was pulled into a knot on the back of her head, and she wore a loose fitting dress and comfortable shoes. She waved him over. For the life of Pete he didn't recognize her. "Are you here all by yourself?" she asked.

"Yes ma'am."

"Well, come on over here and join us. We got plenty a food. Here, have some of my fried chicken and tater salad." She extended a blue plastic plate to him. "You want a beer?"

"No thank you, ma'am. I never eat before I race."

"Then you must be one of the drivers?" she said, withdrawing the plate and sitting it on top of one of the coolers.

"Yes ma'am."

"Ain't seen you here before," she said, studying him. "You new here?"

"Yes, ma'am."

"Well our boy, me and my husband's," she pointed to a man in bib overalls sitting with some others. Pete noticed their talk was loud and bawdy and they were shoveling large mounds of food into their mouths, "Our boy, Ricky, he's racing today, too. He's Number 12. What's yours?"

"Ninety-nine, Pete said, looking around for Jennings, anxious to move on.

"Dick Barnes owns Dick's Garage in Jonesville. He's sponsoring Ricky," she said. Pete had cruised through Jonesville, passing Dick's gas station and garage. It was the headquarters where the local dirt track racers congregated, where the mechanics and the drivers hovered over the souped-up cars or lay under them. "Before Ricky got him for a sponsor, we had to get a second mortgage on our house. It's his dream, you see, to be one of them NASCAR racers. Yep, my boy wants to make the big time, get those big dollars too," she laughed.

"Well thanks for your offer, but I'll be moseying on," Pete said, moving off before she thought of something else to say.

She called after him, "You sure? We got plenty."

When Pete found Jennings, some of the fans were leaving their chairs and empty coolers in the grass and ambling toward the stands. "Warm ups are starting," Pete said to him. "Let's go."

They walked back to the parking area and hopped into Pete's Ford. He drove around to the back side of the track where the cars were lining up. All except two were black Fords between the model years '34 and '40. "That's Bennie Farnes' on that '39 Ford," Jennings said, pointing to the car first in line with the number 1 painted on the doors. Bennie was leaning up against the hood, smoking a cigarette. Pete sneered and muttered under his breath that Bennie wouldn't be so sure he owned that number 1 after this race.

"I warned you Bennie races dirty," Jennings said.

Pete shrugged, "If he had skill, he wouldn't need to use dirty tricks."

"Just be prepared," Jennings said.

"It's my turn in the warm ups," Pete said. He got in the Ford. Jennings waved him off and watched Pete pull onto the track to run his hot laps. When he finished and came back to the wait area, the announcer's voice came over the loud speaker saying the timed runs would begin.

In the qualifying heat races each driver got five laps around the track to establish his place in the lineup for the main event. Pete didn't plan to show his hand by running his best speed. When the main event started, he didn't mind being in the back of the line because he had confidence in his skill as well as his speed. He wanted Bennie to go out over-confident that Pete couldn't beat him. He suspected Bennie was way too cocky to figure Pete might be setting this up. He grinned, watching Bennie strut around, giving other drivers a look under his hood and dispensing advice while waiting his turn. One of these was that kid Ricky, driving number 12, the one whose momma offered Pete the fried chicken. He remembered she said she had mortgaged her house so Ricky could make it to the big time. Pete shook his head. *Wonder if they know that Bennie Farnes will do whatever it takes to win. That boy could end up in the hospital if he gets in Bennie's way.*

Pete actually appreciated the challenge Bennie presented to him. It would require his intense concentration on strategy and skill. At least for a while, targeting Bennie would help him forget, forget that as yet he had no plan to get his ultimate revenge. He was committed. There was no doubt of that. It was just that as of yet he had not found the opportunity. It was the only way to wipe out the constant shame and anger that had tormented him for ten years. Farley's sterling reputation and immense popularity only made Pete more determined. His decision to restore the operation of the Turner farm and his daddy's whiskey business was all part of his dream that included the destruction of Farley Oaks. Once he could get hold of Robert and talk to him, he would get Farley Oaks or else.

Amid the noise of the loud engines and the dusty, oily smell of exhaust, the announcer's voice came over the loud speaker and introduced the drivers for the first heat race. In the stands, a blur of wildly whooping and hollering fans watched the drivers careen around the track, skidding sideways in the turns and throwing up red dust that drifted through the sticky air. After five laps, Bennie placed first. So, he would be first in the lineup for the main event. This was expected since he usually won at this track. In each of the four heat races, ten drivers competed and four of the ten were eliminated from further competition. Of the forty starting out, twenty-four drivers would compete in the main event.

In the second heat race it was Pete's turn. He got in the Ford and pulled onto the track. With his five laps he placed fourth. There were two more heat races to go. Afterwards, during the next hour there would be spectator games and prizes. All this delay was intended to ramp up the growing excitement and sell more hot dogs and soft drinks at the concession stand.

After Pete finished qualifying, he and Jennings walked around to the stands to wait out the interim before the real entertainment began. Jennings stopped to talk to Mack Johnson while Pete moved up the aisle to find a seat. He stepped around rowdy men in bib overalls and unkempt hair hanging out from Red Sox and Durham Bulls baseball caps. The females with them wore low cut halters and skin tight shorts. There were some there in plain cotton dresses or loose slacks, but for the most part respectable women did not accompany their men to the tracks. Pete found a spot and tried to see Jennings. He was still talking to Mack.

Pete moved into an open space in front of a beefy male with two days stubble on his face and his teeth black from Red Man chewing tobacco. As soon as he sat down he felt the fellow's knees pushing into his back. He turned around and gave him a warning scowl. The offender smirked at Pete and the knees continued to press into him. Pete looked around for another place to sit. Then a roar came from the crowd and Bennie Farnes joined the announcer at the microphone. He'd been asked to address the fans with comments about the impending race. Again, all this was to stir the fans to ever increasing frenzy. When the big guy behind Pete stood up to cheer Bennie with four letter expletives for emphasis, he sloshed his beer onto Pete's back. Pete felt the sticky liquid running down his neck and seeping inside his tee shirt. Impetuously, he jumped up and grabbed the front of the fellow's sweaty overalls. The man, spatting foul-smelling curses into Pete's face, flipped out a knife and pressed the point against Pete's throat. People around them scattered, toppling over one another and opening up a space where there had been no wiggle room moments before. "Looka here, pretty boy, ya like yer gizzard cut out?" Pete locked eyes with him, more offended by the nauseating smell of his breath than fear of the knife. Some men came over and tried to separate them, cursing them for distracting from the main event below. The obnoxious fellow uttered a few more expletives and shoved Pete with a force that sent him sprawling into the fans several rows below.

Moments later Jennings appeared. "What happened here?" he asked, extending a hand to pull Pete upright.

Pete jerked his hand free and stomped down the steps.

"You're welcome," Jennings said. Shaking his head, he followed after him, muttering, "If you don't watch it, that temper of yours is gonna get you in real trouble. You didn't use to have such a short fuse."

Chapter Eleven

The main event got under way at 4:25 p.m. The announcer stood on his platform high above the track where the checkered flag fluttered in the slight breeze. He waited for the winner to emerge from twenty-five laps of hard racing. Each man in the competition eyed it with the hope it would wave for him at the finish line. The announcer's voice blared through the speakers, giving the go ahead for the lineup. Over the hush of the crowd, the noise of the engines accelerated, creating sound waves that pounded into the head and chest.

Twenty-four cars in the field began rolling into their starting positions, sending out swirling clouds of red dust above the track. The four drivers on the front row were Farnes, number 1; Donnie Watson, a moonshiner from Martinsville, Virginia, number 15; Massy Taylor, a local guy, number 27; and Ricky Roberts from Jonesville, number 12. They were all racing Fords except Taylor, who drove a Chevy. Several rows back Pete pulled into his place. All eyes watched for the wave of the green flag. At the signal, the line of cars rolled into action.

Within a few laps the field spread out. Jennings stood on the sidelines next to Mack Johnson. Mack said above the drone of the engines, "I thought you were racing this afternoon at Hinton's."

"I changed my mind. Couldn't miss seeing Pete beat Bennie Farnes."

"Bennie ain't gonna let nobody beat him."

"I wouldn't bet on it. He ain't come against no Pete Turner."

"We'll see."

Mack pointed and said, "Farnes is in first position and that Ricky Roberts is behind him in second place. See how Taylor controls third place a car length behind Roberts."

For the next three laps, Roberts vied with Farnes for the lead, but each time Roberts tried to maneuver to the inside lane, Farnes bumped him and Roberts pulled back to avoid losing a tire or spinning out of control.

Before they'd run five laps, the number 10 car lost a wheel and spun into the middle of the track and the yellow caution flag came up. Then car number 3 plowed into the disabled number 10. The red flag came up to stop the race and the crowd rose to its feet, lifting a cry of excitement. The boys with the tow trucks headed out to clear the track while the drivers lined up again in the order in which they stopped.

"We're under the green flag again," Jennings said, intently observing the cars roll into action.

In the next lap, Roberts was forced to pull into the pits to change a tire. Taylor moved into second place behind Farnes, but cautiously avoided the inside lane where Farnes could bump him.

After two more laps Jennings exclaimed, "Taylor's stalking Farnes for first position. See, they're neck and neck. Taylor is inching ahead."

"Looks like number 30 has a problem over there on the other side of the track," Mack commented. "Looks like he's stalled out. Must be engine trouble."

Jennings raised his fist. "Taylor is pulling ahead of Farnes into first position. That-a-boy! He's inching by in the turn. Uh oh. Taylor's fishtailing! He's coming out of the turn, but

he's fishtailing! Look! Oh Jeeze! He's headed for number 30!"
The entire crowd watched as Taylor slammed into number 30.

"Both cars are blocking the track," Mack said.

Pete flew by, swerving to avoid the wreckage. Suddenly
Taylor's car burst into flames and the red flag came up.

For the few seconds, when Taylor didn't emerge from
the vehicle, it seemed he was either injured or pinned inside.
The standing crowd watched in silence. Several crew men
working in the pits, including Jennings and Mack, ran across
the track to help him. Before they got to him, he managed to
climb out the window and run for the sidelines just seconds
before the flames hit the gas tank and exploded.

Again, tow trucks cleared the track and the green flag sig-
naled for the race to resume. Ricky Roberts returned to the
track at the back of the field.

"Turner's moved into eighteenth position," Mack noted.
"He's a long way from first."

Another driver lost control and the yellow caution flag
warned the drivers to slow down. One by one, more drivers
wrecked, burned or pulled off the track with mechanical problems and Pete inched closer to the front.

Mack gave a running commentary, "It's the fifteenth lap.
Roberts is pulling in behind Watson in second position behind
Farnes, but it appears Farnes is pulling into the pits to change
a tire. Now Roberts is in second place behind Watson."

Two laps later he said, "Roberts is unable to close the
gap with Watson in the lead. Now Farnes is back in the race.
Watson's pulled a car length ahead of Roberts and Farnes is
moving up the line in the thinned out field. Oh no! Watson's
developed a problem."

In the seventeenth lap, once again Farnes led and Roberts
held second place behind him. "Pete's just pulled in behind
Roberts!" Jennings exclaimed.

Pete watched Farnes attempt to bump Roberts whenever
he gained the inside position. He understood Farnes felt no

qualms about racing dirty. All week he worked in the mill where rules were strict. On the track the rules disappeared. On the track, he could forget his mundane existence where others controlled his life. On the track, he was in control. As much as Pete had quickly come to despise Bennie Farnes, he realized they shared the same southern values that prized freedom from society's constraints. It was the moonshiners' justification for their right to produce their whiskey. Mill workers weren't daring like liquor runners, so Farnes had more to prove than Pete. He didn't doubt that Farnes, like Ricky Roberts, wanted to race with the big boys, freeing himself from the misery of blue-collar southern poverty and life in the textile mill, but he still didn't like Farnes, even if he believed he understood him. Anyone who praised Farley Oaks was his enemy.

The next time Farnes steered his vehicle toward Roberts to intimidate him, Pete gave Farnes a bump from behind. Roberts attempted to pull around Farnes in the turn, but he couldn't seem to force another ounce of power to get ahead in the straightaway. With Roberts and Farnes neck and neck, Farnes steered toward Roberts to bump his right front. Pete pulled behind Farnes and bumped his left rear, causing his momentary retreat. Roberts then tried for the inside, but Farnes bumped him and Roberts pulled back. Round and round, skidding sideways into the turns and correcting on the straightaways, they continued. In the twentieth lap Farnes controlled the lead with Roberts in second place and Pete a close third. As before, when Roberts tried to push by Farnes, Farnes swiped him.

Jennings exclaimed, "That dirty Farnes has bumped Roberts again, but the boy seems to be holding his own." With tightened jaw and every muscle ridged, Jennings focused intently on the three leading contenders. Then he grabbed Mack's shoulder. "Farnes is bumping Roberts again! The car's not cornering right! He's goin' into the fence!"

Pete swerved to avoid colliding with the out-of-control vehicle. The red flag came up and all drivers pulled into the pits. From there, Pete looked on as some of the workers rushed out on the track. Roberts had not stepped out of his car. It became apparent he had suffered injuries when they removed him from his car onto a stretcher. The race was suspended almost fifteen minutes while the drivers waited in the pits.

After the disabled Number 12 was rolled from the track, the green flag came up. Jennings declared to Mack, "Pete's in second position behind Farnes." They watched Farnes cut some jagged turns, sliding and fishtailing, throwing up voluminous clouds of red dust. Just as with Roberts, when Pete attempted to maneuver to the inside, Farnes bumped him and Pete was forced to back off. Finally, Farnes pulled out half a car length ahead of Pete, who on the next turn steered to the outside to avoid giving his rival a chance to bump him off the track. On the straightaway Pete edged forward and took the lead. "Go Pete!" Jennings shouted.

Coming out of the next curve, Farnes moved in close and bumped Pete. Pete dropped back.

"Farnes has the lead!" Mack shouted.

"Why are you pullin' for Farnes?" Jennings said, irritation in his voice.

"I'm not pulling for him. I just ain't so sure as you that Turner can beat him."

For two more laps Farnes blocked Pete from passing. One more lap around the track and Pete pressed the Ford to give everything in it. He spun the wheel to the left and accelerated through the turn, the rear end sliding and fishtailing. He torqued the wheel to the right and rocketed forward, holding his speed into the straightaway. "Turner has the lead!" Jennings announced, giving Mack a thumbs up.

The fans stood to their feet, shouting. Some were cheering, while others were booing the newcomer. From that point on,

Farnes couldn't catch him. Pete could feel him close behind, but Pete's Ford remained a car length in the lead and he flew over the finish line seconds ahead as the checkered flag came out.

No doubt, Pete thought, there would be fights between those cheering him and those who were furious that Farnes had lost the race. Farnes' Ford roared around to the pits and onto the road leading off the track.

Pete got out of his Number 99 to accept the small trophy, and fans came rushing past the fence to shake his hand. When a bevy of young girls in tight shorts and halters pushed forward to offer smiles and fluttering eye lashes with their congratulations, he ducked his head and brushed past the crowd to find Jennings. He met him coming from the pits, carrying his pack of tools.

"Sorry for Ricky," Pete said. "Hope he'll be okay. Guess Farnes is off somewhere licking his wounds. I know his pride is hurt, and he deserves it, but I'm kinda sorry for Ricky. Guess his momma's upset, too."

"So, you know this Ricky Roberts?"

"Not really. His momma offered me her fried chicken earlier this afternoon. She said they mortgaged their house so Ricky could race. Dick's Garage in Jonesville sponsored him for this one. Losing won't improve his chances of getting a sponsor for the next time."

Jennings raised his fist. "You whipped ole Bennie Farnes' butt! That's terrific!"

Speaking of fried chicken," Pete rubbed his stomach, "I could sure go for that now. Wonder if they have any hot dogs left at the concession stand."

"Let's go see," Jennings said.

By now the stands were almost empty and the crowd was heading toward the cars in the parking lot. Many of the fans wanted to shake Pete's hand. He wasn't comfortable with praise and tried to avoid making eye contact, but nodded to those he couldn't get around. One rude guy grabbed Pete and sneered, telling him Farnes should have won. Before Pete could retort and get himself in a brawl, Jennings pulled him away toward the concession stand. "They're closing up. If you want a hot dog, come on."

A boy with stringy yellow hair and a mustard and ketchup splotched apron was just closing the window. "Can we get a hot dog?" Pete asked.

"Sorry, we've packed up." He nodded toward a truck where a man and woman were shoving boxes onto the back. "Hey, you're Turner, number 99, the driver that won."

"Yeah," Pete said.

"My ma and my pa, they've packed the food in the truck. Sorry, but congratulations. That Ford of yours is got some power."

"Yeah," Pete said. "Come on Jennings. I'll drive you to your car."

"No, it's just as fast to walk. I like to hear what the fans are saying about Bennie losing. You go on. Meet me in the parking lot."

Night was settling over as Pete left the concession stand. He ambled toward the now empty bleachers. He was relieved that the last of the fans had left by way of the short path to the grassy area and from there to the gravel lot. Pete could see a few headlights from the line of departing vehicles. Jennings would be there waiting.

He had to find the opening in the fence to get down the bank onto the track where he'd left the Ford at the finish line. With a smirk he gloated over his victory in showing up Farnes. "Guess Bennie's sore. He won't be bragging so much around Charlie's now, I don't reckon. That'll teach him," he muttered with a sense of superior satisfaction.

Just as he reached the far corner of the stands, the shadows moved. He hesitated, not aware anyone was there but him. A glint of moonlight glanced off metal, and Pete felt the air move over his head. Instinctively, he ducked, a tire iron missing his head by an inch. Someone lunged at him from behind, knocking the wind out of him. He staggered to his feet and whirled around to confront his attackers who were wearing stocking masks. One of them was hefty like the obnoxious fellow who tried to knife him earlier in the stands. "So, you want to take this to the next level, do you?" Pete snarled, rushing at him.

"Hefty" growled and threw Pete headlong into the empty bleachers. "Take this for insulting Farley Oaks," he said. Pete rose to his feet and felt the tire iron impact his nose, making a crunching sound. Blood spurted out. Another tire iron came at him from the right, along with a string of expletives Pete hadn't heard since he got out of the navy. He ducked and staggered forward. He reached to grab the tire iron from his attacker. Pushing against it with all the force he could muster, he felt himself loosing strength and stumbling backwards into the bleachers. He barely managed to keep himself from falling, finally knocking the tire iron from his opponent's grasp. It clattered against cement. Before Pete could grab it and sling it out of reach, the man came at him again and drove a hard fist into Pete's right eye. Pete wobbled on his feet as his face took more pounding. His knees wanted to buckle. Determined to stand, he blocked the next punch. Catching the man's arm, he threw it out of joint and slammed him into the bleachers.

From the corner of his eye Pete could see the second fellow coming at with the tire iron. He whirled around and kicked him in the head. The man groaned, but came back swinging. Pete dodged him and the man lost his balance. Pete grabbed him from behind, bringing his left arm across his neck in a choke hold. Within seconds the man passed out. The other assailant who'd been slow to clear his head, rallied, and came at Pete, but Pete drove a hard blow to the man's stockinged face. He staggered and fell next to his partner.

Pete pulled him up and slammed his fist into the man's face again. He threw him back into the dirt and banged his head against the ground until he was satisfied he wouldn't be getting back up for a while. The taste of blood filled Pete's mouth. He spat and put the tips of his fingers to his nose. The pain exploded. His entire face throbbed. He felt dizzy and nauseous and his left eye was blurry. He forgot about Jennings waiting in the parking area. He thought only of getting some ice and some aspirin.

The last thing he did before staggering to his car was to rip the stockings from the heads of the unconscious goons at his feet. "Hefty" wasn't the jerk who'd assaulted him in the stands during the race. He'd didn't recognize either man.

Chapter Twelve

A light burned in the Crossroads Diner. When Pete saw it, he pulled in. Charlie sometimes stayed after closing when everything was quiet to make preparations for the next day. He had cooked another fresh ham and was preparing to bone it. Pete, covered with blood and red grime, entered through the back. The fluorescent tubes on the ceiling cast a yellow haze over the small kitchen. Charlie paused from his work, laying the knife on the table.

"Charlie, got some ice?"

Giving Pete the once over, he pulled a clean towel from a drawer and scooped some ice from the freezer onto it. He wrapped the ice in the towel and laid it on the end of the table. "Why don't you go over to the sink and wash your face. You're covered in blood."

Pete obliged, gingerly splashing cool water from the faucet onto his hurting face then patting it dry with a corner of another clean towel Charlie handed him. "Got any aspirin? I think my nose is broken."

Charlie touched Pete's nose.

"Ouch!"

"I can put it back in place, but it'll hurt."

"It hurts now. Go ahead."

Pete winced and gritted his teeth as Charlie pushed the cartilage in place. He tossed him a bottle of Bayer and got him a glass of water. Then he brought in a chair from the dining area and placed it in the doorway of the kitchen.

Pete poured a handful of aspirin out and swallowed them. Then he traded the aspirin bottle for the towel and ice, and slumped in the chair. He pressed the ice to his swollen face. "Two goons jumped me after the race."

Charlie washed and dried his hands and picked up his knife. He carefully cut the center out of the ham.

"What's that for?" Pete asked.

"Roast pork plate," Charlie said. He picked up the center cut and wrapped it in butcher paper. Walking over to the refrigerator, he put it on a shelf and closed the door. "Get lots of requests for it. Serve it with vegetables. Tomorrow it'll be collards and pinto beans."

"And you'll make barbecue out of the rest of the meat?"

"Yeah," Charlie said. He pulled up a stool and looked at Pete with concern. "So who beat you up? Somebody sore you won the race?"

"It was dark and they wore stocking masks, but before I left them laid out cold in the dirt, I jerked off the masks. I didn't recognize either of them." Pete ran one hand through his short, mussed hair.

Charlie shook his head. "Looks like you made some serious enemies. What did these fellows look like?"

"I know one was tall and paunchy. At first I thought he was a fan I got into a little altercation with before the race. The other was short." Pete put his hand to his face. "You got a mirror?"

"You don't need to look. I can tell you, you look awful. Maybe you oughta let a doctor check you to see if you got any broken bones. That eye don't look too good either."

"No. It's mostly my nose, but you fixed that. Once the aspirin kicks in, I'll be okay."

Charlie began cutting the outer layer of skin and fat from the ham, leaving a thin skim of fat for flavor. "Some of Bennie's family, I reckon."

"They said it was payback for insulting Farley Oaks," Pete said.

Charlie said, "The tall one sounds like Bennie's older brother. The other one might be Sheriff Money's deputy, Clem Howard. He and Rufus Farnes are thick. Bennie, he's got it in for you after how you insulted him in here the other day, and his big brother's paying you back, especially when you added insult to injury and beat him in the race."

"Whoever they were, Farley put them up to it. Probably paid them to kill me. He forgets I'm not a kid anymore. The other fellows are hurting worse than me I'll bet."

"Maybe, but more an' likely it was payback for Bennie's ruffled feathers after you attacked him in my diner and it hasn't got anything to do with your uncle."

"It could be Farley's wanting to 'encourage me' to leave again, especially if he thinks I've come home to take back my land so there'll be no place for Freddie when he gets out of prison."

"Farley's got plenty of land. He don't need yours."

"He may not need it, but he wants it. It's his way of thumping his nose at Rusty because Rusty wouldn't let him set foot on it while he was alive."

"You do have some notions. How long has Rusty been dead now? You really think a rich businessman like Farley concerns himself about that now? I believe you're the only one who thinks about it."

"I know things that could hurt him."

"Only if you can prove them. Farley's too secure, too entrenched 'round here to worry about the likes of you, especially if you talking about things that happened a long time ago. People tend to be forgiving if it it's no skin off their backs."

"Yeah."

"It's none of my business but I'd like to ask you to tell me one good thing all this anger you're carrying around is doing for you."

"What difference does it make?"

"It seems to me it makes a big difference. It could get you killed. Folks thought you was a bit off your rocker the other day with you whipping up on Bennie just because, like a lot of others, he admires your uncle Farley. You still blaming Farley for your sister's death?"

"He killed her all right," Pete said barely audible. He killed her spirit. Whether he killed her body I don't know. If I'd been there, I would have seen it. I would have seen what that filthy creep was about. I would have killed him, and Mary Kate would still be alive."

Charlie laid down the knife. "Seen what?"

"Nothing."

"Seen what? That your sister was depressed? You trying to do some kind of penance because you weren't there to hold her hand? You were fourteen, grieving for your daddy just like her." Charlie picked the knife back up and resumed cutting away any meat clinging to the bone. "If you insist on taking the blame, at least learn something from your mistakes. If you hadn't been so cotton picking angry at Farley for trying to help Eugenia, you might have been there to comfort Mary Kate. She looked up to you and you going off to live at Jakes didn't make it any easier for her to adjust to your daddy's death. Whatever happened, though, it's too late to change that, but you can recognize that anger is not your friend. Hate for Farley is not your friend."

"Some things are a matter of honor, Charlie, and you don't have all the facts."

"Maybe you exaggerated the facts. Maybe they've been growing out of proportion over the years." Charlie wrapped the meat in butcher paper. "Well I've had my say."

"I'm going back to run the farm," Pete said. "Freddie's gone. My momma's gone."

"I won't ask if you're going to make whiskey. If you are, it's a dangerous way to make a living. Your daddy knew that, but at least it gives you a goal to set your sights on. Maybe you'll get over this anger thing."

"Is Farley behind the sheriff's crackdown on the small bootleggers?"

"I doubt it. Farley Oaks is got bigger fish to fry, like that speedway he wants to build. Not a race track, mind you, but a speedway."

"Where's he keeping himself these days? Folks are telling me he's somewhat of a recluse."

"Could be. I can't say. He was never one to come in here. Could be he just likes his privacy. He's gotten to be some-what of a celebrity around here, especially since he got it in his mind to build this speedway. It's the talk of three counties and that makes it hard for him to try an' carry on like any ordinary citizen. Besides, I understand he's traveling a lot to put the deal together."

"I hear what you're saying about the anger, Charlie. You're right about one thing. My anger is a mean taskmaster. It only gets me in trouble, but there's a part of me that can't let go. It doesn't seem right to let him get off scot free, to watch him admired and praised when I know he's a snake. Under that image he's created for himself, he's a mean, nasty snake. It's not fair. That's all. Besides, I know Farley sent those guys that jumped me."

"I doubt it."

"Because I've been asking questions around."

"What kind a questions?"

"Questions Farley might not want answered."

"And?"

"Well, so far, nothing. People know things. I'm sure of it, but they're afraid."

"Of what?"

"That no one will believe them and...and maybe they're afraid of more than that."

"Let go of it, Pete, before that unforgiveness of yours gets you in worse trouble. Let Divine Justice take care of Farley."

"You mean like God?" Pete laughed, curling his puffy upper lip with a sneer. "I don't believe there's a just God. I believe only in me. If anybody is going to right the wrong done to my family, it's going to be me."

Pete pushed the chair back and got up. "Look, Charlie, thanks for the ice and the aspirin." He picked up the chair and carried it to the dining area. Glancing at the Pepsi Cola clock on the side wall, he saw it was nine o'clock. When he came back through the kitchen he told Charlie, "I'll see you around." He headed for the door.

"Sure. Hope you're still in one piece then."

Chapter Thirteen

On Monday morning Pete ate an early breakfast in the diner. He was hoping to avoid questions about his bruises or conversation about the race. Nevertheless, Charlie's customers seemed to arrive earlier than usual. Pete ignored outright questions which only led to whispered speculations. He'd had enough by the time Walter Hudspeth came in through the front announcing that Bennie was challenging Pete's win. Pete got up abruptly and left through the back. With his hands in his pockets, and cursing his fate that he'd been here a week and had accomplished almost nothing, he strode across the grassy lot behind the diner to go to the motor court. The race, notwithstanding his win, was insignificant in the bigger picture, and in that respect, he felt stalled.

He was glad for the easy money he was earning working for Uncle Jake. A few nights ago he thought he'd seen one of the deputy sheriff's cars tailing him, but Pete still knew dirt roads and turn offs the deputies had never found. Whether it was a tail or not, Pete had quickly lost him, and the money was beginning to add up. Fortunately, Jake was offering Pete a generous cut of the profits since half of his stills were on the land that he assumed was now his nephew's. The money would come in handy when he was ready to make repairs on the farmhouse. There was also the possibility he might have to pay for information incriminating Farley.

Pete got out his key and headed toward his room to brush his teeth and grab his stuff before going out to help Jennings and Mack load up the latest batch of moonshine for tonight's deliveries. Stepping onto the asphalt strip in front of the motor court, he noticed a Cadillac pulling away and out onto the highway. He cursed the day he ever laid eyes on Salvino Pezzo. He knew it had to be the unpleasant Italian. There weren't that many 1954 shiny black Cadillacs around, especially with that tacky Continental kit.

"Now what is he doing still here? Didn't I make it plain enough I wasn't doing business with him?" Pete's inability to answer his question gave him cause for concern. He clenched his teeth. "Since I refused his offer, is that slippery Italian spying on me, helping Sheriff Money, or worse still, Farley? I know those thugs that beat me up worked for Farley. Didn't the big guy say it was for insulting Farley Oaks?" Pete rubbed his chin and swore again. "I'm getting paranoid. Maybe Salvino just likes it here." He stopped in his tracks and growled, "Fat chance of that! Maybe I'll just call Angel. No. Angel's in Italy for his momma's birthday. Just my luck."

Pete started to put his key in the door. There was a card stuck in between the door and the jamb. He drew it out. It was a message from Salvino. "You can reach me at this number, but just for a few more days." Pete crumpled up the card. Inside the room, he flung it toward the waste basket and picked up his toothbrush. When he finished brushing his teeth, he grabbed his pistol, strapped it to his ankle and hurried to the Ford, still fuming over Salvino's impertinent persistence.

Pete left the motor court and headed for Robert's office in Wilkesboro. On the way, he decided he'd find a phone and let his brother know he was coming. Arlene had said he'd be back today. If that Gladys answered the phone, he'd ask for Arlene. That shrew, Gladys, would insist he make an appointment even to talk with his brother. Then, on the other hand, if she knew who he was, she'd never put him through! He wondered if he should give Robert a day to get caught up after being out for a week, but decided not to wait. He was impatient. Time was wasting.

A mile beyond the diner on Hartley Road he could see a large yellow house at the top of a grassy incline. That would be Judge Covington's home. On impulse out of curiosity, he turned onto Hartley. The house was not overly large or pretentious for a judge's home, but nevertheless impressive with four white columns, black shutters at the front windows and a glass transom over the white, double front door. He'd learned from Charlie that Red headed Myra Claire was none other than Judge Covington's daughter.

Pete slowed almost to a stop, but decided he should turn around. Then he saw there was someone pushing a mower across the green lawn up close to the house. Although her hair was tied up in a kerchief, he could tell it was a tall, slender girl, probably the green-eyed beauty he'd seen coming into Charlie's the other day. *She has to be the Myra Claire working in Robert's office.*

Before he took time to reason himself out of it, Pete turned the Ford up the hill. When he reached the circular drive, the girl stopped her mowing and looked at him. As he stepped out onto the smooth pavement, Pete felt painfully aware of how out of place his junk car must look to her in front of the beautiful antebellum home.

With a quizzical look, Myra Claire wiped her hands on the back of her shorts. She obviously didn't recognize him as she walked toward him.

"Haven't we met?" he asked, standing by the Ford. As soon as he said it, he realized it sounded like the dumbest, overused line.

She placed her hands on her hips and frowned suspiciously. "No. I don't think so."

Unable to stop himself, he plunged ahead. "I mean didn't you go to the county high school?" *Dang it! Why was this girl making him nervous? I sound like an idiot.*

"Yes, but I don't remember you."

"I went to school in Wilkes, but your school might have played mine in baseball. I was a pitcher in '42 and '43."

"I don't watch baseball."

"Our paths might have crossed."

"I doubt it. The Judge and momma always told me to stay away from Wilkes County where all those wild bootleggers lived."

"Why 'wild bootleggers'?" Pete asked with a frown.

"They're bad people that operate outside the law, making illegal moonshine and driving like maniacs all up and down the county roads. Anyway," she looked toward the house, "did you come here to see the judge? Tell me your name and I'll go see if he's busy."

Pete leaned against the side of the car. "My daddy was Rusty Turner. Ever hear of him? He made moonshine, the best in these parts and he wasn't a bad man." She folded her arms and tapped one foot impatiently while Pete rushed on. "My daddy, my granddaddy and my great granddaddy made moonshine. None of them were bad people. They were just making a living. It was the government men who were bad, who blew up their stills and put fathers of families in prison because the government wanted to make money off their hard labor." Pete took a breath. "Just to set the record straight."

Myra pulled the kerchief off and brushed it over her perspiring face. "Making moonshine is illegal."

"What if the laws are wrong?"

"Have you heard of due process, the rule of law?"

"Yeah, and I reckon you've heard of civil disobedience. Without civil disobedience and rebellion against unfair laws, the United States would still be under British rule and taxation without representation."

"Sometimes laws are bad, but there's a right way to change them," she said.

"You mean we should expect crooked politicians controlled by rich and powerful men to make laws that benefit nobody but them?"

She placed her hands on her hips. "I hope you're not insinuating that the judge ever accepted graft. If you came here because you've got some gripe against Judge Covington, you better leave right now. He's not in the best of health and he's served this community honestly for many years." By now Myra's expression was angry and challenging, her green eyes sending out darts of fire.

"I don't know about the judge," Pete said, "but for every good politician, there are ten bad ones."

"Gee what a cynic. Not all politicians are crooked, and exactly where do you get your statistics?"

"Life," he said. "There's no justice for the little guy."

Pete realized he'd come across more adversarial than he meant to, and against his will, he couldn't help admiring her spunk. Even with her hair a tangle and her face wet with grime and sweat, she was so darn pretty. Those challenging green eyes, they could take his breath away. "By the way, the name is Pete Turner. You probably don't go to the dirt tracks. If you did, you might have heard of me. Since I came back, I've been winning races at all of them."

"So," she said with a smirk, looking totally unimpressed "you're *that* Pete Turner."

"I am."

"And is that how your face got so cut up and that big bruise around your eye?" Her expression had changed. Her eyes almost held concern.

He rather enjoyed it. "Anyway, we've met at least twice," he said. "I met you coming out of Charlie's diner at lunchtime last Friday."

"No. I don't recall," she said crossing her arms. "Well, come to think of it...there was a guy blocking the doorway. Coming out of the bright sunlight, I couldn't see him well."

"So you see. We have met."

"I'd hardly call that meeting someone."

Pete stuck his hands in his pockets. "We could change that. Maybe you would agree to go to a movie with me." His heart came up in his throat. *I can't believe I said that. My mouth is running way ahead of my brain!*

"I don't know you." She began to tap her foot again.

He grinned. "But I think you know Robert Turner and he's my brother."

"Wait a minute," she said, her expression changing to wide-eyed alarm. "Don't tell me you're that nut that forced his way into our office two days ago claiming to be Robert Turner's brother." She put her hand to her mouth.

So this is *the same Myra Claire.* "I'm not a nut," he said, his eyes narrowing in defiance. "But I am Robert Turner's brother. I don't look like him. He looks like our mother. I look more like our daddy."

"Robert Turner's brother is dead. He says so."

"We'll see about that."

"So you say." She put her hands on her hips and scowled at him.

"If it turns out I am Robert's brother would you go to the movies with me?" *I did it again. She's going to say, "Not in a million years."*

"That's not been confirmed yet."

Trying to get himself out of an embarrassing corner he said, "By the way, how did you come to work for Robert?"

"I know Robert from church. He asked me to fill in temporarily for the summer while one of his secretaries was out having a baby. I teach history and civics at the high school during the school year."

"Did you say *church*? You met my brother at church? What was he doing there?"

"What do people usually do in church? He's a member."

"Oh, no. You mean to tell me Robert's got religion...I guess a lot of things happen in ten years...but I didn't expect that."

"Not religion."

"You just said he's a member of your church. You have to make some kind of religious confession to join a church, promise to believe their doctrine and all that mumbo jumbo." Pete frowned. Religion had ruined his momma.

"If your brother really is Robert, which I highly doubt, you should know that he's received Jesus."

"What?" Pete said, not believing his ears.

"I said he's received Jesus."

"That's not religion?"

"No. That's a personal relationship."

"You're not talking about one of those 'born agains'?" Pete felt disappointment overwhelm him, like his heart sinking into his stomach. If his brother was now one of those born again, Bible-totting fanatics, then this Myra Claire must be one of them too.

"When and if you see Robert," she said, "he can tell you his testimony. Now if you didn't come here to see the judge, if you'll excuse me, I have to cut the grass."

Pete grabbed the door handle of the Ford. "Sure."

She shook her head and walked off.

Pete got in the car. As he drove away, he thought, *Rule of law. Anybody who believes in that is naïve. What could I expect from a judge's daughter? She doesn't watch baseball. She probably thinks racing is barbaric, not to mention how she feels about bootleggers. Worst of all, she's religious.* Pete felt another stab of disappointment in his gut. It was not to be his last one for the day. When he stopped at a pay phone on his way to Robert's office, he learned his brother would not be in until Tuesday afternoon.

Chapter Fourteen

If Pete had bothered earlier to follow the Cadillac when Salvino pulled away from the motor court that morning, he would have seen that sightseeing was all Salvino was up to at the moment. Bored and as impatient as Pete to get on with business, Salvino drove around the countryside and up in the mountains. It was a hot day without a cloud in the blue sky, and the mountain air offered some relief. He pulled off at one of the viewing decks and looked over the edge at the farms below. They appeared like tiny miniatures on a game board. He complained to the breeze how Angel had messed up his life and how all this having to wait around to push Turner over the line was getting on his last nerve. He paced and consoled himself. "It's inevitable, though. With Turner's short fuse, he'll come to me yet. Only I anticipated the explosion would happen quicker. And all this waiting is for what? Chicken feed compared to the kind of payoff I'm used to, but for now, Pezzo, this is your best bet until you get to Florida. There will be new opportunities for you there beyond Angel's influence, but you have to get there first and you can't go a pauper."

Later in the day Salvino ate lunch at the diner. He relished the comments about Pete's broken nose and black eye. Looking very satisfied, he inwardly congratulated himself for his power to make others do his bidding. Although word traveled quickly in the close knit community, no one was claiming to know who beat Turner up, and it was a source of intense speculation. Charlie ignored the talk. When questioned, he said he didn't know anything about it.

Salvino supposed the Farnes brothers would be eager to get their thousand bucks and would be anxiously looking for him to show up at the Bloody Bucket that evening. They didn't know they'd never see three dollars much less a thousand. He'd have to finesse them and keep the carrot dangling until Turner agreed to do business. Once he was done with them, he'd be gone, and those country hicks would soon figure out their windfall had blown away. If he worked it right, he would leave all of them, including Turner, holding an empty bag.

Just as he imagined, after dark on Monday evening, Bennie and Rufus were biding their time at the Bloody Bucket and keeping a lookout for Salvino's Cadillac. The weathered, tin-roofed structure, hardly more than a wooden shack, sat in a clearing that was partially hidden by a cove of tall trees. In the daytime, it looked shabby and indifferent; at night, it came to life, pulsating with lively blue grass music or twanging with Country Western tunes on the jukebox. When night began to descend, the patrons started gathering. The stars and the rising moon gave more illumination than the naked lights hanging from the lamp posts outside, casting shadows appropriate to the business of the place. Like a magnet, it drew the muddy farm trucks and souped-up whiskey cars rolling in to the gravel parking lot. Male voices calling to one another disappeared through the entrance. Some light came through the screened door, banging routinely as farmers and mill workers entered into the noise, smoke and clandestine activity within.

Dimly lit by a few naked bulbs hanging from the ceiling, the shadowy scene inside welcomed the rowdy customers who lounged about the counter, or sat at crude tables and booths to drink and gamble at cards. A handwritten menu posted on the wall listed hamburgers, hot dogs, and club sandwiches for sale. The beverages listed were Coke, RC Cola, and root beer. There were two RC dispensers. Both dispensed beer. If a lawman ever came in prowling and actually requested RC, he'd be told it was out, but he could get Coke or root beer. In the backroom where an interested party might find a card game, there was a barrel hidden behind a fake wall that dispensed moonshine. If the law drove up, word spread like wildfire through the inside, and the customers quickly consumed their illegal alcohol. The occasional lawmen who dared to come in might smell it, but they couldn't find it, and most didn't search too diligently.

Salvino pulled into the parking lot in the front where the Farnes brothers could see the Cadillac. Sure enough, seconds later they came hot-footing it out. Then he pulled around the back where they followed him into the darkest shadows near the edge of the woods. Walking behind his older brother, Bennie chewed a toothpick. Because the owner of the sleek vehicle didn't intend to have them bring dirty boots and grimy overalls into his Cadillac, he opened the door and stepped out gingerly, wincing at the sound of his shoes crunching on the rough gravel. He leaned up against the side. Seeing Rufus, Salvino observed that he carried his arm in a sling. "I told you to rough up Turner, not the other way around, and I warned you he's vicious."

"A thousand smackaroos will ease my pain," Rufus retorted.

"What happened? I hope you've had the good sense to come up with a cover story," he said.

"Clem got a concussion, but he didn't go to no doctor. We're layin' low."

"Did Turner see you? Did he get a good look at you?"

"Don't worry," Rufus said. "Turner don't know us. It was dark. He couldn't of seen much."

Salvino frowned.

"Nobody's gonna know it was me and Clem Howard that beat up Turner."

Salvino looked at Bennie. "I warned you, didn't I, that Turner is vicious? Next time it might take all three of you." He maintained a deadpan expression, despite his amusement. There was plenty more passion in this brouhaha for him to manipulate.

"Next time? You didn't say there was a next time," Bennie said. "When do we get our money?"

"Not until I decide the job is done. Now let's talk about what we do next."

Rufus chewed a wad of Red Man and spat on the ground.

Bennie narrowed his eyes and said, "So, you ain't never said what you got against Turner? What's in this for you?"

"No, I did say. It's my business and nothing that concerns you."

"Yeah. I don't know if I like that." Bennie said.

"So what we gotta do?" Rufus asked.

"Keep an eye on Turner and keep him paranoid."

"Para what?" Rufus said.

"Make him believe his uncle is out to get him. See where he goes."

"Probably to Jake Turner's stills if, as you say, he's haulin' moonshine for him," Rufus said. "But we don't know where them stills are. They could be anywhere up in them hills. It's next to impossible to track anybody up there."

"And if he's hauling moonshine, ain't nobody around here gonna catch him," Bennie said. Bennie picked his teeth and made a sucking sound, swishing his tongue over them.

Salvino looked away in disgust. "Did I say anything about finding the stills? Just make him think Farley Oaks has the sheriff watching him."

"I can get my deputy friend to track him. He'll just be doing his job," Rufus said.

"Then we have to split the thousand three ways," Bennie objected.

"Yeah," Rufus said. "We ain't gonna do that."

"No," Salvino said. "Don't get any deputies involved. Just drop little hints at Charlie's that the sheriff is watching Turner. And always mention that Farley Oaks is behind it. The gossip mill will take it from there. Just don't get any deputies involved. From here on out this has to stay between us, between us. You got that, Rufus?"

"Yeah."

"Rufus, you're sure Pete couldn't identify you from the fight?"

"No. It was dark and he don't know me I told you."

"All right. Do anything you can to harass him."

"Like beat him up again?" Rufus asked, looking worried.

"You don't appear to be in much shape for that, and I'm wondering if Turner didn't get the best of you. I'll leave it to your imagination as to how you harass him."

"Like slash his tires?"

"Whatever you come up with, make him think Farley Oaks is behind it. That's what counts. Continue to feed the rumor that Farley is helping the sheriff close down the stills. You're doing that aren't you?"

"Yeah, we're doing it," Rufus said.

"I don't like lying about Mr. Oaks," Bennie said.

"But you do like the idea of a thousand bucks. No ill is intended for Farley Oaks. It's a trap for Turner. Do what I said. If it works, the payoff comes when you succeed, and be sure you let me know where he goes, who he talks to. Sometimes he doesn't come back to the motor court until just about sunup. That's when he's been making his deliveries during the night."

"We gotta follow him out of town on his deliveries?"

"Just follow him when he's local and find ways to harass him. You understand?"

"Yeah. We understand. How we know you ain't just settin' us up for trouble? How we know you ever gonna pay us our thousand?" Bennie said.

"Look, Farnes, are you in or out? Just say so. I don't have time for cowards who can't make up their minds."

Rufus looked at Bennie. "We ain't gonna get in no trouble just plantin' some rumors. After all, we just tellin' what somebody else tole us."

"Yes. That's what you have to do."

"I still don't like lying 'bout Mr. Oaks," Bennie muttered.

"Our momma always said 'Sticks and stones will break my bones, but words won't never hurt me.' You remember that Bennie?"

Bennie made his sucking sound again, swishing his tongue over his teeth. "Yeah."

"Since I ain't got no work right now, I might as well keep an eye on Turner," Rufus said.

Salvino had to keep a straight face not to laugh at these idiots, especially Rufus. "Keep an eye on Turner," he said. "Find out where he goes, who he talks to, and don't forget to keep him looking over his shoulder for his uncle's bad guys. I'll see you back here tomorrow night."

"What if we don't have nothin' to report by then?" Bennie said.

"Make sure you do," Salvino said impatiently. It galled him to think about all that money Turner was raking in making hauls for his uncle Jake while he had to put up with these nitwits. He needed that money and he needed it now. "The sooner I get what I need, the sooner you get paid." He opened the door of the Cadillac and got in.

Bennie watched Salvino drive away. The sky above the trees was now a dark blanket scattered with twinkling points. The moon had drawn itself into a distant ball of soft light.

"I don't like it," Bennie said. "I don't trust that slick fellow. He's the one dealing all the cards and there's an ace up his sleeve he ain't tellin' us about."

Rufus stuck his hands in his pockets, looked at the ground and spat. "Maybe he's the Mafia man that's lookin' to collect a debt from Turner," Rufus said.

"Why would he need us to do that?" Bennie said, pacing in a circle. "We don't know nothing 'cause he ain't tellin' us nothing. Pezzo ain't the mob guy lookin' to collect the debt from Turner. The Mafia get what they want with muscle and guns. No, Pezzo's got another game goin'. He's after the bootleg money. You can bet on that. How Farley Oaks figures into this, I ain't figured out. Turner hates him. That's for sure, but why does Pezzo want Turner thinkin' his uncle is runnin' him off? What's in it for Pezzo? He don't live here. What does he care if Turner stays or goes? And you think he's gonna give us our grand? Naw. He's gonna use us and take off with the money."

"But if we do what he wants, why wouldn't he pay us?" Rufus said. "Pezzo's loaded ain't he? All them fancy clothes he wears and that fancy car."

"Just cause you think he's loaded don't mean *he* thinks he is."

"A thousand bucks sounds mighty good. Where we ever gonna get a chance to get that kind a money again?"

"We ain't got it yet…but there might be a way to get that and more," Bennie said, breaking his toothpick and throwing it at his feet. "We pretend to go along for now. We'll find out what Pezzo's got up his sleeve. Like you said, you ain't got no job, so you got to be the one doin' most of the spyin'. Get Clem Howard to helpin' you."

"But Pezzo said to tell nobody, to keep our plans to ourselfs, and then we'd have to split the money three ways if we get Clem in on it."

"Howard don't need to know nothing 'cept to help you find out what Pezzo is up to."

"Won't he want to know why?"

"Pezzo's been sayin' he's here representin' a rich customer who wants to build a manufacturin' plant 'round here. Tell Clem you think he's lying, that he's up to no good. That's all you gotta say. If Clem asks a lot of questions, just say you don't know. That's what you gotta find out."

"I sure got a lota stories to keep straight."

Bennie put his hand to his chin and his deep thoughts wrinkled his brow. "Pezzo eats at Charlie's a lot, but he ain't staying at the motor court."

"Not fancy enough for him," Rufus said.

"He's probably staying at some hotel in Winston. It's a big town. Lots of places to fade into the woodwork. Harder to find him."

"A long way to come to eat at Charlie's," Rufus said.

"Not so far. That's how he keeps his ear to the ground. So much gossip at Charlie's. Ain't nothin' much happens around here you can't find out at Charlie's." Bennie rubbed his chin and calculated. "Whatever Pezzo's after, there's money in it. And don't you believe he plans to share any of it with us. But maybe we ain't so stupid as he takes us for. You and Howard find out where that fox is staying and keep an eye on him. It's not Turner we need to watch. It's Pezzo."

"What we gonna report to Pezzo tomorrow night?"

"We tell him just what he wants to hear."

For a minute, Rufus looked confused. Then he grinned. "I get it."

Chapter Fifteen

On Tuesday, Pete's chest felt tight with anxiety about his meeting with Robert. The nervous emotion of seeing his brother after so long a time; the fear of his being scorned for cutting himself off from his family all the years he'd been running away; the uncertainty of whether Robert would dismiss him for wanting to return to the whiskey business; for all of that, Pete could never have imagined this meeting was about to mark a turning point. It would be a decisive moment that would set him on a road he could not have foreseen.

The brown-haired secretary showed Pete to the conference room and closed the door behind her. The scent of Chantilly lingered in the air as did the sound of her clicking heels moving away down the corridor. Neither she nor Gladys made any comment about Pete's first horrendous visit to the office when Gladys tried to have him arrested. Both maintained a polite and professional distance, but Pete felt the uncomfortable suspicion that they still saw him as an imposter. He let out a tense sigh. Surely his own brother would recognize him even after ten years.

Rather than sit, he continued standing. When he'd called here yesterday, after his disappointing encounter with Myra Claire, and then learning Robert couldn't see him for another day, he'd decided he'd better schedule an appointment. He knew Robert was expecting him. His palms were sweating.

To compose himself, he tried to concentrate on the room decor. It was functional, but impressive in its simple elegance. Robert didn't learn this kind of fine taste in furnishings at the Turner farm, and Pete felt the distance between himself and Robert increasing by the moment. He ran his hands over the cherry wood arms of the upholstered chair in front of him and caressed the glossy conference table, its sheen reflecting the light of the brass chandelier overhead. His eyes trailed up to the gold-framed English hunting scenes displayed on the grass cloth above bold chair railing. Festooned in their red jackets and surrounded by the hounds, the foxhunters galloped on their sleek horses over the green hills and rippling streams of the English countryside. Pete couldn't help but be reminded of the hills and streams on the Turner land, hoping it was soon to be his and not in the hands of usurpers. He took a deep breath. The plush Oriental rug under his feet complemented the richness of the maple-stained hardwood floors.

Robert had done well. He had never wanted to emulate Rusty as Pete had. In Pete's opinion, his brother had always acted embarrassed by his daddy's occupation and had tried to avoid the subject when around his school friends whose families had left the whiskey business for legitimate ways of making a living. Apparently, Robert had never complained about taking the whiskey money that paid his way through undergraduate and law school. Although Robert had never shirked his duty while living at home, he didn't hesitate to let Rusty know he meant to follow a different course in life. Remembering this, Pete felt one small ray of hope: Robert would have no interest in the farm. There would be no competition there.

The door opened and Pete took in the sight of his tall, lanky brother. Robert closed the door. With a stern countenance Robert scrutinized him. Pete waited. He didn't know whether to say something or stare back.

Then there was a tilt of Robert's head, a flash of recognition. He smiled, and Pete relaxed with a sigh of relief until Robert's face twisted with emotion as he embraced his younger brother. He sobbed with such deep emotion that his whole body shook. Pete stood stiffly. He hadn't allowed himself to shed tears since his sister's funeral.

After recovering his composure, Robert wiped his face with his handkerchief while he continued to grasp Pete's hand and gaze at him in disbelief, like a thirsty person seeing water and fearing it's only a mirage. When Pete could stand the intensity no longer, he pulled away and began to talk in a nervous rush, making apologies for his long absence, for not letting his brother know he was alive.

"The truth is," Pete said, "I didn't stay in one place long enough to say I'd been there. And I didn't know when the urge to move on would come on me. I was restless, you see."

Robert sat down on the edge of the conference table. He said, "That's not important. What *is* important, you're here now. You have to meet the family," he said with enthusiasm. "I'm married. My wife, Melinda, doesn't know you're home. She only knows I *had* a younger brother. I didn't tell her you'd come back, not until I saw for myself that it was really you. She'll want you to come for dinner. Soon. And you can meet my little girls, Betsy and Lucy. The richest blessings in life come from knowing God and finding joy in family."

Pete's breath quickened. He didn't want Robert to talk about God. Sticking his hands in the pockets of his dungarees, he moved toward the draped window and looked out on a sidewalk where busy pedestrians were passing by. He didn't want to appear rude either and miss this sense of good feeling between them before he could bring up the subject of the farm. He turned back around and stood behind a chair, instinctively placing a barrier between himself and his brother to discourage Robert's touching him. He couldn't handle all the emotion.

Robert continued speaking. "Taking time to enjoy life. That's what's important. I started out working too much, spending too many long hours away from my family, but through Melinda's prayers, I came to see that I wasn't really living. Now I enjoy my work more, not having all the guilt, now having my priorities in order. Our troubles can make us bitter, or they can make us better if we learn from our mistakes." He laughed self-consciously. "I sound like I'm preaching. I don't mean to. We have plenty of time to get to know each other. I'm sure both of us have changed in ten years, but there's plenty of time. I'm just so grateful to God you're alive and you're home."

"Yeah. I heard you got religion."

"From Myra Claire. She told me of, of meeting you." Robert grimaced. "I'm sorry your first visit here turned out to be so memorable, in the wrong way, but we hadn't heard from you, never expected to see you again. Momma refused to believe you were dead. She held onto her life longer than the doctors expected. She was waiting for you to come home."

Pete shifted uncomfortably. *It's just as well she's gone,* Pete thought. He would never forgive her. "You'll let Myra Claire know I'm not some crazy nut, that I'm your brother?"

"Since I haven't kicked you out and called the sheriff, I imagine the office crew has assumed by now you are not the imposter they thought you were. They'll be curious about the details. I'm sure she will be told as soon as she gets in Wednesday."

Pete rubbed his chin. "I'd like to know what she will say, since she was so wrong."

Robert put his arm on Pete's shoulder. "She will laugh. She doesn't take herself too seriously."

Pete said, "I wouldn't have figured that...but I want to ask you about the farm."

"What about it?"

"Freddie's in prison. Momma's...Momma's gone. Unlike you, I've always wanted to follow in Daddy's footsteps."

"Yes, I know you have. I was never ashamed of Daddy like you often accused me of being, but I decided very early that the whiskey business wasn't for me. I'm grateful to him for sending me to college and law school, and by the way, did you ever finish college and get your degree?"

"No. Two years was enough for me. I don't need a college degree to run the farm. I learned everything from Daddy." Pete noticed Robert's eyes reflected a change from mild interest to concern. "You said the whiskey business wasn't for you. Will you disapprove if I want it? It's always been my plan. Will you have a problem with that because you're a lawyer now?"

"Enforcement is not my end of the law," Robert said. "What you do in that respect is on your own conscience."

Pete felt hope flood through him. He let out a sigh. "Then it's settled. I'll make the Turner farm better than ever."

"Not quite *settled*."

"Why not?" Pete asked.

"The Turner land is as good as sold."

Pete's heart stopped. "What do you mean?" But he knew the answer before he asked. He knew who had tried to get control of the Turner land from the moment Farley Oaks learned Rusty was dead. "Not Farley?"

"I'm sorry if you're disappointed. Momma refused him all those years you were away, holding it for you. As her health deteriorated and you didn't come back, we didn't know whether you were dead or alive. Just before she died, she told me Farley could have it. I was busy and I let it slide for months because I knew Momma wanted you to have it, but three months ago I gave Farley a price, which he readily accepted. I drew up the papers and sent them to him. It's been at least two months ago."

"Then the sale hasn't gone through?" Pete asked, hoping it wasn't too late.

"We shook on it, a gentleman's agreement."

"But that's not binding, if the papers haven't been signed."

Robert grimaced. "It's binding if I'm a gentleman."

"Farley's no gentleman."

"I signed the papers. Farley has them. I'm surprised he hasn't sent them back already, but he's tied up with the plans for the race track he intends to put on the Turner land."

"Race track on the Turner land! Pete held out his hands, imploring. You can't let this happen," he said. The blood rushed to his face and he felt his chest constrict as though he were suddenly pulled under water. He grasped the back of the chair next to him. Farley Oaks' hands were squeezing all the breath out of his lungs. He whispered between clenched teeth, "You can't let this happen. You know how Daddy felt about Farley. You can't let him buy the farm. Don't you understand this is one more way he thumps his nose at us. It's his way of giving us Turner's our comeuppance. How could you even think of selling it to him?" Pete put his hands over his face.

"It's already done. There's nothing to stop it now unless Farley should back out, which is unlikely. As far as Farley insulting us, he can't insult us if we don't get insulted. Daddy's opinion of Farley is not something I'm going to carry on. I have nothing against him."

Pete looked up, dropping his hands to his sides in a gesture of hopelessness. "You should. You *should* have something against him."

"Are you going to let Daddy's dislike of Farley affect your life forever?"

"It's more than that."

"Then what? If you're going to abuse the man, you have to state your case."

Pete began to pace. "It's…It's…" But he couldn't find the words to expose his own guilt, his failure to protect his sister and the Turner name. It was all too hideous to reveal. If he didn't speak it, if no one knew…but Farley Oaks knew, and that's why he had to die. Pete swallowed. "Daddy could see beneath Farley's exterior. We should both hate him."

"Don't drink from that cup, little brother. Unforgiveness is poison. It will destroy you. I'm not going to judge him. If he's done wrong, let God judge him. As for me, I'm going to stand by the agreement I made with him in good faith."

Pete looked at Robert with eyes that burned with a hate Robert wouldn't have supposed Pete capable of.

"Farley Oaks will never get the Turner land."

Robert opened his mouth to say again that the deal was settled as far as he was concerned, but he hesitated.

Pete had turned on his heel and was already out the door.

Chapter Sixteen

With one goal in mind, Pete hurried back to his room. Could he find the card with Salvino's number? He remembered throwing it in the trash. If the maid had been in to clean, it was gone. He was seething with indignation at the prospect of Farley building his speedway on Turner land and putting his name there. For Turner land to ever be in the hands of Farley or his heirs was more humiliation than Pete could bear.

He replayed the scene with Angel in the gun shop. He could hear Angel saying to him, "Boy, you have a chip on your shoulder. What is it you're stewing about?" Then Angel gave him that conspiratorial arm around the shoulder, telling him, "If you ever need to eliminate somebody, somebody giving you a problem, I know the right people. Nothing ever traced back to you." Pete had told him thanks, but no thanks. With a pat on the arm Angel assured him if he changed his mind, the offer was on the table. Then he'd written his private number and given it to Pete. Pete knew the "right people" were dangerous mobsters, and he had dismissed the offer as way beyond the pale of any entanglement he cared to involve himself in. Now it seemed not only plausible, but necessary.

Sure, he'd imagined shooting Farley, but he didn't really see himself as a killer. His most rational plan had been to come home and find others who were victims of

Farley's evil. With enough collaborators coming forward, they could expose him, destroy his reputation, humiliate him the way he deserved. The problem was Pete hadn't been able to find them. They were afraid. That had to be the reason. He had made his contempt for his uncle very public, hoping some of those he'd wronged would come to him and say, "I know why you call him scum." Even so, there were moments when Pete wondered if ruining Farley like that would satisfy him. He'd still be a wealthy, influential man. The public was fickle. As long as Farley in some way helped to feather their nest, they'd forgive him. Something Pete would never do.

Now there was no time to wait. He was being forced into action he wasn't comfortable with. He didn't trust Salvino. Although Salvino had overheard the conversation in the gun shop, and he was Angel's right hand man, for any actual deal, Pete would have expected Angel to keep the arrangements confidential. Not even Angel's right hand man should be privy to that. Angel was a careful businessman whose discretion had earned the trust of his clientele. His sending Salvino to pressure Pete without Pete's consent seemed totally out of character. I *don't like it, having to deal with Salvino; but with Farley about to steal the land from under me, and with Angel in Italy, I have no choice but to deal with the sleazy Italian. At least Salvino's contact is Angel's man, or so he claims.*

"I'm Angel's friend," Pete murmured. "Salvino won't dare cheat me. Angel said he takes care of his friends and the people he does business with rely on that about him."

Pete desperately hoped the maid had not been in to clean. He went straight to the wastebasket, but just as he feared, it was empty. He still ran his hand round and round in it, willing the card to materialize. He turned it upside down and angrily beat it against the floor. He looked behind the dresser and searched the nearest corner.

Something had to be done before Farley signed the papers and closed the deal on the Turner land. Pete couldn't stand the thought of that. He grit his teeth. That evil devil would not trample on Turner honor again. He could not allow Farley to take advantage of a Turner ever again. Pete paced the room trying to breathe. His chest was so tight he thought he might have a heart attack.

He slumped back down on the bed. So, he asked himself, how was he to find Salvino now when he so desperately needed to see him. He might have left the state on another mission for Angel, or he might have gone back to New York. He could be anywhere. Fighting total discouragement, Pete put his head in his hands and thought back to his escape from the chain gang. *I knew I needed to come home and settle with Farley. Why didn't I come home earlier, before Robert made the deal with Farley? Why is it I'm always late? I'm unlucky. That's what. And everybody's telling me to forget, to leave Farley in God's hands. The way I see it, scum like that go unpunished and prosper; Good folks get ripped off by them. Farley has all the people fooled, even Charlie, even Robert.*

Pete got off the bed and paced around the room. He had only one hope of finding the Italian. Charlie might have heard Salvino mention where he was staying.

He searched for his keys on top of the dresser where he always tossed them when he came in. He could walk back over to the diner, but he still needed to find his keys. He was so panicked with Robert's news and now the fear of not being able to reach Salvino. He hardly knew what he was doing. He stomped about the room in a daze, looking distractedly here and there. He bent down to look under the bed. Not there. For the third time he rummaged in his shaving kit on the dresser. When his hand did not feel the keys, he zipped up the kit and threw it on the bed next to his duffle bag with the few clothes he owned. He'd already been packing up his stuff since he'd decided to move into the bungalow at the farm to be closer to his work at the stills. Farley Oaks didn't own it yet! He would take his stuff there as soon as he got up with Salvino, but finding Salvino was his first priority.

He ran his hands through his hair and realized he had to get organized. He must have left the keys in the Ford. Moving toward the door, he grabbed his tennis shoes from the floor and threw them by the duffle bag. As he did, a crumpled piece of paper dropped out and fell at his feet. He ignored it and reached for the door knob. Then he stopped and turned back around. His brain was trying to tell him to pick up the crumpled paper. The shoes had been sitting next to the trash can. Something meant for the trash could have landed in the shoe. He should check it out. He snatched up the paper and unfolded Salvino's card!

At nine o'clock Tuesday evening, Pete dozed in a chair in the lobby of the Clairmont Hotel in Winston-Salem. Earlier he had called the number on the card and been informed by the desk clerk that Mr. Pezzo was not answering in his room. Relieved the Italian had not checked out, Pete drove to the hotel to wait for him to return. The furnishings and fixtures were not exactly upscale, although enough to impress Pete. He realized Salvino probably considered the place average or below. It surprised him Salvino has not chosen the best hotel in town. For several hours he paced, or sat watching the guests come and go. Finally, he found the most comfortable upholstered chair, and, despite his efforts to fight sleep, he nodded off.

At nine-thirty Salvino returned from his second meeting at the Bloody Bucket with the Farnes brothers. Without recognizing the sleeping Pete, he walked right past him and went straight to his room.

At two in the morning Pete awoke, groggy, stiff and irritable. The desk clerk refused to disclose Salvino's room number or ring his room at that early hour. Pete considered leaving a message, but decided against it. He wanted no further footprints connecting him to the Italian. Frustrated, he hurried from the hotel. He had work to do at the still. There was nothing to do but wait until later in the day.

By late Wednesday afternoon he had filled a large batch of Mason jars with top quality moonshine. Owners of the speak-easies often cut the good stuff, but usually not when the customer specifically requested Turner product. It was reputed to be the best and loyal customers could tell the difference if it were watered down. Pete left the jars where Jennings and Mack would find them and hurried down the mountain on foot. Since there was no working phone on the premises, he cranked up the Ford and drove out to find a pay phone to call Salvino.

The Italian did not express surprise when he heard Turner's voice. "So, you're ready to do business."

"I'm ready. How about now? You know the Thruway Shopping Center?"

"You get right to the point, don't you Turner?"

Pete gave Salvino directions. "Meet me there at 11:00 tonight in the bank parking lot after the stores close."

At precisely 11:00, Salvino stood in the shadows by the corner of the bank building and watched Pete emerge from the Ford. Salvino put his fingers in his teeth and gave a low whistle.

Pete walked toward the sound. He found the Italian exactly where he'd told him to meet him. Without offering pleasantries he demanded, "How much, Pezzo?"

"Like I said, you get right to the point. And for good reason. You need a job done. I'm the man to do it, but while you were stalling, the price went up, my considering the prominence of your uncle."

"How much? I asked how much?"

"Eight grand."

Pete glared. He'd never seen eight grand at one time. "I can have five thousand by Sunday evening. Do we have a deal or don't we?"

Salvino hummed and hawed. He was used to representing Mafia power and for bigger payoffs than Turner would ever get his hands on. But he had to reckon with being blacklisted by Angel. Nevertheless, Turner was a desperate man. "You can ask Jake for a loan. Surely he could lend a couple of thousand."

"No," was Pete quick response.

Salvino rubbed his chin, forced to play along for now. "I'll see what kind of deal I can fix for you since you're Angel's friend, but these people would consider five grand a down payment. You'll have to find a way to get the rest with interest. Here's how it works. I've set everything up with the contact."

"How is it you've already set this deal up?"

"Let's just say, I had the forethought to make preliminary arrangements, just in case I could be of service to you. I've done this before. It's why Angel sent me. Now do you want to hear the plan or not?" Salvino gave Pete a confident, reassuring smile, setting off alarm bells in Pete's brain.

Pete scowled and nodded in the affirmative, having no other choice.

There's a little out of the way place in Virginia called River Springs."

"Never heard of it."

"Not many people have."

Pete was about to change his mind, but Salvino continued.

"As I was saying there's a small marina there at River Springs. I know the man who owns it. No one uses it anymore but him and his brother and they spend the summer in Europe."

"I'll be coming from Richmond," Pete said.

"Even more convenient. Easy directions from Richmond," the Italian said. "You can take the money there on Sunday night at nine o'clock. Here, write the directions down."

Salvino pulled a flashlight and pad of paper from the trunk of the Cadillac and gave them to Pete. "So Jake does business as far away as Richmond. His business must be very good."

Pete made no comment. He scribbled down what Salvino dictated, folded the paper and put it in his back pocket of his pants.

"There's a small boat partially covered with a tarp. Leave the money in the canvas bag under the tarp," Salvino said.

"I want to meet the contact," Pete said, eyeing Salvino suspiciously.

"That's not how he works."

"I will not leave the money without meeting the contact."

"Leave the money under the tarp. When he's satisfied you're alone, he'll come out to meet you by the boathouse."

Pete set his jaw and speaking between clenched teeth he said, "Don't play with me, Salvino. Angel will hear about it if you try anything underhanded."

Salvino rubbed his chin. "All will go as planned," he said.

"Make sure it does. Or I won't leave the money. And you're sure this is Angel's man?"

"Didn't I tell you so?" Salvino said emphatically, yet he was beginning to worry that if Turner thought too much about Angel, if he got any ideas about contacting him, things could get complicated for Salvino. All Turner had to do was call the gun shop to learn Angel was not in Italy. And if Angel found out Salvino was swindling Pete, Salvino would be the one in the hit man's gun sight. There was reason to believe Turner would not go to the sheriff since his own ambitions were far outside the law, but if Angel found out what Salvino was up to, there would definitely be a problem.

"Nine o'clock at this River Springs marina, Sunday evening," Pete said, looking at the paper where he'd written the directions.

"That's it," Salvino said.

Pete turned and walked back to the Ford.

Late Friday afternoon, Pete came out from the woods to clean up and gather his few clothes for the three nights he'd be on the road. A water hose rigged up in a wooden stall out behind the bungalow served as a shower, and it was cool and refreshing in the July heat. After he toweled off and pulled on some fresh pants, he went inside. He had earlier gathered up the debris Freddie Oaks had left behind, including a collection of unwashed Mason jars lying beside a lumpy recliner. In disgust, he discarded a few more he found under the bed, along the walls, and various other places where they had been scattered. It was obvious Freddie enjoyed the product he was producing, probably the reason he got caught and sent to prison. Most moonshiners did not imbibe. Their work was too risky. At all times they needed an alert mind and eyes in the back of their heads.

Pete entered the bedroom where he dropped his bundle of clothes onto a faded brown spread covering the sagging double bed. It had a plain metal headboard that someone had painted a hideous turquoise blue. Before he left the motor court, he had thought to borrow a set of clean sheets from Charlie's wife, Marie, mainly because he didn't want to sleep on any sheets Freddie had touched. Beside the bed was a distressed black wooden chest containing three ill-fitting drawers. Both items of furniture rested on rough plank flooring without benefit of softening rugs or carpet. The patch-plastered walls were stark white. A closet without a door offered a rod under a crude unpainted shelf. Two naked windows covered only by plain off-white pull-down shades looked out the back side of the bungalow into the wooded landscape.

Pete remembered the scrap of paper with Salvino's directions to River Springs Marina. The last place he put it was in the back pocket of the jeans he'd just taken off at the shower. He ran outside to get the pants. He found the scrap of paper and breathed a sigh of relief that he hadn't lost it. There were so many frustrations plaguing his mind.

Back inside he tossed the pants onto the floor of the closet and read the scrawled note. It says 360 from Richmond and then I get on…it looks like 58. I wrote it in a hurry. He moved to the natural light coming from the window. Yes, 58. He laid the paper on the nightstand while he grabbed his small duffle bag and tossed it on the bed beside his handful of clothes and his shaving kit. Opening the drawer of the chest, he took out his holstered pistol, propped his foot on the chest, and strapped the gun above his right ankle. From under the mattress he pulled out an envelope containing a stack of thirty one-hundred dollar bills. *This is blood money.* His heart came up in his throat. For a moment he hesitated. He had to remind himself why he was about to pay this money. He could see Farley strutting about at the funeral, the great man, pretending to be the grieving uncle. Resolutely he counted out the money, put it back in the envelope and placed it in the bottom of his bag. He threw his clothes and shaving kit on top and grabbed up his gear.

By now, Jennings and Mack would have brought a wagon load of moonshine drawn by a pack mule down from the mountain. They would be at the edge of the woods loading plastic gallon jugs of moonshine in the specially fitted false seat of Jake's '40 Ford. The plastic would not rattle like the Mason jars. Also, the plastic was lighter weight than the glass, meaning Pete could carry more with less danger of breakage.

Walking out into the dusk, Pete saw there were no stars. The night was cloudy. That was good for the job ahead of him. He looked around to check his surroundings. Everything was quiet except for the racing of his heart. He had to admit he felt butterflies in his stomach when he realized this was no ordinary trip. He was about to solicit murder for hire.

Chapter Seventeen

Even after Prohibition ended, many branches of the Turner clan in Windy Gap and Trap Hill were making excellent white whiskey. Their perfected recipes yielded a product that was much more affordable to the common man than the government, highly taxed variety. It had been renowned in Wilkes and in speakeasies in Winston, Charlotte, Lexington and beyond, but that was another time and place. Now, twenty years later, only Pete's uncle Jake and a few others were producing moonshine. Of the shiners who hadn't died out or been run out of the illegal whiskey production, none of them could produce the quality and taste of the Turner brand. That's why Pete had hidden his daddy's recipes. These had been passed down through generations, and he knew Farley was crazy to get his hands on them. But Pete was determined he wouldn't get the recipes—or the land.

Standing in the shadows at the edge of the woods on Saturday evening next to Jake's '40 Ford coupe, Jennings said, "We got the hidden compartment loaded and ready to roll. Want me to ride with you?"

Pete shook his head. "No," he said brusquely.

"How come?" Jennings said, looking offended.

"Got some business. Not coming back right away," Pete said.

"Does Jake know?"

"There's nothing for Jake to know. I'll be back late Sunday. Baring something unexpected, I'll be here on Monday to help at the still."

"When you're hauling liquor, there's always something unexpected. If you want some company, I'll come along with you as far as Richmond."

"How're you going to get back?"

"I got a thumb," Jennings said. "I kin hitch back to here from Richmond. We'll talk about old times."

"Well, okay. Sure. I guess that will work if you really want to come along," Pete said with a shrug.

He got behind the wheel of the Ford and cranked the engine as Jennings scooted in on the passenger side.

"Listen to that baby roar," Jennings said. "Since you replaced the V-8 with the Caddy engine she's gonna fly. Let her roll!"

Without turning on the headlights, Pete pulled onto the highway. The night was overcast and warm, and the moon often hid behind the clouds. Soon Pete turned off onto a dirt road. With the windows down, the loud hum of the engine made it necessary for him and Jennings to almost shout to hear each other. "When I was just a little kid, I came with my brother Tad down this road. He was hauling for my daddy," Pete said. "That was before Tad went to prison. But Daddy didn't know about those times. He would have skinned Tad alive for taking me with him. He hoped I would never be in the whiskey business, and I never wanted to do anything else. Daddy regretted that my brothers had to help in it and put aside all the money he could so they might start a different business later on. Unfortunately Tad and Johnny didn't live long enough for that to happen. Eventually, he had to let me haul; he needed me, and I was good at it."

Coming to a clearing at the end of the county road, Pete turned onto Highway 421, two lanes and paved. "No lights. Just in case," he said.

"We grew up memorizing these roads and we know them like no revenue boys ever will," Jennings said. "Remember how we drove them in the daytime to figure out escape routes so's at night if there was a chase, we could lose them revenuers like we disappeared in thin air?"

Pete said, "You never know if Sheriff Money's men are on the prowl tonight. I keep hearing that Sheriff Money intends to put every shiner out of business. They'd get extra points for stopping me."

"Why is that?" Jennings asked.

"Farley," Pete said.

"You keep saying Farley's men are after you. You think Sheriff Money's in Farley's pocket."

"His father-in-law was."

"I think you're paranoid. Money's different. He's a straight law and order man. I don't believe Farley kin buy him."

"You can buy anything with enough money," Pete said.

"No, you can't. I didn't remember you was so cynical. What happened?"

"Life."

Before long Pete was winding the Ford around the snaky black curves through the Appalachian foothills. The daytime green of oaks, pines, and maples now created a vaulted black corridor, and they could see the night sky only in occasional breaks in the foliage. Once in a while they'd see lights from a store or small shacks set back from the road, but for several miles Pete drove inside a dark tunnel of trees. He could make out the high bank to his right, but the treacherous and deep, rock-filled ravine to his left lay hidden in the blackness, ready to receive the unfortunate vehicle that skidded, flipped over and rolled into its depths to burn.

"So how does it feel hauling again?" Jennings asked.

"Natural, I reckon."

Jennings said, "The foothills with them ravines and hollows are good cover for our back-wood stills, but hauling liquor on the roads to distribution is another matter. Feds is smarter than they used to be, and now they got faster cars and two-way radios,"

"But we can outrun any of them in this car," Pete said.

"I've had my taste of prison. I don't want to do no more time there. I'm looking to get outa the whiskey business. NASCAR's gonna be big. That's my dream."

"Racing hotrods on a track won't ever be like flying on those county roads with the tax boys on your tail!" Pete said. "And many pursuing officers turned upside down in the ditch after overdriving a curve."

"No thrill when them federal boys find your still and blow it sky high," Jennings argued. "Never happened to your daddy, though. They couldn't never find his stills."

Pete remembered Jennings's daddy was not as lucky as his. Their farm was small and the Feds always managed to find his stills and destroy them. Eventually he went to work in a factory. "No thrill when they take you off to prison like they did my brother," Pete said. "I'm not looking for that kind of adventure tonight. Just want a nice, quiet ride to Greensboro then on to Richmond." Holding the wheel steady with his knee, he tried to stretch his arms in the tight space while lifting and stretching his spine.

Before long, Jennings fell asleep. He dropped his head against the top of his bib overalls. His slender torso pressed against the door of the Ford. For a few miles except for the hum of the engine and Jennings' snoring, they were surrounded by silence.

The dark and winding road began to lull Pete into a stupor. He yawned and lifted his spine again. Reaching down to the floorboard next to Jennings' feet, he brought up a plastic jug of water and took a swig, then doused his face with a splash. Just after settling back against the seat, he was suddenly alerted by a flash of light in the rearview mirror. He shook Jennings. "Better wake up."

Jennings roused, rubbing his eyes. "What is it? Do we have company?"

"Maybe," Pete said. "Another car is behind us. Could be just another traveler, but we can't take any chances, though my guess is the driver hasn't seen us."

"Could be another tripper, except this one's riding with his lights on," Jennings said. "Most trippers travel without lights. Like you said, let's don't take no chances."

For the next several miles, the car behind them did not advance or retreat. The lights disappeared in the curves and Pete hoped the vehicle had turned off, but each time his hope was frustrated when the lights reappeared coming out of the curve. "Nobody knows we're making this trip but Jake, you and me," Pete said. *And Salvino*, he thought. *But that Italian isn't about to report me to the sheriff. No. Salvino won't double-cross. Not with Angel involved.*

"Did you hear Jackson Smith went to prison? A local snitch put the sheriff onto him," Jennings said. "When the revenuers were a-running him they shot out his tires."

"Yeah, Jake told me," Pete said. He rubbed his chin. "You see that vehicle is still behind us. It worries me that maybe he's seen us. Could be if he has, he's been on his two-way radio setting up a trap down the road."

"Too dark," Jennings said confidently. "Besides we're just another '40 Ford coupe, still the most popular car on the road in our parts."

Before long, Jennings was asleep again. Pete followed the curving road before him, again with only the sound of the motor and Jennings' snoring to keep him company. Soon his thoughts drifted to a familiar refrain. *Why wasn't I there for her? I filled my days with school, with building cars and drag racing, anything to avoid coming home.* Pete bit his thumbnail. *But soon Farley will be a forgotten memory. After nine o'clock on Sunday, I'll be free of him forever.*

Headlights in the mirror brought him back to the moment. The other vehicle had begun to advance on him. Sometimes other trippers liked to play games, racing to see whose car was faster, but he couldn't count on the car coming up on him being another tripper. He switched on his lights and hit the accelerator. His speedometer got up to ninety. He flew downhill, loving the speed, the feeling of flying, confident he could handle any car. He had turned this one into a road-flying machine. Most farm boys and bootleggers in Appalachia knew how to fiddle with cars, knowing ways to make them faster and faster. They supercharged them with more cubic inches, boring and stroking the engine, putting in extra carburetors, increasing horsepower from a hundred and fifty to four or five hundred. They would modify them top to bottom to outrun the government V-8 powered Fords. Except in Grimly, Pete had earned a reputation everywhere he went for being one of the best of these mechanics. He had a knack for knowing what would work and what wouldn't. Long before he began racing, it was his mechanical skill that had kept him afloat during his vagabond years.

He enjoyed the ride for a few miles, over the hills and down, but unable to completely lose the second vehicle. "I'm betting we have a county car trailing us," Pete said to a snoring Jennings. He nudged him and Jennings sat up. "My best guess is that it's a couple of Sheriff Money's men, probably hired by Farley," Pete said. "I don't think it's a federal car." He pressed the gas, forcing every ounce of speed from the Ford. "We're about to come to a small mom and pop eatery. You remember, just on the far side of it, there's a dirt road. If I can make that, I can lose the other car permanently."

Jennings sat up, grabbing onto the dash. "Yeah," he acknowledged with a yawn.

As soon as they saw the landmark, Pete braked just enough to slide into the dirt road. Turning off his lights, he bumped along until he made another right turn, then a left.

Jennings craned his neck, looking for the other car. "I think we lost him," he said.

"I think we did," Pete said as they bumped along the rough terrain. "I'm betting he was a county man on Farley's payroll."

Jennings looked at Pete skeptically and shook his head.

A mile into the backwoods, Pete pulled off to the side and stopped the vehicle. He reached for the small handgun strapped to his ankle, just to remind himself it was there. He carried the gun in case of trouble on the road. Normally, trippers from where he came from never threatened revenue officers. If one of them had the misfortune to get caught, he just took his medicine and spent ninety days in jail, but Pete didn't have time for jail. He was finally on a decisive course of action, and there was no turning back. They sat watching the dark. Pete drummed the steering wheel.

After a while, he felt it was safe to get back on the road. He backed up and headed to 421. So that he could make up for lost time, he switched on his headlights and drove at full speed. It remained to be seen whether a party awaited him at the bridge. It wasn't far and he knew what to do.

Jennings dropped back off to sleep. He snored and the motor hummed, but by now Pete was wide awake. Topping a knoll, he started down the incline, exhilarated by the speed and the sense of freedom. He felt in control of the powerful vehicle, and after this week end, he'd finally be in control of his life.

As he neared the bottom, he was startled when a huge animal appeared out of the dark in the middle of the road. "What in tarnation!"

Jennings sprang to life. "What? The roadblock?"

In a split second, time stood still as Pete realized his headlights were reflecting in the eyes of the biggest buck he'd ever seen. Jennings saw it and braced himself against the dash. Pete foresaw the huge antlers crashing through the windshield. He slammed the brakes. The Ford skidded. Jennings was knocked sidewinding against the door. For what seemed an eternity, Pete felt the Ford slide toward the left edge of the highway. They were rushing toward the brink of the ravine. Pete jerked the hand brake. The rear end fishtailed. Almost closing his eyes, Pete braced for the worst.

So, when the Ford came to a standstill and they were turned 180 degrees in the road with back wheels just over the edge of the decline, Pete sat in shock, unable to speak or believe they had averted a crash. The buck had evidently bounded into the trees, and the Ford was still in the road.

"Sweeeeet Jeeeesus! Holy Cow!" Jennings breathed.

"Whew!" Pete exclaimed after he caught his breath and found his voice. "So much for a quiet, uneventful ride to Greensboro." He turned to look at Jennings. After a few minutes he took to calm himself, he said, "There could still be a road block up ahead, you know. By the time we get to the bridge, we could be in for more trouble."

"They might shoot out your tires like they did Jackson Smith's," Jennings warned. "And then they'll dump the liquor on the ground," he groaned, "All that work and money in the dirt, but worst of all I hate to think of jail time."

"There won't be any jail time," Pete said, clinching his teeth.

Jennings said. "If the sheriff's men have spotted us, they'll have reinforcements up ahead. You can bet on it."

Pete tightened his jaw and pondered the possibilities for a moment. "When I took that detour onto the dirt road, we probably convinced whoever was behind us that we weren't going all the way to the bridge, but if I can keep from hitting a buck that just appeared out of nowhere, I can beat a road block. So, if they're waiting for us, hold onto your seat!"

Pete stretched his arms above his head and shifted his butt in the seat. "A guy in town once asked me to describe the bootlegger's slide. Well, I told him, you hit the brakes, pull up the emergency brake, turn the wheel, and slide 180 degrees, going in the direction you just came from. This is essentially how I missed that buck."

Jennings breathed a sigh of relief. "We'll be in Greensboro in two hours. We'll finish our deliveries well before dawn and then be on to Richmond to make more deliveries tonight."

"Yeah," Pete agreed. "All our trouble is behind us."

Pete started up the Ford. When they reached the bridge, there was no blockade and they sped across.

PART II

Chapter Eighteen

S tanding at the kitchen sink in her bare feet, eleven year old Frannie contemplated the monotony of this endless Sunday afternoon. What she wouldn't give for a little excitement. She washed the last pot and laid it with the other dishes in the plastic drain rack. Since moving to Virginia two months ago, Wayne Motley was the only kid her age that she'd met, and he was a snotty-nose creep. Her step momma, who called her Frances instead of Frannie like everyone else, did not approve of Ethel across the street. "Find a girl your own age," she said.

Frannie could hardly wait for school to start in a few more weeks. She had often walked around the outside of Stonewall Jackson Elementary two blocks away to get a feel for the place, to imagine her first day. If it weren't for her books and the bus trips to the library downtown, she believed by now she would be a raving maniac from the sheer boredom. *Where is a real person I can talk to,* she wondered.

When she got around anyone who would listen to her chatter, she couldn't seem to stop her tongue. She tried to be quiet, but she could always think of something she wanted to say. She got on her step momma's nerves. When her daddy was home from work, he wasn't a listener. If he was in good spirits, he wanted to do all the talking. If he was low, he retreated to some distant place in his own thoughts, completely unaware of Frannie. If she tried to pretend he was listening, she knew he wasn't and that only made her feel lonelier.

"I'm going outside," Frannie said.

Diane Gregg sat beside her husband on the Naugahyde daybed in a narrow sitting area set apart from the kitchen by a short counter. She wore brown shorts and a yellow cotton halter. They watched a black and white television, purchased on time from Sears, Roebuck and Company where Bill Gregg had recently found employment.

"Did you rinse out the sink?" Diane called to her. "You always forget that. You haven't finished until you rinse out the sink."

Frannie turned on the faucet and swished the grimy residue down the drain with her hand.

"And stay away from the fat girl next door."

"But there's no one else to talk to," Frannie protested, wiping her hands on a dish towel and laying it flat on the counter.

"Geez," her dad interrupted, "could you people be quiet?"

Pointing her finger, Diane got up and came over to Frannie. She spoke to her in a hushed tone, "Frances Louise Gregg, you stay away from that girl next door."

"What's wrong with her?"

"She's a grown-up," Diane said. "You find somebody your own age."

"Who?" Frannie asked.

Diane gave Frannie a warning look. "Stay away from the fat girl. That's all."

"But I don't understand what's wrong with her."

"I just don't like her," Diane said. "And I don't want you hanging around her."

"But you don't even know her. How can you judge somebody you've never even talked to?" Frannie dared to push her sassiness, seeing Diane was anxious to get her out of her hair.

She knew her step momma wasn't likely to start screaming obscenities while her husband was intent on watching the television.

"I know people."

"I guess no one is right for me. I can't have anything to do with Ethel across the street anymore. You say a seventh grader is too old."

Bill Gregg sighed to show his irritation with the continued conversation. Diane grabbed Frannie's arm and pushed her into the hallway. "It's this godforsaken mill town," she said through clenched teeth, "this awful apartment with those nosey Pruitts downstairs. But we have to stay here until your daddy gets better. Now, get outside and don't add to my misery."

Glad to leave the stuffy oppression of the apartment, Frannie hurried through the living room, swiping her hand over the layer of dust on top of the scratched mahogany bookcase as she passed it. She rubbed her hand on the back of her brown cotton sundress. Near the screened door to the outside, she found her sandals half hidden under the sofa and reached for them. Strapping them on and rushing out to the stoop, she skipped down the wooden stairway and into the early August evening.

The sun was low on the horizon. Soon the dusk would settle its shade over the neighborhood. There would be no more fireflies to come out and keep her company. They were gone by August. North Main Street ran in front of her apartment, and cars passed with a regular hum still carrying people home from their evening church services, sporting events or drives in the country. Diagonally across the street at Ethel's house, lights were on upstairs and down. Directly across at Mr. Smith's squat white frame house, no lights were visible. Frannie never told Diane how Ethel always wanted to go over to Mr. Smith's and sit on his lap in his dark, musty living room. Ethel called him "Uncle." He wasn't really her uncle. He gave her money, though, anytime she asked for it. *If I had my own money, where would I go? What would I do?* Frannie shuddered at the thought of sitting on Mr. Smith's lap. She scrambled down the steps two at a time. When her feet reached the bottom, they led her straight to the hedge between the Pruitt two-story brown shingle and the low white frame next door. She peered through at the fat girl sitting on her porch.

As usual her neighbor sat alone at this time of evening, rocking in her wooden porch chair. A voice inside her head said, *No harm in speaking.* Without even a fight, Frannie knew full well she was succumbing to temptation. If she had been in the Garden instead of Eve, she would have eaten the apple. Maybe Eve didn't deserve the bad rap she'd gotten. Frannie felt a real kinship with her. It helped to know she was like somebody. Frannie wondered what the fat girl thought about Grace Kelly marrying a prince. It was in the news. *One question won't hurt.* She hurried around the corner of the hedge. Frannie recalled introducing herself the first time she met her. She had told her, "I'm Frances Louise Gregg, but everyone calls me 'Frannie' except my step momma. She doesn't approve of nicknames." She couldn't remember if the girl said her name. Thus, she echoed Diane and referred to her neighbor as "the fat girl."

"Hi," she said and stepped up on the porch.

"Well, if it ain't Miss Chatterbox."

Frannie took that as an invitation to sit in the empty chair, just for a minute. She observed the girl's huge, round head covered with twisted pin curls of brown hair secured with bobby pins. These, the girl had advised Frannie, she set with perfume to give an alluring scent when she combed them out. Why she cared about that to sit on the porch every evening, Frannie couldn't figure. She wore her mop of curly bright orange-red hair in a ponytail because the August weather was hot and sticky. She believed she'd give almost anything for beautiful, shiny, straight brown hair like Mary Vogels in her fourth grade class back home in North Carolina, but she guessed she was stuck with red curls and the face full of freckles that came with it.

"I wish the fireflies were coming out," Frannie said. "They make the night so beautiful with their dancing, shimmering glow. I wonder where they go in August. When I was younger, I used to catch them and put them in a jar and make diamond rings out of their lights. Not anymore though. I feel sad for them now. They're too easy to catch. It makes me feel sorry for them. They don't fly very fast or have stingers like bees and wasps. And their lights show you right where they are! Have you ever thought about that?"

"Can't say as I have."

Frannie smacked a mosquito on her leg. "They're not like these pesky mosquitoes. Look. That's my blood." She sighed, "Anyway, I can't stay. I'm not supposed to be here, but I was wondering what you thought about Grace Kelly marrying a prince."

"I ain't thought about it," the girl said. "I mean, so what? Why go so far away just to get married."

"But wouldn't it be dreamy to be a princess and wear a crown with diamonds and jewels and live in a palace?" Frannie asked. "I try to imagine what it would be like to be an ordinary girl like me and then marry a prince, just like Cinderella."

"Grace Kelly's a movie star. Ain't nothing ordinary 'bout her."

"I guess so," said Frannie.

"Not ordinary, and very rich," the girl said. "So why does she need to go off to Timbuktu?"

"Monaco," Frannie corrected.

"Wherever. I wouldn't go that far to get married. What if she decides she don't like him. She's got a long way to come home."

"Gee whiz," Frannie said. "Do you always expect things to turn out bad?"

"Yeah, because that's how it is. If ya expect it, ya don't get disappointed. Know what I mean?" To Frannie's look of disapproval, she added, "No. You're just a kid." She stood up, "Say, I gota go inside a few minutes."

"I'd better get going," Frannie said, relieved she hadn't stayed too long in sin.

"I'll be back in a few. I'm going for a walk. You can come if you want."

"A walk? No. I can't...I mean...Will you be back before nine?"

"Probably," the girl said, shrugging her shoulders.

"I have to ask if I can go," Frannie said. "Where are you going?"

"Just a few blocks."

"Exactly how many?" Frannie asked.

"I ain't never counted them," the girl said impatiently.

Frannie jumped off the porch. "And what's your name, by the way?" she asked.

"Jenny. Jenny Daniels."

I'll be right back, Jenny Daniels." Frannie hurried to the steps going up to her apartment, taking two at a time. Half way up, she stopped. *She won't let me go, not with the fat girl.* Frannie stood a minute or two. *No one will even miss me. Diane won't call me in until nine o'clock when the Ed Sullivan show goes off.* She turned around and ran back to Jenny's porch. Without another backward glance, she sat down in one of the rockers and waited for Jenny to come out. In a few minutes, the girl emerged.

"You look different with your hair combed," Frannie said, jumping off the porch to follow her to the sidewalk.

"So whacha think?"

"Nice," Frannie said.

"I wash it and set it after I get home from work," Jenny told her.

"You work on Sundays?"

"Hospitals are open on Sundays. Patients still gotta eat."

Frannie skipped along to keep up. "Say, you move along at a pretty good pace for a fat girl. My step momma says you weight at least 300 pounds."

Jenny stopped and turned toward Frannie. "What business is that of hers? She got something against fat people?"

"You should get more exercise, but don't take it personally," Frannie said. She's always negative about everything. She doesn't like it here in 'this god-forsaken mill town,' as she calls it. Doesn't like living in the apartment above the landlord. We lived in a house before we moved to Virginia, before my daddy had shock treatments."

"Shock treatments?"

"Yes. They electrocute your brain," Frannie said.

"Won't that kill you?" Jenny asked, moving along.

"Apparently not. It's so you can forget stuff you don't want to remember."

"Gee, I'm sorry," Jenny offered.

"It's okay." Frannie kicked a rock. "You said you wouldn't want to move far away. Do you have family? I've never seen anyone over at your house but you."

"My ma never goes out," Jenny said. "She's old and cranky because she has arthritis and she can't half hear. I have to help her. So I guess I'll be an old maid. If I didn't have to stay with her, I might find a prince charming and get married."

"No other family?" Frannie asked.

"Well, I have a half-brother. He comes around when he feels like it."

"So, you said you have a job where you go during the day." Frannie said.

"At the hospital. In the kitchen."

"You like it?"

"It's okay. I think I could have been a hairdresser, but I never got to get the training."

Frannie said. "Do you have any boyfriends?"

The girl laughed. "Boyfriends? You could call them that."

"Hey, there's Campbell Street," Frannie said, pointing. "This is as far as I've ever walked. This Campbell Street is murder. I came flying down it on skates last week. Didn't know Campbell Street is one big hill. Started going faster and faster and couldn't stop myself. I was really scared a car would come in from one of the side streets and run over me. I was afraid if I threw myself onto the side of the road, I'd break all my bones and maybe kill myself anyway."

"So, what happened? You look to be all in one piece."

"I did what my granny always told me to do when you don't know what to do. I prayed! As you see, it worked," Frannie said with a confident tilt of her head. "Not a single car came along until I reached the bottom of the hill."

"That was a lucky coincidence. There's no Great Spirit to hear you when you pray."

"Don't you believe in God?" Frannie asked.

"I don't know. He ain't never done nothing for me."

"Did you ever ask Him?"

"I guess not. I'd feel silly talking to someone who ain't there."

The sidewalk ended and the two trooped single-file along a dirt path with grassy stubble. In a few more blocks they came to a rundown section of town. In the middle of a triangle formed by Main and an intersecting secondary street to the left, a low cinderblock building with boarded up windows sat in the shadows away from the yellow glow of the tall street lamps. Up ahead North Main veered right and crossed the Dodd River Bridge into the business district. Jenny walked toward the back of the deserted building.

"Wait there," she told Frannie, pointing toward the streetlamps.

"Where are you going?" Frannie asked, looking uncertain. "Just wait there under the streetlamp. I have to meet a man for some money he owes me. I'll be back," her companion said over her shoulder as she disappeared behind the building.

Chapter Nineteen

Over the weekend, Pete and Jennings finished their deliveries in and around Richmond without incident. After Pete left his friend on Sunday afternoon and drove onto Route 360 to get to River Springs, a sense of unrest began nagging at him. *I'm getting cold feet. Buck up, man. You want Farley to win? You want him to get off free? You want him to get the Turner farm and turn it into a legacy to him, the Farley Oaks Speedway? Is that what he deserves? No! It's up to you to stop him. You've been a coward long enough. Do your duty!*

Two hours later he was coming up on Route 58 where the road sign indicated an exit to the right going west or to the left going east. Confused as to which way to go, he reached in the pocket of his shirt for the scrap of paper with his directions. Nothing there. *Drat it, where is it?* In his mind's eye, he saw himself in the bungalow when he put the scrap of paper on the night stand just before he reached in the drawer and pulled out his gun. *Did I remember to pick it up?* He searched the pockets of his pants. Nothing there but a few coins. *The address book. I must have stuck it in there.* He had purchased the little book to write in it Jake's and Jennings' and Charlie's phone numbers. He also wrote Angel's private office number there. Angel had told Pete. "I give this number to special people, special ones. You take care with it." Pete pulled the valuable little book from his back pocket and shook it open. He shook it again. Nothing fell out. *I must have left the directions back at the bungalow.* Annoyed with his lack of organization, he laid the book on the seat.

He had reached the intersection where he had to make a decision. "I think Salvino said to go right here. Or did he tell me left? I don't know, but I have to do something." Pete turned to the right. The road signs soon indicated he was approaching Riverton, Virginia. "River town. This must be close to River Springs. Makes sense. I'll keep going."

The Dodd Textile Mill employed approximately one third of the forty thousand population of Riverton. The river divided the town into South Riverton, the more prosperous side, and North Riverton where homes were modest and largely inhabited by mill workers who averaged about two dollars an hour in wages. These were better wages than some mills paid, but far less than the workers felt the prosperous mill should be paying. A few years before, the town roiled with unrest leading to violence when, stirred up by the unions, management and labor butted heads. Management won. Life in Riverton settled back to humdrum regularity and workers settled for less pay than they wanted.

It was getting dark and the sleepy town was quiet. Pete soon crossed over the Dodd River Bridge and drove through the business district. By the lights along the bridge, he was able to read his watch. The time was eight-thirty. He continued to look for signs. There were small stores and businesses, but all were dark. "Nothing yet that says River Springs," he muttered. "Wish I had my directions. If I'm going the right way, I should be there in plenty of time to get to the marina by nine o'clock. Maybe I can find someone to ask, but it looks like this place rolls up the sidewalks on Sunday evening. I don't see anything open."

It had not occurred to Frannie that her friend would bring her to this desolate place and leave her. But no matter, she decided. Jenny said she would be back soon. She only went to meet a man who owed her money. Frannie amused herself for a while, kicking rocks and glass lying in the dirt around the light pole. She was soon lost in her reveries of the time when she would be grown and able to do just as she pleased. "Let's see," she counted on her fingers, "seven more years before I'm eighteen and old enough to go to college." She knew her parents loved her, but they could be difficult to live with. Sometimes her daddy was charming. He was very smart. He read books about history, especially about the War, and he never missed the evening news on the television, but even Frannie realized it was not smart to tell your boss how to run his business. They were fine before he got fired from the hardware store where he was a top salesman. Her daddy tried to get favorite customers to come forward and put in a good word for him, in the hopes his boss would reinstate him, but it didn't happen. Then he and Diane walked the floors of their house. Hour after hour they went over and over the situation, but never deciding what to do. Finally, he had a nervous breakdown, weeping and crying, unable to function even to dress or eat. Then her daddy spent six months in the VA hospital getting those shock treatments. After he got out, he didn't have a job. When one opened up with Sears and Roebuck in Riverton, the family reluctantly left their home in Wilmington, North Carolina and move to Virginia. Frannie wished they had been able to stay in Wilmington. She missed her friends and her granny. She suddenly felt hopelessly alone. It was dark. Even the yellow beams of the street lamps gave limited illumination to her isolated surroundings. She'd read stories about serial killers who grabbed little children and murdered them and dumped them in unmarked graves.

After a while she began to wonder whether Jenny had forgotten her. "Where is Jenny?" Frannie moaned. "What time is it? If Diane calls and I don't answer, if she finds out I've left the yard and with the fat girl, I mean Jenny Daniels, there will be lots of yelling. She'll tell Daddy and he'll spank me with his belt."

The traffic on Main Street was quiet with only a few cars passing now and then. In August, dusk settled over Riverton by eight o'clock. Everyone was already home on Sunday evening, tucked inside their nondescript houses. The dull glow from the half- shaded windows looked out to the quiet street like drowsy, unseeing eyes.

She moved out of the circle of light at the lamppost and crept toward the back of the dark building where Jenny had disappeared. High grass and bushes were grown up around it. There was no sign of anybody, no sound except the crickets playing their maracas. Frannie listened to their music for a moment, longing to be safe in her yard. It was black as ink here beyond the streetlamps.

It was then she smelled cigarette smoke. She didn't know if Jenny smoked. She couldn't remember ever seeing her with a cigarette. Maybe the man who owed her money was with her. Maybe he smoked. She couldn't see anyone, but she knew someone was there. Like the creepy feeling after walking into a spider web, a tingle crept from her neck down her spine. *It doesn't make sense that Jenny should be gone so long. Where is she? What could she possibly be doing?*

The shadows moved. Suddenly, there was a man standing not three feet from her. She could see his dark outline and the red glow from the cigarette ash. Frannie called out in a quavering voice, "Jenny, are you there?" She imagined Jenny emerging from the shadows and saying, "Let's go, Miss Chatterbox." But Jenny did not answer, nor did she appear. Frannie's heart rose into her throat.

The man was not looking in her direction, just smoking and looking at the ground.

Frannie looked back toward the street. With a dash she ran back to the circle of light, drawing herself up against the lamp post, hoping the man wouldn't see her, hoping he would go away. She longed to be at home, sitting in the chinaberry tree, safe and peaceful, but another picture kept coming to the forefront. She imagined a stranger, a serial killer, carrying her off. He took her where her daddy and step momma would never find her and stuck a knife in her heart. As she trembled all over, desperate with fear, the thought came to her to take her granny's advice. She began to pray quietly, "Lord, I know I shouldn't have left the yard. If I had obeyed Diane, I would not be here now. I'd be safe at home, but that's water under the bridge, so to speak. Please get Jenny Daniels, back here. Please send her now."

Then, the stranger came out from the shadows and spoke. "You shouldn't be out this time of night all alone." His voice sounded nice, not harsh or scary. He tossed down his cigarette and ground it under the heel of his boot. He came closer. She saw he wore a baseball cap that hid half of his face. "Has somebody forgot you?" he asked kindly.

"I don't know," Frannie whispered. He didn't seem scary like a serial killer. He seemed nice, even kind. Struggling to speak, she said, "I'm with a friend."

"Well where is this friend? I think you've been forgot. Want a lift?"

Bored and weary of waiting, Frannie considered his offer. She didn't want to walk ten blocks by herself, past those dark houses and shadows in unfamiliar territory. *This man seems nice. Why not let him take me home? I'm going to get a beating if I don't get there before Diane finds out I'm gone. What if Jenny's forgotten me and she's already home without me. He looks sort of strange, but he has a kind voice.* She was about to say "okay" when she heard her granny's words reverberate in her head, "Never, never accept candy or a ride with a stranger." Frannie hesitated. If she had only listened to Diane in the first place, she wouldn't be stuck here. "No, I'd better not," Frannie whispered, barely able to choke out her words.

He held out his hand to her. Softly he said, "I only want to be your friend. I won't hurt you, just you be friendly in return. That's fair, right?"

"Right," Frannie choked, her heart pounding in her ears, her knees growing weaker by the moment.

Then just when she was reconsidering that she maybe could trust him, with a quickness and a firmness that disoriented her, he grabbed her. Covering her mouth with his hand, he pulled her into the dark behind the deserted building. She struggled to resist and he tightened his grip on her. The dark shapes around her, the black deserted building where Jenny disappeared at what seemed liked another lifetime ago, blurred into unreality. He carried her away from the dark building into some tall grass. No one could see her now. If Jenny came looking for her, she wouldn't find her! Frannie tried to scream, but her voice was stuck somewhere way down inside her chest.

He laid her in the grass. She felt her heart pounding under him. She tried again to force a scream, but her breathing came in shallow gulps with the cold, strangling fingers of fear pressing around her throat. He pinned her hands under her while his were groping under her dress. His face covered hers. She felt his warm breath. He was speaking in a coaxing, muffled voice, but Frannie wasn't listening. He was smothering her shallow breath with his closeness, with the smell of cigarettes, sweat, and the sickening odor of his sweet cologne. She fought to arch her body against him and push him away, but she was helplessly overpowered.

His greasy hair and his ear were in her face, in her mouth, so offensive. To struggle against him was useless. His ear rubbed against her lips. The taste of him repelled her and she turned her face away. She felt his ear and hair against her cheek. The odor of stale tobacco assaulted her nostrils.

Then his ear was against her mouth again, and this time she didn't turn away. She opened her teeth. With all the strength in her jaw, she clamped down on his ear and held on...for an eternity... while he screamed...until she thought his jerking would break her jaw. She tasted blood. He began pulling her hair. She screamed, releasing her clamp on his ear. Raising his shoulders, he grabbed the ear and raged curses at her. With his attention distracted, Frannie managed to wriggle to her feet. Blindly, with no sense of direction, she took off into the black, having no thought where to go, only to run for her life.

She felt rather than saw the waist-high grass, as she pressed through it, stumbling over broken concrete and old tires, charging into bushes and pushing them out of her face. Behind her, she heard the grating crunch and crackle of glass from his footsteps, the swish of the bushes as he brushed them aside, the sound of her heart booming in her ears. Moment by moment she imagined his grasping hand on the back of her neck. "Please, Jesus, help!" she cried.

Without really knowing how she got out of the dark, she found her way back to the deserted station and from there to the street. There was no one around. It was quiet. All she could do was to keep running—and he was bound to catch her.

Chapter Twenty

Pete passed through the business district and entered a more affluent area of Riverton. He could tell because the houses were larger and set back from the road. He saw no one out and felt intimidated about knocking on any doors of these large homes and disturbing the people who lived there. He turned around, backtracking over the bridge and entering again into the more modest section of town. "This is one appointment I don't want to miss. I've seen no signs to River Springs and no one to flag down and ask for directions. It's like everyone's asleep." He stopped for a red light. Although there wasn't a vehicle in sight, he took the moment to get his bearings. Up ahead a side street intersected with North Main. He considered going down that way to find a house where a light was on inside, where he could ask directions. The two roads formed a "V" in which he noticed a cinderblock building. Like all the other business around, this one appeared asleep or even deserted. "They must roll up the sidewalks here at dusk," he complained.

The light turned green and he drove forward. Suddenly, an image moved in his headlights. For a moment he was confused because it came out of the dark and he hadn't expected it. He slammed on his brakes. "What the heck! It's a kid!" he yelled.

For a moment he sat stunned, assuring himself he didn't hit her. Then he saw her standing statue like in front of him. He threw open his door and stomped toward her, yelling. "I nearly hit you! I could have hit you! Do you realize that?" The more he yelled the angrier he became. "Where are you parents? What are you doing in the street at this hour?"

In the circle of illumination from the street light he could see she was gasping for breath and shaking uncontrollably. She kept looking behind her.

"Isn't it past your bedtime? Where are your parents? Do they know where you are?"

She stared wide-eyed and speechless.

He caught his breath. "Look. I'm sorry if I frightened you. But I almost didn't see you. I could have hit you. I guess you know that. But you're okay?" She appeared to him to be about ten or eleven. Every few moments she looked behind her toward the dark building, apparently an abandoned gas station. Now he could see the pumps out front had been removed. Only the cement platform remained. "Where do you live, back that way?" He pointed in the direction of the side street.

She shook her head "No." Her disheveled hair appeared bright orange under the lights.

"What do you keep looking at? Is someone with you?"

Again, she shook her head.

"What is it? What's the matter?" he asked, growing impatient. "Can you speak? I'm in a big hurry." She only stared at him like she'd seen a ghost. He sighed. "I frightened you. I'm sorry. Look, let me take you home?" He looked at his watch. *Twelve until nine. Unless River Springs is close, I'm sunk.* "Tell me where you live."

"A man is chasing me," she whispered, barely audible. "He tried to hurt me." She began to sob and to shake uncontrollably.

Pete looked around. "You say a man is chasing you? I don't see anyone." It was then he noticed her brown dress was torn. "I'll take you home. Where do you live?" She stammered and sniffled, "A–b–bout ten blocks. B–back that way." She pointed up North Main, not in the direction he'd planned to go, but he couldn't leave her standing in the street. "Maybe your daddy can tell me how to get to River Springs from here." He looked at his watch again. "Eight minutes to nine," he muttered. *Will the man I'm supposed to meet wait for me to get there?* "Get in. I'll take you home."

She didn't move. He went around and opened the door for her. "Look. I won't hurt you. I had a sister, and she had red hair, like yours."

In a weak voice she said, "My granny told me to never ride with strangers."

"Very good advice," he said. "What would she say about your being out alone in this end of town after dark?"

She sniffled and looked behind her. "Maybe he's not gone," she said, and her body shook all over. Pete thought she might collapse. He reached over to steady her, but she shrunk away like a mistreated puppy.

"I'm sort of in a hurry," he said, "but I can't leave you here. Where are your parents?"

"At my house."

"I either have to take you home or call the police to come take you," he said looking around for a pay phone.

"No. Please. Not the police."

"Then I think I'm your best bet."

"I...I...guess so," she said. With a fearful look of reluctance, she got in the front seat.

Pete closed the door. "Will the contact wait?" he breathed as he ran around to the driver's side. "If the shooter wants his money, I suppose he'll wait. I'm probably small potatoes to these kinds of people, though. If I didn't know Angel... if I didn't know Angel...there wouldn't be any meeting. I probably wouldn't be in Riverton, Virginia on this Sunday night taking this poor kid to her parents." He slid in beside her.

The first car he'd seen since crossing the bridge pulled around Pete's Ford, but it wasn't a good time to flag down the driver. He was too absorbed with the girl. "Point out to me when we get to your street, okay?" Pete put the Ford in gear and drove away from the abandoned station. They passed the first two blocks. "You said a man was trying to hurt you. What happened?"

The child hung her head. "He was smoking a cigarette. Then he pulled me into the grass. He was on top of me."

So, that explains why she ran out in front of me. This poor kid was abducted, maybe raped. "Can you remember what he looked like?"

"It was dark," she said, sobbing softly. "He wore a baseball cap. It came off. He had greasy hair. I felt it against my face. I...I...bit his ear."

"You bit his ear? That's how you got away?"

She shook her head, affirming his question. "Mostly I remember how he smelled, like cigarettes and sweat...and this sweet..." She put her hand to her mouth.

"You gonna be sick?" Pete asked in alarm.

She went on. "His cologne. It smelled...like...I don't know."

"What age was he?"

"I don't know. Not old. Not young."

"Did he have facial hair? A beard? A mustache?"

"No."

"How about scars? Tattoos?" The police with need a description. Your parents will want to call the police."

"It was dark."

"What the heck were you doing alone in this end of town? No place for a kid your age at night. How old are you?"

"I'm eleven." Frannie swallowed. "I didn't come by myself, but the girl I came with left me."

"She left you here in the dark? Alone? What age is she?"

"She's a grown up."

"Do you suppose this man, the one who chased you, did something to her before he got to you?"

The kid turned to him looking alarmed. "Maybe that's why she didn't come back. Maybe he hurt her, but I don't know. She's very large. My step momma says she weighs 300 pounds. No, I don't think he could pull her into the grass. She left me at the lamp post and said she'd be back, that she had to meet a man who owed her money. Then she went into the dark behind the cinderblock building, but she never came back."

"So she had to meet a man who owed her money." Pete clinched his jaw. "And she was gone, how long?"

"It must have been nearly an hour."

"Nearly an hour. Hum…"

Pete slowed down, waiting for her to tell him when he came to her block. "You say you have parents. Do they know you're out like this?"

She sniffled and wiped tears from her face. Pete pulled a handkerchief from his back pocket and handed it to her. She blew her nose.

"I have parents," she said. "They told me not to talk to the fat girl." She began to sob again. Between sobs she told him, "Her name is Jenny Daniels. My step momma calls her the fat girl. Oh my gosh! What time is it?"

"My guess is about nine," Pete said.

"Now I'm going to get yelled at and get a beating," she said with resignation, hanging her head. "My daddy might even get his belt unless Diane stops him. She tells him not to do it, but if he's really mad, he'll do it anyway."

"Does your daddy beat you with his belt often?"

"No. Not often. Just when he loses his temper, when he's really, really mad. If I hurry I can get in before Diane calls me." Then speaking more to herself than to Pete she said,

"She won't notice the torn dress tonight. By tomorrow she'll think I tore it climbing the chinaberry tree. She says I'm awful with clothes, that I should have been a boy."

"Which side of the street is your house on?" he asked.

She didn't answer him but continued to examine her torn dress.

"Which one is your house?" Pete asked.

"It's in the next block. You can let me out here."

"Might as well take you to your door."

"No," she said with fervor.

"I'll take you to your house. In fact, I think I should go in with you. Might as well. The man I was supposed to meet has probably left by now."

"No! You can't go in with me," she insisted. Her hand was on the door handle.   He thought she might jump out before he stopped. He pulled to the curb. "Why not?"

"I can't let them see me get out of your car. I can't tell them about tonight."

"Why not?" Pete asked, looking puzzled. Then he turned to her with eyes that reprimanded. "I get it. You don't want them to find out you disobeyed."

"It's not just that I'll get yelled at for going off with Jenny, but my daddy had shock treatments. I can't cause them trouble right now," she said.

"But this is serious. If a man attacked you, they need to know. Is there another relative or close friend you can tell? You have to let a responsible adult know."

She shook her head "No."

"What if this creep comes after you again? I don't feel good about you not telling your parents," Pete said. "And they'll need to inform the police. I wish you could have gotten a better look at him. They'll need a description."

"We just moved here two month ago," she said softly. "There are no relatives or close friends. We don't really know anybody here except the landlords, the Pruitts, and they're in New York visiting their daughter. Please," she begged, her face twisted in anguish as she reached again for the door handle. "I can't tell them."

"I don't feel right about this." However, the panic in her face and voice convinced him she had been through enough. "First, I'll drive around the block and then let you out wherever you say," he conceded. "I don't think anyone has followed us." As Pete said the words, he had the uncomfortable sense that he shouldn't just walk away. *But I'm not even supposed to be here. And I need to get going now.* "I have an appointment. I'm already late. I don't suppose you could tell me the way to River Springs?"

"You're way off in the wrong direction," she said.

"You've been there before? You can point me in the right direction?"

"Yes," she said. "I've ridden to River Springs with Daddy. He goes there to call on customers. He sells hardware to builders for Sears and Roebuck. Riverton is in one direction; River Springs is in the opposite."

"Driving from Richmond I should have turned left and taken 58 east instead of west?"

"Yes, if you wanted to go to River Springs, you should have turned left."

Coming around the block and back onto North Main, Pete said, "Show me which house is yours. If I weren't already late, I would insist on seeing your parents, but I'll stop two doors down so I can watch you until you get inside."

"It's the two-story," she said. "That short white one on the right is Jenny Daniels,' the one who left me back at the old gas station."

Pete could see lights in the upstairs windows of the two-story. He pulled past and stopped two houses down.

"Thanks, Mister. You saved my life."

"The name's Pete, Pete Turner. Would you mind telling me yours?"

"Frances Louise Gregg, but most people call me Frannie."

"Well, Frances Louise Gregg, you stay in your own neighborhood. Don't be going to that other end of town where winos and bad people hang out. And please tell your daddy. Even if he's been sick, you're his daughter. He'll want to know so he can protect you. That man who attacked you might come back."

"That won't happen," she said. "I've never seen him before. He doesn't know where I live or anything about me."

"I hope you're right," Pete said frowning, but she was already out the door.

He had a scratchy feeling inside about letting her go without making sure her parents were told what had happened to her, but he'd done all he could. Probably she would fess up in a day or two. He got out of the car and watched her bound up the long row of steps to her apartment. From the porch light at the top, he saw her go in the screened door. "She's a spunky little thing. Knows her own mind."

Pete put his fingers to his temples. He felt a headache coming on. He got back into the Ford and turned into a side street, circled around, and headed back up Main the way he'd come. The last time he had looked at his watch he'd seen it was nine-thirty. He sighed, "What are the chances my contact will still be waiting? Who knows? Maybe I'll be lucky for once."

Chapter Twenty-one

The road to the River Springs Marina came to an end where it turned into a gravel lot beside a grey, weathered boathouse. On the far side of the road opposite the marina, two men sat on their haunches and watched the pier.

"We been here since eight-thirty," Bennie said. "What I wouldn't give for a smoke. It's gotta be way past nine. Turner shoulda been here."

"But he ain't," Rufus said. "And we been watching that there dock the whole time. He ain't slipped by us unless he swum." Rufus scratched his arm, raking his dirty nails up and down it in a frenzy. "Them mosquitoes has eaten me alive."

"Ain't nobody been near that boat," Bennie said.

"Why did he tell Turner to bring the money here?"

"I don't know that. I just know what I heard. Maybe Turner thinks the Mafia people are gonna pick up the money here, but we know Pezzo's after Turner's money and he means to get it hisself. Pezzo's gonna double cross Turner just like he thinks he's gonna double cross us." That's why we have to get it first," Bennie said with resolve.

"Maybe you heard wrong 'bout the time." Rufus said.

"They wasn't three or four feet from me," Bennie insisted. "I couldn't hear everything they was saying, but I know I heard that Italian tell Turner to be at the River Springs marina with the money at nine o'clock on Sunday night and to put it in the boat under the tarp."

"They mighta seen you and changed the plans," Rufus said, shifting for the tenth time from a squat to a kneeling position.

Bennie said, "They couldn't see me. It was dark. I was hid in some shrubs. They didn't see me, I tell you." He rubbed his forehead. "Man what I'd give for a smoke, but we can't take no chances of anybody detectin' us fore we get the money. Pezzo could be here somewhere watchin' for Turner same as us."

"And if he is, then what.?"

"We get the money first. As soon as Turner puts the money in the boat, we grab it and run. It's dark and that fat Italian won't be able to catch us."

"You sure they meant this Sunday."

"Whataya think I'm stupid?"

"How much longer we gonna wait."

"You want the money? I bet Turner's coughing up mor'en a couple a grand."

"How much you reckon?"

"Don' know. Pezzo's after it, though."

Rufus scratched his head and neck. "These here mosquitoes is eatin' me alive."

"The wind's picked up. It's gonna storm and blow them mosquitoes away. Think about something else. Think about the money," Bennie said. He sat on the ground and stretched out his legs, rubbing his calves. "I heard Farley Oaks got sick with appendicitis. That's why nobody's seen him."

"Appendicitis won't kill ya." Rufus said.

"Naw. He'll live. You remember Bobby Lee's brother had appendicitis. Got a scar a mile long where they opened up his gut. I'd be honored to go see the great man, but nobody knows what hospital he's gone to." Bennie stood half way. "Man, I could use a smoke."

"Think 'bout something' else," Rufus retorted.

"Suppose Turner got here early even before we got here," Bennie said. We gotta think 'bout this. If Turner came early…"

"Why would he of done that?"

"I don't know. Just because. He could of just got here early."

"We gotta do somethin'," Rufus said.

"And maybe…" Bennie said, "Maybe we're sitting here waiting like dummies and the money's already in the boat."

Rufus stood up, his adrenalin starting to flow. "Then let's go get it!"

"Bennie grabbed his arm. "Wait a minute. Don't forget about Pezzo."

"Unless he already got the money and took off," Rufus opined.

"But I *know* he said nine o'clock. He was expecting Turner to show up with the money at nine o'clock." Bennie scratched his head. "You stay here and keep an eye out. I'll see if the money's in the boat. If Pezzo shows up, you be ready to surprise him with this." Bennie held out a large, heavy flashlight. "Don't kill him. Just fix him so's we get the money and get outta Dodge before he comes to."

"Then he'll come after us."

"What's he gonna do? Get the sheriff to arrest us? And he'll hafta find us first."

"What about them Mafia people?"

"If Turner owes them money, they gonna be lookin' for Turner. Won't know nothin' 'bout us."

"But somethin' don't add up 'bout Pezzo. He gets us to beat Turner up. Next thing we know he's meetin' Turner and tellin' him to bring money here. I don't get whose side he's on?" Rufus said.

"It's like this," Bennie explained. "Not too hard to figure out. Turner come back to Wilkes to get bootleg money to pay these Mafia people who're gonna kill him if he don't pay up. That part of what Pezzo said makes sense. Pezzo plans to get his sticky paws on that money before the Mafia gets it. So he tells Turner to bring the money here. The part I don't get is what all this has to do with Mr. Oaks."

"So what deal is Pezzo talking 'bout doin' for Turner?"

"It don't matter what story he's cooked up to get the money," Bennie explained.

"What if Pezzo *is* working for the Mafia?"

"That I doubt. He'd steal from a chump like Turner, but not them Mafia dudes."

"So we get the money and Turner gets whacked off by the Mafia!" Rufus exclaimed.

"That's right. Remember, watch for Pezzo. I ain't sayin' he ain't slick as grease," Bennie said. "You got that?"

"Yeah. I got it," Rufus said.

Then Bennie trotted off through the bushes to the road. Keeping to the trees, he slunk over to the boathouse and staying in the shadow of it, made his way to pier. When he got to the dock, he steadied the small fishing boat and jumped in. He jerked up the tarp lying in the bottom. "The money! It ain't here," he fumed. "I *know* Pezzo said nine o'clock. He's done took off with it." He whistled for Rufus to come. When his brother got to the pier, Bennie told him, "It ain't here. The money ain't here. Somehow Turner must of got here earlier than we did. I *know* Pezzo told him tonight at nine o'clock. I *know* I wasn't wrong about that, but they must of both come early. Pezzo already got the money and done took off with it."

Swearing, Rufus came aboard to see for himself. Bennie lifted the tarp. "Ain't no money here," Rufus concluded. He spat in the water. "We shouldn't of let that Italian get out of our sight till we got our money." He expressed his disappointment with curses upon God, Turner, and Pezzo as they sat in the boat trying to figure what to do next.

"Nothing we can do. We ain't never gonna see Pezzo no more."

Chapter Twenty-one

Rufus groaned. "All that money—and we ain't never gonna see it neither."

"I know Pezzo told Turner Sunday night at nine o'clock," Bennie said more to himself than to Rufus. He shook his head in severe disappointment. "Storm's comin' and we better get going."

Before they could stand they heard, "Put your hands up and don't move."

They looked up to see Pezzo pointing a gun at them. "Sumbitch," Rufus muttered.

"Funny meeting you guys here. Aren't you a ways from home?" Pezzo said, coming closer. "Carefully reach under the tarp and hand over the money—and don't make any funny moves."

"Where's our thousand bucks, Pezzo?" Bennie demanded. You ain't paid us. You tryin' to cheat us."

The Italian scrutinized them. He said irritably, "Just hand over the money and explain what you're doing here. That wasn't part of the plan."

"You told Turner to come here and put the money in the boat. You meant to cheat us outa our money."

"Who told you idiots I said anything to Turner about putting money in the boat unless you been spying on me you little creeps." He swung his arm and hit Bennie across the face with his fist. "No matter now. I don't need you nitwits. Just hand over the money. Pezzo tightened his grip on his pistol. Turner had pushed his patience to the limit. Now these idiots had to show up. Well it was just too bad for them. "Hand over the money," he demanded.

"Or what?" Rufus said. "You'll shoot us?

"You're smarter than I gave you credit for," Pezzo said. "Now hand me the money."

Rufus said, "There ain't no money, not here."

"Hand over the money," Pezzo said.

Bennie lifted up the tarp. "See for yourself. There ain't no money."

"Turner wouldn't miss this meeting," Pezzo said through gritted teeth. "He's desperate. You've done something with Turner and now you have the money. Now where'd you put it?"

"I guess if you shoot us you ain't never gonna know where we took it now are ya?" Bennie said.

"Get out of the boat," Pezzo said.

With his hands behind his head, Bennie stood up, staggered and fell backward as the wind whipped up and caused the water to slap furiously against the boat and toss it about.

Pezzo cast a glance at the sky. The dark clouds had blotted out the stars. "Hurry up before I decide to drown you."

Bennie kept one hand behind his head. With the other he held on to the side of the tossing boat and hoisted himself up onto the dock. Rufus started to climb up behind Bennie just as a jagged flash of lightning ripped across the sky.

The brothers saw Pezzo's eyes dart nervously toward the heavens. Bennie seized the moment to lunge into Pezzo, knocking him to his knees. The gun flew from the Italian's hand. It skittered across the dock and fell into the water. Rufus stood in the lurching boat and reached under his shirt to pull his own gun from his belt. Pezzo staggered to his feet, and before Rufus could steady himself and aim his weapon, the Italian jumped onto Rufus. Both were locked in an embrace to get control of the gun. Bennie, in the meantime, had run to the boathouse and found an oar leaned up beside it. While Pezzo and Rufus fought over the gun, Bennie walloped the Italian with the oar wherever he could get at him.

As both men wrestled, the gun flew into the air and landed in the bottom of the boat. Rufus started for it, but Pezzo grabbed a pail lying within reach and slung it toward his face. Rufus blocked it with his arm. Rufus and Pezzo dived for the gun in the bottom of the boat that was now rocking and lurching as drops of rain began to fall. The gun slid toward Pezzo. He snatched at it, but Rufus reached it first only to drop it again. Pezzo managed to grab it and, holding to the side of the lurching boat, he pointed it at Rufus. "You, Bennie, you have one second to get back in the boat before I shoot Rufus." Bennie got in the boat. "Now get over beside him and both of you lie down and keep your hands behind your heads." During a momentary lull he attempted to step one foot onto the dock, but he slipped back as another wave rocked the boat. He held to the side, attempting to keep the gun focused on the brothers. "Where did you put the money," he demanded. "Just tell me. You can take your thousand and go."

"You'd shoot us as soon as we told you," Bennie said. "But I tell you now, there weren't no money here. Either Turner didn't show or somebody else got here before we did."

A flash of lightening split the sky followed by a crack of thunder. The brothers could see Pezzo's fear all over his face. The boat lurched, threatening to break from the tether rope. Pezzo braced himself with one hand while he held the gun with the other, waiting for the next lull. The brothers watched for one opportune second to jump him. The next lull came and just as Pezzo put one foot on the dock to climb up, lightening ripped the sky again, followed by another crack of thunder. Pezzo appeared to shrink into himself. With the little boat jumping like a bucking bronco in the rodeo, Pezzo foot slipped. Like an acrobat, the Italian flipped over the side of the boat and fell headlong into the agitated water.

Rufus and Bennie rushed to peer over the side. After a few seconds, Rufus said, "Where is he?"

"Forget Pezzo," Bennie said, clutching his leg, which was bleeding from a gash. "I can't swim and you can't neither. Let's get outa here in case he can!"

The time was almost nine-forty before Pete got back to the intersection where Route 58 turned to the east. It took him twenty minutes to reach River Springs and drive to the marina, located in a tiny inlet on a channel that he thought must be part of a primary or secondary tributary to the Dodd River. At some distance from where the narrow road ended at the marina, he backed the Ford into some bushes and got out. It smelled of rain. He could see that a summer storm had swept through, leaving everything wet. He looked around for some sign that there was anyone nearby watching for his arrival. He heard nothing but some croaking frogs. He began walking.

Up from the river bank, a tangle of kudzu and other bushes climbed the hill to a large hipped-roof house at the top, its outline a shadow against the night sky. No lights shone from it and there appeared to be no other houses in the vicinity. Salvino had claimed he knew the owner of the big house as well as the marina, which consisted of a small boathouse and a pier. Pete reached the boathouse and walked down to the pier. There were two lamp posts, but these were dark. Another storm was brewing and the breeze was whipping up. With its paint peeling and barnacled, a once sleek speedboat bobbled in the water. The name painted on the side of it was *The Madd Hatter*. He stepped aboard. Like everything about the marina, it appeared neglected. He saw the tarp where Salvino had told him to put the money and leave. It was crumpled in the bottom of the boat as if someone had recently moved it. Pete stared back at the pier and the boathouse. He saw no one. Apparently, the contact had looked for the money under the tarp and had not waited when Pete didn't show.

He considered leaving, but he was reluctant, deciding to wait a few more minutes in case the man came back looking to get his money. He paced up and down the pier. His eyes scanned the dark between the road and the boathouse. As the minutes passed, he grew more frustrated. He couldn't stop himself from thinking if he hadn't left his directions, if he hadn't taken a wrong turn, if he hadn't almost run over that kid.

Then, a noise from the area of the boathouse alerted him. A flash of heat lightening momentarily illuminated the dark like someone had turned on the heavens. He could see the pier, the river, and the boathouse as it might look in broad daylight. His pulse quickened. He jumped to his feet and reached for the pistol strapped to his ankle.

The flash dissipated. Shielded again by the dark, Pete move quickly toward the boathouse. He leaned against the side and listened. He inched his way around one corner. There was the sound again.

He peered around the next corner and waited. Rain began to pelt him. Then, lightening lit up the sky. The wind blew a gust and this time Pete saw the source of the noise. He frowned in disgust and disappointment.

A lop-sided sign had broken one of two rusty chains holding it to the metal rod attaching it to the side of the boathouse. At irregular intervals when the wind caught it, the dangling sign and broken chain flapped and banged against the building. After several minutes, with a sigh of resignation, he holstered his gun and walked toward the place where he'd left the Ford. He got in and sat with his head in his hands, while the force of the rain pounded on the top of the car. He'd had such high hopes tonight would be the beginning of the end of Farley Oaks. Several minutes later, the pounding became taps. The cloud burst had spent itself.

He considered his options. There appeared to be nothing in River Springs but this marina. Back at Riverton he remembered seeing a sign for a Shady Lawn Motel. He'd stay the night there and tomorrow, on the chance Angel had come back from Italy, he'd call him to arrange another meeting. If he couldn't get Angel, then he'd have to talk to Salvino. That was based on the uncertain assumption the Italian had returned to New York and could be reached at the gun shop. With that decision, he drove away.

Chapter Twenty-two

The next morning in the half light of his room, Pete awoke, confused by his surroundings until he realized he wasn't in the bungalow on the Turner farm. He was stuck in Riverton, Virginia, an alien little town he only expected to pass through once in a lifetime. It took several blinks to slowly recall the strange evening before and his failure to meet the contact because that kid ran out in front of him. Then there was the mean cuss who apparently ran the motel with his NRA plaques on the wall behind him. He acted like he was doing Pete a favor to take his money and give him a room key. Sour as a persimmon and with grunts rather than words, he examined Pete with a suspicious eye. Then with seeming reticence he thrust him the key. Pete wondered what the inhospitable fellow was doing running a motel.

He doubted he would let him make a long distance call on his room phone, and Pete didn't want to bother asking, but he remembered seeing a pay phone at a nearby laundromat. Thinking about how he really needed to talk to Angel, he rolled out of bed. He preferred to be the one to explain about missing the meeting with the contact and not to have to go through Salvino, who hadn't said when Angel was expected to return from Italy. Pete couldn't wait any longer, not with Farley settling on the purchase of Turner land any day. If Angel was still out of the country, Pete had no choice but to deal with Salvino. That brought up another worry. Where was Salvino? Had he returned to the gun shop or was he engaged in other business for Angel? Pete had two numbers, one for the gun shop and the other to Angel's office at home. This was the number for a private line he had given Pete, the one he only gave out to special friends.

Pete threw on some clothes and hurried out to the Ford to get his address book. To his chagrin, it wasn't on the seat where he last saw it. He ran his hand along the crook of the seat, but the book had not wedged itself there. He searched the floorboard and then the pavement nearby and under the car. He knew he didn't leave it at the bungalow. It had been in his hands when he flipped through it looking for his directions to River Springs and the marina, but after a fruitless search, he concluded it had evidently fallen out of the car either at the marina or when he stopped for the kid. There was no time for his usual morning jog and sit ups. He had to retrace his route. He couldn't afford to lose the book. It not only contained Angel's private number, but also customer numbers and addresses, notes about new orders and where to make deliveries. In the wrong hands, it could be a problem. As soon as he could grab his keys, he headed for the marina.

In the daytime the marina was as deserted as it had been when he left there the night before. He found the spot where he had parked and examined the ground. He retraced his steps to the end of the pier and to the broken sign on the side of the boathouse, but his search did not turn up the black book. He thought back again to the last time he had it in his hands. He was flipping through it minutes before the girl ran out in front of him. If it wasn't at the marina, it must have fallen out when he jumped out of the car to confront her, or when she got out near her house. With a groan, frustrated with another screw up, he got in the Ford and drove back to Riverton as fast as the plodding traffic would allow.

The air was sticky and the heat increased Pete's irritability. Even the slight bit of air coming in the open windows of the moving car felt hot to him. His knuckles were white from gripping the steering wheel. In the slow-moving traffic, he had nothing more to do than to notice the local scene. On one end of the bridge, there were numerous brown brick buildings by the river that composed the offices and production plant for the mill, and on the other end of the bridge, the smaller, less prosperous stores and houses. These in long in need of a face lift, all looked different in the daylight, making the events of the night before seem stranger and more unreal than ever. He came to the fork in the road where the cinderblock gas station sat, looking forlorn as before, but innocent in the daytime. It seemed to say to him, "It's all a made up story." The girl who ran out in the street in front of him might have stumbled upon some sleeping wino and in her fright imagined the rest about an attacker. Children let their imaginations run away with them. What really made him suspicious the more he thought about it was her insistence she could not tell her parents. She did say her daddy had been ill, had undergone some kind of electric shock treatments.

Whatever actually did happen, a complaint should be filed with the authorities. Pete didn't want any involvement with the police, but he felt her daddy needed to act quickly. If there was in fact an abductor, there may have been similar reports from other children assaulted by this man. Even so, pedophiles were difficult to catch because they could easily intimidate their victims. Children were afraid or ashamed to report them. Often when they did tell an adult, the reports were dismissed as fantasy, especially if the perpetrator was a relative or family friend.

If her story was true, Pete hoped she took his advice and told her parents, although she was quite adamant that she could not tell them. He knew from experience the police probably would not actually do anything simply on the word of an eleven year old. She said she could not see what her abductor looked like. She could only remember what he smelled like, hardly anything the police could check out. Whether it was the beating she feared or some other reason why she was reluctant to tell her parents, he would never know. Fortunately, it wasn't his problem, and he certainly couldn't get involved. The last thing he needed was to get the notice of the police. The incident ought to be reported, but not by him. It was his intention to slip through Riverton and River Springs, Virginia without a trace of ever having been there.

Turning into the gravel space in front of the deserted station, he parked and walked down to the sidewalk beside the road where he had stopped the night before. Riverton was more a bit more awake this morning. The traffic rumbled by, stirring up dust and fumes. He searched every inch of space where he could imagine the book might have fallen. Between lulls in the traffic, he searched the curb and the pavement but did not find the black book. Disheartened, he trudged back to the Ford and drove to the neighborhood where the girl lived.

The two-story brown shingle, distinct in the daylight, sat on the right beside the one story white frame house where the Daniels person lived who had left the child alone in the dark. The thought made his jaw tighten angrily, but he reminded himself it wasn't his business. He parked on a side street and walked to where he had let the girl out. Again he searched the ground, the pavement and the sidewalk, even the yards in front of the houses. He bit his lip and tried to think what to do. He supposed he could get the number for the gun shop from the operator, but not Angel's private number. He needed the other numbers as well. He didn't want Angel to know he missed meeting the contact because he forgot his directions, or for Angel to find out Pete had lost his private number. What really worried him was to have evidence floating around that connected him through Angel to the hit man who would take out Farley. Even now, his uncle could have his men watching him. If one of them found the book…The very thought caused Pete's heart to skip a beat. So far, nothing about this trip had gone according to plan. He'd had such high hopes, believing his miseries were almost over. Now with all the delays, he could hardly think what to do. He had to find the book, but he had no more ideas about where to look. Someone could have picked it up this morning. His name was written in the front with Jake's number underneath. If anyone bothered to try to find the owner and called Jake, Jake would wonder why Pete had lost his book in Riverton. He consoled himself; no one would make a long distance call to report a lost address book. It would be better for him if the finder just threw it away. That in Pete's mind was the most likely scenario, but how could he be sure? What he wanted was to find the book. He needed the numbers, but it was preferable that it be trashed than for it to get into the wrong hands.

He looked at his watch. It was just ten now. The gun shop opened at ten o'clock, although Angel never came in before eleven. He decided he would make his call around noon. In the meantime, he would think about where else he might have lost the book and continue his search.

He pulled out from the side street, and a little girl skipping down the sidewalk caught his eye. What made him look twice was the red ponytail bobbing behind her head. *She has to be the same girl from last night. Frannie, she had said her name was Frannie.* It was the same intense red hair, though it had appeared more orange under the yellow street light. Her blue shorts hung on her skinny frame, and a narrow white halter encircled her pale, flat chest and back. She could have been his sister at ten or eleven skipping along. Only a sliver of a girl, she reminded him of Mary Kate in her spunky, but vulnerable innocence. Her walk was confident and energetic the way she held her head high. She knew her own mind. He was impressed with that, despite his suspicion she had spun a story out of her fear, or boredom, or need for attention. Who could tell with kids? She had caused him to miss his appointment, and now he'd lost a valuable possession, all because of her. His admiration was tinged with anger.

He passed her, reminding himself that she was not his problem. He turned into another side street to flip around and head back to the other side of town. As he waited for the traffic, he saw her go into a small market on the corner. The sign above a green awning on the front said "The Corner Market." He was almost certain it was the same child, but it really didn't matter one way or the other. He had to move on. Then, typical of his constant ambivalence, he impulsively pulled into a parking space in front of the little store, if only to satisfy his curiosity that it was the same girl, all the while telling himself not to do it. *It's like feeding a stray dog you have no intention of encouraging.* Despite what his head told him, he waited for the girl to come out. He would get a good look. If she was the same child, he might ask her about his address book. He hadn't thought of that. She might have seen it lying in the grass or by the curb and picked it up.

Chapter Twenty-three

Frannie opened the screened door and entered the dark, cool interior, leaving behind her the impudent white glare of the hot August sun. The air was pungent with a musty odor. She intended to browse before she purchased the potatoes for Diane.

To her right there was a counter where a wrinkled older gentleman with grey hair and bushy grey eyebrows worked the cash register. The shelves behind him held a hodgepodge of popular goods: flashlight batteries, cartons of cigarettes, candy bars, Smith Brothers cough drops in licorice or cherry flavors, and chewing gum. There were dusty, rarely requested items like combs, cards of plastic barrettes, and a couple of tins of Band-Aids. He was ringing up a bagful of items for a tall thin man and a teenage boy. A stooped, elderly woman, who looked to Frannie to be at least a hundred, hobbled up behind them. Under the front window where the only natural light entered the dingy, cluttered store, bushel baskets of vegetables sat along the floor in a row. A few customers moved about quietly as if the dimness required a hushed reverence.

Walking down every aisle, Frannie surveyed shelves crowded with canned goods and bottles and jars of condiments. She felt for her back pocket to assure herself the dollar Diane had given her was still there. She could feel it flat next to her hip. She ambled about, passing boxes of oatmeal, cereals, and her favorite, Kellogg's Corn Flakes. There were bags of rice and dried beans, cans of tomatoes and another favorite, Campbell's chicken soup.

She came to a rack of magazines and looked them over, deciding which one to pick up. She had a habit of reading anything with print on it and here was a whole selection of inviting titles. She reached for an *Archie* comic and read through it. After that, she picked up *Superman,* reading some of the colorful frames as she scanned the pages. At one point, she stopped reading because she thought she sensed a presence near her. She turned around expecting to see someone, but no one was there. A few other people milling around brushed past her. The events of the night before had made her jittery. She turned back to the magazines. On a higher shelf she noticed *True Confessions.* Jenny Daniels had given her a stack of these. When Diane saw them, she snatched them away and ordered Frannie to return the magazines. After that, she told her, "Stay away from that fat girl." Frannie couldn't think what Diane got so upset about. The only pictures were advertisements and the stories she read were silly romances, but maybe in the short time she had them she had missed something forbidden. She was tempted to reach for the magazine, but decided not to, having just escaped getting in serious trouble by the skin of her teeth.

After she saw what was on every aisle, she was ready to spend her nickel on a big Johnny Cake to eat on the way home. But first she would get the potatoes. It wouldn't do to get the Johnny Cake and forget the potatoes like she did last week. She walked to the front of the store to the vegetable baskets under the long window and picked over the potatoes, feeling them for soft spots. She placed five firm ones in a paper sack and walked over to the Johnny Cakes. She unscrewed the lid to the large glass jar containing the round, sweet cookies and picked one.

Moving to the counter with her treat and her sack of potatoes in one hand, she reached for her dollar. Oddly, she felt a slight wad of something, like a piece of cloth. She drew it out and her dollar fell on the floor. She stared in horror at the scrap of material. It was a piece from her brown dress, the one she wore last night. There were spots of dried blood on it! It was his blood from where she bit his ear! She remembered the ripping sound when he snatched at her dress as she wriggled away from him.

Frannie whirled around, expecting to see him standing behind her, ready to grab her and run off with her before anyone knew to stop him. But no one was there. Yet, the piece of cloth was evidence he'd been there, close enough to put it in her pocket. She stared at it. Fear constricted her throat. Her hand shook and she trembled all over. Clutching her bag of potatoes like a shield, she scanned the store, her eyes sweeping the dim interior. Even though she remembered little about him, she was sure she would know him. She walked slowly, forcing herself to look down every aisle. No one remained in the store at the moment except the grey haired man behind the counter. "Did you forget something?" he asked kindly.

She felt dizziness overwhelm her. That awful man had been close enough to touch her. Queasiness rose up from her stomach to her mouth. The room began to spin. She couldn't go outside to walk home. He might be waiting for her! She still grasped her sack of potatoes. Her cookie had crumbled in her hand. She felt her knees drop to the floor. From somewhere that seemed far away, she heard the deep voice of the man behind the counter call to "Violet" to come to the front. The next thing she remembered she sensed a feminine presence, smelling like flowers. Somebody put something under her nose that caused her to sneeze. She fluttered her eyelids and saw wrinkled pink cheeks under a woman's kind eyes. "Child," she said. "Are you ill? Can you sit up?"

"He was here, in the store," Frannie managed to whisper.

"Who?" the woman asked.

"No...no one," Frannie said.

"Do you know where you are?"

"The Corner Market."

"That's right." She helped Frannie sit up. "Where do you live?"

"Two blocks down North Main at 9304."

"I don't think you should walk in the hot sun. Is that what happened? You got over heated?"

Frannie shook her head, "Yes ma'am," she said.

"Can someone pick you up?"

"My momma doesn't have a car."

"You look so pale. If it's just two blocks I can drive you home."

"Thank you," Frannie said.

The woman helped Frannie to her feet and to the door in the back. She called over her shoulder to the man behind the counter that she was taking the girl home. When they got outside, Fannie squinted and covered her eyes from the glare of the sun. The woman helped her into her car, placing the bag of potatoes beside her and the dollar in her hand. "I forgot to pay," Frannie said. "I had a Johnny Cake."

"It's okay. You can pay later," the woman said and closed the door.

Frannie wondered if her abductor was watching. Grateful she didn't have to walk home, she breathed a prayer of thanks. The worry now was that she knew he was stalking her. No longer could she convince herself he didn't know where she lived.

Pete grew impatient waiting for the girl to come out. The sun was hot and he needed to be looking for his black book. *What's she doing in there? She's been inside long enough to buy one of everything in that little store.* He huffed and checked his watch for the third time. *It's been twenty minutes. I'm going in.*

He walked in and looked around, but didn't see her anywhere. He said to the man at the counter, "I'm looking for my little sister, a skinny redheaded kid. She been in here?"

"Yes," the man said. "She was here. She took sick. Must have been the heat got to her. She fell right out in the floor just about where you're standing. My wife drove her home. They left about a minute ago."

Pete thanked the man and walked back to his car. She was inside too long to fall out from the heat. How could she be sick? He'd just seen her skipping to the market. Was this even the same girl from last night? If so, this was a kid that really liked attention. He was bound and determined to find out.

Pete left the Ford parked at the Corner Market and walked the two blocks to the brown shingled house. He went up the wooden steps to the screened door and knocked. After a few moments, the kid stood before him, peering through the screen. "Mr. Turner!" she whispered. "What are you doing here?" She quickly stepped outside, letting the door close gently behind her.

"I wanted to speak to you. It *was* you I saw go in the little store."

Wide-eyed Fannie said, "He was there!"

"He?" Pete said, playing along. "You mean the man who attacked you?"

She put her finger to her lips, indicating he should lower his voice. "Yes." She pulled the scrap of cloth from her pocket. "That's his blood, from his ear where I bit it."

Pete grabbed the cloth from her hand. It appeared to be a scrap from the same dress she wore while she sat in his car, trembling and choking out her story. He recalled the dress was torn. Now he didn't know what to believe. "Did you tell your parents yet?"

"No! I told you I can't."

He wanted to believe she was playing games. This seemed the most likely reason she refused to tell her parents, but could an eleven year old make this up and come across so sympathetic and vulnerable? "You have to tell them now. No fooling around."

Diane called from inside. "Frances Louise, who's there?"

"Just a minute," Frannie called back. Then she whispered, "Mr. Turner you have to go. You'll get me in trouble."

There was something in her presence that was really convincing. He felt pulled one way and then the other. "What if you were my sister? If you're telling me the truth, do you understand you are in serious danger? He's playing with you. You've seen a cat play with a mouse. You're the mouse, and when he's finished playing, he comes in for the kill. Don't let that happen to you. Tell your parents."

Diane called again. "Frances Louise I asked you who's there."

"I have to go. I can talk to you tomorrow, at the library downtown. They let me ride the bus to the library on Tuesdays. I'll be there about eleven o'clock." She opened the screen to go in.

"I won't be here," Pete said. "As soon as I conclude some business, I'll be gone. I hope to leave tonight or early tomorrow."

She turned back to him. "Well thanks for rescuing me. I'll always thank you for being my rescuing angel."

"Don't go out alone. You're in danger," he said as she disappeared into the house.

He heard her momma ask her, "Who were you talking to?"

"Just my angel. My rescuing angel."

"Frances Louise, aren't you getting a bit too old to talk to imaginary friends?"

"But he's not imaginary."

"Really, Frances, I think you're reading too much. I'm beginning to worry that you can't separate the real from the imaginary."

That was all the confirmation Pete needed that the girl's story was mostly in her imagination. She almost had him convinced. She obviously possessed an active imagination. Convincing himself of that absolved him of any feelings of responsibility for her, except for the torn dress and the blood? Did she stage the scene at the market? That was really going some to get attention. It was quite a bit of play acting for an eleven year old.

He walked the two blocks back to his car. Getting in, he noticed a piece of paper under the blade of the windshield wiper. He got back out and removed it. It was a page torn from his black book! Someone found it and left this to inform him. Who would know to leave on this windshield, that this was his car? Why not just leave the book? Immediately, he was suspicious. There was no message written, but whoever found the book must have left it for him in the market. He couldn't figure how to connect the dots, but at the moment he didn't care. The important thing was it had been found, and it was back in his possession. When the contract was fulfilled on Farley, Pete wanted no evidence floating around that connected him to the Mafia. "Whew," Pete let out a sigh of relief. Now he could call Angel on his private line.

The same man he'd spoken to earlier was still there behind the counter. Pete held up the paper in his hand. "Someone found my address book. I assume you have it. I've been looking all over for it."

"Beg your pardon?" the man said, looking puzzled.

"You didn't put this under my wiper blade or know who did?"

"Never saw it before."

"That's my Ford out front. You didn't see anybody put this there?"

Chapter Twenty-three

"No, young man. I didn't."

Pete hit his hand against his forehead, turned on his heel and walked out. Who put the page from his book under the wiper blade? And where was his book now? He got in the Ford and his head slumped against the steering wheel. He felt deflated after such a sense of relief.

Then, reluctantly, it dawned on him. This had nothing to do with Farley. It got there the same way the piece of torn cloth got in the girl's pocket. The stalker, whoever he was, was letting Pete know he and the girl were being watched. "I know who you are," was the implied message. Was that a threat telling Pete to go home and mind his own business? Pete was only too happy to go as soon as possible, but the book in the stalker's hands presented a big problem. What might he do with it to use it as leverage, even to entice Pete into a trap? As much as he hated to think so, he was being pulled into Frannie's situation, and the problems were getting messier.

Chapter Twenty-four

It was mid-day now and the traffic in and around the market had picked up. Pete watched with little interest as people went in and came out. What was rattling his mind was the unbelievable mess he had stumbled into. The pedophile stalking the girl was now stalking him. Furthermore, he had gotten his dirty paws on Pete's address book with all the potentially incriminating evidence, not to mention the inconvenience the loss of it was causing him. He slammed his fist against the dash. If the torn out page on his windshield was meant as a warning for him to mind his own business and leave Riverton, if that was meant to scare him, well, it created the opposite effect. If the pedophile's audacity was a threat to Pete, it was an affront and a challenge as well. Until he had the book in his possession, he *couldn't* leave, and he couldn't proceed with the plot against Farley. He couldn't leave without the book! He was stuck here in this boring little town, yet he had serious business to get on with. He would get the book. He had no choice. No dirty pedophile was going to get in his way.

He knew a lot about them. They often got some of their thrills by taking bold chances. The uninformed public tended to miss or ignore any of the signs. Take Bill Gregg for instance. It was easier for his pride to believe that his daughter was imagining she had been attacked than to admit the horrible reality, but Pete wasn't uninformed. He knew all about pedophiles. The creep would present himself and Pete would be waiting. In the meantime, though, he had to get up with Angel and explain his missing the first appointment with the contact and repair any damage to his credibility.

The question in his mind was where was the contact now? He figured the sharp shooters for hire worked for the Mafia and lived in the big cities, but he supposed the person he came to meet would only be a middle man. It had not been Pete who picked the River Springs Marina for the appointed place, but he could see the wisdom in the choice. It was an out-of-the-way, deserted little inlet. Yet, he could no longer meet the contact there, not while he was being watched. He would negotiate for a new venue far from Riverton once he settled with the pedophile.

Maybe because Pete didn't show up at the marina at the appointed time, Salvino thought Pete had changed his mind about hiring the hit man. Nothing could be farther from the truth. On the other hand, although he hadn't paid the blood money, just based on Angel's good word for Pete, the shooter might already be setting up to pick off Farley. What if the thing had already been done? The scary part for Pete was that the pervert had his book connecting him to Salvino, Angel, and by association, the shooter. How to find the pedophile and get his book. That was a serious problem. The girl had messed up everything.

In one corner of the market parking lot in a shady spot next to a quiet side street, Pete noticed there was a phone booth. He walked over to it and stepped inside. He kept the door open because the afternoon sun still was hot. He'd let the time slip up on him. Maybe he could reach Angel now. Maybe luck would finally favor him and he'd find Angel had returned stateside. Without Angel's private number, Pete's only choice at present was to try to reach him at the gun shop. Pulling out a handkerchief to wipe the perspiration from his face and neck, he dialed the operator and waited while she connected him. He was hopeful when a voice answered on the other end.

"Angel's Goods and Guns."

"Let me talk to Angel. Tell him it's Pete Turner calling." He leaned his elbow against the glass and held his breath.

"Angel's not here."

"So he's still in Italy?" Pete's heart sank.

"Italy? No."

"He's back in country?"

"He was here earlier, but he left with a customer."

"Oh. When will he be back?"

"Not until tomorrow. That's what he said when he left."

Pete swore under his breath. He was impatient for find out what the contact had reported back to Angel since Pete hadn't shown up at the marina. With reluctance he asked, "How about Salvino? Is he around?"

"You kiddin'?"

"What do you mean?"

"I guess you better ask Angel."

"When did Angel get back from Italy?"

"When did he go?"

"For his mother's ninety-third birthday."

"You have some wrong information."

"Angel hasn't been in Italy for his mother's birthday?"

"You better talk to Angel."

"Yeah. You won't forget to tell him Pete Turner called?"

"Pete Turner. I've got it."

Pete sighed and hung up. The fellow at the gun shop either didn't know what he was talking about or Angel hadn't been in Italy. Why would Salvino lie about that? Pondering why this didn't make sense, Pete got out of the phone booth and kicked at the gravel.

It appeared he was going to be biding his time in Riverton until he worked himself out of the mess he was in. There might be a silver lining to the cloud. If he didn't return home until his revenge was complete, when he did go back, he could act as if he knew nothing of the big news of Farley's demise. Plus, it would put distance between himself and Farley's "accident." His heart raced at the enormity of this thought, the extreme and unreal plan to kill his uncle. He must not forget that Farley deserved it. He must not forget that. It was Pete's responsibility to make him pay for the pain and humiliation he had caused Mary Kate, as well as the insult to the Turner name.

While he stood next to the phone booth, he realized he hadn't talked to Robert since learning of the impending sale of the farm to Farley. He got back in the booth and picked up the receiver. Then he hung up. What could he do if the sale had gone through, if Farley had returned the papers? He might already be knocking down trees to build his speedway. Pete slammed his fist against the glass. As helpless as he was at the moment to do anything about it, he had to know. He swallowed. Picking up the receiver, he asked the operator to put him through to Robert's office.

Robert expressed enthusiasm and gratitude that Pete had called. When he inquired of Pete's whereabouts, Pete told him "traveling on business." Robert again reiterated he wanted Pete to meet his family. Trying to sound matter-of-fact over the constriction in his throat, Pete asked if Farley had returned the documents for the sale of the farm. When his brother told him the papers had not come in, Pete breathed a quiet sigh of relief. Apparently, the shooter hadn't killed Farley yet. Like everyone else in the county, Robert would have heard.

As Pete placed the receiver back in the cradle, there was a knock on the outside of the booth. A man about Pete's age stood at the door and said his battery was dead. He wore dungarees and Western style boots. "Can you give me a jump?" he asked.

Pete's antenna went up. Was this the stalker making a bold move, flaunting his belief that he had the upper hand? Pete eyed the man up and down, taking in the longish hair that could be a covering for any bandage or bite wound that might be on one of his ears.

"I'll pay you for your trouble," the man said.

You bet you will, Pete thought. He stepped out of the phone booth and followed him to his black '49 Chevy. Pete raised the hood, took out his keys and scraped some corrosion from the cable connections. "Try her now," he said, watching for any tell-tale sign that he should grab him by the nape of the neck and demand his book or else. The Chevy motor churned but wouldn't turn over. Pete strolled back to the Ford and pulled it up close to the Chevy. He got out and hooked up the cables. "Now try her." The engine sputtered, sputtered, sputtered, and turned over. "I guess you're good to go," he said, still wondering was this the pedophile.

"I need one more favor. Can you drive me three miles up to the Shell station? I'm flat out of gas."

Pete studied him. What kind of man would be out of gas with a dead battery at the same time? Pete eyed him with suspicion. The man seemed ordinary enough, but Pete wasn't going to be fooled. He might be his stalker. *Let him try something. I wish he would. I'm not a bootlegger for nothing. I can take him for a spin he'll never forget.* Pete nodded okay and got in the Ford.

The man slid in on the passenger side. "You won't need to drive me back. My wife works at the cafe across the street from the Shell. She'll bring me to get my car when she gets off for lunch. By the way, the name's Jim," he said. "Sure appreciate your help."

Pete put the Ford in reverse and pulled onto the road.

"You live around here?" the man asked.

"No."

"I'm from a few miles up the way," Jim said. "I've lived in Riverton all my life."

Pete nodded but didn't respond. In a few minutes, he pulled up to the Shell station and let the man out.

"What do I owe you?"

"Forget it."

"Sure appreciate it," the man said, giving Pete a friendly salute.

Pete watched the man walk away. *He's not the stalker. Too bad. If I knew what he looked like...*

Pete drove off, intending to head back toward the motel. Then he had an idea where he might find some clues. He would go back to the place where Frannie was attacked. What might he expect to find? Maybe the creep was a wino or indigent hobo who lived at the deserted station. Even if he found anyone there, how would he know it was the pedophile? He'd have to trust his instincts. He had to do something. His black book might be there, just lying around waiting for him to find it!

When he drove up near the deserted station, he swung the Ford into a side street. He got out and walked a half block. Hoping he would find the creep, he touched his hand to the gun in his ankle holster. Didn't they say a dog always returned to his vomit? Upon reaching the building, he thought again how the daylight disrobed it of any mystery or sense of evil.

To maintain an element of surprise, he crept quietly and cautiously around the perimeter. There was a small door in the back, probably a bathroom. He pushed it open. The stench of urine compelled him to hold his nose as he looked in. Just a broken, nasty toilet and a grimy sink. He shut the door and moved around to the front. Next to the wide, pull-down door, there was another door slightly ajar. He stuck his head in and glanced around at a scarred brown wooden desk, an old beat up file cabinet, and above that some empty shelves. Everything was covered in dust.

He went through a side door of the office into the main part of the garage. An empty rectangular pit remained where the hydraulic lift had been removed. Around that, empty wine bottles, broken glass and food wrappers littered the cement floor. There was no bed roll or clothing, no personal belongings to indicate anyone was staying there, and no black book.

He went back through the office to the outside and around the back where he stood on a space of hard ground littered with broken glass and pieces of cinderblock. To one side he saw a pile of rubber tires. A black snake sunning itself slithered off under them. Beyond, Pete observed a field of tall grass and clumps of overgrown bushes. When the kid was sitting in his car, she had described how she had run blindly through the grass and bushes in the dark. He remembered seeing a fresh scratch on her cheek.

Stepping out into the field, he found old tires scattered here and there and pieces of broken cement hidden in the weeds, just as she had described it. This seemed to confirm her story, or was it her familiarity with the place? There was no one around now unless he was keeping out of sight. Pete heard a woodpecker thumping rat-a-tat-tat on a tree, searching for some bugs for his lunch. Butterflies flitted over the grass. All of nature, so free and peaceful, seemed to mock his predicament. He turned around and went back to his car.

It was now late afternoon and he was no closer to finding his black book, no closer to setting a trap for his enemy. He thought of one more possible source of information. Driving back to the Gregg's neighborhood, he parked again on a side street and walked to the white house where Jenny Daniels lived. Not knowing her work schedule, he took a chance that this late in the afternoon, she might be home. He half expected to see her rocking on her front porch, her hair in pin curls the way the Frannie described her, but the chairs were empty.

He came to the screen door and getting a strong whiff of fried fish and collard greens, he saw a light on in the hall. He knocked and waited. Then he heard a rustle of clothing. Steps were coming toward the door. The person who appeared had to be Jenny Daniels. She weighed about two hundred and fifty pounds. He could see her large head with dark hair twisted into little round disks all over her white scalp and fixed in place with pairs of crisscrossed bobby pins. She looked at him suspiciously, "If ya selling I don't want nothing."

"You know Frances Gregg next door." It was a statement, not a question.

"What's it to you if I do?" she said.

"You left her alone in the dark at that deserted gas station last night and she was attacked by a pedophile."

"You a cop?"

Pete could see fear in her eyes despite her attempt at indifference. "No."

"If you ain't no cop, go away. I don't have to talk to you."

As she turned, Pete said, "Cops might be interested in your business there, and interested in why you left an eleven year old by herself in a rough end of town for some creep to molest her."

He saw Jenny hesitate. "Did you even think about what might happen to her? You had a customer, and you forgot all about the girl."

Jenny turned and faced him with a scowl. "Yeah. Two customers as it worked out. I guess some of us have to make it the best way we can."

"Look," Pete said. "I'm not judging you for the way you make your living."

"Well ain't that real noble of ya," she said with a shrug.

"But," he continued, "you exposed that kid to serious danger."

"Well I reckon she's okay because I seen her a while ago from the kitchen window out back playing in that china-berry tree."

"No, it's not okay. As well as emotional scars she will surely suffer, the attacker continues to stalk her. If something happens to her, you could be liable for neglect of a minor." Pete knew that might not be a solid legal statement, but he figured Jenny Daniels didn't know any better, and it might scare some information out of her."

She stared at him with hostile eyes, but after considering a moment, she said, "I don't want no trouble."

"Do you have any idea who might have attacked her? Did you see anybody around?"

"No, I only meet my johns there. That's not where we… uh…conduct business." She raised her chin with defiance. "And I don't make no social calls on them people that hangs around there," she said with a smirk.

"You saw no one but the person you met?"

"That's what I said, didn't I?" She gave him a condescending look, like he wasn't too bright.

Pete believed she was probably telling the truth. "If you remember anything that might come to you later, will you let her parents know?"

"Why should I? They don't like me. Think they're too good to let their kid talk to me."

"Just remember what I said. You exposed this child to the man who attacked her."

"I don't know nothing and I ain't likely to hear of nothing, but since you're the one so interested, why don't you leave *your* number?"

Pete thought a moment. He didn't really want to give out any information about where he was staying, but he needed his book. "I'm also looking for a little black book of addresses and phone numbers. You wouldn't happened to have found one lying in the grass or by the road, would you?"

Chapter Twenty-four

"No. I ain't seen it."

"Pete pulled out a scrap of paper where he'd previously written the number for the Shady Lawn in case he needed it. "If you think of anything in the next twenty-four hours, you can reach me here." She opened the door and took the paper. "Otherwise make sure you don't repeat what happened."

"What? Oh, you mean leave Miss Chatterbox by herself."

"Pete shot her a warning glance. It annoyed him that she made light of the situation. "Perverts look like ordinary people," he said. "They're devious and daring just because no one suspects them. That makes them difficult to catch and convict. It's their adult word against that of a frightened, confused child."

Shrugging her shoulders, she turned away from the door and carelessly tossed his number on a table behind her. Pete tightened his jaw and left the porch.

Even though he didn't feel much like eating, he stopped at a White Tower for two burgers and a chocolate shake which he consumed driving back to the Shady Lawn. He mentally reviewed the information he had acquired since the morning. The Turner land had not been sold to Farley; however, the stalker, and the book, that was still a problem. Angel was in country, but without the book, he couldn't reach him on his private line. Without the book and unable to talk to Angel, he remained in limbo. He had to find the girl's attacker. If he knew where to find him, he'd take care of him in a hurry. If he knew what he looked like...It was an unnerving feeling not to know what your adversary looked like, yet he could spy on your every move. It made Pete suspicious of everyone he saw. Is he this man? Is he that one? The girl was no help. She couldn't describe him either.

Then he had an idea. It was simple. All he needed to do was follow the bait.

Chapter Twenty-five

Pete jumped out of the lumpy bed early on Tuesday, energized by the certainty he had come up with a sure strategy. He knelt on the floor and sped through one hundred pushups, then jogged a block down College Road to the school and ran two miles on a small track that the waitress at the Red Apple Café had told him about. He began this exercise regimen in the navy, but with all the interruptions in his life of late, he had let it slide. On this morning, however, he was ready to leap tall buildings at a single bound. He felt exhilarating confidence that he would soon conclude his business in Riverton. Everything was going to work out. Soon he'd be out of here and on his way to fulfill his ambition. Just like his daddy, he would earn a reputation for making the best whiskey on the East Coast, the best anywhere, and Farley Oaks wouldn't exist to ever torment him again. Sweating profusely, he finished his run and went back to his room to shower and dress before heading to the Red Apple for breakfast.

A few customers were eating breakfast, but the place was quiet except for the occasional clatter of dishes and the hum of the exhaust fan over the sizzling grill. He imagined it would be noisier and more crowded when the students returned to the college in a few more weeks. A middle-aged waitress in a plain blue uniform took his order. In minutes she slid a plate in front of him with scrambled eggs, bacon, pancakes dotted with butter, and a jug of maple syrup. He poured a liberal splash of syrup over the pancakes and ate hurriedly while he contemplated his plan to follow the girl. The pedophile's shadowing the girl at the market had proved that he intended to lose no time in recapturing his prey. She was the bait. The next time he showed up, Pete would be there for the interception. It would be today. He especially prided himself on the good deed he could perform. He'd get his book back, remove a pervert off the streets, and save the girl. Since he was forced to get involved, he would play the hero.

The girl said she was allowed to ride the bus to the library once a week and that she would be there today about eleven. Her attacker might show up on the bus or attempt to grab her going to or from the library. When he did, Pete would have him. He got up, left his tip on the counter, and paid his bill at the register.

At the Shady Lawn office the sour fellow wasn't around. Pete assumed the bell on the counter would summon him, but to avoid having to deal with the frustrating old codger, he looked around on his own. After several minutes he retrieved the bus schedule from under some magazines on a table near the door.

After figuring out which bus went by her apartment, Pete drove downtown and left his car on a side street a few blocks from the library. Not wanting the girl or the pervert to recognize him, he pulled dark glasses and a baseball cap from his pocket and put them on. He found the bus stop nearest the library. Right on time the red and white lumbering beast of metal and tires swerved toward him. It stopped, and the hot acrid exhaust filled his nose as the door opened with a hiss and a clang. Pete mounted the steps. He plunked his coins in the metal box. The money jangled down as the doors rattled and hissed in closing.

He was still feeling the optimism of the morning. Trembling with anticipation, he made a quick survey of the few people on board, none of which were males, except the driver. He was a wide, square man, with brown hair shaped like a donut around his pink, bald scalp. Making his way down the aisle, Pete passed a tall, thin woman with grey hair and wearing a wide brimmed, flowered hat. She was seated behind the driver on the long bench that ran parallel to the windows. Across from her on the opposite bench seat, a young mother read a Golden Book to her young son. Pete noticed the title was *The Little Engine That Could* and recalled his mother reading it to him, remembering that as a good time for the Turners. He surveyed the two-person bench seats, facing front and lined up on either side of the aisle. A long bench stretched across the back where two Negro women sat with bulging shopping bags on their laps. Their closed parasols lay on the seat beside them. There was no indication on this bus that Rosa Parks' sensational defiance in Montgomery, Alabama last December had caused any changes in Riverton. As the bus lurched forward, Pete grabbed the metal poles along the aisle and pulled himself toward the back.

He found a seat two rows from the middle. Settling next to the window to watch and wait, he unrolled his newspaper and passed the time staring at the print. He peered out from behind it when each new passenger climbed aboard. Two heavy-set, well-dressed and perfumed older women got on. The one in front greeted the driver with a jovial "Good day, Mr. Jones." She put change in the box for herself and her sister, and with heavy breaths, grabbed a pole and plopped onto the bench beside the woman in the large hat. The sister sat down beside the young mother and her boy as they moved over to make room for her.

The bus roared to life again. When it passed the brown shingle where the girl lived, Pete looked out the open window. He was expecting to see her standing at the corner. She wasn't there. His heart sank. They passed The Corner Market. She wasn't anywhere in sight. There was always the possibility something prevented her coming today—or that the attacker had already kidnapped her. Pete pushed the thought from his mind. Surely the event in the market had frightened her into caution. The buzz cord sounded and the bus pulled to the curb. The young mother and her son got off. At each succeeding stop passengers disembarked. At the end of the line the driver pulled to the curb to wait five minutes before beginning a new circuit. The two Negro women from the back exited, leaving Pete the only passenger aboard. He stood up to stretch his legs.

The driver turned to Pete, "Where're you headed?"

"Library," Pete said.

"You got on near there. You already passed the library way back other side of town."

"Yeah," Pete said. "Just passing time, taking a tour of your fair city."

"Well, enjoy yourself, then," the driver said and turned back around.

Pete went to his seat, frowning. He wasn't feeling quite the same exhilaration as earlier. He decided maybe his idea to play Sherlock Holmes wasn't working out. The girl's parents must have had other plans for her today.

The time was ten-thirty when the driver swung the bus around and headed back toward downtown. Several passengers got on, two women and two men. One of the men was a frail Negro with grey hair and the other was a white boy too young to be the girl's abductor. Pete realized the pedophile probably knew the kid would not be on the bus. He no doubt was better informed of her whereabouts than Pete. When the bus reached her block, Pete looked out the open window beside him. He saw an elderly gentleman with a cane. Then, behind him, he saw a small figure with a red ponytail. She held a bag of books. To his relief, it was the girl.

He settled back, taking up the entire seat to discourage company, especially hers. He didn't want her to see him until he was ready to reveal himself. Hiding behind his newspaper, Pete glanced around it to see the grey haired man with the cane slowly and carefully making his way onto the bus. Then the girl's red head emerged as she flounced up the steps. Dressed in a simple blue cotton print dress and brown sandals, she dropped her coins in the box and moved down the aisle as the bus rolled forward. She didn't look in his direction, but took the window seat in the middle section behind the elderly gentleman. As soon as he was seated, she leaned toward him and began talking, probably continuing a conversation she had begun with him while waiting for the bus. Pete strained his ears to hear bits and pieces of the conversation above the roar of the motor and intermittent voices of the other passengers.

One block after her stop, a thin, bespectacled, teen-age girl got on carrying a stack of books. She was another one bound for the library Pete guessed. He thought that Frannie might know her, but she was too engrossed in her conversation with the elderly man to notice. A pretty blonde haired woman came down the aisle and sat beside Frannie. Then, a block down the line, a man of medium build got on carrying a hard hat in his hand. He wore brown work pants, a thin cotton tee shirt, and heavy brown work boots. His dark hair was sweaty and covered his ears so that Pete could not tell if one ear was bandaged. This was the first passenger Pete considered to be a possible suspect. His heart rate quickened. He hid his face behind the newspaper, but managed to keep one eye on the approaching suspect. The man sat down across the aisle one row up.

Pete could hear the girl's chatter. He heard her tell the blonde haired woman that she was going to the library. He made a mental note to tell her not to broadcast information about herself in public where everyone could hear.

When a Negro woman got on and took a seat in the rear, Frannie asked the woman next to her if she thought Negroes should have to sit in the back of the bus. In a gravelly voice, the woman said it had always been that way and she could see no reason why it should change. "Just makes for trouble," she said. Frannie declared passionately that it was wrong and unfair. The woman turned her head with a frown, obviously not wanting to continue the conversation. Frannie picked out one of her books from her bag and held it out to the woman. *"The Adventures of Huckleberry Finn,"* she announced.

"I never read it," the woman said without interest.

"Oh, you must," Frannie said. "In the story most of the people believed slavery was okay. You don't think that, do you?" Frannie asked her.

The woman ignored the question.

Frannie continued anyway, "But Huck helped Jim, a Negro man, escape down the Mississippi from his owner, Miss Watson because he saw slavery was wrong. Like making Negroes ride in the back of the bus is wrong." Frannie looked away. "I wish I could ride a raft down the Mississippi and save a man from slavery," she said with a sigh. When the woman continued to ignore Frannie's chatter, she turned to watch out the window.

Pete continued to keep an eye on the man with the hard hat across the aisle who leaned back against the seat with his eyes closed. He appeared to have no interest in the girl, but he could be waiting for her to get off the bus. Pete assumed there were bushes and shrubs planted all around the grounds of the library where an abductor could hide, waiting for an opportune moment to grab her. For this girl, the man would have only to strike up a conversation to lure her off the path, especially when she didn't know what he looked like and didn't seem to have any hesitation about talking to strangers.

The bus rumbled down Main Street, then crossed the bridge and the Dodd Mill conglomeration of buildings. When it passed a grassy hill covered with colorful tents, Frannie pointed out the window and addressed everyone who could hear her. "Oh look! A carnival! See the Ferris wheel? Oh, imagine riding so high up you could see all of Riverton!"

As the bus wound its way through downtown, it turned and followed several back streets. Across from a construction site where steel girders rose up toward the roofs of other one and two-story buildings, a passenger pulled the buzz cord. The bus came to a stop and the man Pete had hoped was the girl's attacker joined those getting off. He slumped in disappointment, the departure of the suspected passenger leaving him completely deflated. The bus rumbled on past the United States Post Office that covered half a city block. Next it stopped across from the library. Pete waited for the girl to get off and then followed some distance behind her. He clenched his jaw with impatience, but he reasoned, sooner or later the pedophile would follow the bait. There was still time for him to show up today.

Chapter Twenty-six

The Riverton City Library was a two-story beige stucco building with brown trim and a flat brown roof. The building and its grounds covered much of a city block. Following a good distance behind, Pete pinned his eyes to Frannie as she crossed the street and walked up an asphalt driveway beside a manicured lawn dotted with tall trees. Neatly trimmed shrubs lined a brick walkway to steps that led up to the front entrance. No one sprang from behind any of the bushes or trees to accost her.

He removed his sunglasses and hat when he followed her inside, staying along the periphery where he could be inconspicuous and yet keep Frannie in his line of vision. She deposited her books at the return desk and tried to strike up a conversation with the librarian about the carnival tents and the Ferris wheel she had passed on the bus. The librarian put a finger up to her lips to shush her. Frannie mouthed an "Oh," and backed off toward the stacks. She ambled among the rows, collecting a new armful of books. After fifteen minutes of watching her, Pete grew impatient because the pedophile had not shown himself. He had hoped not to have to wait around for two hours and follow her on the return trip home.

He had already reasoned with himself that the pervert must have seen Frannie get out of the Ford on Sunday night. He couldn't have seen Pete in the dark, yet he knew Pete's car at the market. How did he know the black book belonged to Pete? Had he observed it on the ground where the girl got out? It gave Pete the creeps to know someone he could not identify could recognize him and was spying on his every move. He wondered how many watching eyes were spying on him. Were Farley's men here in Riverton keeping an eye on him as well as the girl's abductor?

Pete gave it another five minutes that seemed to him like thirty while Frannie continued to browse among the stacks. Finally, she checked out her books and carried them to a table and sat down. Frustrated, Pete decided the pedophile wasn't going to show up in the library and he hurried over to her.

"It's Pete Turner," he said in a whisper.

Frannie looked up. "What?" She blinked. For a moment she was speechless. He pulled out the chair beside her and sat down. "Mr. Turner!" she exclaimed. People at the next table looked up. "Oh, sorry," she said, lowering her voice. She whispered, "I didn't expect to see you. I thought you had left."

Pete felt that all eyes in the library were now on them. "Look," he said. "Let's go outside. It's too quiet in here." Frannie hopped up, gathered her books into her bag and led him out a back way.

The tall leafy trees, longtime residents from the looks of their height and broad trunks, shaded much of the grounds close to the building. These stretched in a line along the left perimeter in the back and lead to a quiet garden of flowers and shrubs. Two wrought iron chairs and a similar bench provided a private conversation spot in the shade of a huge magnolia. Pete sat in one chair and Frannie took the other. "Mr. Turner, I thought you were leaving," she exclaimed with obvious excitement at the unexpected diversion.

"Do me a favor," Pete said. "Don't call me Mr. Turner. Call me Pete."

"Oh, I couldn't," Frannie said. "My step momma would skin me alive for calling a grownup by his first name. I'll call you Mr. Pete."

"I guess that will work. It's better than Mr. Turner. That makes me feel old."

"I thought you were leaving."

"My business got delayed, but I hope to leave soon. I followed you on the bus, hoping the scum who attacked you would show up like he did at the market."

Frannie immediately frowned and looked down at her feet. When she raised her head she asked, "You were on the bus?"

"Yes, and by the way, you shouldn't be broadcasting where you're going so the whole world can hear. You never know who's listening."

"I'm a chatterbox." Frannie said matter-of-factly, slumping her shoulders. "Everybody says so, but sometimes I wish there was somebody to talk to. I miss my friends. There were lots of kids my age in the neighborhood where we lived in North Carolina. I miss my granny. We lived next door to her before we moved here."

"He's bound to show up again," Pete said.

Frannie jumped up from her seat. "Isn't is beautiful here?" She twirled around. Walking toward a flower bed she said, "Look at those pretty impatiens," and she put out a hand and touched one. Walking further away and shading her eyes, she pointed. "And those tall red canna lilies over there soaking up the sun. Can you smell those sweet petunias when the breeze sends their perfume this way, just like in my granny's garden?"

"Look, kid, this is serious. Do you understand?"

Frannie turned around reluctantly, "Yes."

"This man is a sicko. He preys on little children. I know what I'm talking about. A bad man like this one..." Pete stopped himself. "Have you remembered anything else from the other night?"

She bent down and fumbled with the buckle on her sandal. "It was dark. It's still a blur. Mostly I remember running."

"He's dangerous. You remember that he assaulted you, took you against your will, dragged you into the grass in the dark. I know it's painful to talk about."

She picked up a turtle crawling through the grass.

"Try to remember. Did he have any scars or tattoos?"

She shook her head. "I already told you he didn't." Then she smiled up at Pete. "You were my rescuing angel."

"I'm anything but an angel," Pete said, looking flustered. "And I'm not Robin Hood and you aren't Maid Marian either. I'll have to be leaving." He pointed his finger at her, "and if he doesn't show up soon, you must always be aware of your surroundings. Don't go places alone, and certainly not with that Jenny Daniels."

Frannie placed the turtle on a rock and studied him intently. She gave him some grass. The turtle ignored it, waddled to the edge of the rock and fell off. She let him go and turned back toward Pete. "Tell me, Mr. Pete, when you leave here, where are you going? Where are you from?"

Pete sighed, frustrated he couldn't get through to her. He put one arm up on the back of the bench. "When I was your age, I was growing up in the beautiful foothills of the Appalachian Mountains."

"Ohhh," Frannie said. "That's where the bootleggers made moonshine."

"How do you know about that?" Pete said.

"I read about it in a book."

"My daddy made moonshine."

"Your daddy was a bootlegger?!" She gasped. "That's so romantic!"

"Not romantic," Pete said. "It's a hard life. It's how my daddy died, in a crash when the federal agents were chasing him."

Frannie's brows knit together. "I'm so sorry. I guess that's why you don't think bootlegging is exciting."

"It's a means to an end, a way to make a living, but I'd rather talk about you and how I'm not going to be here to watch out for you. You can't think of me as some kind of guardian angel."

"If you go, Mr. Pete, I have a real guardian angel."

"Frannie, you're smarter than that. Bad things happen to people all the time. Where are their guardian angels?"

"My granny says if I believe, Jesus will take care of me."

Pete let out another deep sigh.

"Mr. Pete, do you know Jesus?"

"What?"

"I said do you know Jesus. Do you believe in Him?"

Pete looked over her head toward the library. "I went to church as a boy. My momma took me. My daddy didn't have much use for religion."

"Was that because he was a bootlegger?"

"Lots of our neighbors were bootleggers. Anyway, what are you, some kind of child evangelist?"

"God sent Jesus so we could be saved from hell in the hereafter and enjoy a good life here on earth. You need to get saved."

"Why? So I can believe in a myth?"

Frannie frowned at him and folded her arms.

"Sorry. I don't mean to hurt your feelings. You're just a kid. I'm worried about you trusting in make-believe religion when you're in real danger."

"Christianity isn't a religion."

Pete looked at her curiously. "You're the second person to tell me that just lately…but enough about that." Pete stood to his feet. "My stomach's growling. You hungry?"

"Not really."

"I'm hungry enough to eat the rear end out of a rag doll."

Frannie giggled, "The rear end out of a rag doll! Mr. Pete! That's so funny."

Pete grinned to think he could make someone laugh even if she was only eleven years old. No one had thought of him as humorous in quite a while. "What do you say we walk over to that carnival and get a hot dog? It's not a long walk and we can get a drink and some food."

As soon as the words were out of his mouth, he regretted them. There were plenty of places closer around to get food. Nevertheless, he had a couple of hours to kill before he could try to reach Angel, and he needed to leave a quick message for Jennings to say he might be gone another day or so. Since it didn't look like the perp was going to show up and his day was wasted anyway, he might as well entertain her. She had a strange pull on him. She reminded him so much of Mary Kate.

"Oh! Mr. Pete, could we?"

The way her eyes sparkled when she was happy made Pete feel good inside in a way he hadn't felt in a long time. Nevertheless, he reminded himself he must not get more involved in her situation than he already was. He had serious business to take care of, and if it weren't for almost running over this kid and then his address book falling into the hands of the perp, he wouldn't be sitting here at the Riverton Library on a Tuesday morning. "What time do you have to be home?"

"Sometimes I stay here until around three," she said.

"He looked at his watch. "It's almost twelve-thirty. Let's go."

Frannie hurried to her seat where her stack of books lay. She swept them up. "I'll be right back."

"What are you going to do?" he called as she started across the grass.

"To leave these with the librarian until we come back," she said as she ran off.

The kid was as flighty as a butterfly and he could not seem to get across to her how cautious she must be. He knew it paid to be suspicious and alert. He'd learned that working with his daddy. He stood up to follow her, remembering he'd seen a pay phone inside where he could leave a message for Jennings.

It was then Pete saw a man through the shrubs right behind where he and Frannie had been sitting. Pete stiffened. The man wore overalls and whatever the length of his hair, it was tucked up under a straw hat. He was holding a trowel. He got up from his knees and began gathering up his tools.

He didn't try to follow Frannie, but sauntered off in the opposite direction toward a copse of trees.

Pete sighed. *Probably just the gardener.*

He sprinted toward the building to catch up with Frannie.

As soon as she and Pete disappeared inside, the man in the straw hat with the gardening tools circled back to a narrow street behind the library. He got into a black paneled work truck. When he took off, he drove in the direction of the carnival.

Chapter Twenty-seven

Pete led Frannie to an alcove near the library's main entrance where earlier he had noticed a pay phone. He situated her in a place where he could see her while he dialed the operator. He gave the operator the number for Jennings' landlady. Fortunately he had this number memorized. When she answered and Pete asked if he could give her a message for Jennings, her response was puzzling. She said, "I've gotta see if he's up to coming to the phone." He hadn't expected to talk to Jennings. *Why isn't he working at the stills?*

In a few minutes a muffled voice asked, "Pete? Where are you?"

"What's going on?" Pete said. "Why aren't you at the still?"

"Monday night…I'd been out with some guys…" Jennings sounded groggy. "Got back here." He paused, as if struggling to collect his thoughts. "Outa nowhere these two thugs grabbed me. Asked me where you was. I said I didn't know. They roughed me up, like shovin' me aroun' and saying I was lyin'. They kept saying 'Where's Turner?' I said you went to Richmond and that's all I knew. Either they didn't believe me or they just wanted to be sure you got the message that they were lookin' for you, but anyways they broke my arm and busted my jaw. Had to take off work a couple of days."

Pete threw his head back in frustration. "You got beat up because of me? What did they look like?"

"Well, it was dark, and they threw a bag over my head."

"Those chicken-livered jerks. They don't have the guts to fight fair. I know it's Farley's men. It's the same ones that busted my nose and roughed me up after the race a week ago."

"One fellow said to warn you that their people ain't playin' games. He said you either pay up or die. He said 'tell 'im the arm of the Mafia's long.' Why did they say that?"

"It's Farley's men. They're the same ones that tried to beat me up. I know they're working for Farley. They said as much."

"Well, these guys implied they're working for the Mafia."

"They're lying. They're working for Farley."

"Just where are you, Pete?"

"Long story, and it's best you don't know. All I can tell you right now is watch your back."

"You aren't getting involved with the Mafia, are you Pete?"

"Why would I do that?"

"I don't know why you hate Farley so much. What's it gonna cost you, Pete? If you're messing around with those kinda people, you could end up going to prison—or dead. It don't make sense."

"I told you those were idle threats. It's just Farley's thugs trying to throw you off."

"If you say so, but they'll probably be back. They say you owe money and I believe they mean to find out where they can collect it."

"Like I said, just watch yourself. I'll get back with you." Pete hung up. Jennings' words rang in his ears. "Mafia... you could end up going to prison...or dead." *I'll never go to prison. Not for Farley Oaks.* He sat a minute to calm himself. Then he motioned for Frannie and they left by the front entrance.

She skipped her brown sandals along the narrow sidewalk, stepping over the section lines and trying not to step on the cracks, at the same time attempting to keep up with

Pete's long strides. Beside them, Main Street hummed with downtown traffic and the noise of trucks rattling by, spewing exhaust fumes. They felt the heat of the sun and the moisture on their skin soaking their clothes. Occasionally, a Wednesday afternoon shopper brushed past them. As they approached the green, rolling terrain where the tents were set up, the whimsical music of organ, bells, and drums floated toward them like an overhead cloud. "I hear the music," Frannie exclaimed. Just around a corner they came to a temporary metal fence enclosing the event area, creating an entrance and exit passageway into the arena. The crowd, moms with young kids, grandparents, and lots of teenagers out of school for summer vacation, were entering the way into the carnival. The numbers weren't comparable to what they would be on a weekend, but the carnival was obviously popular in this small town.

"It's the smells grabbing my attention," Pete said. "I'm getting the aroma of grilling onions and hot dogs." He paid the fee to get inside and they entered a different world. Let me have your ticket stub. We need to save these so I can go out to that service station across the street and make another call at one-thirty." Frannie gave it to him and he stuck both of them in his shirt pocket.

Just inside the carnival grounds, there were many small tents where crafts, prize jellies, pickles and other food products were on display. They saw smelly prize pigs and pumpkins as tall as Frannie. As they wound their way through the cacophony of carnival sights, sounds, and smells, Pete had to smile in amusement at his small companion's pointing in awe and delight at every scene along the grassy path. A carnival worker standing in front of a game booth called out, "Play the game. Everyone's a winner!" Down the line another cried, "I can guess your age within two years or you get a prize!"

"Is that true?" Frannie asked.

"In your case it is. Even I could do that."

Chapter Twenty-seven

She smiled. "What about old people like you? I mean adults?" she said.

"Thanks a lot. He might guess it if he's lucky," Pete said.

"But he said a prize if he misses."

"That's because you pay him a quarter for a prize that's worth maybe five for a dime, but that's part of the fun," Pete said. "Do you want him to guess your age?"

"Not yet," she said. "We just got here. I want to see everything first."

A fortune teller beckoned to them from in front of a booth curtained with strings of gold beads. "Show me your palm. I will tell you your fortune," she said in mysterious, deep voice. Her long black hair fell onto a bright yellow shawl draped over her rich purple blouse. Large gold earrings dangled to her shoulders. As they passed her, she called after them, "I can see it. You're going to meet someone dangerous."

Beyond the fortune teller, they could hear a carnival barker with a megaphone announcing, "Ladies and gentlemen! You're about to behold a sight so strange, so horrifying, so deformed!" As they drew nearer, they saw him on a raised platform in front of a black curtain. "Get your tickets! See the baby with two heads!"

"Is that real, a baby with two heads?"

"I hope not. Probably not," Pete said. "Haven't you been to the carnival before?"

"No. Diane, my step momma, says it's a gyp."

"Well, in a way she's right. You have to suspend your disbelief. I haven't been to one of these since I was a boy, Pete reminisced. "I always liked to throw the basketball, but most of all I liked to watch my daddy try to ring the bell with the big hammer. He could do it, too."

They paused a few minutes to watch the bumper cars bang into each other and then spin and crash against the wall. It didn't take them long to walk the entire length of tents, booths, and rides. At the end of the path, they came to the largest tent on the grounds. A sign posted out in front indicated the next circus performance would be at four o'clock. Frannie peered inside the tent flap to see a sawdust-covered ring surrounded by empty bleachers and a worker picking up paper cups and food wrappers. Pulling her head back outside the flap, Frannie said, "I wish we could see the circus."

"Too late," Pete told her. "We have to leave before three o'clock to get you home."

"I know," Frannie said with a sigh.

"This won't be Barnum and Bailey. You can go to a real circus sometime. Here you might see a juggler, tumblers, maybe some dog tricks, nothing exotic. And clowns. You can't have any circus, large or small, without clowns."

They ambled back onto the main path when Pete heard, "Get your hot dog! Get your corndog!" He took Frannie to a cluster of tables under a shading canopy.

"Let's eat."

"I'm not hungry," she said. "I'll have a lemonade."

"You're sure?"

"Just lemonade. I guess I'm too excited."

Pete felt something strange tug at his heart. It was another one of those good feelings he wasn't used to. "I don't want you getting sick on me."

"I feel fine," she said.

"Well, I'm starving," he said. "Wait here in the shade. I'll get in line."

Keeping his eyes on Frannie, Pete moved to one of several food stands in a row. Frannie watched the succession of people passing: young children with adults, strolling teenage boys eyeing giggling girls or younger boys chasing each one another, zig-zagging through the crowd.

Pete came over with their order and sat down, placing Frannie's lemonade in front of her. She sipped while he inhaled his hot dog and washed it down with gulps of Coke. He finished the last bite and was considering another round of food when Frannie suddenly dashed off toward an organ grinder with his pet monkey coming up the path. Pete dropped his trash in a nearby container and sprinted after her. He didn't want to lose her. She would be hard to miss with her red hair, but she was small, and there was always the chance that their stalker might be watching them. Pete had all but forgotten about him. They were in a very public place with people all around, and it would be difficult to just walk off with her. However, Pete intended to play it safe and stay close. He felt for the pistol strapped under his pant leg.

The organ grinder was as wiry as the little monkey sitting on his shoulder. He wore a red jacket and black bowler that matched the monkey's vest and red fez hat. Frannie asked, "Can I touch him?" His owner consented and Frannie gingerly reached out her hand. From his master's shoulder to the top of the organ to right in front of Frannie's face, he let her pet him and shake his hand. Then he pulled a marshmallow out of the organ grinder's pocket. When Frannie reached to take it, he popped it in his mouth and scampered back onto his owner's shoulder. Frannie giggled.

"Are you having fun, Mr. Pete?" she asked.

"Sure if you are. I came to eat," Pete said.

"I wish my daddy and Diane would come, but they can't right now."

Other kids with their accompanying adults began to gather around the organ grinder, and Frannie and Pete moved away to make room for the others to get close. They meandered down the path to a game booth. A sign advertised three throws of the basketball for a quarter. Pete stepped up and paid a burly man with a hard, stubbled face and a mouth with brown or missing teeth. When he gave Pete the ball, Pete first asked Frannie if she wanted to try. She shook her head. "No." He made all three baskets and the fellow offered him a small brown bear. Pete frowned, "How about the big one up high for my little friend here?"

The man said, "You have to pay again for the big one."

Pete smirked. "I have to pay again? And how many times after that?"

Expressionless, he waited for Pete to pay his quarter.

Frannie tilted her head to one side and raised her eyebrows at Pete, "I can't take the big one home," she said. "I'll take the small one with the blue bow."

"Okay." He nodded reluctantly and the man gave her the one she chose.

"Thank you, Mr. Pete," she said, hugging the bear to her heart.

They ambled along and met a clown wearing a frizzy orange wig and a baggy, bright yellow suit with puffy orange buttons. On his feet were floppy black shoes. He walked up to Frannie, took her hand, and placed it on his round red nose. He told her to squeeze it. She hesitated, but giggled. He said, "It's okay. Go ahead," in his funny, high clown voice through his painted red smile. She squeezed it, laughed, and squeezed it again. He picked a pink balloon on a string from a colorful bunch he carried and handed it to her. Pete reached in his pocket for a nickel, but the clown waved it aside. He made a deep, solemn bow toward a smiling Frannie and drifted into the crowd, his balloons bobbing along behind him.

Pete looked at his watch. It was almost one thirty. He didn't know what part of the afternoon Angel was expected back at the gun shop, but he was anxious to try to reach him. He said to Frannie, "I have to make a phone call. Let's go back to the gate where we came in. This shouldn't take long. We'll still have some time to come back when I finish."

They passed out the exit and crossed the street to the pay phone booth. "Sit here on the grass, and don't talk to anyone," he told her.

Holding the bear, she sat down. Pete deposited his coins at the operator's request. After a minute the quick buzzing in the receiver told him the line at the gun shop was busy. He put down the receiver, waited a minute and tried again. It was still busy. He slammed the receiver back in the cradle. Since Frannie was occupied looking for four leaf clovers, he decided to call Robert again, anxious to know if the signed papers had been returned since yesterday.

He asked the receptionist for Robert. When his brother answered, Pete asked if he'd heard from Farley. Robert said that Farley had not returned the papers, but that he understood Farley had been in Mexico and had only recently come home. "Just as I told you, he's a busy man, but I expect to have the papers in my hands in a day or so."

Although distressed by the further delay, Pete said he'd check back tomorrow and hung up. He wondered how long had Farley been in Mexico. It was obvious to Pete that Farley's spies had been reporting to him, informing him that Pete was back in Wilkes and asking questions. Pete didn't doubt for a minute that Farley knew about his tussle with Bennie Farnes in the diner. Now with Farley having returned from his travels, he would waste no time in signing the contract to buy the Turner land. It was more urgent than ever for Pete to get up with Angel. Immediately, he dialed the gun shop. The line was still busy. Pete hung up.

Since he'd promised to take Frannie back to the carnival, he would go now. He realized it would be less distracting to talk to Angel without having to keep an eye on her because he never knew when she would take off on an impulse.

Pete stepped out of the booth. "Let's go kid," he said, trying to smile in spite of his worries. "We have about forty-five more minutes. Then we have to get back to the library."

Pete showed the gatekeeper their ticket stubs and re-entered the carnival grounds.

"Let's ride something. What do you want to ride?" he asked. "There's the carousel."

She wrinkled up her nose. "That's for children," she said.

"Excuse me. I thought that's what you were."

"I'd like to ride the Ferris wheel."

"The Ferris wheel it will be," he said.

Pete paid at the ticket booth then helped Frannie into the seat. Getting in beside her, he latched them in. After a few minutes, they began to move. The air was cooler as the great wheel began to roll them to the top. Frannie expressed awe at the broad view of Riverton where all the streets, buildings, the river and the bridge appeared to be tiny miniatures. She pointed at the tiny cars on the roads. When she did, her balloon floated from her hand. While she watched it drift up toward a cloudless blue sky, she held the bear tighter.

The wheel stopped to let some riders off and others on. Looking down on the world below, Pete was thinking he was almost having fun. The carnival seemed far away and so did Farley Oaks, and Angel and hit men. If life could be so simple, he thought, as the wheel began to move again. He couldn't remember if Mary Kate had ever been to the carnival. Pictures of her began flashing through his mind, the happy, beautiful girl she was before Rusty's accident when everything changed. Then, his reverie was interrupted; it was their turn to get off.

Pete tried to interest Frannie in other rides or cotton candy or a snow cone. She said, "No," at each suggestion as if anything so tangible would disturb her fascination with all that was around her. She seemed really grateful. It had been a long time since Pete had enjoyed such an elated feeling at someone else's pleasure. He checked his watch. He could hardly believe it was time to go. "We need to leave to get you home by three," Pete said. They started back toward the gate where they had come in.

In an open space where two grassy paths crossed, a group of boys and girls Frannie's age and younger were gathered around a clown pulling coins out of their ears and making bright colored scarves disappear and re-appear. Frannie tugged at Pete's sleeve, "It's that nice clown who gave me my balloon." She moved closer. He checked his watch. "Five more minutes," he said.

Nearby the smell of mustard, chili, onions and cooking meat wafted toward him, reminding him he didn't get his second hot dog. He told Fannie, "Don't move from this spot. I'm going right over there to that stand to get another hot dog. Then we have to go."

Watching as the clown pulled a nickel from behind the boy's ear beside her, she said, "Okay." Her eyes followed the yellow suit moving toward to a little girl with blonde hair. She wore a pink sundress. He held out a black hat and told her to reach inside to verify that it was empty. She did. Then he turned it upside down and shook it. When he turned it up again, he pulled out a pink scarf and waved it before the mesmerized kids. They oohed with one voice.

Then he motioned for Fannie to step forward. She pointed to herself. "Me?" He nodded "Yes." He indicated she was to reach inside the hat. She did. "There's nothing in it," she said. This time he pulled out a rubber chicken. As quickly as he made it appear, he made it disappear again. Frannie asked, "How did you do that?"

He pointed to a wooden fence a few feet behind him. "If you walk over there, you'll find my rubber chicken on the rail. Get it for me and I'll tell you."

Frannie ran to the fence and held up the rubber chicken. Again all the children exclaimed with amazement. She beamed with happiness at all the attention.

A hand on her shoulder startled her. It was the nice clown's. He pointed to something further down the path.

Pete had been watching the entire proceeding, keeping his eyes fixed on Frannie. He turned away just before Frannie ran to the fence, but only long enough to pay the girl handing him his food. When he looked back and saw an empty spot where his charge had been standing, he froze.

Chapter Twenty-eight

Pete dropped his food on the counter and rushed toward the first child he came to. "Where's the kid with the red ponytail?" he asked him.

"With the clown," he said.

"Where? Which way?" he asked. The child pointed in the direction he had seen them go.

"Pete caught another boy walking away. "Where's the girl with the clown?" The boy shrugged and Pete stood looking around, not knowing in what direction to dash off to first. He felt a tug on his shirttail. "Frannie," he said, turning around. "I thought I told you…"

But it was the girl in the pink sundress. "You looking for the girl with the red hair?"

"Which way did she go?" Pete demanded.

She pointed down the path. "She was helping the clown find his rubber chicken."

"Which way? Which way?"

"The clown pushed her. She didn't want to go, but I saw him push her. They went that way," the girl said.

Pete sprinted off in the direction she indicated, helter skelter dodging the people in his path while scanning the crowd for an orange wig. *I shouldn't have left her, even for a minute, knowing how she is. She thinks everybody is her friend. I don't see her. Where would he take her? People are all around.* He stopped where two paths intersected. *Where? Where?* He looked in both directions. He saw the circus tent. *The empty circus tent!* He ran that way, pushing bodies out of his way.

When he reached it, he threw back the flap and dashed inside. He blinked several times to adjust his eyes to the shadows. Then he noticed movement in the middle of the arena. It was the yellow suit and orange wig. The clown was carrying Frannie towards the backside of the tent. "Stop," Pete yelled as he reached for his pistol. "I have a gun. Stop or I'll shoot." He saw him throw Frannie to the ground. Pete rushed to her as he watched the flash of yellow and orange disappear through the tent flap. "Are you hurt?" he asked, bending over her.

She seemed dazed, but said, "No."

He helped her sit up. Pete looked toward the exit. "I want to get him. Can you sit right here and let me try to catch him before he gets away?" She nodded assent. Pete dashed after him, hopping over guy ropes, and between the trailers parked behind the tent. He spotted the yellow suit climbing a high wooden fence at the rear of the carnival grounds. Pete raced toward the fence, but before he could aim the gun and fire a warning shot, the pedophile was gone. By the time Pete reached the fence, he found the orange wig and a pair of oversized rubber shoes lying on the ground. He shinnied to the top, but Frannie's abductor was out of sight. "Drat it. I've been so close and I still can't say I've seen him."

He went back to Frannie in the tent and helped the shaking girl to her feet. "Are you okay? I want to see the carnival manager. Do you feel like walking with me?"

"Okay," she said.

"We'll find out if this creep works for the carnival. My guess is he doesn't."

He took Frannie's hand and let her set the pace. When he found the manager's trailer, he knocked on the door. After a few seconds a man with shoulder-length dirty blond hair came out. He had a large snake tattoo running up his arm. Pete said, "I want to register a complaint about the clown walking around the grounds and doing the magic shows."

The man frowned. "A clown doing magic shows on the grounds?"

"Yeah," Pete said. "The one with the orange wig and yellow suit."

The man shook his head. "Our clowns perform with the circus. That's the only time you can see them."

"Just as I suspected," Pete said.

"What is it you wanted to complain about?"

"Nothing now," Pete said, turning to go. "More than likely he won't be back."

"That's it?" the man asked.

"Yeah," Pete said. Taking Frannie by the hand, he led her through the circus tent and along the path to the exit. "You feel like walking back to the library. My car's there."

"But you rode the bus."

"Yes, I rode the bus from the library."

"Oh," Frannie said, ambling along. He exercised patience, although he found it tedious to keep her slow pace. On the inside, his engine was revved to go, yet at every turn he felt stalled in time. At the library, he went inside with her to get her books from the reference librarian.

They walked around the side to Pete's car. He checked his gas, figuring he was probably low. He didn't want to get stranded and put her through any more walking or make her any later getting home than she already was. "Look, we're running late. It's almost three o'clock now. I spent my cash at the carnival, so I have to drive back to where I'm staying and pick up enough money to buy some gas."

"I'll just tell Diane the time slipped up. It's sort of the truth. She won't worry about me. She'll think I was reading and forgot to check the time."

"If that'll work," Pete said and took off.

At the Shady Lawn Pete pulled up in front of his room. "I'll just be a second," he said and hurried inside. Frannie got out of the hot car to stand in the shade and admire the pansies and impatiens planted in beds around the motel. When she saw a yellow tabby cat resting in the flowers, she reached down to stroke it.

Pete came back bringing a glass of water to her. "It's not cold."

She took two sips and gave back the glass. She handed him the bear she had managed to clutch throughout her ordeal. "Keep this for me, please. I'd better not take it home."

Pete took the glass inside and tossed the bear on the bed. He hurried back out to help her into the Ford. Then he drove to the gas station near the laundromat. After he filled the gas tank, he headed for town and across the bridge.

"I'm going to start calling you 'Frannie the Cat' because you have nine lives. I just don't know how many you've used up now."

"I'm not a cat," Frannie said. "You're my rescuing angel."

Pete looked at her with concern. "I won't be here to save you again. I'm leaving. Do you understand?"

"That's what you said before and here you are."

"I'm only here because my business was delayed, but it will be finished soon, maybe by tomorrow night."

"If you leave, my guardian angel will look after me."

"Where was your guardian angel today? I want to know."

"He sent you."

Pete sighed. It seemed useless trying to make her understand. She was going to believe what she wanted to and he didn't know how to get through to her.

He stopped a few doors from her apartment because she insisted. Before she got out he found himself saying, "We have to talk to your parents. This evening. With or without your consent, I have to tell them you're in serious danger."

She lifted sad eyes to him. "It won't be how you think, Mr. Pete." And she was gone, trotting up the sidewalk with her arm load of books.

He watched her go up the steps to her apartment. When he saw she was safely in the door, he pulled off to find a pay phone. It was time to try again to reach Angel at the gun shop.

Chapter Twenty-nine

Pete stopped at the first pay phone he came to. He put in his coins and dialed the operator. He waited while she connected him to the gun shop. When the dial tone indicated the line was open, his spine straightened. He felt hope. A different voice from before answered. Pete gave his name and this time he was told, "Angel's been expecting you to call for the last two hours, Mr. Turner."

"I tried but the line was busy," Pete said.

"He wants to talk to you, but he had to leave. Said tell you to call him on his private line at home this evening."

All Pete's expectation flew from him like somebody knocked his breath out. "His private line?"

"Yes. You must be somebody special if you have Angel's private number."

"Yeah. Thanks." Pete said. He slumped forward, resting his head against the glass booth. Then he hung up.

Dragging back to the Ford, he threw himself in the seat. Putting his head in his hands, he lamented that the pervert had caused him to miss making another connection. Now he really needed that black book.

He drove back to the motel and dropped down across the bed. Despite the churning on his insides, after a while he fell into a fitful sleep. He dreamed Mary Kate was running, out of breath and running. She was thin and pale like she was the last time he saw her alive right after he came home from the navy. Around every corner there was Farley reaching for her. Then he saw his daddy's face and heard him say, "Pete, boy, what were you thinking? With me gone you were supposed to look out for your little sister, not let those awful, dirty things happen to her at the hands of Farley." Then he saw a trembling Mary Kate leaning against a closed door. Farley was knocking, knocking, and threatening her if she didn't open to him. His sister began sliding the latch to open the door.

"No! Don't!" Pete woke up in a sweat. He shook himself, but the knocking continued. It took him a minute to realize the knocking came from outside the door of his room. He jumped up, grabbed his pistol, and jerked the door open, but instead of Farley or the two thugs who assaulted him and Jennings, there were two plain clothes detectives standing there, showing their badges.

"Hand over the gun and step outside," one of them said. Pete handed over his gun while the second detective frisked him.

The older of the two who was doing the talking said, "You Pete Turner?"

"Yeah, I'm Turner. What's this about?"

"You know Frances Gregg?"

"I know her," Pete said. "Has something happened to Frannie?"

"We received a report from a concerned citizen that you abducted her from the Riverton library this afternoon."

"A concerned citizen?" Pete smirked. "He's concerned all right."

"We need to take you downtown for questioning. Her daddy's real upset. He's probably gonna press charges."

"For what? You can't press charges for walking around the fairgrounds."

"You put her in your car," the lead officer said.

"She got in my car. I didn't force her."

"Where is she? Is she here in this room?"

"Wait just a darn minute," Pete said. "We walked from the library to the carnival a few blocks away. I didn't abduct her."

"Is she here with you now?'

"If you phone her parents' apartment, you'll find she's at home. For a couple of hours I walked her around the carnival and then drove her home."

"Can we look inside?"

"Help yourself. You won't find her here." Pete stepped away from the door.

The two officers went in and looked around. The second officer, a young guy about Pete's age, scowled with contempt when he saw the stuffed bear still lying on the bed where Pete had thrown it earlier, "One of your lures, Turner? That how you got the girl in here?"

"I won it at the carnival," Pete shouted. "I'm not the pervert!"

The young officer checked the closet and the bathroom. He pulled back the shower curtain. "She's not here," he announced.

"What have you done with her, Turner?" the lead man questioned.

"I told you I took her home, not more than an hour ago."

"How do you know this girl? Her parents never heard of you."

"I just met her. If you want to know, two nights ago, Sunday night, a man abducted her, but she got away from him just long enough to run in front of my car. I almost hit her. After she told me what happened, I did what any reasonable person would do and I drove her home. However, her abductor is still stalking her. He grabbed her again today at the carnival. That's your pervert."

"And you saved her? Is that your claim?"

"Why don't you ask her?"

"Was this reported to the police?"

"No."

"Why not?"

"Ask her."

"I'm asking you," the detective said, flipping his pen back and forth against his notepad. "If you knew this girl was abducted, why didn't you report it?"

Pete ran his hands through his hair. "I told her to tell her parents. She didn't want to, said her daddy had received some kind of electric shock treatments. She didn't think he could handle it right now."

The lead officer looked at his notes. "Her daddy, William Gregg, called the motel here threatening the owner. Said the man in Room 34, this room, had kidnapped his daughter from the library and brought her to his motel. The owner, Frank Tillman, called the police when he saw you take the girl into your room. That was a little before..."

"Correction," Pete said, feeling heat rising up his neck and flushing his face. "She did *not* come in my room."

"Take it easy, Turner."

"She stood outside playing with a cat she saw lying in the flower bed. I came in here two minutes to pick up something, some money, to buy enough gas to take her home. Why don't you call her parents now? I let her out a little after three."

"The fellow who runs the Corner Market says a man came in there yesterday afternoon looking for the girl just before she took sick and his wife drove her home. Was that you, Turner? Did she take sick because she was afraid you were outside watching for her?"

Pete showed his exasperation with a long sigh. "The pervert is the one behind this. He's setting me up to get me out of his way so he can get to the girl. Did he report this in person? Not likely. Did he give you his name?"

The officer looked at his notes. The tip came by phone. The man said his name is Tom Luce."

Pete laughed contemptuously. "Right."

Chapter Twenty-nine

"Then the father called us. We talked with him at his home, 9103 North Main."

"So," the younger officer asked. "It was you that went after her in the market? You fit the description the owner of the market gave us."

"I refuse to answer any more questions without a lawyer."

The other officer looked back at his notes. "You're not from around here. Tillman said you checked in Sunday evening late, around eleven o'clock. What's your business in Riverton?"

"I'm not answering anymore questions without a lawyer."

The two detectives stepped away from Pete and conferred. The younger one walked to the police car. When he came back he said, "The girl is home. She's okay."

"What did I tell you?" Pete said with a smirk.

The lead officer said, "The sooner you leave Riverton, the better. In the meantime, don't go near Frances Gregg. If you do, we're gonna lock you up. We don't want your kind around here." The detectives turned and walked toward the parking lot. Pete watched from the door of his room until they got in the patrol car and drove away.

"The feeling's mutual," he muttered. He went inside, slamming the door. He banged his fist against the wall. "That sour old Tillman called the police on me without even talking to me or getting his facts straight." Feeling like he was about to explode, Pete paced around the room. He knew what he had to do. He jerked open the door and strode toward the motel office, muttering under his breath, "I'll give that scrawny jerk a piece of my mind. He'll think twice before he calls the cops on me again."

He marched into the office, slamming the door behind him, the bell on it clanging loudly. The noise suited Pete just fine. He wanted Tillman to feel the full impact of his anger. He was sitting behind the desk reading the evening newspaper and looked up scowling. Pete reached over and slapped away the newspaper. He grabbed Tillman's knit shirt at the neck, jerked him up from his seat, and pulled him against the counter. With their faces two inches apart and through clenched teeth, Pete demanded, "What do you mean calling the police on me?"

The man made no response, his eyes defiant, glaring like he might spit in Pete's face any minute. Before Pete could push him back in his seat and further harangue him, someone taller and bigger than Pete took the back of Pete's shirt. Giant hands shoved Pete away from the desk and up against the wall. "We don't want no aspersions cast on this here establishment," the voice behind him said.

Pete looked up to see a huge man a head taller than himself standing over him. "Right," Pete muttered. "This is such a high class *establishment* and all."

He gritted his teeth to brace for a blow, but instead the fellow tightened his grip at Pete's neck and said, "The girl's old man called here raving that you had abducted his daughter. Then you showed up with her. So, my brother called the police because we don't like perverts and don't want none of that kind staying here. Now get up and get out." He shoved Pete toward the door.

Pete caught his breath. "I'm not the pervert. Don't you thick-headed people understand English? I'm not the pervert."

"So what's your story?" the big man said, "and make it good and don't waste my time."

With passion and exasperation, Pete explained, "A man abducted Gregg's daughter Sunday evening. She got away from him and ran out in front of my car. I almost hit her. She told me what happened. I drove her home."

"What about today? Why were you with her today? Why did you bring her here?"

Pete said, "My business in Riverton got delayed. I felt sorry for her. I thought maybe the creep who attacked her might try again and I could at least provide a description of him to the police. He did attack her, but he was wearing a clown costume." Pete tightened his jaw and grimaced. "Couldn't tell much about him."

With probing eyes and rapt attention, the big fellow listened while Pete told his story. When he finished he said, "Just the thought of some pervert abducting a little girl makes me sick to my stomach."

"Yeah," Pete said. "Tell me about it."

"But I believe you're telling the truth. So what made her daddy think you were the bad guy?"

"Obviously, the perp is doing that. He saw her with me this afternoon. He took the opportunity to report it to her daddy."

"But you were the one who rescued her from the abductor and brought her home last night."

"Yes, but she didn't tell her parents about any of that. She doesn't want them to know." Pete said. "Her daddy's been sick. She doesn't want him upset right now."

"Sounds like she's got herself in a heap of trouble. Her daddy needs to know. He needs to report this to the police."

Pete said. "But I couldn't persuade her to tell and I saw she'd been through enough. I couldn't force her. Besides, what factual evidence is there for the police to go on? Nothing."

"Can't the girl describe her abductor?"

"No. She said it was dark, but besides that, I think she's blocked out most of what happened to her. She only remembers running, and..." Pete sighed. "she remembers how he smelled."

"How he smelled?"

"Yes."

"Seems she'd want her parents to know so they could try to protect her."

"I'm not sure she's realized her danger before today. She's trying to block it out, but after what happened at the carnival, maybe she's beginning to see."

"So you say he abducted her again at the carnival? If she was with you, how did that happen?"

"He was dressed as a clown. I took my eyes off her one minute, and she was gone."

"Then you saw the clown with her, taking her against her will?"

"Fortunately I carry a gun. I threatened to shoot. He let her go, but he got away."

The big man held out his hand. "I believe you're telling the truth, Turner. Sorry for the misunderstanding."

Pete shook his hand. "Okay," he said.

"Name's Harvey. You've already met my brother here." The man nodded without smiling. In a lowered tone Harvey said, "My brother's got some suffering in his back. The doc says it's Sciatica."

Pete nodded that he understood.

"So," Harvey said, "this pervert is still after the Gregg kid. Is there anything we can do to help?"

"I don't know what anybody can do. We don't know what he looks like. He doesn't work for the carnival, at least not as a clown. The kid didn't see what he looked like Sunday night because it was dark. I'm leaving here as soon as my business is finished, maybe in another day or two. I'll keep an eye on her until I leave, although the Riverton cops say they'll lock me up if I go near her."

"Did you tell them what you've told me?"

"I tried, but I'm not sure how much they heard. They've already decided I'm the pervert."

"Like I said, let us know if we can do anything."

"If I come up with something, I'll let you know," Pete said. "I hate to think what's going to happen to that poor kid. I'm inclined to speak to her daddy even if it's against her wishes. I can't just go away without at least doing that."

"I agree. Even if her daddy's been sick, he needs to know."

Pete shook hands again with Harvey, nodded at the brother and walked out of the office.

Back at his room he checked his watch. The time was seven-thirty. He paced back and forth over the thin carpet. It bothered him to have to worry about the police. Too many eyes were watching him as it was. He had enough to worry about from the pervert who he had to assume was holding his book with Angel's number in it, though it was doubtful he had any idea how valuable it was to Pete. If he got any idea how incriminating the book could be for Pete, there'd be the devil to pay for sure. All of this was holding up the plan to arrange Farley's demise. That resolution continued to sit just beyond his reach, keeping him in Riverton, just a different kind of imprisonment. Would he ever be free?

Pete bit his lower lip. He went over the problems again in his mind. He needed to catch the pervert, get back his book, call Angel, and reschedule the meeting with the contact, and he didn't need the police nor any of Farley's henchmen complicating these matters, The Gregg girl was the bait for catching the pervert, but now that her daddy had filed a complaint to keep Pete away from her, any attempt to go near her meant he might end up in jail.

Finally, reaching for his keys on the dresser, he decided what he had to do. He would talk to the girl's daddy and explain the situation to him just as he had to Harvey Tillman. He gave himself a thumbs up and hurried toward the door. Seeing the teddy bear on the bed and remembering the cop's remark, he grabbed it on his way out and flung it in the back of the Ford. No doubt Gregg could be reasoned with, and Pete could convince him to withdraw his complaint with the authorities. With the police out of the way, it was only a matter of time before he could trap the pervert and get his book. Then he'd have done the Greggs a service as well. The pervert would be identified, locked up, and the girl would be safe. Most important, his plan to erase Farley would be back in operation.

He lived for that revenge!

Chapter Thirty

From the moment Frannie stepped inside the apartment, she sensed something was in the air. Now as she washed the dinner dishes, she pondered what it could be. Neither Diane nor her daddy had said a word to her about her late return from the library. She had gone straight to her bedroom and carried one of her newly borrowed books out her window into the chinaberry tree where she stayed until dinner. All through the meal she'd felt uneasy, sensing something was brewing. It had been strangely quiet, and Frannie, who usually filled any interval of silence with her chatter, was afraid to utter a sound. She wondered why her daddy had been home from work early. Maybe he got fired like on his last job. Maybe her parents were in the middle of an argument. Nevertheless, after the meal, as was the pattern this time of the day, they appeared to focus on the evening news on the television. Frannie made every effort not to call attention to herself. Remembering to rinse out the sink, she finished the dishes and tiptoed down the steps into the warm evening.

When she reached the bottom, she thought she heard someone call her. She listened. It was Jenny Daniels speaking from the other side of the tall box shrubs separating the Pruitt's two-story from the Daniels' squat white house. Frannie walked over to the line of shrubs. Although she had no desire to test the Almighty's patience, having gotten by so far without any detection of her crimes, she could not resist the chance to socialize with someone calling her name.

"Come over to the porch," Jenny said. "I have a question for ya."

"Can't," Frannie said. "I might already be in trouble."

"Why'd you cut out on me the other night?" Jenny asked.

Frannie looked behind her toward the apartment. Her parents would still be watching television. She hurried to Jenny's side of the bushes and together they walked to the porch. Frannie said she could only go as far as the steps. There she plopped down, her heart heavy with her burden of guilt.

Jenny carefully lowered herself into one of the porch rockers, then sighed from all the effort.

"I got tired of waiting for you to come back," Frannie said. No use to tell Jenny about her trouble. She didn't want to talk about it, not even to Jenny.

Neither seemed eager to press the matter and let it drop. Then Frannie piped up, "I went to the carnival today. A monkey kissed me and I rode the Ferris wheel."

"No joke," Jenny said dully.

Frannie decided not to mention the clown either. "My new friend took me."

"Is he a real friend or one of your made up ones?" Jenny said.

"He's not made up," Frannie said emphatically. "His daddy was a bootlegger and my friend hauled moonshine with his brothers. They had to outrun government agents to make deliveries to the people who wanted to buy it. Isn't that amazing?"

"You're makin' that up," Jenny said.

"No," Frannie said, indignant. "Some of his family still makes moonshine. They are famous in the mountains where he grew up. He said his daddy made the best white lightening, that's another name for moonshine, around those parts. And they didn't make it just at night under the moon either because they hid their stills so well in the mountains that the government agents couldn't find them. People from all up the east coast wanted to buy their moonshine."

Jenny looked skeptical. "If you say so. Are you sure this ain't somethin' you read about?"

"Did you know some moonshine will make you sick, even kill you?" Frannie said.

"I thought all moonshine was bad stuff."

"No," Frannie said. "The Turners made good stuff, but some bootleggers made theirs with Clorox. Can you imagine drinking Clorox?"

"Turners...Where did I just hear that name?"

"Can you imagine drinking Clorox?" Frannie repeated. "That would be awful."

As Frannie spoke, the sun, big and pink, like a dollop of ice cream, was melting into the western horizon. "I miss the fireflies. Don't you?" she said. Without waiting for a reply she stood up and looked toward the upstairs of the brown shingle. "If this were June they would be coming out about now, twinkling their lights, but I'd better go before I get in trouble. I'll sit in my tree and imagine I can see them lighting up. I can tell them all about my day with Mr. Pete. He's my friend forever."

"Pete Turner. Now I remember," Jenny mumbled. She eyed the girl quizzically, watching her jumped off the porch and run toward the hedge.

Sticky with sweat, Pete crossed the bridge and turned onto North Main. He drove to the brown shingle and parked behind what he assumed was the Gregg's battered '51 Studebaker.

He mounted the wooden steps to the door of the Gregg's apartment. Thinking her daddy might ask why he had not informed them of the girl's abduction before now, he tried out several possible answers. He didn't want to blame her and say she asked him not to. That sounded weak when compared to the danger she faced. Saying he was late for an appointment and he didn't have time to bring her to her parents sounded callous. He'd just have to wing it. He wasn't sure how he would explain his tardiness in letting them know. Whatever way he approached it, he wanted to convince them he was coming to them because he knew it was the right thing to do regardless of the inconvenience to himself, and to let them know he had saved the girl from her abductor, not once but twice. He felt confident as he knocked on the screen.

Diane Gregg came to the door. She was a petite woman with dark hair whose eyes appeared distant and worried. "Yes?"

"Evening ma'am. I'm Pete Turner. I wonder if I could speak to you and your husband for a few minutes. It's about your daughter, Frannie."

He saw her hesitate before she spoke. "Wait there," she said and turned into the dimly lit room where only a small lamp burned. Through the screen he could see her walk to the door between the living room and what appeared to be a hall. He could hear the television coming from that direction. She said, "Bill, Pete Turner is outside. He wants to see you."

Gregg said, "Who?"

"Pete Turner," she repeated.

"Who's Pete Turner?" Gregg demanded in a loud voice.

Diane whispered, "You know."

"What?" he said. There was another brief conversation and then Gregg let out a growl. "You mean that pervert that abducted my daughter? He's at the door? Our door?"

"Yes," she said.

Stomping down the hall and into the living room, a storm raging on his face, Gregg screamed, "I'll kill him!" He stopped when he saw Pete through the screen and shouted, "You have a lot of nerve. What are you doing here? Diane call the police." With a trembling hand, Gregg snatched up an iron poker from the fireplace. With the other he threw open the screened door.

"Look," Pete said, grabbing the poker and using it to push Gregg backward. "Could you just put your weapon down? I'm not the man who abducted your daughter."

Gregg staggered from the force of Pete's shove. "Diane, have you called the police?"

With a look of fear and horror on her face, Diane had backed away toward the hallway, but stopped to hear the exchange.

Regaining his balance, Gregg said, "What do you mean taking my daughter to the carnival? I don't know you. How old are you?"

"Thirty-two," Pete said.

"Thirty-two! Way too old to have a healthy interest in my eleven year old daughter." He drew back the poker again but refrained from swinging it. "Didn't the police tell you never to come near my daughter again?"

"Can you listen just one minute?" Pete said. He judged Gregg to be between forty and forty-five. He wore thick wire rim glasses and was dressed in an undershirt and some wrinkled shorts. Looking disheveled and wild-eyed, Gregg continued to grip the fire iron.

"Whatever you have to say, say it fast—before the police get here. I don't know why they haven't already locked you up."

"Because I haven't done anything they could arrest me for," Pete said. He opened the screen and stepped inside although he had not been invited to do so.

Gregg, still brandishing the fire iron, warned him, "Don't sit down; you won't be here that long."

Pete looked Gregg eyeball to eyeball. "I met your daughter on Sunday night when she ran out in front of my car. She was a very frightened little girl and out of breath. She said a man had abducted her. She had bitten his ear and managed to get away."

"And where did all this take place?" Gregg demanded. "Out front here?"

"Where North Main forks," Pete replied. "There's an old cinderblock gas station there."

"I know exactly the building you mean," Gregg said. "What would my daughter be doing in a place like that? And did you say at night? She was never there, never."

"She was left there by the girl next door."

"Who?"

"That fat girl?" Diane whispered.

"Yes," Pete said. "Her name is Jenny Daniels."

With eyes blazing Gregg yelled, "I don't care what her name is. My daughter is not allowed to speak to her. Isn't that right, Diane? You're talking about the worst end of town. What kind of parents do you think we are? Fannie's never been near any such place, and certainly not with that fat girl. You're lying through your teeth."

"Nevertheless," Pete said, trying to remain calm, "Frannie was there on Sunday evening and it would be to your benefit to believe what I'm telling you."

"Get out!" Gregg screamed. "You're lying and you're just trying to cover your own butt."

"It's too late for that," Pete said. "The police you and the real bad guy sicced on me already suspect I'm the pedophile."

"Then why didn't they lock you up?" Gregg said.

"Because I'm not the pervert and they have no evidence against me. Frannie will tell you that."

"If she does, it's because you've charmed her and deceived her. Besides she's said nothing about anybody abducting her. My god, man, she would have told us about something like that."

"This time she didn't," Pete said. "She didn't want you to be upset because she said you'd been sick."

"Sick? She knows I'm fine now. Frances knows she can come to me about anything, anything at all."

"And would you even believe her? Call her in and see if she doesn't confirm my story. If you're fine, then you'll want to know the truth. You'd want to know if your daughter was in danger."

With murder in his eyes, Gregg made no move to back down.

Pete sighed irritably. "Listen, would you? You need to believe me. A man has tried to abduct Frannie twice. Not only did he grab her on Sunday night while she waited for Jenny Daniels at the deserted gas station, but, dressed in a clown costume, he grabbed Frannie at the carnival. Fortunately, I saw quickly enough. I tracked her down and he let her go, but I don't think he's going to give up. That's why he wants me out of the way and why he wants you to think I'm the pervert. I'm warning you to be watchful. She's in great danger."

"So, you're the hero now. You saved her twice. We're to thank you for taking our daughter without our consent. We knew Frances was in danger when we learned a stranger abducted her from the public library, a perfectly respectable place, and carried her off in his car to the carnival. You lured an innocent eleven year old from the library. You must be some real sicko." Again Gregg snarled and drew back the fire iron.

Exasperated, Pete yelled. "What's your problem? Can't you put down your weapon and your defensiveness and think about the fact that your daughter could be in serious trouble? Doesn't that matter to you, that it might be true what I'm telling you?"

Gregg thrust out his chin, scowling in defiance. "Get out. Get out and don't ever come around Fannie again." He yelled to Diane, "Have you called the police like I told you?"

Pete felt himself getting angry enough to punch Gregg and knock some sense into him, but he couldn't afford to do that. He turned and stomped out, slamming the door behind him. "You'll be sorry," he called to Gregg as he ran down the stairs. Frannie had been right all along in knowing her daddy would not be able to handle the facts.

Chapter Thirty-one

On Wednesday morning after his exercise routine, Pete showered and ate breakfast at the Red Apple. Then he took his few clothes to the laundromat near the college. In the rectangular room, a row of plastic chairs and a couple of similar tables covered with out-of-date magazines faced a wall of washers and dryers. A window air conditioner at one end did little to cool the room with three of the six dryers running. Pete's wet shirt stuck to his back. After he bought some detergent from a dispenser and put his clothes in the washer, he shuffled through the magazines and found only *Ladies Home Journal* and *Good Housekeeping*. There was no *Hot Rod Magazine* or anything he liked to read. He plopped down in one of the chairs, and sighing with frustration, he watched the clothes and soap bubbles through the glass door of the washer as they whirled around going nowhere…just like him.

Down the row of chairs, he was distracted by two young women sitting together chatting. Despite the noise from the machines, coupled with the hum of the air conditioner, he caught a few words about fall classes they hoped to get. He figured they must be in-town students. Both of them were probably early twenties and neither wore wedding rings. Then an idea began to germinate. These young single women appeared wholesomely dressed in knee length shorts and blouses. One wore her hair in a short bob; the other wore hers twisted up on top of her head. If he had a girlfriend, just temporarily, he might convince Gregg he was a normal guy and not the sicko who preyed on little girls. Then maybe Gregg would call off the police, and he could proceed with his plan to use Frannie as bait to catch the pervert. When he made his next move, Pete would be ready this time. The old disguise wouldn't work the next time.

He hadn't figured how he would trap him. He'd have to think about that, but having access to Frannie without worrying about the police breathing down his neck was essential. He reached down and touched the pistol strapped above his ankle. He'd force the creep to tell where he'd put the black book if he had to beat it out of him. Then he would turn him over to the police. He relished the thought of seeing that young officer's face when he produced the real pervert with an "I told you so." Frannie would be safe and Pete could call Angel. As it was, he kept missing Angel every time he tried to reach him at the gun shop. Each time his subordinate gave Pete the message, "Call the private number in the evening." Pete couldn't say he'd lost the number, and he couldn't ask the subordinate for it; he wouldn't know it anyway. Just special people Angel had said. Everything depended on catching the pedophile.

The problem was he didn't have a girlfriend. He hadn't bothered with girls much during his years on the run. He didn't stay in one place long enough, and they always got around to talking about commitment which he was not in a position to make. During the time he spent in South Carolina he did kinda like this girl named Emily, until she started psychoanalyzing him, telling him he had an anger problem. She gave him a book, *How to Win Friends and Influence People*. Pete broke up with her, and he didn't read the book. Maybe once he got his life back, he could be as happy as his brother claimed to be with a wife and family.

But here were two single girls. What if one of them would pose as his girlfriend just long enough to convince Gregg to call off the police. He began to imagine walking over and striking up a conversation. *Excuse me. Do either of you have change for a dollar? And by the way if you don't have any-thing to do this afternoon, would one of you pose as my girl-friend? I need to catch a pedophile.* They'd think he was a kook. What if they reported him? He came out of his reverie and realized they had turned to look at him. He must have been staring. Pete blushed. He fumbled through the maga-zines, feeling like a complete idiot for even thinking such craziness.

In a few minutes they got their clothes from the dryers and folded them into their plastic laundry baskets. Shortly after, they walked out. He watched them through the front window as they carried their baskets to their car. He felt hope-less, watching his only option pull out of the parking lot. As he moved his clothes from the washer to the dryer, he remem-bered the pay phone out front. He realized he was lonely. He'd never realized it before, but coming back home after ten years of running had stirred up feelings and connections he had intentionally suppressed. That huge anger on the inside that he had nurtured and fueled for so many years was the only thing he could feel—until now.

He went outside to the phone booth situated close to the road away from the building. It was hot inside the booth. He left the door open in spite of the noise from the traffic. He recalled the last time here when the man needing his bat-tery jumped had banged on the outside to get his attention. Was he the pedophile, taunting Pete? The pedophile had all the advantage. He could shadow Pete and remain invisible because Pete didn't know what he looked like. Frannie was no help at all. As Pete dialed Robert's office, the only number besides Jennings's he knew by heart, his fingers seemed to act independently of his brain, so chagrined was he for his hanging in limbo with no idea how to get free.

When Robert's secretary, Arlene, answered, Pete didn't know what possessed him to do what he did next. He must have experienced a moment of temporary insanity when he asked for Myra Claire.

Chapter Thirty-two

It was another hot Wednesday evening just before sunset. The air remained humid and miserable. Frannie felt the confinement of the apartment closing in on her, and her thin body glistened with sweat. She curled up on the brown sofa next to the brass floor lamp in the living room to read a book of her daddy's, *A Soldier's Story* by Omar Bradley, whoever he was. Before her eyes reached the bottom of the page, her mind had wandered to her present worries. She put the book down with a sigh and shuffled to her room. Plopping on the bed, she curled her legs under her and began a letter to her best friend back in North Carolina. "Dear Pattie." She sat for a while, flipping her pencil or drawing circular impressions on the blue chintz spread with the end of her finger. Nothing came. She could think of nothing happy to report. She walked to the window and looked out into the branches of the chinaberry tree growing up past the roof. It was like a good friend with those huge limbs wide enough for Frannie to sit in comfortably for hours, a private sanctuary where she felt safe, where she could dream. Picking up her rag doll, Sally, she unhooked the screen and stepped out onto the rough asphalt tiles on the roof. There were those unspoken thoughts of her parents. What were they *not* saying to her? So far she couldn't put her finger on what it was. Diane told her there would be no more trips to the library since she would be starting school in a couple of weeks. She said Frannie needed to organize her closet and take an inventory of what clothes she had, what she needed to mend and wash. She also told Frannie not to leave the yard. Frannie didn't protest. It saved her from making excuses for sticking close to home. Organizing the closet took about ten minutes since she had only unpacked from the move two months before, and this morning before leaving for the library, she'd already mended and washed her few clothes.

After she secured the screen back in place to keep out the mosquitoes, she stepped onto the closest limb and climbed down to a lower one with a broad crook that hid her among the leafy foliage. She related to Sally all about Mr. Pete and how his daddy was a respected bootlegger except by the agents who ran him over the side of the mountain where he died. But Sally couldn't talk back, and eventually Frannie grew tired of supplying both sides of the conversation. She climbed down through the branches and jumped to the ground. Hot, miserable and bored, she imagined Jenny Daniels would be sitting on her porch, but she knew not to even think of going there.

In a few minutes, despite her misgivings, she found herself peering through the hedge. Jenny was there on the porch in her usual rocker, but there was a man sitting in the one beside her. She was curious to know if this was Jenny's sweetheart, although Jenny insisted she didn't have a sweetheart. Frannie's curiosity overwhelmed her. She darted around the front of the hedge and called to Jenny, "Hey." As Frannie approached, Jenny's visitor got up and went inside, letting the screen door bang behind him.

"Who's that?" Frannie asked grinning. Your sweetheart?"

"My sweetheart?" Jenny laughed with a smirk. "Girl, the real world ain't that imaginary world you keep your head in."

"Oh," Frannie said, a little bit disappointed. She scooted into the empty rocker. There was a radio playing inside.

"That's Elvis Pressley singing *Heartbreak Hotel*." Jenny told her about the time she saw Elvis Pressley on the Ed

Sullivan show. Frannie listened for a moment with some interest, but something began distracting her. She realized it was an odor. Sitting in the chair, she was picking up the peculiar smell of cigarettes and cologne.

"Did you see him on TV?" Jenny asked.

"Who?" Frannie said.

"Elvis. Are you even listening? Have you seen his wiggle?" Jenny raised her eyebrows and laughed.

"No," Frannie said, trying to focus. "No, but I saw a clown do magic tricks at the carnival yesterday. He could make a chicken appear out of nowhere and then land on a fence twenty feet away." She hadn't meant to tell Jenny about the clown.

"So, what does that have to do with seeing Elvis?" Jenny asked.

"I said I hadn't seen Elvis, but I was telling you something amazing that I did see," Frannie said swallowing, trying to understand why her heart was racing.

"Amazing?" Jenny said scornfully. "It was only a trick. There was two chickens. The clown planted one chicken on the fence before he made the other one disappear."

"I wondered about that, but how do you know?" Frannie said.

"My brother who was just sittin' out here with me before you come over, he used to fool me with that trick when we was kids, 'til I figured it out. It's just a trick. No magic to it."

"Your brother?" Frannie said, licking her dry lips. The cologne and cigarettes. It was *his* smell, the man who attacked her in the dark at the old deserted gas station! She felt her heart go down to her stomach and the blood drain from her face. She got up from the rocker. "I have to go."

"Sure," Jenny said, giving her a quizzical look. "You okay?"

Frannie jumped off the porch. "I just remembered I have to go," she said as she disappeared around the hedge. Running up the steps to the apartment just as fast as she could, she thought about how she had asked her daddy last night if she could go back to Wilmington and live with her granny. He said she couldn't go, that the family had to stay together. She knew she had to find a way to change his mind.

Pete ran the track at the college as if he had wings on his feet. He usually did his running in the morning rather than late in the day when the still air hung hot and sticky, but he was about to explode with nervous energy. He tried to stop thinking about his brief conversation with Arlene at Robert's office. If it hadn't been Gladys' afternoon off, she would never had been as forth coming as Arlene. What possessed him to ask for Myra Claire Covington? Of all the stuck up people he could have come up with! What a stupid blunder. He'd blurted out her name before he had a chance to think about how dumb that was. When Arlene told him Myra Claire wasn't back, why hadn't he dropped the subject? He didn't though. He just plowed on ahead, getting himself deeper and deeper into a messy situation he didn't want or need. Now he couldn't get the conversation out of his head, and every time he replayed it, he felt more agitated.

"Not back? What do you mean?" he had persisted.

"Mr. Turner said Myra Claire wouldn't be back until next week, but she left a number where we could reach her if we needed any information about what she'd been working on."

"She left a number?" Pete asked. *But of course I'll bet Miss Covington is the type to never overlook any detail.* "Let me have it, will you?"

"Sure. Hold on a minute." He heard her rustle papers. Then she said, "Here it is. It's a Durham number 421-0623."

"She's in Durham?" *That's just an hour from here.*

"Her grandmother's death wasn't unexpected, but it's not something you're ever prepared for."

"Death?"

269

"Yes," Arlene said. "Myra Claire was very close to her grandmother."

"Well, thanks," Pete said, feeling a disappointment he couldn't explain. Now it would be rude to call her, probably the best thing, but it didn't solve his problem with Gregg and the police standing in the way of his getting his black book from the pedophile. Frannie was the bait to catch him, but not with the police looking over his shoulder, ready to lock him up for the slightest excuse.

After he hung up, he cursed himself for even mentioning Myra Claire Covington. What was he thinking, that he could ask her to come and pose as his girlfriend? He didn't even like her and he was sure the feeling was mutual. The problem was he hadn't come up with another solution. For that reason the temptation to call her, rude or not, kept tormenting him. Then he'd think about how ridiculous he'd feel.

Except for one thing he kept turning over in his mind. These Christians were such suckers for wanting to earn their brownie points with God by their good deeds. This one thought, that Pete could play up the poor child being stalked by a pedophile, might move her to come, not to help him, but to help the girl. She might just as easily laugh at him, and the idea made his face burn with humiliation. Hadn't he already humiliated himself by even mentioning her to Arlene?

Besides the fact that he had obviously had made a bad impression on her, her grandmother had just died and it wasn't a good time to ask for a favor. Furthermore, there was another concern. He didn't want Robert or anyone else to know where he was and to start asking questions about his business here, but at least Myra Claire was used to confidentiality from working in a law office.

Pete finished his run and collapsed on the ground exhausted. What was he supposed to do next? Time was wasting. His life was on hold. He was sick of this crummy town.

He walked the two blocks back to the Shady Lawn. When he went in the office to see if there was a newspaper he could take back to his room, Harvey greeted him and asked for an update on the girl and her situation.

"I talked to her daddy last night. He's in denial. He's concerned about himself and what people will think of him. He can't even consider her danger." *Aren't you doing the same thing you're judging him for?* "What?" Pete demanded, looking around to see who spoke behind him.

"I didn't say anything," Harvey said.

It wasn't Harvey. But someone spoke to me. I heard it loud and clear. But there's no one here but Harvey and me. Pete tried to compose himself. "Yeah," he said. "Bill Gregg can't see beyond the end of his own nose. It's a shame." *You're doing the same thing you're judging him for.* "There it is again." Pete didn't look around this time. He was getting too stressed out and it was affecting his brain.

"There's what again?" Harvey asked.

"Nothing," Pete said. "I was just thinking, if I wanted a friend to come and help watch out for the girl, where could she stay? Here wouldn't be a good place since I'm staying here, and it's a motel and all. She's a very respectable young woman."

Harvey grinned and cocked one eyebrow in a knowing look. "I have the very solution. The caretaker at the college is my brother. He would let her stay in one of the dorm rooms. None of the students will be back for a couple of weeks. She would have complete privacy."

"I'll let you know," Pete said, wondering if Harvey's other brother was as ornery as the one at the motel.

He walked outside. Instead of going to his room, he went in the direction of the laundromat. When he got to the phone booth, he toyed about whom to call. Finally, he dialed the operator and gave her the number for the gun shop. No answer. The tone buzzed and buzzed. No answer. He slammed down the receiver and leaned his head against the inside of the booth.

Then he walked outside for a breath of air. It was beginning to cool only slightly. He paced back and forth, daring himself to make the call to Myra Claire. He ran his hands through his wet hair and hesitated before he went back inside the booth. He hesitated a moment more, then picked up the receiver, swallowed, and dialed the operator. "I'd like to make a person-to-person call to this number, 421-0623, in Durham North Carolina for Myra Claire Covington." His voice croaked as he said the name.

After a couple of seconds a male voice answered, maybe Myra Claire's boyfriend, or fiancé. Pete almost hung up, but he held on. He heard the operator say it was a person-to-person call for Myra Claire Covington from Pete Turner.

The man said, "Hold on. She may have left already."

There was a part of Pete that hoped she had. He held his breath. Sweat poured from his face and dripped into his mouth. It rolled down his neck and back. His sleeveless t-shirt was already too saturated to absorb the wetness that dripped off him.

"Hello."

"Miss Covington, uh this is Pete Turner, uh Robert's brother."

"Yes, I *do* remember who you are. You can call me Myra Claire. Is there something wrong at the office or with Robert?" He could hear the concern in her voice.

Pete cleared his throat. "No. This is a personal call."

"Mr. Pete Turner, I hope this isn't about going to the movies with you is it? My grandmother passed away on Monday. I came here for her funeral. It was this morning."

"I know this is a bad time to bother you. My sincere sympathies to you and your family."

"We are sad because we'll miss her," Myra Claire said. "but Grandma is a Christian. We know she's rejoicing in heaven right now. I'm sure she and Grandpa are holding hands and he's showing her around to see all the amazing sights and sounds up there."

Pete rolled his eyes. *Nice sentiment for gullible people.* "Arlene told me, about your grandmother. I'm sorry to intrude. Maybe I shouldn't have. I called because—because I—I need your help."

"What can I possibly do for you?"

"A little girl, eleven years old, is being stalked by a pedophile. I'm trying to convince her daddy that I'm not the pedophile. Instead, I'm trying to help her. This may sound crazy to you, but I need someone to pose as my girlfriend for a couple of days to help save this little girl. I thought of you because you seem like the kind of person who would care, and you have the kind of respectability that might sway her daddy and the police."

"The police? Hum. And you're asking me? I would think you'd have lots of girls you could call on."

"Actually I don't. I've been kind of a rolling stone for a while. I'm not asking you to do it for me. Really it's for the girl. She's in eminent danger. It's a matter of life and death, but there would be no danger for you. All you would need to do is come with me to try to make her daddy understand that I'm not the bad guy and that the real one is stalking her."

"Well, I must say this is a surprise. It sounds intriguing, and awful for that little girl. I suppose if I could really be of help."

"Does that mean you'll consider it?"

"Where is it you are proposing I come? Are you in Wilkes? Robert said you were staying at the Turner farm."

"No. I'm about an hour away from where you are in a little place called Riverton, Virginia."

"Yes, I'm familiar with Riverton."

"You are? I'm staying at the Shady Lawn motel, but I can arrange for you to stay at the Asbury College in a dorm room."

"I know exactly where the Shady Lawn motel is, but I would assume all the dorms at the college are closed. Summer school is over and all the students have left for another two weeks."

"Let's just say I've got some connections."

"I see."

"Look, if you drive here and I tell you the whole story and you don't get a good feeling about staying, I'll understand."

"As long as we have that agreement, I'm curious enough to at least hear your story, and, as you say, you're only an hour away."

Pete let out a slow breath, hardly daring to breath. He could not believe she was actually saying she'd come. "And Miss Covington, I mean Myra Claire, one thing that's very important. I'd prefer no one else knows my whereabouts right now."

"Well, I really should tell Daddy in case he needs me, but if you're talking about a day or two, I'll arrange for a friend to drop by and see him."

Pete certainly didn't want her telling anyone about him being in Riverton, especially the judge. "I guess that will work. How soon can you get here?"

"How about late tomorrow afternoon. I'll be at the Shady Lawn about four-thirty."

"I'll be on the lookout for you. What will you be driving?"

"A blue and white 1955 Oldsmobile convertible."

"Nice car."

"See you tomorrow then."

Pete hung up the phone and leaned his head down. "Whew. One problem settled. At least one. There are others to be worked out, but about these Miss Myra Claire Covington must know nothing."

Chapter Thirty-three

Turning the Ford onto a side street not far from the Gregg's apartment, Pete parked and came around to hold the door for Myra Claire. Their first meeting had gone well enough if he had to be bothered with her at all. He had taken her to the Red Apple Café for dinner and given her a summary of his encounter with Frannie on Sunday evening when she ran out in front of his car and of the clown abducting her at the fair. He explained as modestly as possible how he rescued her. She expressed a passionate desire to help Frannie. That made him nervous. She came on too strong. He'd prefer consent without all the tears watering her eyes. Pete hoped he'd made it clear all he needed for her to do was to pose as his girlfriend for one or two meetings with Bill Gregg, just enough to satisfy him that he had no perverted interest in his daughter. He wanted Myra Claire to leave as soon as Gregg was willing to call off the police.

They walked the half block to the plank stairs going up to the Gregg's apartment. Pete indicated that he would lead the way and that Myra Claire should stand behind him. If Bill Gregg came brandishing his fireplace poker, Myra Claire might have second thoughts about getting involved with these crazy people. "Gregg's unpredictable," he told her. "I don't want you in his line of fire should he do something irrational." Pete knocked, wondering if Frannie would answer the door and ask him to go away. All in all, it was a risky venture and Pete took a deep breath.

However, it was Diane who came to the door. She peered through the screen. "You again," she whispered. "What do you want? Haven't you caused enough trouble already?"

"Diane Gregg, I want you to meet my—my girlfriend, Myra Claire Covington," Pete said. "And I want to talk to you and your husband."

Diane hesitated. Then she turned around and walked back into the dim room behind her. Pete put his hands in his pockets and waited. He could hear low voices in the hall, Diane whispering and then Gregg's response in tones not so soft. "What? You're telling me Turner's back? He's at our door? His girlfriend? Ha! Who does he think he's fooling?"

Bill Gregg came to the screen wearing the same wrinkle Bermuda shorts and sleeveless undershirt he'd worn the night before. He turned on the porch light and frowned at Pete. "Didn't I tell you to stay away? We don't want you here," he yelled. When he saw Myra Claire, he softened his tone slightly. Between clenched teeth he said, "I didn't think we had any further business. I told you Frances is an imaginative child. There's nothing going on in her life I don't understand and have full control over."

"Bill Gregg, I'd like you to meet my friend, Myra Claire Covington. Could we come in? We won't take much of your time."

"Well," Bill said scornfully, "if this is a social call, I'm really not in the mood for the occasion." He grimaced. "You know I have to work all day. I have to relax when I get home."

He seemed ready to turn away when Myra Claire spoke up. "Mr. Gregg, we can come another time. I'll be happy to meet you and your wife when it's more convenient for you."

Pete froze in anger. He was ready to jab Myra with his elbow. He didn't want to wait for Gregg's convenience.

Bill took a second look at Myra Claire, frowned and unlatched the screen. "Might as well make it now. I'm not an unreasonable man, but I think I know my daughter, and I don't need" he glared at Pete, "your friend here meddling in our family business." Bill opened the door and stepped aside.

Pete leaned into Myra Claire's ear, "I thought you were going to blow it."

She whispered back, "A soft word turns away wrath."

Bill took Myra Claire's arm and guided her to an upholstered chair, obviously the most comfortable and least faded one in the room. There were no pictures on the walls and the mahogany coffee table and a simple wooden bookcase filled with books needed a good dusting. Pete sat on the end of a pea green fabric sofa next to Myra Claire's chair. Bill sat on a straight chair across from her. When Diane came in, before she could sit on the opposite end of the sofa from Pete, Bill ordered her, "Diane, get them some tea."

Pete and Myra Claire both declined, saying they had just finished having dinner. "We won't take up much of your time. I expected to leave Riverton before now, but I still have some business I'm waiting to tie up and I need to stay another day or two longer. I wondered if we might communicate civilly. What I want to know is, with Myra Claire accompanying me, would you permit us to visit Frannie and keep an eye on her, just in case there is an attacker?"

Bill smiled at Pete as if he were indulging someone slow of comprehension. "You talk to Frances for long, you'll see she has a great imagination. She's young, only eleven. She gets fact and fiction mixed up." Bill gave Myra Claire a big smile. He had nice teeth. "However, if you have this lovely young lady with you, I suppose it won't hurt for you to prove just what I've been telling you. You'll see I was right about Frances. She's my daughter and I'm proud of her. She's smart as a whip, reads all the time. She's probably in her room reading a book right now. Diane, go get her. Tell her to come in here. There's someone wants to meet her." Diane left the room. Bill turned to Myra Claire. "Now tell me, young lady, where are you from?"

"A little crossroads outside of Winston-Salem. I work for Pete's brother in the summer as needed at his law firm."

"Her daddy is a judge," Pete interjected.

"During the school year," Myra Claire continued, "I teach history and civics in the local high school."

"So, you're a school teacher, and your daddy's a judge." Bill paused, nodding and stroking his chin as if to show approval. "And how do you like Winston-Salem? I've never been there, but I've heard it's a pretty place."

"I've lived around there all my life. It's home."

"Isn't that where the Moravians settled sometime in the 1700's?"

"Yes," Myra Claire said. "In Salem you can visit their settlement. They make these marvelous crisp ginger cookies, thin as paper. I always buy them at Christmas."

"Sounds delicious," Diane said as she took a seat on the sofa.

"I'll send you some," Myra Claire offered.

"Well, that's very nice of you," Bill said, again nodding approvingly at Myra Claire.

Pete shifted in his seat. *Was Myra Claire ever snowing Gregg!* He felt a little annoyed that her social graces obviously outstripped his, but he guessed he should be grateful he'd had the forethought to ask her to come.

"Now Diane, here," Bill nodded at his wife, "she hates Riverton. She's from Wilmington where I was stationed during the war before they shipped me off to India. That's where I met my first wife, Frances's mother. When she died, I married Diane, her best friend."

Pete didn't mention his short stint in the navy a year before the war ended. He didn't want to get this guy started with competing stories, knowing how he liked to talk about himself.

Bill turned to Diane. "Maybe we should have moved to Winston-Salem. Maybe you would have liked it better there than this 'god-forsaken town'—as you call it. Did you tell Frances to come? Is she coming?"

"She's climbed up in that tree again. I heard her singing, but she didn't answer when I called. Should I call her again?"

"No. Let her alone. She can meet Myra Claire another time." Turning back to Myra Claire, he said, "Actually Diane wants to go back to Wilmington, and we will soon."

Pete shifted again. *By that time it may be too late for Frannie. Why didn't she answer? I wanted her to meet Myra Claire.*

"Anyway," Bill went on, still addressing Myra Claire. "I appreciate your interest in Frances. Don't we Diane?" He nodded in Diane's direction and she acknowledged his question with a slight smile. "If Turner wants to play the detective, well, I guess he can." He turned back to Myra Claire. "Now if Frances went off with that fat girl the other night and got a scare, she knows she wasn't supposed to associate with her, much less go off with her. She talks to everybody, but Diane told her to stay away from that girl."

"More to the point," Diane said, "the girl is too old for Frances. I've told her to find friends her own age."

Bill winced that his speech had been interrupted. He turned to Diane. "Now Frances tells me you won't let her play with any of the neighborhood kids." He turned back to Myra Claire. "It's unfortunate that we have to live in this neighborhood and in this tiny apartment, but it's only temporary. We've had a run of bad luck, but everybody has trials now and then. It only makes us stronger. Don't you think so, Miss Covington?"

"It depends," Myra Claire said. "Our trials can make us better or bitter, depending on how we respond."

"Yes," Bill said, studying Myra Claire and if wondering if she had agreed with him or contradicted him. "My sentiments exactly."

Pete stood up. "As I said, we don't want to keep you. If we have your permission to come by, if it is all right to talk to Frannie, we'll let you know if we find out anything useful."

"Sure," Bill said with enthusiasm, looking at Myra Claire. "Bring Myra Claire. Come anytime. Come just to visit. Like I said, we appreciate your interest in Frances."

As Pete led Myra Claire to the door and she stepped outside, Gregg slapped him on the back. In an audible undertone, he said, "Nice girl, your friend, Myra Claire. You must be okay after all. Guess someone played a joke on us, huh? You might, though, have asked us about taking Frances to the carnival. We're good parents. You can be sure of that. Bring Myra Claire tomorrow. You can see Frances then."

When Pete and Myra Claire got outside it was dark. Pete said, "So what did you think? He's a little irrational, isn't he? One minute he tries to kill me with the fireplace poker and the next, he's slapping me on the back. No doubt he was taken with you."

"Based on his having had shock treatments according to what Frannie told you, he suffers from depression, so he's probably on meds," Myra Claire said. "These can cause highs and lows. That might explain his behavior somewhat."

"It's too early to take you back to the college unless you're tired, with your grandmother's passing and all."

"I'm wide awake," Myra Claire said.

"Same for me. There's nothing to do around here. They roll up the streets in Riverton at sundown. I've noticed there's a neat place here on the porch. Frannie tells me the landlord and his wife are away in New York visiting their daughter. If you're up for it, we can sit there and talk about how to best keep an eye on Frannie. When the pervert makes his move, we'll be waiting for him." He led Myra Claire down the stairway and around to the front. Noticing a rose bush, he stopped to pick a bloom, pricking his finger in the process. "Ouch! You deserve a bouquet for impressing Gregg, but I hope this will do." Myra Claire smiled, accepting the flower, and held it to her nose.

They discovered a swing at one end of the porch and sat in it. With only a glint of light coming from the street lamps, it took a few minutes for their eyes to adjust to the dark. Pete pushed the swing forward with his foot, just enough to give it a gentle sway. "The incident at the carnival must have scared some sense into Frannie," he said. "She seems to be keeping close to home. I've driven through the neighborhood several times today and she hasn't come out. She talks like she spends a lot of time in a chinaberry tree in the back yard. I've caught a glimpse of it and it's huge. I hope she's safe there. Apparently there are no kids in the neighborhood suitable for her to play with."

"So you haven't spoken with her since when?" Myra Claire asked.

"Not since I brought her home after the carnival. She doesn't know I'm still here. I almost wish I could keep it that way."

"Why? I had hoped to meet her."

"And you will. It is just that Frannie talks to everyone. She doesn't know to be discreet, not that the pedophile doesn't know everything I do."

"He can't watch you all the time."

"No, but it feels like he does because I don't know he looks like. I don't know what to be looking for. Does he drive? He might just be her neighbor for all I know. She mentioned some story about this older man across the street and a girl named Ethel a few doors down. She sits on his lap and calls him 'uncle.' He gives her money."

"Sounds suspicious," Myra Claire said. "This porch would be the ideal place for surveillance. These thick Wisteria vines surrounding this porch make a perfect cover. Now that they're past blooming, they don't attract the bees. No one could tell we were here, day or night."

"I'm not too good at sitting in one place for long," Pete said, "but if you've got some good stories, we can come here some."

"I would think my stories would be dull compared to yours. After all, what can I tell about teaching school that would compare in interest with bootlegging whiskey?"

"I wouldn't think you would find stories about bootlegging suitable for your innocent ears."

"It's not like I'm going to drink it if I hear about your escapades," Myra Claire said with a raised eyebrows and a playful smile. "When is the landlord expected back?"

"Frannie said they'd be back in a week or two."

Pete continued to gently push the swing. *Myra Claire sure did charm Bill Gregg. She can be very personable after all, not as stuck up as she seemed at first. And she's pretty, darn pretty.* He became uncomfortably aware of her closeness and the delicate scent of her perfume. He breathed it in, but then reminded himself her daddy is a judge. *If she knew...I can't get involved, and she probably has a boyfriend anyway. There's no ring on her hand, so no fiancé.* To put some space between them, he got up and walked to the wooden railing. Leaning his back against it, he said, "The Greggs really liked you. Tomorrow you'll meet Frannie."

"How long will you be here?" Myra Claire asked.

"I'd be glad to leave now, but I'm waiting...for some things to fall into place. Until then I'm stuck here."

"When your business is done, what if the pedophile hasn't been caught? Will you let the police know?"

"The police aren't going to believe anything I say. They are convinced I'm the pedophile. Even if Gregg were to agree to get them involved, the police aren't going to do anything. Frannie can give them nothing to go on. They don't have the manpower to watch after an eleven year old that might just have an active imagination. Gregg could hire a private eye, but I doubt he would, even if he could afford one, and I don't think he can. Anyway the pedophile is going to make his move again. My stepping into the situation only enhances the challenge for him, like a red flag waving at a bull."

"How do you know so much about pedophiles?"

"I've done the research."

"Why such a gruesome subject?"

"I've got my reasons."

"Does it have something to do with why you were gone all those years, letting your family think you were dead?"

"You ask a lot of questions."

"What else do we have to talk about? Did somebody... were you..."

"No. Lord no!"

"Do you know Him?"

Pete lean forward scrunching his eyebrows together, puzzled. "The pedophile? What do you mean?"

"The Lord. Do you know Him?"

Pete gave her an indulgent smirk. "Obviously not like you and my brother claim to."

"What if the pedophile hasn't showed up by the time your business here is finished?"

Pete shifted uncomfortably. "At some point I have to leave. She's not my daughter."

"Will you be able to just walk away?"

"The creep is going to try again. I know it. I'll be expecting him the next time."

"I see," Myra Claire said thoughtfully.

Frannie climbed in her bedroom window from the chinaberry tree. From her bedroom door she heard her daddy talking to Diane about somebody named Myra Claire. Frannie didn't want to talk to anyone right now. She needed to think how to persuade her daddy to let her go to her granny in North Carolina. She fell across her bed. With school starting in a couple of weeks, he was not going to agree to her visiting, and he'd already said the family had to stay together, that she couldn't live with her granny. When the Greggs could move back, she could spend time with her then. She went over and over in her mind every argument she could think of to change his mind, none of which he was going to approve. She walked to the window and stared through the chinaberry branches at the sky. The stars were very bright tonight. The apartment was hot. She went to her door and tiptoed down the hall and out the front screened door to sit on the stoop. Then she scooted to the bottom. There were voices coming from the porch. *Were the Pruitts back? But they just left.* She listened. Two voices, a man and a woman. *It sounded like…Mr. Pete talking…but it couldn't be. Didn't he say he was leaving? But he said that before and he showed up at the library.* She crept toward the front, keeping low behind the shrubs. It was unmistakable. She jumped up. "Mr. Pete! Is that you, Mr. Pete?"

"Frannie?" Pete said coming down the steps. "I'm so glad to see you. I want you to meet my friend, Myra Claire."

"Is she your sweetheart?" Frannie asked.

"Well, she's my…my girlfriend." Pete swallowed.

Frannie grinned at him.

Myra Claire came down the steps and even in the moonlight Frannie could see Myra Claire's red hair. It was the first time Frannie ever imagined a redhead could be so beautiful! She held out her hand. "Pleased to meet you," she said.

Chapter Thirty-three

Myra Claire clasped Frannie's hand. "It's a pleasure to meet you, too."

Turning to Pete, Frannie demeanor turned serious. "Oh, Mr. Pete, I'm so glad you're here. I wanted to tell you...it's Jenny Daniels' brother." She cast an apprehensive eye in the direction of the Daniels' place.

"What about Jenny Daniels' brother?" Pete asked.

Frannie lowered her head. "The man who attacked me. He's Jenny Daniels' brother."

"You're sure?" Pete said.

She shook her head and said emphatically, "Yes."

"Come on the porch and tell us how you know this," Pete said.

PART III

Chapter Thirty-four

Shortly after Frannie's disclosed to Pete and Myra Claire that her attacker was Jenny Daniels' brother, they heard Diane call her. "Frances Louise Gregg, are you outside again? Come in now!"

Pete took her by the hands and enthusiastically praised her for her sharp observation. She smiled modestly, obviously pleased with his attention. "Now go!" he said, "before you get both of us in trouble."

After she left, Pete peered through the Wisteria vines. There were lights on inside at Jenny's. "The creep may still be over there."

Myra watched him pace back and forth across the porch. Periodically he peered through the vines toward the Daniels' house. "I'm going to talk to Jenny again, but right now she's probably gone to meet one of her johns. Maybe I should go knock on her door. We've as good as got him now," Pete muttered. He looked through the vines again. A light came on at the porch. "Myra Claire," he whispered. She moved behind the swing to stand beside him. They saw Jenny come out the front door and down her porch steps. "I'll be back," Pete said. He dashed to the end of the hedge. When Jenny was at the sidewalk, he called to her. "Jenny! Over here."

Her head flew up. Slowly she turned around. Moving closer, she could see Pete. He was standing in a circle of light from the streetlamp on the side of the hedge away from the view of the Daniels' house. "You again. I told you I don't know nothing. You can't get blood out of a turnip so leave me be."

"Jenny, this is important. Where's your brother?"

"My brother? How should I know? He was here earlier, but he ain't around now. What you want with him?"

"I know who attacked Frannie," Pete said matter-of-factly.

Jenny's expression changed from irritation to mild curiosity. "So? Who?"

"I'm saying your brother is the pedophile who has abducted Frannie twice."

"You accusing my brother? How do you know he done it? What's your proof?" she asked, her double chin stretched forward in indignation.

"Frannie has identified him. He'll do it again. If you know anything, you'd better come clean. Remember you could be considered an accessory as well as negligent in the care of a minor."

"She ain't never even laid eyes on my brother."

"She saw him on your porch this evening."

Jenny squinted her eyes as if trying to process the information."

"Does he live here?" Pete asked.

She shrugged. "No. He just shows up when he feels like it. I reckon he gets lonely out there in them woods where he lives."

"Tell me his name."

She looked over her shoulder with a worried expression, then turned back to Pete. "Orville," she whispered.

"Daniels?" Pete questioned.

"No. Orville Wooten. He's my half-brother," she said, glaring at him. "My ma married his daddy 'fore I was born.

He left her when Orville was a baby. Then she married my pa. He got her pregnant with me then he took off. Men are all the same. Ain't one of you worth two cents."

"Is he married?"

"Far as I know he ain't. How come I gotta answer all these questions? He ain't gonna like it 'cause he don't want people knowing his business."

"Yeah," Pete said. "Would you rather tell me or the police?"

Jenny swallowed. "No police," she said.

"Tell me where he lives when he's not here. I want to know where he lives and where he works."

"In a trailer," she said barely audible.

"In a trailer where?" Pete demanded.

"Off Burris Road in Rougemont."

"Where does he work?"

"He works for hisself, *Wooten Plumbing*."

"How does he get business? Is he in the phone book?"

"I reckon. It's mostly word of mouth. And there's another thing. That number you gave me where to reach you."

"What about it?"

Jenny looked back over her shoulder, then quickly back at Pete. "He must of took it. I laid on the table in the hall, but it's gone. It ain't there no more."

"Great." Pete said with a grimace. "What does he drive?"

"A black paneled delivery truck. Looks like an old paddy wagon or a hearse."

"Where does he park his truck when he's here at your house? I haven't noticed any truck."

Jenny whispered, her voice quivering with fear. "He parks it in the garage 'round back."

"Does he sleep here?"

"Sometimes, in the back bedroom."

"So he stays in the back bedroom and spies on Frannie."

"It's where he sleeps," she said, her indignation returning. "I don't know nothing about spying. Can I go now?"

"Where's Rougemont?"

Jenny sighed. "It's way out in the boonies toward Carterville. You have to go Route 41 then cut off on Burris Road. I ain't never been out there but onct. It was a long time ago. But he ain't moved."

"Is there a box number for his place on Burris Road?"

"It's 2305."

"What? I couldn't hear you," Pete said.

Jenny cleared her throat. "2305."

"Are you sure? If you haven't been there in a long time, how do you remember?"

"Sometimes he leaves his mail here and I seen the address is still the same. He wouldn't like me telling you this stuff. He don't like nobody snooping in his business."

Pete thought a minute. "That will do for now," he said, "but don't go anywhere too far in case I have more questions, and don't tell him I talked to you about him." He knew she wasn't about to tell him. He turned and sprinted back toward the porch. Jenny stared after him momentarily, then with head down and shoulders hunched, trudged down the sidewalk.

Pete considered his next move as he walked up the porch steps. With Frannie's information, if she was correct, the picture for him had vastly improved. Before, he had no choice but to wait for the phantom to strike and hope he was in the right place at the right time. Now, however, the culprit might no longer be a phantom. Wooten was definitely somebody to check out. Pete was ready to follow Jenny's directions to Burris Road, and Myra Claire would be a liability.

He knew that once Wooten realized he was on to him, the stakes would be raised. Then the creep would be more determined to get Pete out of the way permanently. Pete could take care of himself, but Myra Claire would be in the way. He was grateful for her greasing the wheels with the Greggs, but he didn't need two girls to worry about, and besides, the judge's daughter asked too many questions. Her regular job as a history teacher would begin in a couple of weeks. It was better if she left now before she became a target as well as he. That would totally complicate Pete's life even more than it was. He would tell her in the morning that she could leave right away. All she needed to do was let the Greggs know. She could say she'd received a call that the old judge needed her.

Chapter Thirty-five

At seven o'clock on Friday morning, Pete left the Shady Lawn and drove three blocks to the Asbury campus to pick up Myra Claire. The sky was as blue as a robin's egg and the overnight temperature was the lowest it had been since June. The early cool promised a pleasant day with lower humidity.

Frannie's new information had given him a measure of excitement. He needed a break in the gridlock. If the child was correct, Pete had a lead, something to go on. Jenny's brother being the attacker made sense. He would have known where Jenny met her johns and could have seen Frannie tagging along on Sunday evening. He would have anticipated that Frannie would be left alone in the isolation of the deserted station for a window of time, giving him the perfect opportunity. From Jenny's place he had the ideal proximity to observe all the kid's comings and goings, as when she went to the corner market, or carried her books onto the bus on Tuesdays. Her attacker had to be the man at the library where he was posing as the gardener. He was hidden by the shrubs when he overheard Pete and Frannie say they were walking to the carnival. So, the big bad wolf got there ahead of them and swiped the clown costume.

Of course, none of that conjecture *proved* anything. And despite Frannie's unshakable certainty, neither Wooten's being familiar with the common sleight of hand trick nor that he smelled like her attacker, would impress the police. Lots of men smoked and had the odor of tobacco on them. Many probably used the same cologne. It wasn't much to go on, but it was enough to get Pete's adrenalin pumping.

He had been in Riverton five days and it seemed like forever. He wanted to believe he had almost come to the end of this inertia, this nightmare of being stuck here in Riverton. If this Orville Wooten was the sicko like Frannie believed, Pete would find a way to prove it. Then he'd get his address book, call Angel, and set up a new meeting place with the contact far away from Riverton. Then he'd be gone. It couldn't happen soon enough that his uncle would be history, and Pete could go home where everyone would be talking about Farley's tragic demise.

Myra Claire was waiting in the parking lot in front of the dorm. When Pete saw her, he caught his breath. The red-headed beauty was impeccably dressed in white Converse tennis shoes, black Bermuda shorts and an unbuttoned yellow and black plaid shirt over sleeveless yellow top. Today she had pulled that untamable red hair into twist behind her head. Even so, saucy squiggles bounced about her face. She smiled at him with the same piercing green eyes. He couldn't help but notice she looked as fresh as the morning. He had to admit he found her appealing.

Hurrying out to open the door for her, he wondered whether she had a steady boyfriend or even a fiancé. Then he reminded himself it didn't matter. He couldn't afford romantic notions about any girl, especially this one. His business had to remain close to the vest, and she had already been asking too many questions. She would never understand how he was honor-bound to avenge the Turner name. It was good she had fixed things for him with the Greggs, but her usefulness had passed. He would tell her this morning. Then she could say her goodbyes to Frannie and the Greggs. She had wanted to meet Harvey to thank him for arranging her accommodations at the college, and he would arrange for that, but he had decided that by this afternoon she should be ready to leave.

She slid in the front seat of the Ford. When he got in behind the wheel, she said, "Are we playing detective on an empty stomach, or are we getting breakfast?"

Pete said, "Does a cat have a climbing gear?"

"I guess that means you're hungry, too?"

"Starving. I started to ask if you wanted to go somewhere last night after we left Frannie, but like I said before, Riverton rolls up the streets about eight o'clock. There's the little café where we had dinner last evening and where I've eaten breakfast every morning since I came here. Soon, when the students return, the place will probably be crowded, but so far, I've gotten good service and good tasting food."

"The food was good before," she said.

"You hardly ate anything. I ate mine and most of your burger. You picked at a few fries."

"That's because I was so drawn into your story of Frannie's abductions and the mysterious moves of her stalker. The Red Apple is fine. Food anywhere sounds terrific," Myra Claire said.

In five minutes Pete pulled in at the café and parked in the front. He opened the passenger door for Myra Claire and then the door of the café, stepping aside to let her go ahead of him into the cozy little eatery. Inhaling the smell of bacon cooking and fresh baked bread wafting toward them, they took a seat in one of the booths. The waitress in a crisp blue apron and with "Molly" stitched on her shirt pocket came immediately and took their orders. When she left them, Myra Claire spoke in a soft voice, "Do you think Jenny will try to protect her brother, tell him you're asking questions, and warn him away? And are you going to talk to the police now?"

"Jenny's not going to tell her brother that she talked to me, and it's too soon to go to the police. What's there to tell them, that Frannie suspects this man because she thinks he smells like the one who abducted her and does the same ordinary magic trick she saw the clown perform at the carnival? All I saw was the man wearing a clown suit. We don't have anything that proves this Wooten is the bad guy–yet."

"But you think Frannie's right."

"It's a place to start. More than I've had before, and it makes sense logistically. From Jenny's place he had the opportunity to notice her."

"So," she said, "what's the plan? Think we'll have any trouble finding her brother's trailer, or have you decided we should stake out the Daniels' place from the Pruitt's porch?"

"I've been thinking about that and, well you know, I appreciate your coming here and charming Bill Gregg. You completely won him over."

The waitress sat two glasses of water, two cups of coffee and a small pitcher of cream down in front of them. "Thanks, Molly," Myra Claire said.

Molly smiled. "Sugar's on the table and your orders will be right up."

Myra Claire stirred cream and sugar in her coffee. "We could keep an eye on Frannie if we watch out for him from the Pruitt's porch and then follow him. Like you said, that could mean long boring hours. I hope you have lots of entertaining stories to tell me about yourself."

Pete glanced down at the table and picked up his spoon. "There's nothing to tell about me." The conversation wasn't going in the direction he wanted. He looked up at her. "Maybe you could tell me stories about you. Who's missing you back home? There must be a special fellow in your life, someone you want to get home to?"

A serious expression crossed Myra Claire's face. Her eyes looked off in the distance. "I was engaged to someone, a soldier. He was killed in action in the war." Then she looked at Pete and smiled. "He was a wonderful man. However, I'm sure your adventures bootlegging moonshine are more exciting than anything I've ever done. I had a very normal childhood, went to college, got my degree, and now I teach history in a small, county high school. I like my job teaching, but it's not what I want to do forever."

"What's that?" Pete asked pouring white crystals from the clear glass container into his coffee.

"Someday I'd like to open a Christian retreat and a summer camp for kids."

"Sounds like an ambitious project for someone on a teacher's salary," Pete said. In spite of the fact that his question didn't lead back to the subject of her leaving, Pete felt an unexpected satisfaction in finding she apparently wasn't involved in a serious relationship. Again, he inwardly admonished himself not to go there. What would be the point anyway? Too complicated with her being a judge's daughter and him in the process of hiring a contract killer. He needed to settle it with her that she had to leave. She had taken Frannie and her plight to heart, but she had done what he needed her to do. He stirred his coffee. "Look, Myra Claire, all I really needed you to do here was to smooth things over with the Greggs. You've done that. Once Jenny's brother knows I'm on to him, he will just get bolder in his attempt to get me out of his way, and I can't expose you to that danger. "

"So, are you trying to tell me you're sending me home?"

"As long as you tell the Greggs you're leaving, you should go right away. That's the safest plan."

"What if I want to stay? If the pedophile is going to get bolder, then you need somebody to watch your back."

Pete sighed. "I don't need two girls to worry about."

"I'm not a girl. I'm an adult. I care about Frannie and I'm not leaving." She spoke with finality.

The waitress brought their food and they ate in silence except for Myra Claire's favorable comments about the crisp bacon, the eggs scrambled just right, and the fluffy pancakes topped with maple syrup. Pete finished before his companion, one he needed to figure out how to get rid of. He requested a second cup of coffee. He would be firm and not take "no" for an answer. "Myra Claire, you can't stay. It's too dangerous. If something happened to you, I'd never forgive myself for bringing you here. Robert wouldn't forgive me. And what about the judge? He's getting older. Doesn't he depend on you?"

"The judge is adamantly independent. I guess I tell myself I look after him to feel needed. Now you need me and so does Frannie. I'm not afraid. And I'm staying."

Molly brought the steaming coffee and sat it on the table before him. He took a sip. He decided to hide his frustration for the time being. He'd think of some way to get rid of her. "I guess if your mind's made up, there's nothing else I can say, but only for one more day. You can help me check out Wooten this morning. After today, you should plan to leave."

Myra Claire smiled. "I'm glad you see it that way."

"I'm going from here to find Burris Road," Pete said.

Myra Claire blotted her lips with her napkin. "Do you want me to watch out for the bad guy from the Pruitt's porch? I'll take a book to keep me company. I can walk back to the campus and get my car."

"What would you do, follow him in your Buick convertible?" he asked with a smirk.

Myra Claire ignored his sarcasm. "Is Frannie going to be okay without one of us there to watch out for her?"

"I told her to stay home until we got there. She said she would, and Diane has more or less grounded her."

"So, you're going to let me go with you to find Burris Road. That's the plan?"

Pete shrugged. "Do I have a choice? I don't want the Greggs feeling sorry for you all alone for hours on the porch. I just hope you understand what you're getting into." He took another drink of his coffee. "And I hope Frannie's right and this is a break in a string of bad luck. Up till now, the pedophile's been holding all the cards, but the sun don't shine on the same dog's hiney all the time."

Myra Claire arched her eyebrows, but there was a twinkle in her eyes.

"Sorry," Pete said. "Just an expression my momma used to say."

Myra Claire's twinkle left. Her eyes narrowed. "Robert said you didn't come back for her funeral."

"What?" He frowned and shook his head. "I didn't know anything about it."

"It must have been very difficult for her not knowing you were dead or alive. Did you ever think it might be a good idea to let your family know?"

Pete bristled. "She didn't deserve to know." He hit his fork on the table. "I didn't speak to her for ten years after... but never mind. You wouldn't understand."

"Try me."

Pete spoke with a sharp edge in his voice. "You wouldn't understand."

Molly came to their table. "Anything else I can get you?"

Pete looked at Myra Claire. "Want another cup of coffee?"

Myra Claire folded up her napkin and laid it beside her empty plate. "No. I'm good to go."

"Just get our check," Pete said to the waitress.

Molly pulled her order book from her apron pocket, tore out a page, and placed it in front of Pete. "Thanks a lot for coming in," she said.

Pete picked it up and reached for his wallet. "Well, Orville Wooten, here we come. We'll see him in jail where he won't be a threat to Frannie or any other little girls. In a small town like this, he'll be lucky if they don't lynch him. He doesn't deserve any better."

"You don't mind passing judgment on others, do you? Don't you know when you point at someone else, three fingers point back to you?"

Pete laughed. There was bitterness in his voice. "You're one to talk."

"I know it," she said with a grimace. "I need to do better."

"Anyway," Pete said. "I was only saying it's a real probability. Even criminals don't cotton to pedophiles. One thing for sure, I don't think we'll find Jenny's brother is a big shot in Riverton with the police on his payroll."

"Like your uncle Farley?"

"What makes you say that?"

"Oh, rumors that you don't care for him; that you think he has people in authority in his pocket."

"Yeah. You're the judge's daughter. Maybe you are privy to some of my uncle's secrets."

"Sorry to disappoint you. I only know him by reputation, that he's a humanitarian and an entrepreneur who's done a lot of good for the community, but the scowl on your face says it all. You really don't like him, do you?"

Pete stood up. *If this girl wasn't so attractive...she could really get under my skin. Every time I start to like her some, she annoys the heck out of me, like all those Christians.* "You ready? If you insist on coming, we've got work to do."

Chapter Thirty-six

Pete started up the Ford and before driving two blocks from the cafe, he noticed a squeak coming from under the hood. He gave a sigh of impatience. "That squeak," he said to Myra Claire. "could be a belt breaking. I'll pull in at the Shady Lawn. You can meet Harvey while I check it out."

He rolled into the parking lot and got out. When he raised the hood and confirmed the belt was splitting, he opened Myra Claire's door and led her to the office. The old man was behind the counter, but Harvey had seen them and came out from the office to greet them. Pete could tell that Myra Claire immediately impressed Harvey. This irritated him. It irritated him that in minutes Harvey seemed to be bowled over by her. He told himself, a person couldn't always pick up on Myra Claire's self-righteous smugness at first. Even the old man was grinning at her. Myra Claire thanked Harvey for making the arrangements with his brother Marvin for her to stay at the college. "It's so quiet and the campus is lovely," she said.

"I'm glad I could help," Harvey said with a big smile. After I found out what Pete here is trying to do, well, he's doing all of us a service to get the creep who's after that little girl, and now I suppose you're going to help him."

Myra Claire nodded an affirmation, eyeing Pete like the cat who swallowed the canary.

Harvey frowned. "You be careful, young lady."

Pete left them chatting while he left to figure out what to do about the squeaking belt. As it turned out, he had to borrow Myra Claire's Buick to drive to the nearest garage to buy a new one. When he came back to the motel, he saw Harvey had shown her to some lawn chairs in the shade.

All the while Pete worked in the heat replacing the belt, he could hear them laughing and talking. Sweat ran down his face and bare chest. He was more annoyed than ever that everyone liked Myra Claire.

When he was done, he went to his room to clean up. According to the clock sitting on the dresser, the time was pushing ten o'clock. He drew back the window curtain and glared at Myra Claire's animation and Harvey's obvious enjoyment from whatever she was telling him. "While she's occupied and not trying to stick her nose in my business, I'll call Angel," he muttered. "It's time for him to come into the shop." Not trusting the privacy of the phone line at the motel, he took off, sprinting to the laundromat pay phone.

He asked for Angel and to his surprise, he was told, "Hold on. I'll get him."

His heart beat quickened. This was good news. At last his luck was changing!

"Young Pete," Angel boomed in his ear. "You finally caught up with me. You ready to let me back you in the big NASCAR races?"

"Angel, I called to explain why I missed the meeting with the contact. You see, this kid, this eleven year old girl ran out in front of me."

"Wait a minute," Angel said. "You missed what meeting? What contact? I'm the one missing something here."

"You know, the meeting Salvino set up at the marina."

There was a momentary pause, then Angel said, "I fired Salvino months ago."

"You fired Salvino ...But you sent him...You always said if I needed...that you knew some people. Salvino said you sent him." Pete ran his hands through his hair.

"You think I sent Salvino? That liar? That cheat? Those fellows that worked him over should have finished him off, but he won't set foot in the State of New York again. He'll never do business anyplace where my name is known. My customers have blacklisted him. We don't do business with ungrateful cheats."

Pete swallowed the huge lump in his throat. "Salvino came to me. He said you sent him."

"I hope you didn't give that rascal any money?"

"No, because I missed the meeting."

"Good thing. So, you need a problem taken care of young Pete?"

Pete let out a nervous sigh. "Right."

"And you have the money?"

"I've got the five thousand Salvino said to bring to the marina."

Angel laughed. "Five thousand! We're talking pros. These people won't touch a job for more than ten thousand plus expenses."

"Ten thousand! I've never seen ten thousand." Pete continued to run his hand through his hair. "I can make a down payment."

"If I could lend you the money, your word would be good enough for me, Pete. But I'm just the messenger in these deals. I don't put up any money. You understand? In case something goes wrong."

"But Salvino said," Pete swallowed, realizing that Angel had made clear he shouldn't trust anything Salvino had told him "that they don't make mistakes."

"Sure they're pros, but, young Pete, there's always a risk. You understand? Who's the target? Somebody 'round your way, up in Wilkes County?"

"His name is Farley Oaks," Pete said in a whisper. "He's my uncle. He plans to build a big speedway in Wilkes on the Turner land."

"Wait a minute!" Angel said. "I've heard that name before, around the tracks. Prominent fellow in your area. That'll cost you at least ten thousand."

"Listen, Angel. I'll get the money. The sale of the Turner land will happen any day now. I can get that much for it." Pete rubbed his chin, his thoughts whirling through his brain. *At least Farley won't be able to enjoy the benefit of it. Kind of ironic if I hire his killer with his money. I'll buy the land back after Farley's rotting in his grave.*

"I'll do this much, Pete. I'll send one of my guys to check him out, put his ear to the ground, so to speak. Give me a couple of days, and then we'll talk again."

Pete hung up the phone and wiped his sweaty arm across his wet forehead. At least the plan was in motion for real. Next he had to get his book out of Wooten's hands. He still didn't want Angel to find out he'd misplaced it. Besides that, his name was in the book along with Angels. He didn't want to leave any evidence connecting him to the gun dealer or the dangerous people Angel was associated with. He'd heard if you crossed up those Mafia people, if they even thought you'd crossed them up, they'd come after you just like Jennings said they would.

Chapter Thirty-seven

Mid-morning on Friday, Orville Wooten drove his black paneled truck along Route 58 on his way back to his trailer. He'd spent several hours unstopping an old lady's sink and installing a toilet for another customer. He was thinking about his next move to net the kid with the red hair. She had slipped through his fingers twice because of that Turner fellow's interference, but he'd met up with obstacles like this before. It only made his game more interesting. He didn't know why Turner hadn't gone to the cops, but it didn't matter if he did. No one was going to believe him. There had been accusations in the past. Eventually all whispers and finger pointing against him amounted to nothing, treated by the authorities as vague rumors without substance. He never left any incriminating evidence, and he minded his own business. He had earned a reputation for doing good work and charging fair prices. No one wanted to believe evil of a man like that. They could feel good about themselves for thinking well of him. To question his character and to imagine him capable of hurting little girls was unthinkable when they liked his work. It meant they would have to reconsider their own judgment, and he'd found most folk's convenience and pride stood in the way of them doing that.

As he drove along, he noticed a bulldozer entering the highway from a dirt road where nothing but woods existed a few weeks ago. He left off his musings to satisfy his curiosity, whipping the truck around into a quick U-turn. The road was newly cut through a wooded area, green with pines and maples. He saw right away two lots had been cleared.

A pickup truck filled with mud covered shovels, picks, wheel barrows, and the like was parked near the construction. Wooten left his vehicle at the side of the road and walked toward two men digging footings. He watched several minutes, calculating when the footing might be poured. The workmen took no notice of him, but kept on with their digging.

He was about to walk back to his truck when he heard, "Hey! You don't get paid to stand around. Grab a shovel and get to digging." Wooten looked up to see a tall husky fellow coming toward him. He assumed this was the boss who was yelling at him.

"You don't get paid to stand around," the scowling man repeated.

Wooten, of slight build and medium height, was dressed in work pants, work boots typical of laborers, and a nondescript grey shirt. His dark brown, slightly wavy hair fell just below his ears. It was matted and greasy. Despite a days' growth of beard, his face was ruddy from working out of doors digging wells and water lines.

"This ain't my job," Wooten said.

"You're not here to work?" the man asked with slightly less edge to his voice. "What do you want then?"

"My business is plumbing. Guess I musta got the wrong address," Wooten said with a shrug. Then he turned and walked back to his truck.

"Be a couple of days before the footers are done for both lots," he muttered to himself. "Then they'll be pouring if it don't rain much. Timing is everything." With these thoughts, he drove off.

Eventually he turned off Route 58 onto Route 41, a winding, narrow road. Passing only an occasional dingy trailer or small wooden hut, he followed in this direction until he turned onto Burris Road. Soon the paving ended. Wooten bumped and bounced along the ruts until he could see a narrow driveway through the woods to his trailer. He followed it through the thick foliage. With Turner's interference, he took care as he approached to observe that his place appeared deserted and undisturbed. He assured himself, "No need to worry about Turner. I know all about him, but he don't know me, and I mean to fix it so's he don't never know." Wooten gave a satisfied grin. He pulled in behind the trailer and got out. From the truck he removed two cases of empty Mason jars and stacked them on the ground.

Used to talking to himself, he declared, "That old darkie James said he could fill these this afternoon and get them back to me. He'll come to the trailer to get them. He said a couple of dollars for two cases. I told him that was highway robbery charging two dollars for this rot gut. Probably kill you if you're not use to it, but quality isn't what matters," he snickered. "It'll turn the key on that Turner feller. Tried to scare him off so's he'd quit snooping in my business, but, no, he's gotta be a hero. He thinks I'm scum. I know it. Let him think what he wants. He'll have plenty of thinking time sitting in that jail. By the time he's free, he won't never find the brat."

Pleased with himself, he got back in the truck and pulled it around into the woods out of sight. Then he got out, and pushed his way through the overhanging branches to the trailer.

"Red headed brat turned out to be more trouble than she's worth. I didn't want to get rid of her just yet. Pretty little thing. Saw her playing. Then when she goes with Jenny, knew it'd be easier than if I had planned it." He clomped up the steps and pushed open the unlocked door. "Just wanted to be friends...but the little brat bit my ear."

Inside, he leaned his shoulder against a small Formica table and removed the boots, letting each one fall with a thud. Then in his sock feet, he padded to the refrigerator. He pulled out a can of beer and used a can opener to make two triangle openings on either side of the top. Taking a long swig, he bent over in front of a small black and white TV sitting on a fruit crate. Switching it on, he fixed the sound to barely audible.

He sat down in the one padded chair and propped his feet on another crate topped with a pillow to watch *As the World Turns*. When he was settled, he drew a pack of cigarettes out of his shirt pocket, lit up, and sat smoking and drinking his beer while he stared at the TV screen.

By the time he finished two more beers and ate a peanut butter sandwich, he pulled his work boots back on and went out back behind the trailer, then into the woods to a vehicle parked a hundred feet from the plumbing truck. It was a flatbed contraption with wooden latticed sides. He climbed into the cab, cranked the engine, and rattled back out through the woods to the dirt road. After following it for half mile, he turned into another narrow truck path so obscured by the foliage that one had to know it was there in order to see it.

With good directions from Harvey, Pete had no trouble finding Route 41. After a thirty-minute drive, the green rolling landscape changed to rocky hills dotted with patches of Mountain Laurel and small pines. The Ford wound around steep mountain curves. Since Harvey wasn't too sure about Burris Road and Pete's map didn't show it, he told Myra Claire to watch out for it.

Pete pointed. "There's a sign. What does it say?"

"It says 'Burke Road.'"

"Too many 'B' roads," Pete said, "Unless Jenny told me the wrong name."

The signs became scarcer and scarcer. None of them said 'Burris Road.'

Eventually, Myra Claire pointed. "There's a sign. It's bent. I can't read it."

Pete didn't see it and kept going. He was getting impatient. He ran a hand across his forehead. The further he drove, the more convinced he became that Jenny either didn't know what she was talking about, or she intentionally deceived him. He continued on for another fifteen minutes until they were going up into the mountains in the next county. Pete groaned. "We'll never find this road. I think Jenny may have sent us on a wild goose chase. Maybe I was wrong. Maybe she *is* protecting her brother."

"There was a road sign back about fifteen minutes ago I couldn't read."

"That's probably not it."

"How do you know?"

Pete slowed down looking for a place to turn around. "We'll check it out. This is our last shot. If we don't find Burris on our way back, I'll go back to Jenny and choke it out of her."

"You won't be much help to Frannie locked up, will you?"

"Jenny's not going anywhere near the police."

"You're sure about that?" Myra Claire said.

Pete made no comment.

When he saw a mom and pop restaurant, he turned around. "You want anything to eat?"

"No thanks. Big breakfast. You could go in and ask directions."

"No. I don't believe Burris Road exits," he said and switched back onto Route 41 the way he had come.

She rolled her eyes, but said nothing until a few minutes later. "That sign I saw was somewhere along here."

"I don't see any road or sign," he said with annoyance.

After a couple of miles she said, "We must have missed it."

Pete sighed again, "What did I tell you?"

Chapter Thirty-seven

However, a few hundred feet further, she pointed. "There. Up ahead. Slow down."

By now he wasn't expecting to find it, but reluctantly he followed her directions and slowed down. "Now I see it. The sign's bent all right."

"Pull over," she said. "I'll get out and see if I can read it." When she got back in, she said, "That's it, Burris."

On the paved part of the road there were occasional mailboxes but the numbers weren't in any rational order. "How's anybody supposed to figure the numbers out?" Pete said. "Jenny told the truth when she said he lived in the boonies. Why would anybody stay in this remote place unless he had something to hide? Unfortunately though, that doesn't prove he's a pedophile."

When he hit the dirt road, it narrowed immediately. Like a bucking steer, the Ford bounced and jumped, rattling the teeth in their heads. Neither he nor Myra Claire saw any trailer. Pete shook his head. "Jenny has lied to us for sure. This has to be nothing but a wild goose chase. No body lives around here. I'm going to turn around if I can find somewhere to pull into without getting stuck or puncturing a tire. All we need is to meet another vehicle on this narrow road."

"I saw something," Myra Claire said, looking behind her. "Just then. Might have been a trailer."

"There's nowhere to turn around," Pete said. He began to mutter under his breath. All at once, the road came to a dead end. "Now what?" He rested his head on the steering wheel.

"I think there's just enough space to make a turn if you pull between those trees," Myra Claire said.

Pete raised his head. "Might as well give it a try." With some effort, he was able to pull into some bushes and turn around. "Now what?" he said.

"Okay. Go really slow. I think I might have seen something through the trees," Myra Claire said.

Pete sighed, but he did as she suggested.

"There!" she pointed. "I'm sure it's a trailer."

"You might be right," Pete conceded. He stopped and began to back up. "I won't leave the Ford in view and tip Wooten off if he comes along. I'll back up to where I turned around and I'll hike to the trailer."

"What do you mean *you'll* hike? I'm coming with you."

He clinched his jaw but didn't try to protest.

When he got back to the dead end, he hid the Ford in the bushes, and he and Myra Claire got out. They kept in the cover of the woods until she pointed through the trees to a faded green trailer. Seeing no path at first, they found it difficult to move quickly through the dense growth. The only sound was the squirrels shaking the leaves as they flitted through the tree branches. Pete could go faster than Myra Claire because his legs were longer. Then he spotted a narrow driveway. "Here. Over here," he called to his tagalong.

"This is better," he said, after she caught up to him.

What they found was an old house trailer. It was small and looked deserted. He walked up the two wooden steps to the door and tried the knob. It wasn't locked and he pushed it open easily. Pete stuck his head in and immediately noticed a stale tobacco odor and mustiness. "You keep a look out. I'm going in." He proceeded cautiously. It was obvious someone lived here, but he saw nor heard no one.

Myra Claire stayed just inside the door and kept watch.

The kitchen area was untidy with unwashed dishes in the sink. Empty beer cans sat on the red linoleum counter top. There was a scorch mark in the linoleum where a hot skillet or pot had burned a hole and the wood showed through. On a grey Formica table he saw a knife beside a jar of peanut butter. There was fresh peanut butter on the knife blade. It was covered with ants. Someone had been there a short time ago. Pete opened the doors of the two cabinets over the sink and found the usual household items: a few chipped dishes and bowls, jelly jar glasses, a box of cornmeal, a bag of flour, and a box of corn flakes. A loaf of bread sat on the narrow counter that separated the kitchen from the sitting area. He walked through the sparse layout past a stuffed chair in front of a little TV with rabbit ears. The TV sat on a fruit crate. To one side there was a freezer, the only other item in that section of the trailer.

"Now what did a single man need with a freezer?" Pete wondered aloud. The freezer was padlocked. He'd found it strange that the door to the trailer was unlocked, but the freezer was padlocked. He supposed if Wooten hunted deer and game that it made sense the meat would be the only thing of value here. His eyes scanned everything where he might find his address book. He had a moment of excitement when he spotted a small book on top of the freezer. With his heart racing, he snatched it up and almost shouted with glee. *But no! This isn't it!* It was a book about the size and color of his, but when he flipped through it, he found it was all about the signs of the Zodiac. He dropped the book back where he'd found it. "What makes people believe in such foolishness?" he muttered to himself.

He ran a mental list of the things he was pretty sure he knew. The pedophile was in the Corner Market when he put the piece of Frannie's torn dress in her back pocket. Since the pedophile was there, he must have been the one to put the page from Pete's book under his windshield wiper. Otherwise, he had no hope of finding his book. He knew Wooten was Jenny's brother and that Frannie was convinced he was the man who grabbed her at the old gas station. However, he wasn't finding anything here that would incriminate him. He shook his head, discouraged, wondering if he was chasing the wrong rabbit. He moved on down the narrow hall and noted the trailer's small sliding windows near the ceiling. They were open with screens over them. He found a single bed with dingy, yellowed sheets and a closet that held several pairs of work pants, a few shirts and a pair of western boots. These could have been the ones Frannie said he wore the night he grabbed her, but nothing about them was unique. Any store selling boots might have a dozen pair like them.

"Hey!" Myra Claire called in an undertone. "I hear something. A truck. Someone's coming."

"Is it a black truck, like a hearse?"

"No. It's a flatbed truck."

"There's only one way out of here," Pete responded. "We have to climb out the window. I'll give you a boost." He put his hands on her hips and pushed her up. "Knock out the screen and when you hit the ground, run for the trees." The screen made a squeak and then a slight bump as it fell.

"Wait!" she said when she saw the flatbed truck rattling around to the back just a few feet from the window.

"What?" he said sharply.

"It's him. He's just outside this window."

He lifted her back down, grabbed her hand, and pulled her to the front of the trailer. "Let's make a run for it while he's in the back. Head straight for the trees—and hope he doesn't see us!"

When they reached the cover of the trees just beyond the trailer, Pete looked back. "So that's the creep," he said, making a mental note of Wooten's scruffy appearance as he emerged around the side of the trailer.

Wooten stomped up the steps into the kitchen. At the sink he splashed some water in his face and dried it with a dish towel. He started past the table, but turned and picked up the knife, gooey with peanut butter and the crawling little invaders. He wiped it with the dish cloth and stood for a moment, holding it and thinking about making another sandwich. Suddenly, he threw back his head and sniffed. There was a faint feminine scent in the air like the odor of flowers. Laying the knife quietly back on the table, he moved cautiously down the narrow hall, on full alert. Everything appeared to be as he'd left it.

He went back down the hall to make his sandwich when he happened to notice the screen missing from one of the windows. "Someone has been here," he announced. He walked outside, brought the screen in and replaced it. Then, shrugging it off with a few expletives, he turned his attention to his appetite. He made his sandwich and was just about to take a bite when he heard a knock at the door. He laid the sandwich on the counter and pulled a sharp blade from under his shirttail out of the waistband of his trousers. He held it behind him as he pushed the door open just enough to see the short, black man standing on the stoop.

He relaxed his grip. "Old James, it's just you, is it? I was ready to slice you up. You ain't been inside my trailer snooping around have you? Didn't push out that window screen for some reason did you?"

James's eyes widened into huge white orbs.

"Okay." Wooten laughed in his menacing way. "It won't you. You don't smell like flowers. You can get those jars from out back behind the trailer."

James bowed slightly and turned to go to the back.

Wooten pushed the door shut. He walked over to the TV and turned it on for company.

He sat in his chair and took a big bite of his sandwich. "Somebody's been here," he mused while he chewed. "Whoever it was, I musta just missed him." He swallowed and took another bite. Could be old James was lying. Nothing here he wants." He got up to get a beer.

"And that don't explain the smell of flowers."

Chapter Thirty-eight

P ete and Myra Claire got back to the Ford. After they endured the bumpy ride back to Route 41 Pete relaxed some and said, "That was close! The question is will Wooten know we were there. I don't think he knows about you, Myra Claire. He couldn't have seen you last evening at the Gregg's. It was almost dark when we got there, and late when we left the porch."

"That might make me more useful because he doesn't know," she said.

"Maybe," Pete said skeptically.

Against his will, during all the ride back to the campus, he couldn't stop remembering the firm, yet soft feel of Myra Claire when he lifted her up to the window of the trailer. Just the thought of it made his pulse quicken. There was the faint, fresh smell of flowers that came from her hair. He still felt the clasp of her smooth hand in his as they ran leaping over dead branches and dodging limbs and briars. He felt himself wanting to give in to her allurement and make friends with her. That temptation infuriated him. He wished she'd leave. She was only complicating his life more, and at the same time, he wanted her to stay. Her stubbornness annoyed him, and he almost liked that about her too.

"You think you can drive this whiskey car?" he asked. "You could take the Ford and keep guard over Frannie from the Pruitt porch the rest of the afternoon. We know where Wooten is right now, but he could go on the prowl any time."

"And where will you be?" she asked.

"I have some business to attend to," he said, wishing she didn't ask so many dang questions.

"Sure," she said, watching him, noting his tense grip on the wheel. "I guess you don't want him to see my car and start figuring there are two of us on his trail."

"If you drive Jake's car and Wooten sees it, he'll think I'm there at the Greggs'. Like you said, no use giving him any clues you're involved. You'll be safer that way."

He pulled into the parking lot at the college. "I'll come to the porch at dinner time and relieve you. I'll drive your car, but I'll park it on a side street, Maple Street, about a from the Greggs' apartment."

She said, "I'll stick around after you get to the porch. I have nothing to do at the dorm except read a book. I can do that this afternoon, unless Frannie comes around and wants to talk."

"You can still leave Riverton, you know?"

"Not a chance," she said.

"Then I'll bring some dinner when I come. Burgers from White Tower okay?"

"Yes."

"I'm warning you, if you stay, there could be danger."

"I've been warned," she said.

At the college he got out and opened her door. She reached for her purse and gave him the keys to her car. Then she slid behind the wheel of the Ford. He got in the Buick and watched her drive off. He knew why he disliked her. She was unattainable. Even without a special someone in her life, she belonged to another world, one where people didn't hire contract killers. There was a great gulf between them, and it was not passable.

He drove to the motel, parked her car, and walked to the pay phone at the laundromat to make a call to Robert. He knew his brother was often in court in the mornings, but it was afternoon now and Pete was dying to ask about whether Farley had returned the signed papers. Although he hadn't wanted Farley to buy the farm, things had taken a new twist. Now he needed the proceeds from the sale to pay the blood money. At least he had the consolation of believing that Farley would never enjoy his purchase. How many days would it take for all the legal knots to be tied before he could put his hands on the money? He didn't know, but Robert could tell him.

When Pete got Robert to the phone, his brother knew the question before Pete asked it. "No. The papers haven't come in. I'll admit I'm surprised, but Farley's busy, and he's just come back from his travels in Mexico. There's no telling how many deals he's involved in at the same time."

"If he's not going to pee, I wish he'd get off the pot," Pete said. "I need the money." He knew Robert would ask why, and he did. Pete already had a lie thought out. He told him, "Since you're selling the Turner farm to Farley, I'm buying some land elsewhere."

He told himself that lying to his brother didn't bother him. The end justified the means, but he felt a twinge of regret. His daddy was admired for his honesty because he always told the truth. People knew when Rusty Turner gave his word or told you something, you could count on it. He'd keep his word to his own hurt.

"Oh." Robert sounded disappointed. "I hoped you'd come back to settle around here, but if you need money, what about the trust fund? Last time I checked you had seven or eight thousand in that."

"What did you say about a trust fund?"

"Your trust fund, the one daddy set up for you just days before he died so you'd have money to go to college. I assumed when you went on the G.I. Bill, you didn't need any of it." The silence on the other end of the line prompted Robert to ask, "You didn't know about it?"

"How soon can I get the money?"

"It's Friday afternoon, but I can have it in a few hours if you're sure you know what you're doing."

"Robert, get the money. I'll have Jennings pick it up at your house this evening. Give me your address."

"Another thing," Robert said. "I received something in the mail here that belongs to you. It's addressed to Pete Turner in care of Robert Turner and it's postmarked Riverton, Virginia."

"I don't know anybody in Riverton," Pete said too hastily. "What is it?"

"It's a small package that came special delivery. It felt like a book. I gave it to Adelle to hold for you the next time you came in."

"A small book? It came special delivery?"

"Correct," Robert replied.

"Send it with Jennings, will you?" Pete said, wondering if it could possibly be his address book. "And let me speak with Adelle." He listened to Robert buzz the secretary and tell her to pick up on Line 2. *Now I can get Angel's private number!*

"Yes, Mr. Turner, what can I do for you?"

Pete noticed her hesitation when she said 'Mr. Turner'. She probably still had reservations that Robert's dead brother had really come back to life. "You have an envelope for me? Would you go ahead and see what's inside?"

He heard her open a drawer, then rattle paper.

"It appears to be an address book."

"I lost it and somebody took the trouble to mail it to me. How it got in Riverton, I can't imagine," Pete said. He rubbed the bridge of his nose, trying to figure why Wooten would have mailed the book. He could come up with nothing that made sense. *Unless he tossed it and someone else found it. That's the only thing that makes sense. Wooten tore out the page to let me know he was on to me. Then he tossed it aside and someone else found it and took the trouble to mail it.* "Is there a note from the sender?" Pete asked.

"No. Just the book."

My name's in the front of the book, but the only address I wrote in it for myself is 'Turner farm, Wilkes County'. The person who sent it must have assumed Robert and I were related with the same last name, and seeing Robert Turner, Attorney at Law they supposed Robert would be likely to get the book to me.

"Mr. Turner, what did you want me to do about the book?" Adelle asked.

"Uh, there's a number in it I need." He reached in his shirt pocket for a pen and paper and pulled out Harvey's directions to Burris Road. "You see 'Angel's Goods and Guns'?"

"Yes."

"There's a number under that one. Give it to me."

He scratched it down as she read it off. "One more thing, give me Robert's address." She dictated and he wrote it on his paper.

Pete hung up the phone and dialed Jennings first, crossing his fingers he was still recuperating at the boarding house from the assault at the hands of Farley's men. While he waited for an answer, he wondered whether Jennings was doing well enough to drive.

The landlady answered and said she'd get him. Pete breathed a sigh of relief. When his friend answered, he remembered to ask how he was doing.

"I ain't able to lift nothing, so I can't work at the still yet. I'm going stir crazy."

"Can you drive?"

"I haven't, but I'm going to make some deliveries for Jake tonight."

Chapter Thirty-eight

"Up this way by any chance?"

"I'm making the run to Richmond since you ain't here."

"Before you leave, I need you to do me a favor. I need you to pick up a package from my brother Robert and bring it to me. Be careful with it because it contains a big sum of money and an important little book. Then tell me where I can meet up with you."

"I'll leave here 'bout midnight and make deliveries around Richmond. After that, I should make it to Roanoke by dawn. I'll sleep a few hours at a motel there, get up and come home."

Pete thought for a minute. "There's a dirt track outside of Roanoke called Bentley's. They'll be racing tomorrow afternoon. Meet me at the ticket entrance about 3:00."

"Bentley's," Jennings repeated. "Let me give you a number for the motel in Roanoke, just in case."

Pete wrote down the number. "Don't worry. I'll be there."

"Does Robert know what you're gonna do with this money?" Jennings asked.

"Yeah. I'm buying some land."

"And this doesn't have anything to do with that money you owe those Mafia guys?"

"Didn't I tell you that was a lie? Those are Farley's men who said that, and they'd love to get their hands on my money. Be sure they don't. Don't tell anybody about meeting me. Okay?"

"Right."

Pete hung up. Things were changing fast. Finally! He dialed the operator and read off Angel's private number. When he heard the Italian's voice he told him, "Angel, it's Pete. I've got the money. All of it."

"Young Pete! What'd you do? Rob a bank?"

"Daddy set up a trust fund for my college education before he crashed. My brother just told me about it. I didn't know. So, where do I deliver the money?"

"What does your brother know?"

"Don't worry. I didn't tell him why I really wanted it."

"I'm not worried about me. Like I told you, I'm just the messenger. When the money passes hands, I'm out of the picture. The man who'll do the job will get in touch with you. He'll tell you where to take the money. And as of now, I'm calling my man home."

"Has he seen Farley?"

"No. He's watched his house, but nobody comes or goes but one man, a big muscular guy, apparently a body guard. He picks up mail and buys groceries."

"It's not like Farley to be a recluse. He's got to come out sometime, but he's just returned from Mexico. Maybe he's hiding from somebody, somebody besides me who's found out what he's really like."

"Well, whatever the situation, my connection ends soon. Call me on this private line on Monday evening after six o'clock. I should have some information for you then."

"Not until Monday?"

"By then all arrangements will be in place. Then you take the money to wherever the caller tells you. Within twenty-four hours—Boom! It's all over for your adversary."

"Twenty-four hours, you're sure?"

"Relax, young Pete. Get a positive attitude!" Angel laughed a hearty, belly laugh.

Easy for you to say 'relax,' Pete thought, but Angel was gone. In a second Pete heard the dial tone, then the operator asking him if he wanted to place a call. Pete hung up.

Chapter Thirty-nine

Pete got back to the Shady Lawn and stretched across the bed. He was restless with too many thoughts running through his head. Eventually, he dozed off into a fitful sleep.

While Pete napped, Wooten pulled into the parking lot and looked around for the Ford. He saw a slick blue Buick convertible and a few less notable cars in the lot, but no black '40 Ford. "He's not here. Could he of checked out? I'm looking for the true pleasure of seeing Mr. Hero go to jail for hauling booze." Picturing the Mason jars full of old James' rotten whiskey, Wooten touched his sore ear. He looked toward the office. "There's more than one way to skin a cat," he muttered and hot footed it in that direction.

Harvey was manning the desk. "You need a room?" he asked as Wooten came in the door.

"Naw. I's supposed to meet a fellow here. Turner's his name. You got a Turner staying here?"

Harvey started to answer in the affirmative, then checked himself. Knowing what he did about Pete rescuing that little girl from a pedophile, he responded, "We don't reveal our guest list unless one of them specifically tells us he's expecting a visitor."

Wooten narrowed his eyes and a look crossed his face that Harvey could only describe as sinister. "I just wanna know if this is the right place. You can't answer that one little question and tell me if he's staying here?"

"That's right." Harvey said, his suspicion growing by the minute. He pointed to a conversation area over to one side with a sofa and two chairs. "If someone's supposed to meet you here, you are welcomed to sit down there and wait."

Wooten's mouth twitched like he'd tasted something sour. Turning on his heel and letting the screen slam behind him, he stomped back to his truck. "If he's not here, could be he's gone for good, but I don't think so. If Turner hasn't left Riverton, he's with the brat." He cranked the engine and roared out of the parking lot, headed for the north side of town.

As he usually did, he reached Jenny's by a back alley that ran behind the houses fronting North Main. He parked in the sagging garage behind the Daniels' house. Then he went to the hedge to look for Turner's Ford in the Pruitt's driveway. "He ain't here unless he parked somewhere's else." After considering the situation for a minute, he pulled back out of the garage and drove around the neighborhood looking for the Ford.

At the time Wooten missed seeing the Ford, Myra Claire had taken Frannie for a drive in it. The girl was eager to get away on an adventure with Myra Claire and ride again in a car that had been used to actually haul bootlegged whiskey. She told her new friend she had been too upset to savor the experience the first times when Pete brought her home. Myra Claire was glad to get a change of scenery from the porch. Frannie kept her entertained with her chatter, telling her she'd read about how the bootleggers hid the moonshine inside a false back seat. "Did you know Pete's back seat, well not his, but his Uncle Jake's, is really a compartment for hiding moonshine? He told me so. He won't care if I told you."

"What are you saying? We aren't carrying moonshine, are we?" Myra Claire asked, her eyes wide with alarm.

"Frannie laughed, "Not now!"

Myra Claire smiled. *This precocious kid never runs out of commentary.* "I should hope Pete wouldn't tell me to drive his car if he were carrying moonshine in it."

After they explored several miles out North Main, she decided they'd better turn back, although she wasn't eager to return to the porch. She hadn't seen any sign of Wooten thus far. Even so, she decided maybe she shouldn't leave Pete's gas gage on empty. He might have occasion to follow the suspect later in the evening. They stopped at a grocery store to get snacks and then settled in at the Pruitt's for more surveillance.

A large black and white cat was stretched out in one of the porch rockers. Frannie picked him up and began stroking him. "This is Sylvester," Frannie said. "The Pruitt's call him 'Boots' but I call him Sylvester because he looks just like Sylvester in the cartoons. They're paying me a dime a day to feed him while they're away."

Myra Claire reached down and stroked Sylvester. He purred for a few minutes, then jumped off Frannie's lap and ambled down the steps.

"I know what!" Frannie said. "Come see the chinaberry tree in the backyard."

"Is that your special place you've been telling me about?"

"Yes," Frannie said. "Come on, I'll show you."

Myra Claire looked over toward the Daniels' house. She hadn't seen anyone over there all afternoon, but Wooten could be there watching them. She directed Frannie to go to the side of the house away from the Daniels'. Frannie took her hand and happily led Myra Claire to the backyard. She removed her sandals and hoisted herself onto a limb. When her companion didn't hesitate to climb up after her, she clapped with delight and scampered barefoot through the branches like a squirrel. She showed Myra Claire all the neat bends and curves where she liked to sit.

"This is better than the porch," Myra Claire said, looking down and surveying the Daniels' place from her bird's eye view. However, she could not see part of the Pruitt front yard and the end of the driveway that was blocked by the roof.

While she and Frannie were up in the chinaberry tree, Wooten had come back to Jenny's. Walking from the garage, he heard voices coming from the chinaberry tree and recognized Frannie's. He crept quietly to the front and spotted the Ford parked in the shade that spilled over into the Pruitt's driveway from a large oak tree on Jenny's side of the hedge. He hurried back to his truck and removed a case of Mason jars. He carried it to the space between the hedge and the side of the Ford. Squatting close to the ground, he tried the door. It was unlocked as he expected. He knew from Pete and the brat's conversation behind the library that Turner carried his moonshine in a false back seat. He hurriedly tried to pull the seat out, but it wouldn't move. As he pulled and pried, he realized he was picking up the scent of flowers. He paused and sniffed. "Hum. How about that." He stopped his search long enough to check his surroundings again. The coast was still clear.

Thinking maybe he'd misunderstood about there being a false seat, he tapped the floor to look for a false bottom. Nothing there. He felt along the sides of the seat again, deciding there had to be a catch or release of some sort. Nothing. Sweating profusely, he sat on his haunches and scratched his head. "It's here and I'm gonna find it." He tried again, running his hand up and down and across the sides of the seat until his hand touched a small protrusion. "This is it!" He moved it. Nothing happened. Again he checked his surroundings. There was no one coming. After he tried several pushes and pulls, the latch finally snapped and he lifted the top. Peering inside, he saw a couple of sandbags for keeping the rear end from riding too high when the whiskey car was not full of moonshine, some rags, and a quilt to cushion the jars and keep them from rattling The compartment would hold many more cases than what he had, but any amount found by the cops was all that was needed to get Turner arrested. Wooten grinned.

He grabbed the crate of moonshine to stow it in the compartment, and in his haste, he dropped it on the ground with a crash. He looked around to see if he'd alerted anyone to his business. All remained quiet and he quickly stowed the crate in the compartment. Then he noticed one jar was cracked and leaking. "Whew! This stuff stinks!" He cursed and removed the broken jar from the crate. "Can't be helped," he muttered. Now the quilt and crate were wet the inferior whiskey. "It'll evaporate, but I don't know." Again he checked to see that no one came. "Still clear," he said, "but I gotta fix this mess." In a panic he grabbed one of the rags and soaked up as much of the spillage as he could. "It still stinks." Then he had an idea. He threw the rag onto the back floorboard behind the front seat. "He might not remember puttin' that rag here, but maybe he won't go looking for those jars before the cops do. Gotta alert them pronto. Can't do it while he's parked here at the brat's. Too obvious, but this evening or tomorrow when it looks like he's out to make a delivery." Then he heard Diane call Frannie to dinner and he disappeared around the hedge.

"Miss Myra Claire, I'll ask Momma if you can have dinner with us. She knows you're here. She's probably expecting you to eat with us."

Myra Claire grimaced to gently make a refusal.

"Please?" Frannie pleaded.

"Well thank you, Frannie for the invitation, but Pete's bringing dinner."

"Oh," Frannie said, looking downcast. "I guess you'd rather eat with your sweetheart. I understand."

"Frannie, that's not how it is with Pete and me. We're just friends."

Frannie's brows came together in a furrow. "Mr. Pete's not your sweetheart?"

"My sweetheart, the man I had hoped to marry," Myra Claire said, "died fighting for our country and our freedom during the war."

"Oh, Miss Myra Claire, I'm really sorry. Is he in heaven?"

"Yes. I was young when he went away, only twenty. He was older. It's been a long time now."

"Then Mr. Pete can be your sweetheart."

"Myra Claire laughed. "It doesn't work quite like that."

Frannie tilted her head to one side. "Are you a Christian, Miss Myra Claire?"

"Yes, I sure am," she said.

"I don't think Mr. Pete is," Frannie said, frowning. "So I guess he can't be your sweetheart. I'm praying for him."

"Me too," Myra Claire said.

As Myra Claire climbed down and jumped to the ground, she assumed Frannie was coming behind her. When she didn't, she looked up in the tree to see limbs moving as Frannie climbed higher and higher up. The tree grew past the top of the house, one of its sturdy branches spreading over the roof under an upper story window on the left. Myra Claire held her breath, watching the branch shake. Through the foliage she saw Frannie stretch out on the limb and pull open the screen. In a split second, the spry little creature scrambled through the window.

When Myra Claire got back to the porch, Sylvester was in his chair washing himself. "You must have just finished your dinner," Myra Claire remarked as she sat down in the swing to wait for Pete. With the days getting shorter, the sun was beginning to set and dusk was coming on. She wondered if Pete had forgotten her.

Chapter Forty

While Wooten performed his mischief in the Pruitt driveway and Myra Claire entertained Frannie, Pete at the Shady Lawn fell into a terrifying, unsettled sleep, finding himself surrounded by a wall of fire. Futilely, he searched for a way out, but each time he found an opening through which to escape, it disappeared like a mirage. Once again the stifling flames closed in around him, smothering and stinging him like a thousand hornets. He had never known such fear and such a sense of helplessness, yet the worst part was the cacophony of faceless, anguished cries and piercing screams that came out of the blaze. It was the most desperate, hopeless sound he could ever have imagined. Finally, he shook himself awake. Soaked in sweat he rushed for the shower.

The cool water ran over his body and relaxed him. Remembering the dream, he tried to laugh off his fear. "I guess Myra Claire would tell me that was a premonition of the hell fire awaiting my lost soul." However light he made of it, he couldn't shake the sense of heaviness the dream had stirred in him, even after he dressed and left the room.

Outside dusk was coming on. He realized he hadn't eaten since breakfast. As he started for the Buick, ready to get dinner for himself and Myra Claire, Harvey came running out to him. "Some fellow was asking about you. Said he was supposed to meet you here at the Shady Lawn. I refused to tell him anything. I hope that was okay."

"What'd he look like?"

"Slight build. Dark brown hair."

"About medium height?

"Yeah."

"Good. I'm glad you didn't tell him anything."

"Is he the bad guy?"

"Unfortunately he is," Pete said, "but I can't prove anything yet."

"Good luck," Harvey said and Pete got in the car.

He stopped at the White Tower for burgers and RC Cola. Myra Claire mentioned she liked RC Cola.

When he got to the north side of town and parked on Maple Street, he discovered the alley running behind the houses in that block of North Main. He followed it to the Pruitt porch where he found Myra Claire in the swing, stoking Sylvester.

She put down the cat. "Time for my dinner, old boy," she said. He stretched himself, and swishing his tail, he jumped off the porch and wandered off.

Pete sat down next to her. He couldn't avoid noticing the scent of flowers about her. It was warm out and her skin was moist, and yet there was a freshness about her that was so nice. He found himself wishing she liked him better. Immediately, he reminded himself that if she had softened at all in her opinion of him, she would thoroughly despise him if she knew his secrets. That thought made him angry and resentful, but he tried not to show it. If he could just keep his focus a couple more days, he'd be free of Farley, free of Riverton, and free of Myra Claire.

He set the bag of food between them.

"Have you eaten since breakfast?" she asked.

"No. What about you?"

"I had a snack. Frannie wanted to take another ride in a real bootlegger's car. She's such a romantic, and she's so bored and lonely. But we didn't use all your gas, and we were hoping we weren't carrying moonshine."

Pete gave her a disdainful look for even thinking he'd do that to her and Frannie. "I just hope you were careful of Wooten. He doesn't know about you. He could be watching."

"I must confess we left the porch after we came back," Myra Claire said. "Frannie wanted to show me her chinaberry tree. You should see how she scoots up those branches like a squirrel. In fact, I think you ought to come take a look. There's a way she gets inside her bedroom from the tree that bothers me."

"Before we eat?"

"Before it gets too dark for you to see. It's important."

He followed her around the back. Again they kept to the shadows, intending to avoid Wooten's evil eyes if he happened to be at Jenny's spying out a window.

The huge chinaberry tree grew near the left corner of the house and towered over the roof. Myra Claire pointed. "See how those branches hide that second story window. That's Frannie's bedroom. She leaves the screen unlatched so she can go out the window into the tree. She calls it her sanctuary. Apparently, she spends a lot of time up there. She gets back in the same way."

Pete said, "I can understand they have to keep the windows open with the hot weather, but you're right to be concerned. She should keep the screen latched when she's inside. If she can get in that way, he can too."

Myra Claire said, "I'll point that out to her and get her to promise."

"If the man we observed from the cover of the woods going into the trailer is the pedophile, he'll have no more trouble getting up that tree to that window than Frannie," Pete said.

They lingered another minute and then walked back to the porch, pondering the tree as a dangerous access instead of a sanctuary. Pete opened the bag of burgers. Soon the aroma of beef, onions and barbecue sauce captured his attention. "I got RC Cola," he said.

"You did? That was thoughtful."

Pete said, managing a smile. "I have a few good points."

"You have many good points, Pete."

"I'm glad you've noticed," he said, not meeting her eyes. Her compliments made him feel like a hypocrite.

"You rescued Frannie. Who knows where she might be today if you hadn't come along when you did, and you're still here watching over her."

Pete squirmed. "I've had business here. I *couldn't* leave."

"So you said."

"Speaking of that, I have to make a trip tomorrow in the afternoon. Are you up for surveillance?"

"I still have my books, and Frannie." Myra Claire laughed. "I declare that girl never runs out of talk, although I do remember Diane is taking her shopping for school clothes in the morning. I don't think they have a lot of money right now, but Frannie's growing and she has to have a few things to start school. I wish there was some way I could give her some errands so I could pay her and not offend the Greggs, but I haven't thought of anything yet."

"Right now she needs to stay close to a safe adult. We have to warn Diane she can't take her eyes off her when they're out. If Wooten was brazen enough to take her at the carnival, he can do it again," Pete said.

"I'm not sure Diane and Bill believe the story about the clown at the carnival," Myra Claire countered. They still think there's some other explanation and that Frannie's imagination played a large part in that. Even so, they can't imprison her in the house. Besides, she's got to go to school in two weeks."

"We will catch him before then," Pete said with a scowl.

"You're pretty convinced Wooten is the one," she said.

"Not totally, but we'll know soon if he is. He'll make his move again."

They ate in silence for a few minutes. When they finished, he collected their trash in the White Tower bag. Myra Claire got up and went to the steps.

Pete asked, "Where're you going?"

"I got Moonpies when I was out with Frannie and the driveway was shady, so I hope the chocolate didn't melt."

"Moonpies! How did you know I love Moonpies?"

"I didn't know, but I like them."

"You're going to share?"

"Maybe."

"RC Cola and Moonpies. My favorite."

"Yep."

"You like RC Cola and Moonpies?"

"My favorite."

"I would have you figured for something more sophisticated, like a spot of tea and crumpets, whatever crumpets are."

Myra Claire laughed. "Fooled you, didn't I?"

"And not the first time," Pete said wistfully. "Let me get them. Even though it's getting dark, Wooten hasn't seen you. We don't want to give him information he doesn't need."

As soon as Pete opened the door of the Ford, he was met with a strange odor. "What in tarnation! What have they spilt in my car?" He grabbed the bag with the Moonpies and went back to the porch. "Did Frannie spill something in my car?"

Myra Claire looked puzzled. "No."

"It smells like some kind of awful disinfectant."

"Frannie sprayed the porch all over with bug spray for the mosquitoes, but she didn't spray in your car."

"It's a strong smell. Reminds me of a hospital, and hospitals remind me of death and people dying."

"Does the thought of dying frighten you?" Myra Claire asked, taking the bag.

331

Pete remembered the dream he'd had earlier. "I don't think about dying, except in hospitals. What about you? Oh, that's right. You're one of those who believe there's a heaven where people are playing harps and floating around on clouds."

"Where did you get that idea?"

"Don't I remember you said your grandma is in heaven now, walking on streets of gold?" Pete smirked as he said it.

"I didn't say anything about clouds and harps. Saints will be working, ruling and reigning."

"You lost me there," Pete said.

"Read Daniel and the Book of Revelation," Myra Claire said.

"Nobody understands that stuff."

"God does, and He reveals these things by His Spirit to those who believe in Him."

"If you say so."

"You know, it doesn't cost you anything to ask God to show you if He's real. If He's not real and He doesn't respond, you've lost nothing...but what if you're wrong?"

"I believe in God, but not a just one."

"Then you don't know the right God. The only way to the true God of the Bible is to know Jesus. He is a picture of the invisible God, revealing what He is like, compassionate, always desiring to do us good, if we'll let Him. You have to invite Him into your heart, but He will respect your right to refuse Him entrance."

Pete let her statements pass without comment. He didn't want to get into a big argument about religion. He had to get along with her for another day or two and he hoped to make the best of it.

When they finished the Moonpies, to lighten the mood, Pete took his handkerchief and wiped chocolate from the corner of Myra Claire's mouth. Then she took the handkerchief and wiped his chin. "Now. We're presentable," she said.

Pete pushed the swing with his foot so that it moved just slightly. Myra Claire leaned her head back. "It's cooling off. That's what I love about August. The days are warm, but the nights are cool and pleasant."

Pete continued to push the swing with his foot, but Myra Claire's closeness made him restless. Abruptly, he stopped pushing and jumped up. "I'm going snooping. I'm determined to find something to either prove Wooten is our nemesis or clear him of suspicion."

Without an invitation, Myra Claire followed him down the steps. Lights in the Daniels' house shinned through the opaque shades at the windows. They crept toward the garage. Carefully, Pete opened the door a crack. It made a squeaking sound that pierced the silence and reverberated across the yard. They waited for some reaction, but there was no movement of the shades and no one came outside. Pete put his head in. He could see well enough to discern Wooten's black paneled work truck. He tried to look in the truck, but there wasn't enough light. "I have a flashlight in my car. I'll get it."

He came back with the flashlight and crept back inside the garage. Carefully and quietly he opened the door of the truck and shone the light in its interior. His cursory search revealed only tools useful to the plumbing trade. After several seconds he clicked the door shut. He flashed the light around the walls and corners of the garage and couldn't see anything besides a push mower, a shovel, an old tire, some paint cans and a rusty bicycle. He switched off the light. He slipped back out the door and closed it. "Nothing here," he whispered to Myra Claire.

"What did you expect to find, bodies hanging from the ceiling?" she asked with a grin.

Then they heard someone open the back door of the Daniels' porch. Pete grabbed her hand and pulled her behind the garage. After several minutes when no one came, Pete realized he was still holding her hand, and he was standing close to her, breathing in her presence. For a moment an engulfing wave of regret washed over him, a distaste for everything he was plotting to do, the full panoply of his adult life's ambition, all the anger, hate and fantasies of revenge. He dropped her hand and stepped away. *She doesn't even like me. She only wants to save my soul!* "I'll walk you to your car," he said irritably. "Can you get back to your dorm room okay?"

She nodded, then returned to the porch to get her purse. When she came back, they moved quietly along the hedge and into the dark alley. Even though it was a clear night and the stars were out, Pete switched on his flashlight to find their way to Maple Street.

"You told me Diane is taking Frannie shopping tomorrow. Before I leave town in the afternoon for the rest of the day, I'm going back to Wooten's place in the morning and look around again. You can stay at the college."

"You didn't turn up anything suspicious earlier. What do you expect to find?"

"I wish I could say. Who knows, I may be chasing the wrong guy, but I don't think so. Anyway, I'm going back and look around again."

"Actually, I'd prefer to tag along."

He hesitated to agree, but what could he say? Reluctantly, he nodded consent, still feeling the touch of her hand in his like a brand burning into his flesh.

Chapter Forty-one

Early on Saturday morning Wooten came out of the trailer and disappeared into thick bushes to get into the flatbed contraption with wooden, latticed sides. He cranked it up and rattled off through the woods. At the unpaved section of Burke Road that passed his property, he did not turn right to go toward the main road, but to the left, following the dirt lane that had led Pete and Myra Claire to a dead end. However, a half a mile before the road ended, he turned into a narrow truck path so obscured by the foliage, one almost had to know it was there to find it. Small branches and briars made scraping sounds against the cab of the truck, catching in the side rails as if attempting to halt an intruder. Wooten bumped along deep into the woods until he emerged through the thicket in front of a small hunting cabin, constructed of logs and capped with a dark tin roof. Wooten bought the land after he discovered the cabin. It was where the former owner brought the deer he killed for hanging and skinning.

He drove the truck to the back and parked. Hurrying to the front, he reached up in the crook of a branch to bring out a key. With it he unlocked the heavy door and pushed it open. All the windows were boarded up except a small one near the apex of the ceiling. A lantern hung on the inside of the jamb. He took it down, lit it, and sat it on a rectangular work table in the center of the room. The light from the lantern revealed tools hanging on the walls: a game pole with hooks for hanging the animal, a game hoist to get the buck onto the hooks, a coil of rope and some saws. He opened a drawer in the table. It contained a Buck knife, a skinning knife, a boning knife, and a tool knife with a bone saw on the back of it. He counted each one and slammed the drawer shut.

Then he walked over to a spool of rope and cut off a length, tossing it in a corner of the room. He went back out to the truck, climbed up into the back and dropped an armload of netting over the side. He took it into the cabin and threw it inside near the door. Then he went back to the truck to get a gallon can of kerosene for the lantern. He brought that inside and set in a corner toward the back of the room. Then he sat down in the chair, crossed his legs, pulled a pack of Lucky Strike cigarettes from his pocket, and lit up. While he smoked, he muttered, "Redheaded brat bit my ear." He reached up and touched his left ear, rubbing it and emitting a string of expletives. He got up from the chair and paced. "She's gonna disappear, but first I gotta deal with Turner. Not so easy to make him disappear. It's takin' me some planning, but I'll fix him! It's early still. Once I do what I gotta do here, I'll go to that motel where he's staying and as soon as I see him drive off in that Ford loaded with moonshine, I'll call them Riverton cops and report the suspect carrying illegal whiskey in his hidden compartment. They already suspicious of him. Thanks to me for keepin' them informed. They'll throw him in the slammer and I can get on with what I gotta do with the brat." He looked over at the rope and the chair. "She's gonna pay!" After he finished his smoke, he hurried back to the truck and headed to his trailer for something he'd forgot.

Pete finished his one hundred pushups, showered, dressed in some new dungarees and drove over to the college to pick up Myra Claire. He was still in his sullen mood of the evening before. His sleuthing had amounted to nothing. He had definitely underestimated Wooten, and he was running out of time. Once he was gone, he had little confidence Frannie's parents would protect her, seeing as how they were unconvinced of her danger.

Besides his uneasiness about Wooten having unimpeded access to Frannie once he left, he was having nightmares about the step he was about to take. Once he got the money from Jennings and delivered it to wherever he was told to take it, he would be connecting with dangerous people. If anything went wrong, he could be charged with solicitation of murder for hire. It had an ominous sound. He could go to prison *if* anything went wrong. He kept telling himself nothing was going to go wrong. He was paying ten thousand dollars for a professional, most of his trust fund. Nothing was going to go wrong. Another thing he found annoying was that Angel was so quick to disassociate himself from the arrangements. Hadn't Angel been the one to say, "If you ever need someone eliminated, I know the right people." He sighed. He always came around to the fact that life was hard. There was always some catch.

Then there were his mixed emotions about Myra Claire. He didn't like her, and he did. Surely it would be a case of out of sight, out of mind. Yet, there was that nagging thought that once he crossed that line and disposed of Farley, he would be killing any chance of a future relationship with her. But he couldn't let that be a consideration, as remote a possibility as it was anyway. He was bound by family honor to a duty he must perform. He should have protected Mary Kate when there was no one else to do it. With his daddy cold in the grave and Robert in law school, he had been all she had, and he wasn't there when she really needed him. He had been so completely focused on his own problems with Farley, he'd neglected her and let her suffer the worst fate imaginable. *Just what you are about to repeat with Frannie*. He'd heard that before. It came from deep inside. "No!" he said aloud. "My purpose is clear. It's to do my duty." It was a quiet voice. He heard it again, *Mary Kate is gone and nothing you do will bring her back. Frannie is here*. He grabbed his head. These were the wavering thoughts that tormented him. Frannie reminded him so much of his sister, the way he remembered her best, when life was good, when Rusty was still alive...before Farley intruded into their lives.

He opened the door of Harvey's old green truck and climbed in. Harvey had insisted he drive the truck this morning when Pete had described the rough terrain where Wooten lived. Pete accepted it gratefully and considered the advantage of Wooten not recognizing it. He cranked it and headed to the college.

Myra Claire, also wearing dungarees, was her usual cheery self. Their last experience had taught them they needed covering from the mosquitoes and briars despite the warm temperatures. He acknowledged to himself that he was grateful for her company. He needed something to keep his mind off the afternoon meeting with Jennings. He held the door for her to get in. "Where'd you get this?" she asked, and he explained Harvey's offering it.

He drove the truck past the site of Wooten's trailer and to the dead end of Burris Road, making sure their vehicle was hidden from view. They got out, keeping in the trees and out of sight as they made their way in the direction of the trailer.

Myra Claire slapped a mosquito on her neck. "At least we haven't seen any snakes, just squirrels and blue jays," she said.

"And mosquitoes," he said, slapping his cheek.

After they'd been half a mile, Pete pointed, "Driving sure is much faster, but the trailer is just beyond that bend if I remember."

Then in a cloud of dust, a flatbed truck like the one they had seen Wooten driving the day before came from the road behind them and rattled by. "Hum," Pete said. "Where did he come from? There's nothing back here but a dead end. Maybe we should turn around and take another look. He knows the area and we don't. It's like the Feds trying to find my daddy's stills. If you don't know where they're hidden, it's close to impossible to locate them."

So, they turned around and began retracing their steps through the trees and undergrowth to find a hidden road. "Sure hope he didn't spot Harvey's truck," Pete said.

"What do you think he would do if he did?"

"Maybe slash the tires if he suspects I came in it. Then we'd be stuck out here and it would be a long hike to civilization. On the other hand, if he thinks it's a stranger, he might leave it alone. Who knows what his sick mind would think."

"It was hidden pretty well."

"If there's any kind of a road, it's hidden pretty well too," Pete said, "but Wooten didn't just fall out of the sky."

Thirty minutes later Pete decided, "We're almost back at the dead end and we haven't found anything. I'm about ready to go." He looked at his watch. "I don't have all day, remember. We should have followed Wooten. He could be stalking Frannie and Diane, and here we are being eaten alive by mosquitoes."

"There must be something down here," she insisted. "Like you said, he didn't fall out of the sky."

They searched for another ten minutes. "Let's go back," Pete said. "I'm really worried he saw us somehow when we parked and he's done something to the Harvey's truck. We could find we have a hot, miserable trek ahead of us." *And I have to meet Jennings.*

Pete noticed a hawk swoop down into the woods. "He's after something," Pete remarked with a tired sigh. "Reminds me I'm thirsty and hungry." Just as they got within a stone's throw of the dead end, Pete stopped and extended his arm to halt Myra Claire. "Wait a minute. I think I see an opening!" He hurried to pull back some bushes to uncover a narrow truck path. "So,"

Pete said. "So this is where Wooten came from. I think we've found something!"

"I knew it!" she exclaimed. "Like you said, he didn't fall out of the sky."

He grabbed her arm. "I'll get the truck. You wait here."

Pete took off in a run. His hands shook with excitement as he unlocked it and cranked it up. As soon as Myra Claire heard the truck and made sure it was Pete, she came out from a clump of bushes. He paused long enough for her to slide in beside him. He turned into the newly discovered road and together they began the bumpy ride.

After several minutes, she said, "I guess you saw the 'no trespassing' sign."

"That's for hunters, to discourage hunters from coming on his land. Anyway, if we run into anybody, we'll say we got lost and we were trying to turn around," Pete said with a grin. Then frowning he said, "Who knows? Maybe Wooten has some kid shackled up here, a prisoner for his perverted use."

"This is certainly out of the way," she said with a grimace. "I hate to think of him with Frannie. No. I can't think about it." She shuddered. "I can't even think it."

"But it happens."

Myra Claire put her hand to her heart and tears welled up in her eyes.

"There!" Pete pointed. "What's that through the trees?"

"I see it!" she whispered.

He followed the narrow road around to the back of a crude, weathered cabin and cut off the engine. "Let's hope Wooten doesn't come back. There's only one way out of here." They got out of the truck and listened for a moment. No sound except the rustle of leaves as squirrels darted about. Pete put up his hand to stay Myra. Then he moved quietly from one corner of the back to the other and peered around the sides. He came back to Myra. "There are two boarded up windows. Does that mean the place is abandoned, or someone wants it to appear that way? You stay here, just in case there's an occupant inside who doesn't hesitate to shoot trespassers. I'm going to work my way around to the front."

At the front, Pete found the door padlocked. He put his ear against the door. Not a sound from within. He whistled for Myra Claire to come. "See. There's a padlock. It looks pretty heavy duty." He leaned his head against the door and called out, "Is anyone in there?" They waited. There was no sound but the shaking limbs from grey bushy tails flitting through the trees. "Unless Wooten is holding a prisoner inside, there's no one here. I don't have anything to break the lock with," he said, looking around. He picked up a stone, but tossed it down. "I don't want to break the lock if I can avoid it." He moved around to the side and tried to pull a board loose from the window. It was nailed securely, but he kept working until he pulled it free. He came back to Myra. "It's dark inside. I can't see anything. I could pull enough boards off the window to climb inside, but then he'd be able to tell we've been here. I'd rather he didn't know until we have some kind of evidence to convict him."

"You know how people hide keys under the door mat, but there's no mat here," Myra Claire said. "That would be too obvious, of course, but there could be a key hidden somewhere." She began looking around for a hiding place and Pete joined her. They scoured the outside walls, feeling for a nail with a hanging key. She felt along the top and bottom of the door frame.

"Think of Wooten's height," Pete said. "He's shorter than either of us. He would hang the key just above eye level for him and he wouldn't hang it higher than his reach."

After a fruitless search, Myra Claire said, "Maybe we're looking too high. Maybe he buries it. We don't even know that this is Wooten's cabin."

"You're right. We could be trespassing on someone else's property. Hope we don't get shot," he said with a mock tone of fear.

"Wooten came from this direction. This has to be where he'd been. Where else would he have come from?" she speculated.

"That's true," Pete concurred.

She felt along the bottom of the door frame. Then she searched the ground, systematically spreading out from a circle close around the cabin to the edge of the woods.

"Maybe he keeps it with him," Pete said, "and we're wasting our time."

"We could come back later with some tools," she offered, "but you're leaving this afternoon for your trip. How can we bear the suspense of not knowing what's inside until tomorrow?" She stood up to brush herself off, and her head hit a low hanging branch of a large oak. She moved aside and scowled at the offending branch, at the same time seeing a sort of hole or pocket in the crook of it. "Wait a minute. I see something," she said. With a curious expression, she felt in the hole. Her hand touched metal. "I think I've found it!" she announced to Pete and handed him a key. "This has to be it."

He grabbed it from her hand and ran to the door. When the key fit and he turned it in the lock, he called back to her, "Right you are!" Once again he grudgingly admitted to himself that Myra Claire had proved to be an asset. He pushed open the door and they walked into the musty darkness.

Pete stood a minute, adjusting his eyes. He moved toward what appeared to be a work table in the middle of the room. There he felt around and found a lantern and some matches. "Let's see if there's kerosene in the lantern." He struck a match and lit it. The light opened up the room to reveal ropes with large hooks hanging from the ceiling and other paraphernalia for aging large game. A crude center beam extended from one end of the cabin to the other. "Know what this place is?" he said. "This is, or used to be, a hunting cabin. This is equipment used to hang a deer carcass for drying and aging." Pete shined the light around the interior and on the work table. "Everything's too clean. The lantern, the table. From the looks of the windows outside, you would think this place had been abandoned." Pete rubbed his hand across the table. "Too clean. There would be a layer of dust. I'd say it's been used recently, but not for hanging deer. It's not the season. Too warm. Most hunters wait for cooler weather when the heat and mosquitoes are gone."

"You think Wooten's a hunter?" Myra Claire said. "My uncle was a hunter. I've seen all this equipment before."

For the next ten minutes, Pete searched every corner of the cabin, determined to find some evidence linking Wooten to his pedophilia. Finding nothing, he leaned against the work table and frowned. "If Wooten is a hunter, where are the guns? Most hunters take pride in their guns. There were no guns hanging on the walls of Wooten's trailer. No guns here."

"You're assuming this is Wooten's cabin." With that statement, Myra Claire stepped over to the door and peered out, just to make sure no one was coming.

"True," Pete agreed. He walked over the dirt floor back and forth, and circled the room several times again. Finally, he threw up his hands. "There's nothing suspicious here." He went over to the work table and opened a drawer, finding various knives and tools for skinning and butchering. Using his handkerchief, he examined them one at a time. "Here's something!" he said.

Myra Claire came over to see. She looked at the knife in his hand and then at him. "Blood? But animals bleed."

"They hang them up to drain the blood, so butchering won't be so messy. I'll take this knife. A lab can determine if this is animal blood." He wrapped the knife in the handkerchief.

"Well, let's go," he said. "I don't think we're going to find anything else."

They started for the door just as it swung open and Wooten appeared in the opening.

Chapter Forty-two

"Y ou folks lost or something?" Wooten asked his two guests. Myra Claire looked startled. Pete, attempting to appear nonplussed, deadpanned.

Wooten held out his hand, "I'll take that," he said, referring to the skinning knife Pete still held.

Pete looked at the knife and slowly handed it to Wooten who dropped it on the worktable. "We were just taking a drive, exploring the countryside, you know, with my girlfriend here. We got off on this road. Not a good place to turn around. When we found this truck path we hoped it would wind around or that we would come to a place where we could get out."

"That the reason you parked your truck and broke into my cabin?" Wooten asked.

"Well, one thing kind of led to another," Pete said. "Once we stumbled upon this place it was too tempting not to look inside. We easily found the key in the crook of the branch. It seemed to invite us to open the door and come inside."

"With them keen eyes of yours I reckon you didn't see them signs that said 'no trespassin'?" Wooten said.

"We did see them," Pete admitted, "but we figured that meant hunters. There was no one around, and we thought we might find some water. We're pretty thirsty."

Wooten pulled a pack of Lucky Strike cigarettes from his pocket and started to put one in his mouth. He stopped and offered it to Myra Claire, who said, "No thanks," and then to Pete.

Pete held up the flat of his palm, declining.

Wooten proceeded to light up his cigarette. He took a deep drag, giving Myra Claire the once over as he exhaled. "You got red hair," he said, blowing out a puff of smoke. "I kinda like red hair."

Myra Claire made it obvious with her glaring frown she didn't appreciate Wooten's attention.

"I kinda think I've seen you folks visiting next door to my sister's place in Riverton. You sure got yourselves a long way from there."

"Yeah," Pete said.

"So, you found the key, you say, and let yourself in. Didn't think nothing of trespassin' on my property."

"Like I said, we figured that meant hunters."

"'No trespassin' means 'no trespassin''" Wooten declared, taking another draw on his smoke. "Well," he said on the exhale, "since you folks are visiting…you from outa town I reckon?"

Pete nodded. "You a hunter?"

Wooten made no comment. He continued smoking. Then he spoke up, "Maybe I won't press no charges, this time."

"That would be very considerate of you," Pete said. He turned to Myra Claire, putting his hand on her shoulder, pushing her toward the door. "Let's go. I've got places to be this afternoon."

"Just one problem," Wooten announced.

They stopped and Pete turned around. "What's that?"

"I got you blocked in." He laughed, showing his tobacco-stained teeth. "Didn't want no trespassers escapin', you understand. I reckon you can't leave till I move my truck." Wooten pulled another draw from his smoke. There was an awkward silence while Pete and Myra Claire held their breath. Was he going to let them go, or was he merely playing with them? Maybe he was going to kill them. Pete thought of his gun, inconvenient to get to since it was strapped to his ankle. *It's two of us and one of him. If I can distract Wooten...*

Suddenly, Wooten drew a knife from under his shirt. Pete instinctively pushed Myra Claire behind him. With one quick, smooth movement, in the blink of an eye, the knife sailed through the air across the room behind a bag of dry cement. For a moment, Pete and Myra Claire froze. Then Wooten exhaled and strolled over to the corner where the knife landed. "Got him," he proclaimed, lifting up two halves of a copperhead snake, still writhing.

Myra Claire tottered on her feet, holding onto to Pete.

After another drag on his cigarette, Wooten threw the snake out the door and motioned for them to follow him. He got into his truck. With a salute and a grin, he said, "Be seein' you folks. Oh, and would ya lock the door and put the key back where you got it?" Seconds later, Pete and Myra Claire watched his truck bounce off into the woods.

"Let's get out of here," Pete said. He locked the door, replaced it in the tree, and pulled Myra Claire toward their ride.

When they reached Burris Road, she let out a slow breath and said. "When he held up that knife, I thought I was going to be seeing Jesus and my grandma."

"He either wanted to impress us with his skill or scare the heck out of us. Maybe some of both," Pete said. "He did kill the snake. He has a sharp eye and a quick hand."

"You were very chivalrous, by the way. You thought first of protecting me, not thinking of yourself, and before you suggest it, even though I wasn't much help to you today, I'm not going to leave. It can't hurt to have another pair of eyes. You need me to watch your back. I should have been the look-out today. The place seemed so isolated. It was easy to let down our guard."

"Wooten seems to materialize out of nowhere," Pete said. He's doing a more skillful job of tracking us than I am of him. Anyway, by the time you would have seen him coming, we couldn't have gotten out in time. I learned better from my daddy to be more aware and cautious. I must be slipping."

For the next few minutes they both got lost in their own thoughts. With mixed emotions Pete anticipated his meeting with Jennings later in the afternoon. It was satisfying in the sense that he could soon go home, and terrifying at the same time. He couldn't leave Riverton until Farley had been taken care of. Everybody who knew Pete at all, knew he hated Farley. He realized he should have been more discreet. That was hindsight. At first he meant to keep this interlude in Riverton a secret when he expected to deliver the blood money here. Now that was no longer a concern. Even though he didn't know where yet, it wouldn't be Riverton. He would insist on that. Trying to save Frannie gave him an alibi. There were witnesses to his being here, so when Farley disappeared or whatever was going to happen to him, Pete would not be a suspect. Then he would go home, as shocked as everyone else about Farley's misfortune. Sometimes he wished there was some other choice, but there wasn't. He couldn't pretend certain things had never taken place and just try to live a normal life. For the present, so that he could get on his way, he needed to get Myra Claire back to the college

"Other than Robert, did you have other siblings?" Myra Claire asked.

Pete came out of his reverie. He considered her question, realizing she sensed his low mood and was trying to distract him. "My brother Johnny got killed in a knife fight at a place you've never been I'll bet, the Bloody Bucket. It wasn't even his fight. He just happened to be in the wrong place at the wrong time. That was before my daddy died, before his whiskey car flipped over and rolled down an embankment.

Eugenia had three other sons, but they died young. I don't remember them."

"Why do you call her Eugenia?" Myra Claire asked.

"I can't call her "momma," not anymore, because she let Farley Oaks come into our home after my daddy died. She betrayed us. I could have run the farm and the whiskey business. I knew how my daddy did everything. After all, I had watched him work since I was old enough to follow him around. But no, she said I had to go to school and she let Farley put his brother Freddie in charge, and she let Farley into our home. My daddy didn't dislike many people, but when he was alive, he would not let Farley onto our property because he could see into creeps like him. He knew Farley wasn't what most folks believed he was." Pete swallowed. He realized he'd said too much. These matters were private, and yet he couldn't seem to stop the flood of words.

"How old were you at the time of your daddy's accident?"

"Fourteen, going on fifteen."

"I can see why your momma said you had to go to school. You were too young to quit school."

"I'd already had all the school I needed. I never wanted to do anything else but run the farm just like daddy did. Eugenia could have said it was a family hardship."

"The illegal whiskey business is dying out. It's not like it was in your daddy's day."

"There will always be a demand for Turner moonshine. My daddy made it then, and now my uncle Jake makes a superior product and sells it for less because they don't have to pass on to the customer the unfair government tax."

They rode in silence for a while, then Pete said, "I had a sister, you know?"

"No, I didn't. I don't think Robert ever mentioned her."

"Yeah. She died too."

"Pete I'm so sorry. I'm trying to make you feel better and I've asked the wrong questions. You've had a lot of tragedy in your life, a lot to deal with at a young age."

"Farley Oaks killed her." *I shouldn't have said that! I'm saying too much! Why do I need her approval? What do I care what she thinks?*

She jerked around to face Pete. "What? How could that be true?"

"You mean how could he be walking around free if he killed my sister? You tell me."

"Was there an investigation into your sister's death?"

"No. The sheriff, Sheriff Money's father-in-law, said it was suicide, but Farley Oaks killed her as sure as if he put the rope around her neck."

"Oh," Myra Claire said.

Pete drove the next mile without speaking, embarrassed he had told her these things.

When he pulled in at the college, Myra Claire turned to him. "Farley did something awful to your sister, didn't he? I remember our conversation about justice by the law. This terrible thing that happened to your sister, that's why you say you have no confidence in due process. It may not be perfect, but as far back as the Greek and Roman civilizations, men came to realize that law beats getting justice by revenge." Myra Claire eyes were wide with alarm. "What are you planning, Pete? What is this business in Riverton you keep mentioning? You intend to get your own justice, don't you?"

"No. Of course not. Don't try to figure it out, Myra Claire. It's not your concern."

She got out without waiting for Pete to come around to open her door. Leaning toward him, her eyes wide with passion and worry, she said, "Let it go Pete. Nothing you do to Farley will bring your sister back. You think revenge will bring you peace? It won't. You need to let it go. Forgive your uncle. There is a higher justice that won't fail you if man's does. If you could just believe it!"

"Forgive? Are you crazy? He killed my little sister, a beautiful girl who could sing like an angel, and she's dead in the cold, hard ground while my uncle is alive and prospering, an upstanding citizen in the community. Ha!" Pete looked ready to spit. "Did your law fix that? No! And what of divine justice? Is there any divine justice in that? You're right about me; if I want justice, I have to make my own."

"Is it justice you want or revenge because *your pride* is hurt over the insult you feel *you've* suffered? Does it gall you because he's alive and prospering? Don't you see that hate and unforgiveness will destroy you? Let it go, Pete. Hate and unforgiveness are deadly. Think about how you have been a slave to hate and unforgiveness all these years, separated from your home, your family. If Farley Oaks caused you pain years ago, he's still doing it and you're letting him! Even if you have some dire revenge in mind, you will bring disaster down on yourself, Pete. Ask God to help you forgive and He will."

Myra Claire turned and ran across the parking lot to her entrance.

Pete sat in the car, fuming at her last remark, fuming at himself for opening himself up to her, allowing her to judge him, wondering what had come over him to practically tell her what he was about to do. *Nobody will be able to prove I'm involved, but she'll know.*

Chapter Forty-three

As soon as Wooten left the cabin, he drove to his trailer and watched to see the green truck roll by in a cloud of dust as Pete and Myra Claire headed for the highway. Then he pulled out and drove over to old James's shack. He said to himself, "I can play your game of switcharoo, Turner." When the grey-haired Negro came out, Wooten pointed to a beat-up brown sedan. He said to James, "I'm gonna leave the flatbed here and take your car for a spell. Key's in the truck." James nodded and went inside to get the key to the sedan. Wooten got his toolbox from the truck. When James came out and handed the key to Wooten, he threw the toolbox in the back floorboard, got in the car, and drove off.

Before making the call to report Turner for bootlegging, he had to find out what was up with Turner and the green truck. "Did he trade the Ford or just use a borrowed truck to spy on me?" he muttered. Unsure whether Pete had gone to the motel or directly to the brat's house, he drove first through the parking lot at the Shady Lawn. He spotted the Ford. At the time Pete was still in Harvey's pickup taking Myra Claire to her dorm room at the college. "Well, he hasn't traded it. He was trying' to fool me so's he could spy on me. Guess I messed him up." He laughed. Then he frowned. "So, where's he now?" Wooten parked on the street a hundred feet from the entrance and waited to see if Pete would come. He didn't want to report Turner's bootlegging while the Ford was parked at the Shady Lawn. It had to appear he was in the process of transporting it. Then the cops would pull him over, discover the moonshine and Turner would be permanently out of the way. But how long was Turner gonna use the green truck? He let loose a string of expletives.

He was making up his mind to go on to Jenny's when the green pickup pulled into the lot and drove around to the back of the motel. A few minutes later, Turner came striding to the front to enter his room. "So, now how long's he gonna be?" He had no idea whether Turner was in for the day, but he doubted it. It was only twelve noon. Soon he bet he'd be heading to the brat's or to get the flower girl wherever she was. He meant to be tailing Turner in the Ford when he saw with his own eyes the Riverton cops pull him over. As time passed without any sign of him, Wooten would catch himself nodding off. He'd shake himself awake, smoke a cigarette, and then dose off again. "Old James ain't got a radio in this beat up jalopy to keep me from dozing."

Finally, Turner emerged from his room. "Now get the Ford, Turner. Get the Ford." To Wooten's satisfaction, Pete got in the Ford and drove away in it. Wooten rubbed his hands in glee and followed. "I've got you now! Let's see if he's going' to babysit the kid. If so, I gotta wait 'til he leaves later this evening to call the cops." Much to Wooten's surprise, Pete turned in the opposite direction from Frannie's side of town, going west on route 29. "This is perfect! I'm gonna catch this fish now!"

At the first gas station where he saw a phone booth, Wooten jumped out and called the Riverton Police Station. He said, "You want to catch a bootlegger? You better send out an alert to grab him. He's driving' west on route 29 in a '40 Ford, North Carolina license plate E-26-915. There's a false back seat with a stash of illegal whiskey."

"Do you want to give your name, sir?"

"No." And Wooten hung u

The officer at the station put down the phone. Looking at the information he'd written down he said to no one in particular, "I bet that's that same informant that reported Turner had abducted the little Gregg girl. That proved to be somebody's idea of a joke, probably this fellow's, later the girl's daddy confirmed it was a false report."

He took the information to his supervisor anyway. When he showed it to him, the supervisor crumple the paper and shook his head. "This fellow's a nut. We ought to lock *him* up."

After making the call, Wooten felt exhilarated. With a sense of expectation, he ran to get back in the car and drove west to catch up with Turner. He wanted to see when the cops pulled him over, so that he could enjoy the moment when they slapped on the handcuffs and took him away. Once Turner was under lock and key, he could get down to business with the kid. He soon caught up to the Ford and trailed it for two miles. At last he saw a Riverton black and white cop car pulling out from a small grocery store onto the highway. He began pounding the steering wheel with excitement as he watched the car move in behind Turner. "Those boys are on the ball!" Wooten exclaimed. "Now do your job boys!" He expected the officer to turn on his red light and pull Turner over any second, but instead, after the patrol car trailed a half a mile behind Turner, it exited onto a secondary road.

Screaming out a string of expletives, Wooten kept trailing. In another three miles Turner pulled onto Route 58. "Now where's he going?" He followed Turner another few miles without seeing a single cop car. When Turner passed by the turn off to Route 41, they were way beyond Riverton jurisdiction. "He'll be in Carterville before long!"

Further down the highway, Pete pulled into the parking lot of a mom and pop store, busy with vehicles coming and going. He pulled around the back and Wooten followed in James's brown sedan. Wooten watched Pete get out, go to the front and go inside. "No Riverton police are going to get him way off here." He muttered more curses. "But I'm not out of ideas." He hurried out of the car and grabbed a screw driver from his toolbox. When he could scoot in behind Turner's Ford without being seen, he crouched down and unscrewed the license tag. "Now that ought to get him stopped. It's not sure fire. They might not look for moonshine." He threw the plate in his borrowed car and pulled off to the side to watch for Turner. "If he sees the tag's gone, I might as well give it up for today."

Pete came back to the Ford with an RC Cola and a sandwich. Without noticing the missing tag, he got in and turned back onto Route 58. Wooten followed. "If the cops don't see the missing plate...the mountain's not far. I'll cut his brake line when he stops again. That'll fix him, but it's not my preference. It'd be better for the cops to put him away. Might get messy otherwise."

With a worried expression, Wooten lit up a cigarette and followed Pete for another few miles. He finished his smoke. As he threw the stub out the window, he saw a Carterville patrol in his side mirror. It was coming from behind around a bend. Wooten slowed down and the patrol car passed him. It pulled in behind the Ford and trailed for half a mile. Just as it appeared to Wooten the cops were going to go around Turner, they pulled back behind him and sounded their siren. "Get him!," Wooten yelled.

Pete heard the siren behind him. In his rear view mirror he saw the Carterville patrol car with the cherry red light on top. He slowed down and pulled over to the side. Wooten pulled apace down the road and turned into a tire and auto parking lot where he could see what happened next.

"I wasn't speeding and I'm not hauling. Now what's this about?" Pete huffed, watching two officers stroll up to his window. A tall blond officer spoke, "Mr. Turner, did you know you're missing a tag on the back?"

Chapter Forty-three

"No, Sir."

"Can I see your license?"

Pete handed it out the window.

The officer studied the license. "Says here Wilkes County." The officer looked back at Pete. "Can't drive this vehicle without a proper tag."

"When I left Riverton where I've been on business for the last week, the tag was on the car," Pete said. "I've got an important appointment this afternoon."

"Sorry for the inconvenience, but the vehicle can't be driven without a tag. I'll have to ask you to drive it over to the police station. You can call someone to pick you up there."

Pete put his hand to his head. He'd have to call Jennings to come get him, if he could even reach him.

The blond officer continued in a friendly manner, his brow creased in sympathy with Pete's dilemma. "This '40 Ford's been a popular model, especially up in Wilkes with bootleggers. We don't see much bootlegging around here anymore. Those boys up in Wilkes still making it?"

Pete didn't respond. He was obviously distracted, running his hands through his hair.

The other officer was a short, dark haired man with a scar down one side of his face. "Officer Watson asked you a question," he said. "Maybe we ought to take a look."

The blond officer furrowed his brow again, studying Pete with a sympathetic expression. "You said you came here from Riverton."

Pete muttered under his breath, "These fellows are looking for something to do. Maybe they've got all day to chat, but I need to be on my way."

"What was that?" the short fellow asked, tauntingly. "How about you step out of the vehicle."

Giving the officer an irritated stare, Pete complied.

The short officer stuck his head inside on the driver's side and looked around. Then he walked around to the passenger side and looked in the back. He bent down and began sniffing where Wooten had thrown the rag he'd used to clean up the spill from the broken Mason jar. The officer drew back and stood up. "Watson, what do you make of that smell?"

Pete hadn't taken the time to try to clean up the odor from what he'd assumed was Frannie's bug spray. He'd either been using Harvey's truck, or his mind had been too absorbed with other matters to worry about it, and he'd simply ignored it.

Watson stuck his head in the Ford, sniffed and turned back to Pete, "What's that smell?"

"Bug spray. I don't know," Pete said.

"You don't know?"

"I didn't spill it."

Watson turned to his partner. "What do you suppose, Smitty?"

Smitty turned to Pete. "You're not hauling any of that Wilkes County moonshine in this '40 Ford are you, fella?"

"No," Pete answered with confidence, glad he was clean.

Smitty said, "The smell's here in the back floorboard. No secret tank under here is there?" He bent down and looked underneath the Ford. Finding no secret tank, he took another look inside the car. Then he went around and lifted the trunk lid. "Nothing back here." He closed the lid. "What about inside that back seat? You got one of those hidden compartments under there?"

Pete let out a sigh of frustration. "There is a secret compartment, but nothing's in it."

Smitty gave Pete a beckoning sign with his index finger. "Open it," he ordered.

Pete snorted at the unnecessary harassment, but willing for the search to be over so he could be on his way, Pete moved to comply. With Smitty watching from the other side, Pete pulled open the top of the seat.

"Bingo!" Smitty exclaimed.

Pete was overwhelmed by the sight of the Mason jars. His chest contracted like a clinched fist. He reared back from the Ford and declared, "It's not mine. I've been set up, and I know who did it!"

Officer Watson motioned Pete aside and took another look. Smitty removed the case with the Mason jars. He unscrewed one of the lids, sniffed the contents, and passed it to the Watson. "Bug spray, huh? Smells like booze to me." Watson sniffed and nodded his agreement.

Officer Watson, looking chagrined, said, "I'm gonna to have to take you in." He unhooked the cuffs from his belt. "Mr. Turner, let me have your keys. We're taking you in for carrying illegal whiskey."

"It's not mine. I've never seen it before," Pete insisted.

"Tell it to the Federal marshal, Smitty said.

Smitty frisked Pete and discovered the gun strapped to his ankle. He told Pete to hand it over.

"I'm carrying that legally," Pete said and handed the weapon to the officer.

Officer Watson snapped the handcuffs on Pete.

Pete had no choice but to endure the indignity.

All of this Wooten watched from the window of the brown sedan. He could hardly control his enthusiasm as he watched the short cop put Turner in the back of the patrol car drive off with him. "Have a nice stay!" he shouted. The blond cop got in Pete's Ford and drove off in it. Wooten headed back to Riverton. He laughed hysterically for half a mile. Then he wiped the tears from his eyes and gleefully attempted singing his own version of *Don't Fence Me In*, enjoying how Turner was just that, fenced in and out of his way.

The Carterville jail was a two-story, square brick building typical of small towns. The officer took Pete through a back door. The Carterville sheriff was a big man with broad shoulders and a wide girth that dwarfed the wooden desk where he sat, his large, round head bent over some paper work. Four front windows were open, and a fan rotating on a pole whirred quietly. A wooden nameplate on his desk said "Sheriff William Patton." He looked up when Smitty brought Pete in and explained the arrest.

"So you hauling moonshine, boy? You from Wilkes?" Patton asked in his slow mountain drawl.

Pete didn't comment.

"We're pretty tough on bootleggers around here. Those that produce and distribute illegal whiskey, we put in prison."

"The whiskey's not mine. I didn't know anything about it. It would be an insult to the Turner name to produce that rotten stuff."

"How do you know so much about it if you didn't make it?"

"I could smell it. Besides I know how it got in my car."

"Yes. You said you were set up."

"That's the truth, and by the way, I wouldn't drink any of it. It'll probably corrode your insides. At best it'll make you real sick."

Sheriff Patton gave Pete an amused look. "You need to make a phone call?"

"What are you going to do with me?" Pete said.

"Monday morning I'll turn you over to the Federal marshal. You can tell him your story. Due process, that's what you'll get here."

"My brother's a lawyer," Pete said.

"That so? You're free to give him a call, but it won't do you much good because my boys caught you red handed."

Pete declined to make the call. He didn't want Robert asking questions, what he was doing in Carterville and whose moonshine was it if it wasn't Jake's? Pete wasn't sure he could tell a face-to-face lie to his brother if he should decide to come to Carterville. Over the phone it was hard enough. Besides, Pete didn't have time for due process. He had to get out now. His only hope was persuasion or bribery, or whatever worked.

The sheriff took Pete down some stairs. He took out his keys, unlocked the door to one of the unoccupied cells, and motioned for Pete to enter. There were a total of four cells, three of them empty. The one other prisoner appeared to be sleeping on his cot.

Pete hesitated. Once that door closed behind him, he would miss his appointment to meet Jennings. Finally, he'd gotten everything arranged to get the money from Jennings so that he could deliver it once he received the phone call telling him where to take it. While the first appointment had been a ruse set up by Salvino, this time if he dropped the ball, it would make him look unreliable to Angel and the people he dealt with. Desperate, he turned his jailer. "Look. I'm sure you're a reasonable man. I told you somebody planted that whiskey in my car."

"Not my decision," Patton said. "You were caught with the booze in your possession. Not up to me."

"Somebody set me up! He's a pedophile and I'm trying to keep him from hurting this little girl. If you don't let me go, she could die."

"Tell it to the marshal."

"When will that be?"

"Can't say. Not before Monday."

Pete ran his hand through his hair. "That may be too late."

"Don't be stalling. Get in," he barked.

Clinching his jaw, Pete walked into the cell.

The iron clanged when the door slammed. The sheriff locked it and turned to go.

Pete whipped around and grabbing the cell bars, he called after him, "That little girl could die!"

"You got a good story there," Patton said. He shook his head and walked away.

In the cell there was a small cot and a bucket. Pete looked up at the one tiny, barred window. Then he dropped on the side of the cot, head in hands. He told himself, "Think. You've got to get out of here. Wooten set this up. Now with me out of the way, he'll get Frannie. It'll be a cinch for him." He began to pace in the confined space. "Myra could be in danger as well." He ran his hand over his hair. "And the meeting with Jennings, if I miss that, with Jennings I can reschedule, but if I miss the phone call about where to take the money, I won't get another chance." Pete walked over to the bars and looked out. There was no one around. "I have to get out of here!" He continued to run his hands over his hair. "Frannie. She's brought me nothing but bad luck because I stopped to be the Good Samaritan. What about this divine justice Myra talks about? I don't see any."

In the afternoon, Pete heard the sheriff rattling his keys. He jumped up from the cot and looked out of his bars. He was unlocking the door to another cell. "Come on, Billy," he said. "Your brother's here to take you home." Pete couldn't see, but he heard the cell door slam shut and the scuffle of shoes going down the short hall. He went back to his cot. He sat there for ten minutes. Then he got up and called for the sheriff. There was no answer. He pounded the bars until his hands were bruised, but no one came.

Sunday morning, Pete heard the jingle of keys. One of the officers was bringing him some scrambled eggs, toast and orange juice for breakfast. Pete noted the ashen color of his face. "You don't look so good," Pete said, but the man gave him the food without commenting.

After a while, Pete heard the keys again. Like a nervous cat, he jumped up to try to see through the bars. Pete called out, "That you Sheriff Patton?"

Patton strolled over to Pete's cell. "What you want?"

"I could use some coffee."

He nodded approval.

"Your boys didn't get into that moonshine now did they, Sheriff? The one brought my breakfast looked kinda grey. If they smell like bleach, you know they've been some kind of sick. I warned you it was bad stuff."

Patton eyed Pete curiously. While Pete had his attention, he said, "I didn't make that stuff. I told you I was set up, but I've got connections. I can get you some 90 proof. I don't drink it, but people tell me it goes down like water."

"You said you don't drink it. If it's so good, how come?"

"Moonshiners don't drink their product. Too dangerous. They have to have a clear head all the time."

"I've seen moonshiners that liked their product just fine."

"Not the ones that produce the good stuff. I bet you've never tasted whiskey so smooth that it goes down like water, now have you?"

"Ninety proof, huh? How do I know you're not lying? How do I know if I let you go, I won't ever see any 90 proof?"

"Check me out."

The sheriff shook his head. Pete didn't know what that meant. When he walked away, Pete sighed and went back to his cot and waited.

About noon the sheriff came back to put a drunk in the cell next to Pete. The door slammed and Pete rushed to the bars. "Say Sheriff, did you check me out?"

He sauntered over. "Ninety proof, huh?"

"I can get it. A whole case."

"I talked to Sheriff Money in Wilkes."

Pete held his breath. Sheriff Money didn't particularly like him.

"He knows you Turners. Big moonshine family from way back, he says. Your old man killed in car crash trying to outrun the Feds. Too bad."

Pete maintained a deadpan expression while the sheriff with narrowed, intent eyes and a pondering expression studied him.

"I've got to say one thing you told the truth about. I haven't got a man can hardly move this morning. They all sick as dogs, moaning and cussing."

"I told you the truth about everything. Somebody set me up, somebody who wants me in jail and out of his way so he can molest a little eleven year old girl." Even as Pete said the word 'molest,' the impact almost took his breath. He had used Frannie's danger to get the sheriff's ear. Other times he had seen it as an inconvenience, but for the moment, he truly felt concern for her, knowing Wooten's intention in getting him jailed was to have a clear path to her. Now it might be too late to save her.

"Money tells me you've got connections. You're some big shot's nephew, he says. Farley Oaks. Says Oaks is a big man around your parts. Lot of influence." The sheriff stood, scratching his forehead, and continuing to scrutinize Pete.

Pete held his breath, trying to figure where this speech was headed.

"So you making stuff that's 90 proof?"

Pete gripped the bars. "Not me, but I can get it."

Patton rattled his keys. "That right? Well, now, about that little girl, the proper authorities need to be involved." He unlocked the cell and opened the door.

Is he letting me go, or does he have the feds waiting in the next room?

"Of course, you've got to have evidence against the man you're accusing. Innocent until proven guilty. It's the law. Come on to the desk and get your personal belongings."

With his heart racing, Pete followed him to the desk. He was still wondering whether the sheriff was mocking him, or was he really going to release him. However, he handed him his watch, his keys, pocket change and his gun. "You got a temporary tag on that Ford," he said. Then he offered his hand. Pete shook it. He marveled at this good fortune which he apparently owed to Farley's admired reputation, the only time his uncle's reputation had proved advantageous.

"Don't be trying to get that bad guy on your own, and don't you forget about that 90 proof. My men will be pleased to get it."

"Thanks, Sheriff. You can count on it."

"Good luck, now."

Pete was out the door in a hurry.

Now that he had been released, he faced a dilemma. He debated with himself. "I should go straight to the Greggs because I know Wooten is ready to move on Frannie. I care about Frannie and Myra, but what am I going to do about getting the money? I can't be in two places at once. I have to be ready with the money when I get the call."

Impulsively, he started in the direction of Roanoke, knowing there was something out of kilter about his reasoning because he felt like he'd swallowed a lump of tar. To feel better about himself, he stopped as soon as he saw a gas station with a phone booth out front. He surmised that Jennings had already gone back to Wilkes since Pete didn't show on Saturday evening at the Bentley dirt track. So, he first tried Jennings' landlady. When she answered, she told Pete that Jennings had left a message for him. "He said call the number he gave you."

"The Roanoke number?" Pete wanted to be sure he'd heard right.

"He just said tell him to call the number he gave you," she said.

Pete hung up and dialed the number.

When Pete heard Jennings' voice he asked, "You still in Roanoke?"

"Still in Roanoke, waiting on you."

"I thought you'd be long gone."

"You just caught me. I'd given up, wondering if those Mafia guys was holdin' you someplace. Where you been?"

"It's a long story."

Jennings said irritably, "It always is. I don't like having to keep up with all this money."

"I'm in Carterville right now."

"What you doing in Carterville? I know–it's a long story."

"There's a dirt track close to Galax. I think it's called 'Rudy's.' Meet me at the track in about two hours. It's a small one, but at the stand where you pay to get in, look for me close to that."

Jennings said he'd be there.

Pete hung up and leaned his head against the glass, his mind replaying the past twenty-four hours. *This time Farley's reputation was my get-out- of- jail-free card. Thanks to that, I can get the money that will pay for his demise. That's destiny.*

Next he called the Greggs. No one answered. *It's Sunday. Guess they're in church.* He called Harvey at the Shady Lawn. "Can you get a message to Myra at the college?"

"Sure thing."

"Tell her to be extra careful and to keep Frannie close. Wooten is about to make his move. Tell her I'll be back this evening. I'll see her at the porch. She'll know what I mean."

Chapter Forty-four

At Rudy's dirt track outside Galax, Jennings handed Pete the envelope from Robert. The exchange was brief. Pete ignored his friend's sullen manner and clipped words. He understood his delay had caused Jennings to wait around a whole twenty-four hours, restless and anxious with concern for his welfare. That Pete continued to offer no explanation did not assuage Jennings' irritation in the least, Pete realized, but he knew Jennings would get over it. He watched him spin away on two wheels, tires squealing and dust flying.

Pete hid the envelope behind a special panel in the Ford created especially for holding the bootlegger's profits, then he got back on Route 58 to head back to Riverton and wait for the all-important phone call from the contact.

The drive back to Carterville proved uneventful. Tall green pines and leafy oaks formed a corridor along the highway, shielding him from the mid afternoon sun. Although he felt the urge to step hard on the gas because he was anxious to know what was happening with Frannie, he dared not press his luck, but drove just under the speed limit. He'd had enough of dealing with sheriffs and jails. He also kept an eye out for any suspicious vehicle that might be tailing him. He wasn't putting anything past Wooten, although Pete was counting on Wooten's believing that he was languishing

behind bars in the Carterville jail. He smirked at the thought.
He turned on the radio and sang along with Elvis Pressley's
You Ain't Nothin' but a Hound Dog. He lost the station as
Teresa Brewer pumped out *Let Me Go Lover*.

Coming into the Carterville business district and passing
by the jail, he felt anxious to get beyond Sheriff Patton's
jurisdiction. Just before leaving the city limits he was about
to relax when a Carterville patrol car pulled in behind him.
He would almost swear it was that cop, Smitty behind the
wheel. There was no siren or red light, but the car stayed on
his tail for another mile. Pete began to sweat. Soon he was
out of the Carterville jurisdiction, but the car was still behind
him. Since he was accustomed to operating just outside the
margin of the law, he had reason to always be suspicious of
authority. He began to sweat. As soon as he spotted a short
order drive-in, he turned off the highway. The patrol car
did not follow him and Pete breathed a sigh of relief. With
the smells of food drifting toward him, he realized he was
hungry. He hadn't eaten since having a very bland breakfast
in the jail.

The place where he stopped was unusual. With tall grey
turrets, it was named "The Castle." Cars and pickups rolled
into the parking lot. Some drivers were there to get food.
Others were merely cruising through to get attention from
the females. The combination created a bustle of traffic and
congestion.

A slight brunette about twenty, wearing knee length shorts
and black and white saddle oxfords, came to his window. He
ordered a Castle burger and some fries. The establishment
didn't offer RC cola, so he settled for a root beer. While he
waited, now that he had his money from Robert in hand, he
thought he'd better check on Frannie and Myra Claire as
soon as he finished eating. At least he had sent Myra Claire
a message through Harvey. Just the same, he would like to
know the girls were safe.

The waitress brought a tray of food and attached it to his window. He paid her and ate quickly, putting aside the empty feeling that came to mind when he remembered the pleasure of Myra Claire's company that he had enjoyed lately. Despite his morning victory persuading the sheriff to release him, the old heaviness descended on him like a cloud. Certainly, aloneness was his norm.

There was a phone booth on the edge of the lot, but with all the traffic, it was too noisy here. He drove to the first gas station far enough from Carterville to cause him no concern and dialed the Greggs. Bill Gregg answered. "Bill, this is Pete Turner. Everybody okay?"

Bill let out a long, emotional sigh. "Dead!"

Pete nearly dropped the phone. "What? Who's dead? Frannie? Tell me it's not Frannie!" Pete's heart sank into his stomach. He could barely stand on his feet.

"Oh, she's all upset. I reckon those Pruitts will hold us responsible. Even though it was just a mongrel."

"What?" Pete demanded. "What are you talking about?"

"That mongrel cat."

"Cat?" Pete said. "The cat's dead, but Frannie, she's okay?"

"Well, no."

"What do you mean 'no'? What's happened to Frannie?"

"She's not stopped moping and sniffling since she learned about the stupid cat."

"That's all? How about Myra Claire?"

"That Myra Claire, she's a nice girl. She took it pretty hard herself."

"Let me talk to her," Pete said.

When she came to the phone, Pete asked, "What's going on?"

"Wooten knows about me," she said. "It was awful. I stayed at the college this morning while the Greggs went to church. I didn't want to impose, and their church is more formal than I'm used to. Then, this afternoon, I came out to my car to drive over here. Sylvester, poor Sylvester..." Myra Claire stopped to clear the catch in her throat. "I could hardly believe my eyes. At first I couldn't imagine what was hanging from my antenna. It was Sylvester, hanging by…" She swallowed. "He was hanging by his neck. It was shocking. It was awful. Frannie's taking it pretty hard. She feels responsible."

"She shouldn't. There's no way she could have prevented it."

"I told her that, but it hasn't helped her feel any better."

"So, Wooten not only knows your car, but where you're staying. Is this enough to convince you to leave as soon as you can?"

"Not a chance. Wooten is demented. I feel sorry for him, but he must be stopped before he takes his meanness out on Frannie instead of a cat. It makes you wonder what happens to a person to make him so filled with anger and hate, but then I guess you could answer that question."

"I'm on my way," Pete said, relieved it was just a dead cat they were all concerned about.

He reached Riverton, thinking about how to keep Wooten in the dark concerning his release from the Carterville jail. If he drove the Ford and Wooten caught sight of it, he would know Pete was free. Wooten evidently now knew both his and Myra Clair's cars and that they parked them on Maple Street. He'd seen Harvey's green truck when he caught them snooping at the hunting cabin. Wooten always managed to be more aware of their comings and goings than they were of his. They rarely saw his vehicles, yet he seemed to show up out of nowhere. Pete admonished himself that he should have been more careful. Then he blamed his carelessness on Myra Claire. It was cumbersome having to work with another person. Though, with his usual ambivalence, he had to admit, she had been helpful at times.

He stopped first at the Shady Lawn to see Harvey. The old man was manning the desk. "Where's Harvey?" Pete asked.

"Dunno," the old fellow said without putting his paper down.

Pete knew better than to persist. He wouldn't get a straight answer. He walked back outside and sprinted around to the back of the motel. He found Harvey and his wife sitting in two wooden outdoor chairs near a bed of canna lilies. They appeared to be relaxing and enjoying the quiet. Pete hurried toward them. His gait and body language indicated he had serious purpose on his mind.

Harvey greeted Pete and introduced him to his wife, Margaret, a well preserved, petite woman with a pleasant face. Pete judged her to be around fifty. "Something I can do for you?" Harvey asked.

"You have a car I could borrow tonight? In fact, I need to hide mine for a few days."

Harvey pointed to a blue '53 Chevy with a white top. "That's mine, if it's not against your principles to drive a Chevy rather than a Ford."

"It is," Pete said, "but this time I can't be choosy."

Harvey reached in his pocket and pulled out some keys. He took one from the ring and handed it to Pete. In exchange, Pete gave his the keys to the Ford. "I'll take your Ford to my friend's used car lot and park it there."

"What will you drive?" Pete asked.

"I've got the truck."

"That will be a big help. Thanks," he said.

"Anything I can do to for that little girl."

Pete nodded, turned and sprinted to the blue vehicle.

On the way to meet Myra Claire at the porch, he passed the deserted gas station and noted that the entire episode in which he was presently entangled had begun at this place. He knew the very spot where Frannie had dashed out of nowhere in front of his car only a few evenings ago, yet it seemed like months. He remembered the fear and aggravation, fear because he almost hit her, aggravation because he had to stop and get involved in her situation. Now he noted with consternation, the meeting at the marina that he was so agitated over missing, had never existed, at least none Angel knew anything about. *Just where is that shyster Salvino now? I'd love to get my hands on him!* As he neared Maple Street he decided to find a new parking place, since he knew by now that Wooten was sharp enough to take notice that the blue Chevy wasn't normally parked there. Right away he might get suspicious. Pete didn't want to give him any cause to think he was anywhere but the Carterville jail. *This cat and mouse game is getting tedious. It's got to end soon.*

As he drove past the Greggs' apartment, he remembered the brick school across from the Corner Market and went there. He pulled around the back near the ball field, got out, and locked the door. Keeping to the shadows, he hurried to the Pruitt porch.

He got there, and found Myra alone, trying to read a book with the illumination from the flashlight he had left with her on Friday night when they had investigated the Daniels's garage. She put down the book and switched off the light.

"You'll ruin your eyes like that," he said, trying to get off to a friendly start. She smiled slightly. He asked how things had gone for her, other than the bad experience with the cat. She said "uneventful." It was becoming obvious to him that her usual sparkle was replaced by a stiff reserve, all because of his stupid blabbing when he took her back to the college on Saturday after their encounter with Wooten at the cabin. In spite of her coolness, he gave her a summary of his overnight stay in the Carterville jail. "I'm planning to be invisible so Wooten won't know I'm on the loose again. You can bet he's congratulating himself that he figured out such a cunning device to get me out of his way, and he'll be making a bold move any time now. Frannie's got to be extra cautious, and we have to drum that into her."

Myra listened attentively, but asked no questions and made no comments. He tried to make further conversation, but she wouldn't lighten up. It annoyed him. He'd spent time alone in the jail and on the road, and he had been looking forward to seeing her. If she could just mind her own business and not try to preach at him, they could pass the time pleasantly.

Finally, Myra said she was going back to the college. He offered to follow her there, but she refused, telling him he needed to stay and keep guard over Frannie. Not willing for her to walk alone in the dark alley, he insisted on accompanying her to her car. She let him come as far as the edge of Maple Street. "Don't take any chance being seen. Wooten might be watching my car. You don't want him to see you."

"I'll stand right here in the dark until I see you drive off," Pete said.

"There's one more thing," Myra added. "I think it's time we should go to the police. I need to leave and get out of your hair. As you have made the point, I've done what you asked me here to do. I have to leave anyway to get ready to go back to my teaching job. And you'll be leaving too. We can't just abandon Frannie without doing our best to make her safe."

"The problem with going to the police is what will we tell them, that we think Wooten is her abductor and the one who's stalking her? What proof do we have, the word of an eleven year old who says Wooten *smells* like the man who abducted her? That won't get much action from the police. Even her own parents believe the abductor is a product of Frannie's overactive imagination."

"But you're an adult. You can tell them what happened at the fair."

"Yes, I can do that, but I can't prove that Wooten was the clown. Wooten isn't stupid. In fact he's smarter than I'd like to think. We have nothing solid to identify him as Frannie's abductor."

Myra gave a deep sigh.

"But I do have the perfect solution," Pete said. "There's one more thing you can do and again, it involves Bill Gregg. You need to convince Bill and Diane to send Frannie to her grandma's for an indefinite length of time. Tell them to let her start school there. That's what Frannie wants to do anyway."

"Me? You want me to convince them?"

"If anybody can persuade them, you can. They like you. They might listen to you."

Myra made a circle in the dirt with her foot. "I'm going to pray about this," she said.

Pete's brow furrowed. "Is that all?"

Myra huffed. She gave him an impatient look, pursing her lips. Then she said, "I'm going to pray that God will soften their hearts, make them realize this is the best thing for Frannie right now. I'm going to pray because Bill is so dead set against it and it's going to take a miracle."

"But you will talk to him, to Gregg, as well as..." Pete pointed up. "As well as the Man up there?"

"If the Holy Spirit gives me the go-ahead."

"Time is of the essence."

"I know, but God's never late. We just need to trust Him."

"Right" Pete said, looking down. He knew it wasn't the time to roll his eyes and get sarcastic.

Myra turned toward her car. He watched until she drove away.

Chapter Forty-five

After Pete saw Myra Claire get to her Buick and drive off, he went back to his guard post on the porch. Sitting in the swing, he was getting a faint whiff of her flowery scent. He got up and moved to one of the rockers. Without anyone to talk to, he propped his feet up on the porch railing and leaned his head back. He was vaguely aware of a rising wind and the frenzied flapping of a wire hanging from the ceiling brace. At one time it must have dangled a wind chime or some other ornament, but now it whirled and danced naked in the breeze of a brewing summer storm. Pete's thoughts drifted off to his return home. Would the Turner farm be sold and in the hands of Farley's heirs. Would the heirs sell the farm back to Pete? Those Oaks were stupid and mean, all of them. Farley had been the only one to better himself, at least on the outside. He'd made a lot of money. On the inside, Pete knew he was rotten to the core just like all the rest of them. Before long he caught himself nodding off. Then he heard footsteps coming up on the porch. He shook himself awake.

Bill Gregg's appearance surprised him. Except for the phone conversation about the dead cat, he hadn't seen nor heard from him since he and Myra Claire left the Gregg apartment on Thursday evening. Pete surveyed him with concern. Gregg didn't say anything for a few minutes. He just sat in the other rocker, the one Sylvester had preferred, and stared into the dark.

Pete decided to break the silence. "By the way, you should get the Pruitts to have that branch on the chinaberry tree cut back, the one too close to Frannie's bedroom window. Anybody could get in just like Frannie does."

"Yeah, how much you think that would cost?" Gregg said. "The rent here's high enough, but you wouldn't know anything about that, being a single guy."

"I told Frannie to always lock and close her window. Really, she should keep it that way and go and come through the front door," Pete said.

After another silent interlude, Gregg said, "I guess after this cat incident, it's time to get the police involved. I don't know what actually happened to Frannie. You've seen she has such an imagination, but this cat thing was weird. It has me worried. The police should be informed."

Pete didn't want the police too close for comfort. They had always been the enemy. He just naturally didn't trust them, and he knew Gregg would expect him to talk to them. However, he couldn't use a direct approach with a stubborn know-it-all like Gregg. He said. "What do you think the police will do?"

"Investigate," Gregg said with conviction.

Pete tried not to laugh or speak with sarcasm. "Investigate? A dead cat?"

"I'm a taxpayer. Yes. I expect them to investigate."

"Well, I guess you can try," Pete said, biting his bottom lip.

In a few minutes, Gregg got up and walked off without another word to Pete.

"Hum," Pete said, "Speaking of weird...and will Gregg decide to contact the police, or will he not go to the trouble? Who knows?" Pete propped his feet back on the railing to wait for the approaching storm. The humidity all day had felt miserable. A storm would cool the temperature down. Too restless to be still, he got up and peered through the Wisteria vines at the Daniels' house. There were some lights on, but no sign of anyone coming or going. He walked off the porch and around the side of the house to check the backside of both houses. All was quiet. He hurried back to the porch as a few drops of rain blew in his face and sat down again in the rocker. The loose wire from the porch ceiling continued to whirl and slap against the wood post. Hypnotized by the lashing wire, Pete dozed off. Moments later he jerked awake. "Man, I need some company," he muttered, "someone more entertaining than Gregg. I guess Frannie's in bed." The air smelled of rain as a downpour began pelting the rooftops. A flash of heat lightening lit up the sky, followed by a rumble in the distance. Pete stood up and leaned against the porch railing to watch the rain. Ten minutes later the storm ended as quickly as it had begun. He went back to the rocker. There was still the breeze and the dancing wire. Soon he shut his eyes and his head fell forward on his chest. In his dream he was trying to grab the wire, but it kept dancing out of reach. It was like trying to catch the loose ends of his life, always seeming to move out of his grasp.

By the side of the house a shadow crossed below the porch. It was Wooten walking with a purpose to the back yard where he could hear Frannie singing softly in her lyrical, child-like soprano. She was climbing out of her window into the chinaberry tree.

"Somewhere over the rainbow, way up high, birds fly over the rainbow, why then oh why can't I?" Her music floated on the breeze left from the storm.

His shadow flickered unnoticed across the grass where a faint light shone down from the upstairs windows.

Pete made a determined effort to grab the illusive, devilish wire. Furiously he snatched it from its hook at the ceiling and wound it around his hand. He already knew what he was supposed to do with it.

He slipped off the porch and crossed the hedge to the Daniels' house, but the Daniels' place looked much like the

Turner farmhouse. A tall man stood on Jenny's porch. Pete felt confused because Wooten was not tall. He was putting a key in the front door lock. It was Farley! What was he doing here? Of course, Farley was in cahoots with Wooten! He should have known! Pete sprang out of the shadows, looped the wire around Farley's neck and pulled the wire tighter and tighter. Farley was choking. "You won't get away now," Pete said, "and you won't hurt anymore little girls." Then he felt Myra Claire's hand pulling him back. He tried to push her away. Then he woke up.

He saw the wire was still attached to the ceiling, hanging quietly now that the storm had passed. The air was still and humid again. He got up and stretched himself. He walked back and forth across the porch, thinking he would leave for the Shady Lawn and get some sleep. He walked down the steps and started for the school to get Harvey's Chevy.

In the backyard, Wooten spoke, "Hey, Kid, come down. I want to show you something."

Frannie's song stopped in midsentence. There was no answer.

Wooten waited.

Still Frannie made no sound.

Then Wooten spoke again, "Kid, come down. I just want to be your friend. You haven't given me a chance to show you what a good friend I can be. You let that Turner fellow be your friend. I can be just as good a friend as him and he's not going to be round for a while. I can be just as good a friend as him," Wooten said. "I would have taken you to that fair. Now come on down. Let's be friends."

"Go away," Frannie said. "You tried to hurt me. Now go away."

"No. I ain't gonna hurt you." Wooten laughed a low, confident laugh. "Who was it got their ear bit? Now you tell me that."

"Go away," Frannie repeated.

Wooten spoke again, this time with more impatience, "I'm not a bad person, but I can be. Come down. If you don't, I'm coming up."

Wooten moved closer to the tree. Grabbing the lower limb, he pulled himself onto a lower branch. "All I ask is you be nice to me and I'll be nice to you. You'll see. Do you like to go to the movies? How about a new doll?"

Just before Pete took off for the school, he recalled his words to Gregg about admonishing Frannie to close and lock her window. The question was, had she done as he told her? He decided to take one last look before he left for the night. He turned around and sprinted toward the back of the house. The moon had waned. A rectangle of light shone from one of the upstairs windows of the two-story. The house and the great chinaberry tree cast shadows over the yard. The dark room was Frannie's where Pete assumed she was sleeping. Then he heard her voice, "If you come any closer, you'll be sorry."

"Does that girl ever go to bed?" he murmured. "Who's she talking to?"

"I can come up and get you down."

"That's Wooten's voice!"

There was breathless pause. Pete's heart began racing with excitement. He took a step forward. He heard Wooten rustling the branches. He was climbing up into the tree after Frannie! *I have him now! As soon as he takes her against her will, he can't claim he's a friendly, curious neighbor drawn over by her singing!* Pete pulled his gun from the ankle holster.

"I'm giving you my last warning," Frannie said.

Pete wanted to tell her it was okay to come down. "We can catch this creep now in the act!" he whispered. "As soon as he tries to abduct you this time, we have our evidence!"

Then Pete heard the strangest sound, like the earlier pelting rain. What was going on?

377

Wooten laughed again, but it wasn't a friendly laugh. "This isn't being nice. I said if you were nice, I'd be nice to you. Come on now. Cut it out." More thumps hit the ground. Frannie was pelting him with something! Wooten jumped out of the tree, ducking his head and shielding himself with his arms to avoid being hit in the face. Pete could see the silhouette of the wiry man crouching as he turned away from whatever was raining down on him. Wooten hurried away from the tree, laughing his low, bitter laugh.

As he came toward Pete, Pete stooped behind a bush and reached for his gun. Above him, Pete heard Frannie scramble through the branches. Then her window closed with a thud. She was safely inside!

With his back to Pete, Wooten struck a match and lit a cigarette. Then he hesitated, listening as though he sensed Pete's presence.

It was all Pete could do to keep silent and not jump out of the shadows. He wanted to beat the man's face in, but he had to restrain himself. It wouldn't do to accost Wooten now. He put his gun away. The chance to catch him had been lost again.

Wooten took a couple of drags from his cigarette, then walked on toward the Daniels' place and disappeared around the hedge. Pete followed, slinking in the shadows. He saw Wooten enter at the Daniels' back door. Soon a light came on and shone through the opaque window shade, probably where the creep slept when he stayed overnight. Pete hurried back around the hedge and to the chinaberry tree. He climbed up to Frannie's window and tapped.

"Frannie, it's me, Pete."

She came to the window and Pete pressed his face close to the pane. When she saw it was Pete, she raised the window.

"Don't hit me with your ammo," he whispered with a grin.

"Mr. Pete?"

Chapter Forty-five

"Yes, I am here. I saw Wooten. I heard him."

She came out on the roof and Pete said, "Follow me."

The branches shook as Frannie made her way after him. He jumped to the ground and she hopped down beside him.

"Frannie, what were you doing outside. Isn't it time you were asleep?"

"It's hot inside. It's cool out here. Is Miss Myra Claire with you?"

"No. She had to leave. What were you pelting Wooten with?"

"I keep two sand buckets of chinaberries and rocks handy in case this kid up the street, Wayne Motley, comes around. He's a creep."

"So, you keep ammunition on hand for creeps," he said with a slight smile. "It worked. You discouraged him long enough to escape to your room." He looked toward the Daniels' and could see the light go off.

He turned back to her with a stern expression. "Promise me you'll be careful," he said. "Stay out of the big tree at night, and even though it's warm, keep your window closed and locked. It's too exposed, even if you have to sleep in another room. He could climb into yours by way of the tree just like you do and come in your open window. All he'd have to do is remove the screen." Frannie shook her head that she understood. "Don't be out alone at night, or anywhere. During the day, if you have to walk to the Corner Market, be aware of your surroundings and run like heck if you see Wooten or anyone acting suspicious. Remember Wooten is capable of using disguises. Better still, don't go anywhere alone."

"I understand, Mr. Pete. I'll do what you say."

"You know what I'm going to do? I'm going to find a comfortable perch in your tree and keep on the lookout at least for a while longer, just to make sure Wooten doesn't try again tonight. If I have to stay until morning, I will, but you should still keep your window locked. Don't sleep in your room, not until this creep is behind bars."

"Okay, Mr. Pete." She gave him a quick hug and scooted up into her tree and through the branches.

He heard her pull down the window and lock it. Thinking of Frannie pelting Wooten with chinaberries made Pete laughed like he hadn't laughed in he couldn't remember when.

An hour later at midnight, the Gregg's apartment and the Daniels' house were dark. "Wooten's turned in for the night. So has everyone else. Frannie's window is closed and locked. I heard her do it." He climbed down from the chinaberry and headed for Harvey's Chevy behind the school.

Chapter Forty-six

The following day, to avoid any possibility of being seen by Wooten, Pete stayed around the motel. He thought Harvey's blue Chevy could use a tune-up, so with Harvey's permission, he spent most of his morning with his head under the hood, tweaking the engine and changing the oil. When he finished that, he washed the Chevy. He needed to keep busy because this was the evening Pete was to call Angel to find out where to take the ten thousand. A shiver ran through Pete as he contemplated what that meant, the demise of his uncle, that fine, upstanding humanitarian and admired entrepreneur, Farley Oaks, who also molested young girls. When Pete saw Farley in his mind, so confident and so powerful, he wondered if he were dreaming to think he could really be rid of him. Somehow, he couldn't get his mind around Farley being caught off guard by any hired killer, no matter how professional and expert a marksman. Farley was a survivor. Pete felt his fear choke him like the wire he'd dreamed of twisting around Farley's neck. He buried himself in his work.

When the sun was almost overhead and he was sweating profusely, Harvey came out to tell him that Myra Claire was on the phone wanting to talk to him. He wiped his hands on a towel and followed Harvey through a back entrance and into a small, private office. Myra Claire came straight to the point. She said she would get to the Gregg's about one o'clock.

"Until then," she said, "Frannie promised to stay inside and not go anywhere until I get there. I'll let her know that I'll be leaving early tomorrow morning and that I can spend the day with her until you get here later this evening."

"Uh, did you get any word from the Man Upstairs on what we discussed last evening?" Pete asked.

"I prayed off and on all night. When I got up this morning, I hoped to get a sense of peace, a confirmation that I should speak to Gregg, but I didn't."

"So you won't speak to Gregg?" *I guess she needs handwriting on the wall.*

"Actually, my confirmation came another way."

"How's that?" *Handwriting on the wall, I'll bet.*

"A growing sense of impending danger confirmed to me Gregg should act without delay."

"Does that mean you *will* speak to Gregg? I've been telling you that Wooten's going to make his move, now that he thinks the way is clear of me." Then he told her about Wooten's attempt to abduct Frannie the night before and how Frannie drove him away with chinaberries and pebbles.

"As soon after Bill gets home from work and has his dinner, I'll speak to him. I hope he'll put Frannie on a bus as early as tomorrow or at least by Wednesday."

"I want to see her off, to make sure Wooten's not on that bus. Please do caution Frannie not to talk about it, not even mention it. Wooten heard us talking behind the library the day he showed up at the carnival. I wouldn't put it past him to get on the bus even down the road at one of those many stops those Trailways buses make. He's clever in a sinister way. I don't put anything past him. Tell Frannie to keep mum about her plans."

"I'll encourage Bill not to tell Frannie she's going until they're on the way to the bus station. That way she can't spill the beans."

"Good idea."

"Well, I guess that's it," Myra Claire said.

After Pete talked to her he felt mixed emotions, a sense of relief where Frannie was concerned and confusion about his feeling toward Myra Claire. He had to be glad about her leaving, yet he wished they could have parted on friendlier terms. He had all the confidence Gregg would do whatever she suggested. By early tomorrow Frannie would be out of Riverton! At least he could be pleased about that.

As Pete started to leave the office, Harvey stopped him and asked, "Don't you need to be keeping an eye on that little girl? What you gonna do about her when you leave here?"

"Myra Claire's holding down the fort today, and early tomorrow Frannie's daddy will send her to stay with her grandma for a while. That's the safest solution. Wooten will have no idea where she is as long as Frannie doesn't disclose it to Jenny or anybody where he might overhear."

The rest of the day, Pete busied himself helping Harvey around the motel. Finally, seven o'clock came and Pete went to the pay phone at the laundromat to call Angel on his private number.

"Where are you?"

"At a pay phone."

"Give me the number."

Pete read off the number printed on the center of the dial.

"Wait ten minutes," Angel told him. "The caller will give you instructions."

"Got it," Pete said. He heard Angel say, "Good luck." Then there was a click and he was gone.

After that, Pete paced just outside the door of the booth. Cars passed by on the road, but the phone was situated to one side of the parking area away from the noise. There were a few cars parked in front of the laundromat. He looked at the phone, willing it to ring. His heart raced. He would actually be speaking to someone with a connection to a killer-for-hire, maybe even the killer himself. He was crossing a line and he knew it. Ten minutes passed. When Pete wasn't staring at the phone and willing it to ring, he stared absently at the people who came and went, carrying in their baskets of clothes, or coming out and driving away.

He popped his knuckles. His mouth felt dry and tacky. He didn't dare walk away to get a drink from the machine inside.

Fifteen minutes passed. He kept thinking he heard the ring, but it always turned out to be in his mind.

Twenty minutes passed. He ran his hand through his hair. He tried to think positive thoughts about getting back to his farm to produce his daddy's famous brew. He imagined all the old customers congratulating him, glad to be able to get Rusty's whiskey, but inevitably, his thoughts could not shut out the voice in his head. *He's not going to call. He's not going to call. You're the target. Farley's men, Salvino, even Angel could have been bought off by Farley.* His uncle had that kind of power.

Pete was about to hyperventilate when the phone jingled. He took a deep breath.

"Yeah," he answered.

"Who's this?" a voice with a Jersey accent said.

"Turner."

"Do you have the money?"

Pete didn't trust anybody, especially not this faceless caller. If he couldn't trust Angel, how could he be sure there wasn't somebody waiting to assault him as soon as he claimed to have ten thousand dollars in his possession? "I'll have it tomorrow," Pete said.

There was a pause on the other end.

"I said I'd have it tomorrow. Just give me the instructions," Pete said.

"Ever been to Union, in Pennsylvania, in the northern part of the state?"

"I'll find it," Pete said.

"A place near there is called Gillie Hill Road. Come alone and follow Gillie to the sign that says Galway Creek. Turn right and go to the dead end. You'll see a large, white farmhouse. Go around back to the dry well. Place the money in the bucket, lower it, and leave. If the money's not there by midnight on Tuesday, the deal's off."

There was a click. Pete finished writing down the directions and hung up. He stepped out of the booth and started sprinting back to the Shady Lawn. It worried him that Angel was in such a hurry to distance himself. He thought of Myra Claire sitting on the Pruitt porch. The distance between them just got wider as well. The closer he came to resolving his Farley problem, the wider the gap grew between them, but that was how it was. Myra Claire was leaving in the morning. Before long she'd be a memory. She was an amazing person, but she was not in the cards for him. He would meet the contact and pay the blood money. As soon as Mary Kate and the Turners were avenged, he could go home. After all these years, he told himself, his ordeal would be over. Thinking how he'd expected euphoria once he got the call, he realized he felt worse than crap.

Pete returned to his new room on the backside of the Shady Lawn. Harvey had suggested Pete change rooms as well as cars. From the room, he picked up a brown paper bag Harvey had packed with sandwiches for Pete and Myra Claire and a cooler packed with ice and RC Colas. Pete shoved the bag and cooler in the trunk of Harvey's Chevy and headed for the place behind the school where he had parked the night before.

As he drove, he wasn't surprised that his feelings were confused at the thought of saying good-bye to Myra Claire. The sandwiches and RC Colas would be the last meal they shared, but he knew it was for the best. Why prolong the inevitable? She was different from anyone he had ever known, completely herself and comfortable being who she was. He was confident that, unlike him, Myra Claire had no secret other self, but she had already figured out Pete had secrets. She knew too much about him as it was.

Behind the school, he got the bag of sandwiches and two colas from the trunk and, keeping in the shadows away from the street lights, he sprinted to the porch, At the Greggs' he noticed Myra Claire's Buick parked in the driveway. He found her sitting in the swing. When he came up on the porch, she stood up. "No sign of Wooten all day. I think everything's all set. I talked to Bill Gregg. I did the best I could. I hope our friend will be on the early bus in the morning, and Bill said Frannie wouldn't know anything until they were driving to the station. He agreed that's the only way to be sure she doesn't broadcast it."

"I knew you could do it," Pete said matter-of-factly.

"We'll see. So, I guess this is it," she said, picking up her purse and a book.

"Guess so," Pete said, sitting the bag and the colas on the rocking chair. "Harvey sent some sandwiches and RC Colas for our dinner."

"That was sweet of Harvey," Myra Claire said, "but I had dinner with the Greggs."

"Oh," Pete said, with disappointment in his voice. "So, you're leaving? Now?"

"Yes. I'm going early in the morning. Might as well call it a day."

"I'll walk you to your car."

"Well, it's right there in the driveway. My sleuthing is done, so why bother hiding. You, on the other hand, need to keep out of sight until she gets on that bus, so stay here."

"I'll stay close to the hedge," he said. "You said you hadn't seen him."

He followed her down the steps to her Buick and opened her door for her. She got in. Looking up, she said, "Be safe."

Reluctantly, he stepped back and watched her back out onto North Main and drive away. Then he went back to the porch. Frannie came out to tell him good night. She told him her daddy was acting really weird making her go to bed so early. Pete promised to keep watch in the chinaberry tree until he was sure Wooten wasn't coming around.

"Thanks, Mr. Pete. You're my guardian angel."

Pete started to object, but saved his breath.

"If you're gone to get some sleep when I wake up in the morning, you'll be back later?" she asked wistfully.

"We'll see what tomorrow brings," Pete said.

Myra got to the campus and parked. Back in her room, she looked around. So much had happened since Friday. It had been an adventure, meeting Frannie and the Greggs and tracking a pedophile. Romance had almost bloomed, and died in the bud. There had been a spark, but he'd clearly lost interest, and it was just as well. She was attracted to Pete, but because he was so bound up with guilt and anger, as appealing as she found him, he was not someone she could consider as a life partner. She knew the business that brought him to Riverton had something to do with retaliating against his uncle who years before had molested his younger sister. Ironically, another pedophile intent on destroying a young girl had delayed Pete from his purpose. Frannie had thrust herself into his life very inconveniently. What a coincidence. Or was it divine intervention? Deep inside Pete had a good heart, but that wasn't enough to compensate for the bitterness that drove him, eating him up. No, Pete Turner was not someone to fall for. Whatever his business that had brought him to Riverton, it was not good. She feared he could end up in prison for the rest of his life.

Myra Claire gathered up her books and carried them out to her car. She went back inside, retrieved blouses hanging in the closet, and carried them to her trunk. If she wore her same clothes in the morning that she had on, she could put her suitcase in the car now. At daylight, all she'd have to do is pile the dirty linens in the bathroom and go. Mary, the caretaker's wife, had told her when she got ready to leave for good, not to bother to lock the door. Just leave the key on the dresser she said.

She carried her suitcase to the Buick. As she lifted it to stow it in the trunk, she noticed dim headlights coming around the bend and realized it was the second or third time a vehicle had passed. She'd been too engrossed in her thoughts to pay attention. This time she looked up to see a black truck pass under the street lamps. As it went by, she took a deep breath. If it wasn't Wooten's truck, it looked like his. She watched to see whether he would come around again. He didn't. He could be parked somewhere on the campus watching her. He must have followed her from the Greggs. That he already knew where she was staying was evidenced because of what he'd done to Sylvester the cat. Had he meant merely to warn her, or to spy on her? Well, after tonight, she wouldn't have to worry about him again, although, the thought occurred to her that when Frannie was safe in North Carolina with her granny, some other child would become his prey. She didn't have such a good feeling inside when she considered that. She wished there was something she could do, but at least Frannie would be on the bus in the morning, and Wooten would never find her.

Seeing the caretaker's lights on in the cottage, she decided to speak to him about keeping an eye out for strangers, just until daylight when she'd be leaving. She would feel better knowing someone was alerted to the possibility that Wooten might try to cause her trouble. She crossed the road to the modest white rancher. Marvin answered the knock. She introduced herself. She and Pete had met the wife, but not Marvin. "Would you keep an eye out? Make sure no strangers come around? We've had a bit of trouble." Then she told him about the incident with poor Sylvester."

"My brother told me about some pervert trying to hurt that little girl. Is she okay?"

"For now," Myra Claire said.

Marvin promised to call the police if he observed anyone strange hanging around and looking suspicious. Myra Claire thanked him and walked back across the street and parking lot to go to her room. No doubt with Wooten thinking Pete was jailed in Carterville, he was feeling bolder than ever.

After seeing Myra Claire off, Pete came back to the porch and met Bill sitting on the steps.

"I still say Frannie probably exaggerated the abduction story," he said.

"What?" Pete responded, still thinking of Myra Claire.

"Myra Claire came to talk to me, asking my advice. She wanted to know what I thought about sending Frannie to stay a while with her grand momma and to start school there in North Carolina. Now, I've been dead set against that because I think families should be together. There are appearances to consider, but the old lady is getting up in age. She's my first wife's mother, and she's a spry old soul, but it wouldn't hurt for somebody to be there to help her around the house. She wants Frannie to come, and frankly, Diane wants some relief. All this talk about abduction makes her nervous. If I'm going to get any peace, I'd better let her go."

Gregg sat without speaking further, just staring ahead as if he were pondering some deep problem.

"So?" Pete said. "She'll be on the bus in the morning?"

Gregg nodded. "The bus leaves at six o'clock, and she'll be on it." Then he got up and walked off toward his apartment.

Pete breathed a satisfied sigh.

Chapter Forty-seven

Not long after ten, all the lights went out in the Gregg apartment. The Daniels's house was dark as well. Pete climbed up in the chinaberry tree. The huge tree limbs, like comforting, open arms, offered numerous crooks where he could sit comfortably. No wonder Frannie found the tree so inviting. When he told her he would be guarding her window tonight from her special tree, her face gave way to smiles despite her sadness at Myra Claire's leaving.

Diane would wake her early for Bill to get her to the bus station and on the bus to Wilmington by six o'clock. Pete intended to get there before Frannie's bus arrived to scope out the place. Then he would board with her to make sure Wooten was not among the passengers, but he'd be in disguise. The thought crossed his mind, Wooten himself might be in disguise as well. This could turn into a real game of charades. Once he was satisfied Wooten was not on the bus, Pete would disembark before the bus pulled out, but he would warn her to speak to no one and to inform the driver if anybody tried to bother her. He would say "good-bye" to her then.

As soon as she was on her way to her grandma's and out of Wooten's reach, he would return Harvey's car and have Harvey drive him to pick up the Ford from the used car lot. He was anxious to get past the trip up north and making the ten thousand drop off. After that, he didn't anticipate remaining much longer in Riverton. Maybe he wouldn't come back. Maybe he'd just take his time, meandering to some of the small town tracks where he'd raced before. He might even see how Jake's Ford performed on some of them. Soon the Riverton episode would be a strange memory. He and Myra Claire had said goodbye, not on the best terms, and in the morning, Frannie would be on her way to the North Carolina coast. Summer was coming to an end. He'd left Wilkes County just over a week ago and it seemed as if a lifetime had passed. Myra Claire would return to her teaching job in about two weeks. By then he would be working again in the stills for Jake, unless by some fluke of luck, Farley's demise occurred before he had returned the signed papers and before the farm had come in the hands of his heirs. That was a hopeful thought.

Either way, Myra Claire would not care to associate with a bootlegger. He wondered if their paths would ever cross again. He recalled the first time he'd seen those piercing green eyes and flames of untamable red hair as she was coming in Charlie's Diner. It would be best if he avoided the diner. He didn't want to run into her.

Pete shifted in his seat in the bend of a sturdy limb and looked over the area below. No one stirred. There were no sounds but the crickets and the frogs. The Daniels's house remained dark. Myra Claire hadn't seen Wooten come or go. He began thinking about a cold bottle of RC Cola left in the cooler in the trunk of Harvey's car. He wasn't drowsy. Diane had brewed him a thermos of coffee earlier. He had finished that. What he really wanted was that cold bottle of cola. The more he thought about it, the dryer his mouth felt. He wondered if he dared sprint two blocks to where he'd parked behind the school. He kept telling himself he'd wait, but the temptation to get that refreshing drink was almost overpowering. He jumped to the ground, telling himself he only wanted to stretch his legs in an attempt to divert his thoughts.

Once on the ground, it was easy to see himself making a quick run to get the bottle of cool drink buried in the ice in the Igloo cooler. He calculated he could get down to the Corner Market in three or four minutes, get the drink, and be back in just over five minutes. It would take Wooten that long to climb the tree, if he even dared to chance another pelting with the chinaberries. Pete laughed again. That Frannie was a smart cookie. He continued to ponder the wisdom of leaving his post to get the drink. Frannie had promised to close and lock the window. She should be okay for five minutes.

During this debate with himself, Pete peered through the hedge and saw the beam from a flashlight. Someone was going toward the garage. Pete moved closer. It was Wooten. Pete could tell from his size and walk. He could see the longish hair. He had apparently approached through the back alley. Now he was going into the garage. Wooten didn't even look around, so confident was he that Pete sat behind bars in the Carterville jail. The door squeaked open. A shovel clanged as it landed in the back part of the truck. Pete watched the red tail lights of the flatbed truck as it backed around and rumbled out onto North Main in the direction of the bridge and downtown. Pete remembered having seen the truck before.

He paced around the yard, wondering if Wooten intended to return. If he didn't come back, Pete would call it a night and head to the Shady Lawn until time to meet Frannie's bus. He waited ten minutes, to make sure the pervert hadn't gone on a short errand to buy some cigarettes, if there was any place in Riverton open past ten o'clock. Then he thought about the shovel he heard thrown in the back of the truck. That would indicate Wooten was probably leaving. After another ten minutes, Pete felt sure his adversary was gone for the night. The neighborhood was quiet. He looked toward Frannie's window, dark and hidden for the most part by the chinaberry foliage.

At five minutes after midnight, he took off sprinting through the darkened yards, past the Corner Market to the side street, and across it to where he'd left the Chevy behind the school. When he got to trunk of Harvey's car, he unlocked it and pulled the cool, wet bottle from the Igloo. He took several long swigs before he shut the trunk and jumped in the car, anticipating an uneventful trip back to the Shady Lawn.

However, just before the bridge he approached a flatbed truck with the hood of the cab raised. It was pulled to the side of the road. Pete's antennae went up. A man holding a water can slammed down the hood. *Radiator must have overheated.* Pete could see it was Wooten! He must have walked some distance for find water. Most of the gas stations were closed.

Just beyond the next intersection Pete drove in behind a small grocery store to wait for Wooten to pass. *Vampires and evil creatures do their work at night. I'll track him for a while.*

As soon as the truck sped by, Pete kept his distance and followed Wooten across the bridge trailing him through town. It was a good thing he still drove Harvey's Chevy. They passed the library and on toward the far side of Riverton. Pete debated whether to turn in at the Shady Lawn. If Wooten was headed to Burris Road, he had no intention of following him there. They passed the Shady Lawn with Pete staying just in view of Wooten's tail lights. He kept thinking he would turn around. *When he gets to Burris Road, I'll turn around.*

But in a few more dark miles, contrary to Pete's assumption that Wooten was headed to his trailer, the truck turned off the highway onto a dirt road. Pete slowed the Chevy, and after giving Wooten plenty of distance, he made the turn without headlights. The area appeared undeveloped. He pulled into the edge of the woods while his eyes followed Wooten's red taillights a short distance down the road. Then Wooten swung around and came back. *He's scoping out the place to make sure he's alone. So what's this creep up to?* Then Wooten pulled off the road and shut off his engine. When he turned off the truck head lights, the area was in pitch dark.

Pete stuck a flashlight in the waistband of his jeans and hustled on foot to where he'd seen Wooten park his truck. At first he stumbled along on the unfamiliar ground, but soon his eyes began adjusting to the pitch dark. He ascertained they were on a construction site. Wooten had parked in the driveway of one of two cleared lots. Pete edged closer, then dropped to his knees and elbows and crawled as close to Wooten as he dared. He could see where footings had been dug. Wooten appeared to be digging. *What in tarnation is he doing? This isn't a job. He's not working this time of night.* He watched Wooten dig for the next twenty minutes. When he laid the shovel down, he came back to his truck and removed a burlap bag. He carried the bag to where he'd been digging and dumped it in the hole. Then, he proceeded to fill it up. When he finished, he went back to the truck, threw in the shovel, and left the site. Pete had to know what Wooten had buried.

Frannie, having closed and locked her bedroom window just as she'd promised Mr. Pete, tried sleeping in the living room. The sofa proved uncomfortable. Because of the backward slant of the seat, she couldn't keep her face from rolling into the crevice between the seat cushions and the sofa back, making her hot and unable to breathe. She shifted and turned. A broken spring kept poking into her stomach and side, depending on which way she lay. Knowing Mr. Pete was on guard from her tree, she got up several times to look out, trying to see him in the dark branches.

When the dial on the mantel clock showed eleven, she got up to get a glass of water from the kitchen. She finished drinking, rinsed out the glass and left it in the sink. Then she decided to get a quilt down from her closet shelf. It was a patchwork quilt her granny made for her. She hugged it to herself, breathing in the smell of her granny's house that she could only imagine and wish that she were there. She carried the quilt to the living room to make a pallet on the floor. Tossing her pillow down, she stretched out and slept until one-thirty when she woke up chilly and shivering.

All the windows in the apartment were open with the exception of the one in her bedroom, and with the late August temperatures dropping into the mid-sixties, she felt miserably cold. Finally, she gathered up her bedding and shuffled to her room. It was plenty cool now, even with the window closed. She gratefully fell into her own bed and pulled a light spread over her. Before long, she sank into a peaceful sleep.

On his way back to North Main, Wooten exalted in his progress. "Now with Turner out of the way, safely behind bars, the brat is mine to do with her as I please," he exclaimed. "He won't be interfering any more. And with her boyfriend in jail, the chick with the cool set of wheels must be leaving. Saw her packing the car." He grinned and rubbed his chin, thinking how he'd outsmarted the nosey pests. "Now for the brat! If she'd only wanted to be friendly. But no! She had to bite my ear and then get that Turner interfering. She shouldn't of done that."

He parked the truck on a side street behind his black paneled work truck. He got out and scanned the dark surroundings, circling the building. He didn't want to be seen by Jenny and one of her customers. But it was late even for Jenny. Once he determined no one was around, he hurried through the tall grass and old tires to the back alley.

"She won't be throwing any berries at me now," he said, scowling and touching the knife tucked in his boot. He strode through the back yard to the chinaberry tree and hoisted himself up, climbing from limb to limb until he reached the window he knew to be her bedroom. Again, he hesitated and listened. All was quiet. There were no lights on anywhere in the neighborhood. Most of the world, at least in Riverton, were asleep. Quietly, using the knife blade, he removed the screen and let it drop. It only made a slight swoosh before it clunked softly to the ground.

Although he could see the window was closed, he didn't expect to find it locked. He tried to push it open, but it wouldn't move. He cursed it. "I could break out the bloody pane, but not without making a noise. What happens if I knock real gentle? Will she open to see who it is? Does she even know Turner's in jail?"

Through the window, he could see her dark form in the bed. He tapped lightly on the pane. She didn't stir. He tapped again, slightly harder, and waited. No response. He knocked again. *I gotta get in there!* Just then he saw a shadow. A light from a flashlight came on and shinned around the room. *That must be the daddy.* The girl sat up. The light came close to the window. Wooten stepped down to a lower bough and waited. After minutes went by, he moved back up and carefully raised his head to see through the window. There was no light. He waited. There was no movement. The daddy had left. He tapped, tapped on the glass. This time the girl got up and came to the window. He heard her unlock it and raise it just a crack.

"Mr. Pete? Mr. Pete is that you?" Frannie whispered.

Wooten answered softly, "Yeah." Then Diane appeared in the doorway of Frannie's room.

"Frances, what are you doing out of bed? You're keeping your daddy awake and he has to work tomorrow."

"I can't sleep, or I couldn't sleep on the couch."

"Well, since you're back in your room now, go to sleep. You're disturbing us. Get back in bed and I'll rub your back." Frannie looked back at the window.

"Frances, get back to bed."

Frannie closed and locked the window.

Diane began to rub Frannie's back and legs and hum a soft tune. All Frannie could think about though was whether Pete was still outside her window and she was terribly curious to know why he'd knocked. What did he want? Not knowing made her more restless than ever, but she tried to be still and not further irritate Diane. In a few minutes, Diane got up and went back to her room.

Frannie wondered if Pete would knock on her window again. She was going to miss him and Miss Myra Claire. Pete kept saying he was leaving and one day soon she knew he would, but Miss Myra Claire promised to come for a visit in a few months when she brought the Moravian cookies. Maybe Mr. Pete would come too. With that pleasant prospect in mind, she closed her eyes and snuggled under her quilt.

And then...the tap, tap, tap.

Frannie sat up. "Mr. Pete?" She hurried to the window, unlocked it, and pushed it open.

Chapter Forty-eight

As soon as Pete observed Wooten drive away, he hurried to where he'd seen him digging. Batter boards outlined the footings for the foundation of a five room house. "These are ready for the concrete," he murmured. He scouted along the trenches, keeping the flashlight low to the ground until he saw where the dirt had been disturbed. "Here! He buried something here…in the burlap bag. Whatever he put in the ground, he doesn't want it recovered because probably by tomorrow it will be under concrete. I've got to get a shovel!"

He didn't want to knock on some stranger's door this time of night, but he remembered seeing a small ranch style motel along this highway that might be open, even in Riverton. Breathing hard with excitement, he ran back to his car and pulled out to the main road. Passing patches of undeveloped woods interspersed with an occasional business closed up until morning, he said, "I know that motel is along here somewhere. If they don't have a shovel…" Then he saw the neon sign flashing "vacancy." He swerved into the parking lot in front of the office and ran for the door. Inside, there was no one at the desk, but there was a bell on the counter. He hit it hard with the palm of his hand. It clanged, blasting the silence. After a minute, he hit it again and waited, still breathing hard, his heart racing. After another couple of minutes, a sleepy-eyed attendant came through a door behind the desk. "Okay. Okay. I heard you the first time."

"Do you have a shovel? It's an emergency."

The young man rubbed his eyes. "Well, yes, but I can't just give it away."

Pete threw a two dollar bill on the counter. The attendant picked up the money and led Pete through the office to the back of the building. He unlocked a storage shed and took out a shovel. Pete grabbed it. "Thanks." He followed the man back inside, then shot past him and out the front to his vehicle. He threw the tool in and took off.

Back at the construction site, he pulled the Chevy into the same place where Wooten had parked earlier. He jumped out and grabbed the shovel. Quietly shutting the door behind him, he sprinted over the uneven ground. At the footings, he leaped into the ditch and began digging furiously. About five feet down he hit the burlap bag. He threw down the shovel and jerked the bag from the hole. It was weighty and cold. *The freezer in Wooten's trailer.*

When he untied the burlap he saw it contained a black plastic bag. This was closed with a tight knot. He tried the knot but couldn't get it loose. He switched on the flashlight to look for a sharp stick. It took a minute, but he found one and hurried to puncture the bag enough to tear it open. Still holding the light, he shinned it in the bag. When he did, for several moments he stared in disbelief, unable to take his eyes from the contents of the bag. Then, dropping the light and the bag, he gasped, hung his head over the side of the ditch, and vomited on the ground. He vomited until he had nothing in him to come up but dry heaves, until he was too weak to stand. He knew he would never get the image out of his mind, the blonde hair, the dismembered body parts. It was the little girl's face. Even distorted in death he recognize her as the one that he had seen three weeks ago with Wooten in Charlie's diner. Something then about that little girl had made Pete skeptical of Wooten's story about her being his dead sister's girl. The child had seemed frightened. Pete knew now that it wasn't that she *couldn't* talk. She was too terrified to speak. She'd been threatened.

Pete sat many minutes with his head hung over the side of the ditch, feeling numb, as though his body was elsewhere and he was just a lump of nothingness.

After a while, his numbness gave way to an overwhelming anger. Finally, he dragged himself to his feet. He carefully laid the bag in the hole and shoveled in the fill dirt. "I've got to phone the police. By sometime tomorrow she'll be forever buried under a slab of cement, and I can't even prove Wooten's responsible." He clenched his teeth. "I saw him bury her, but it's my word against his. The Riverton police think I'm the pedophile."

Pete trudged back to the car. At the first gas station he came to, he pulled up to the phone booth and called the police station. He reported the buried child at the construction site, giving details of the exact location. When asked for his name, he hung up, fearing any entanglement with the police. If he had real evidence that Wooten was the perpetrator, he'd let Gregg take the credit, but after tonight, it wouldn't matter. Frannie would be in North Carolina and he'd be gone from this place forever.

For a moment he lingered, leaning his head against the side of the booth. He was shaking. Finally, he got back in the car. It was up to the police from this point on. He headed to the Shady Lawn to clean up before time to make sure Frannie got safely on the bus to her granny's. And then it was on to Union, Pennsylvania to deliver the blood money. He just wanted to get it done and get on with his life.

As soon as Frannie slid the window up, Wooten forced his way inside. She knew it was him, even before he spoke. She smelled him! "You're...not...Mr. Pete!" she gasped and then felt the breath go out of her.

"Don't make a sound, he said, and nodded toward the parents' bedroom, "or they die along with you." Frannie felt the sharp edge of a knife against her throat. He stuffed a handkerchief in her mouth. It smelled of stale tobacco and Wooten's sweet musk cologne. She felt bile rise up in her throat and tried to cough, but the cloth filled her mouth and throat. He pulled a rope from his back pocket and tied her hands behind her.

He pushed her toward the door and into the hall. The parents' bedroom door was partially closed. The daddy was snoring and the sound was loud enough to mask any creaking of the floor boards.

Wooten shoved Frannie down the hall and into the living room to the front screen. He unlocked it and pushed her onto the stoop, then dragged her shoeless and in her shorty pajamas down the steps and into the yard. Feeling the wet grass squish between her toes, she shivered, as he forced her into the dark alley. There the rocks and other debris cut into her bare feet. When they reached the tall grass behind the old station, the ground rose up before her eyes and her knees buckled under her.

When she came to, she was lying in a tight, dark space. She wondered if she were dead and closed in her casket.

Chapter Forty-nine

On Tuesday morning before sunrise Diane wrapped a cotton robe over her nightgown and poked her feet into her bedroom slippers. She padded into the kitchen to start making breakfast so Bill could get Frances on the early bus to Wilmington before he had to be at work. She could hear him in the bathroom running the shower. He'd leave it in a mess, with wet towels and puddles of water all over the floor and shaving cream with black specks of his freshly shaved beard coating the sink. She sighed and opened the refrigerator to get out a pack of bacon and a carton of eggs. The smell of bacon frying would draw Frances out of bed. She'd soon be in the kitchen to get out glasses and pour the orange juice. Diane allowed a small smile to think how the girl had no idea the surprise that awaited her this morning. She would be chattering a mile a minute when she learned she was going to stay with her grandmother for a while. Diane had packed one large suitcase with enough clothes to get her by for a couple of weeks. Later, she and Bill would have to drive to Wilmington to take the rest of her things.

She put two slices of toast in the toaster but didn't push down the lever. Bill liked his bread warm so his butter would melt. She measured coffee in the aluminum percolator and set it on the stove, then turned on the gas to boil the water.

Bill came in smelling of soap and shaving cream. He pulled out his chair and sat down. When he saw his glass was empty he frowned. "Where's Frances?"

"Still sleeping," Diane said.

"Why haven't you gotten her up?"

"I thought she'd be in here by now. Sometimes she stays in that tree until after we go to bed. At 3:30 last night I found her at the window talking to Pete. It's a good thing she's going away for a while." She pushed the lever down on the toaster.

"Yes," Bill agreed. "I'm ready for Turner to go."

"It's not proper for him to be hanging around her like he has," Diane said. "I suppose he means well, but you're right. This whole business with Turner needs to stop. It doesn't look right."

Bill pushed back from the table, his chair making a scraping sound on the linoleum. "I'm going to get her up." He hurried down the hallway to his daughter's room. Not there. "Must be in the bathroom," he muttered. "No, the door's open. She's not there. Now, where the devil is she?" He stomped through the apartment calling her name. He went back to her room. "If she's in that tree…" He stalked to the window. It was open and the screen was missing. "What the…?" He called her. When she didn't answer, he stormed back to the kitchen. Diane had filled his glass with orange juice and he took a gulp.

"You sit down and eat. I'll find her," Diane said and put a plate of scrambled eggs and two strips of bacon before him. She poured his coffee and got a jar of grape jelly from the refrigerator. "I'll check the stair and the porch," she said.

When she got to the living room she found the screen door unlocked. "Frances must have gone out this way." However, her stepdaughter was not sitting on the stoop nor on the steps. Diane padded down the stairs. She was getting annoyed having to appear outside in her night clothes in front of the neighborhood, not to mention the passing traffic on Main Street. "I love the girl, but she can be so…

so…irrational." Complaining to herself about having to get her bedroom slipper wet, she went through the dew soaked grass to the front walk then up to the front porch steps. She called, "Frances, are you on the porch? Don't get your daddy riled up this morning. He has a surprise for you." She waited, expecting an exuberant girl to come bursting out to the sunlit yard. Frances do you hear? We have a big surprise for you, but if you don't come on you're going to miss the bus to Wilmington."

Perturbed, Diane stomped up the porch steps, but Frances was not on the porch. She ran back to the apartment, through the living room and into the kitchen. "Bill, she's nowhere to be found."

After both of them searched the apartment and the yard again, Bill said, "You don't suppose that Turner has taken her somewhere?"

"But he knows she's to get on the early bus to Wilmington."

"You said he was outside her window at 3:30 this morning."

"Yes, I came in her room because I heard a noise. She was standing at the window and I distinctly heard her say his name."

Bill slammed his fists against the wall. "I was right about that guy from the first." He cried out in anguish as he paced the floor. "Turner has deceived us all, even that sweet Myra Claire. She's not part of his deception. I'm sure of it. She's been deceived about his character too. He's led us all to think he was trying to protect Frances from a pedophile when he's been the pervert all the time. He wanted to build up our trust and cast suspicion elsewhere so when he took off with her, we wouldn't suspect him."

"I don't know, Bill. Pete is a bit strange in some ways, but I don't agree he's a pedophile."

"Well, I know he is. He has Frances." In between curses Bill said, "If we find him, we find her. I'm calling the police." With a quavering voice and shaking hands he picked up the phone and dialed the operator. "Get me the police. Yes, I want to report a missing person," he broke down. When he managed to compose himself he choked out, "My eleven year old daughter."

Chapter Fifty

The warm shower cleansing Pete's body could not wash away the sickness on the inside of him. It was like Mary Kate's death all over again. He couldn't let himself imagine Frannie ending up like the sad little blonde girl. Even though he couldn't feel glad at the moment, he knew he was relieved and grateful Bill had agreed to send her to her grandma's. In just an hour, she'd be on the bus and she would never again have to fear Wooten. Then Pete could be about his own business.

Stepping from the shower, he dried himself and wrapped the towel around his middle. He threw the duffle bag on the bed and pulled out his last pair of clean Levis. Fortunately, he was leaving or he'd have to go back to the laundromat. He could hardly believe it was only a few days ago he was there thinking of talking to those college girls to persuade one of them to pose as his girlfriend. It seemed like weeks he'd been languishing in Riverton. That was the day he called Myra Claire…*Myra Claire…if things were different, maybe they might have…but no use going there.* That reminded him, when he came in he'd found a note that Harvey had left under the door, something about Myra Claire. It was on the bed. He reached for it. "Hum," Pete said, frowning. The note said Melvin had called Harvey to report that he had met Myra Claire last evening. She had come to him to request that he keep an eye out for anybody hanging around the dorm. A vehicle like Wooten's driven by several times while she was packing her car to leave in the morning.

"That would be today. She should be leaving just about now if she's not already on her way," Pete murmured.

The note went on to say that Marvin could assure Pete that Myra Claire was safe because, unbeknown to her, Marvin had spent most of the night guarding her door, and Wooten did not return. Pete put down the note. "Wooten was too busy at that construction site. That's why. At least I can feel relieved that both Myra Claire and Frannie will soon be where Wooten won't know where to find them."

He threw his toiletries in his shaving kit and everything else in the duffle bag. Harvey had Jake's Ford parked out back. Pete was about to pick up his keys when there was a forceful banging on the other side of his door. A voice called, "Open up, Turner! This is the police!"

Now what? Pete dropped his bag. If there had been a back window, he would have given them the slip. He jerked open the door. The same two detectives who'd threatened to arrest him a week ago stood in front of him. This time they had their guns drawn. *They found that blonde girl's body and they automatically suspect me!* Pete sighed. "You, guys, haven't we already played this scene? What is it this time? What are you accusing me of now?"

While one officer kept his gun pointed at Pete, the older lead officer pushed Pete aside and entered the room. "Where's the girl, Turner?" He began searching the room. Pete stood watching, smirking at the ridiculousness of the situation. *It would be funny if I weren't in a hurry. I have to get to the bus station. Somehow I have to get rid of these fellows.*

When the officers' search failed to turn up the girl, the lead demanded, "Where is she? We know you have her. The mother said she was talking to you from her bedroom window early this morning."

"You're disgusting and weird, Turner, you know that?" the other one chimed in. "What's your interest in an eleven year old girl? What were you doing before daylight outside her bedroom window? Wasn't it the same as your reason for taking her to the carnival, to lure her under your control?"

The lead officer said, "Thought we told you a week ago you were to leave Riverton and stay away from the Gregg girl."

"Look, I resolved that with her parents. It was a misunderstanding instigated by the creep who's really after Frannie. They are aware of that now, that my interest in her has been only to help her. So, I don't know what you're doing here. It's harassment and I'm getting pretty sick of it."

"What we're doing here is that the girl is missing, and you're the prime suspect."

Pete's heart leaped into his throat. The smirk fell off his face, displaced by a look of concerned disbelief. "You say Frannie's missing? What are you talking about?"

"Apparently, the girl's stepmother went to get her up this morning to go on a bus trip only she was gone. Turner, what were you doing at the girl's window?"

Pete was no longer listening. The detectives' voices droned off in the distance. *Does Wooten have her?* In his mind's eye he saw the blonde child like a butchered animal. The vision hovered in his thoughts like clouds of a stalled storm.

"Turner, answer the question. What were you doing at the girl's window?"

"I wasn't at her window, not at the time you're talking about," he whispered, still seeing the plastic bag and the distorted face of the blond child.

"Where were you at 3:30 this morning?"

Pete tried to focus. He could see the two officers, but they appeared like images in the crazy mirror at the carnival, all warped and wavy. His voice seemed to come from outside him. He didn't want to imagine Frannie in the blonde child's place. Surely, there was another explanation. Frannie was going to be on that bus to North Carolina in an hour and then safely in Wilmington by early afternoon. He snapped back to the present scene and the need for quick action. "Look. I know where she might be." He started through the door. "We're wasting valuable time. Follow me and I'll take you. Hurry before it's too late."

"Forget the wild goose chase," the spokesman declared. "This time you're not going anywhere but to police headquarters. He unclasped his handcuffs from his belt and moved toward Pete.

Pete lifted his hands submissively, but on impulse he lunged into the officer and knocked him into the one behind him. As they toppled over one another, one detective's gun clattered to the floor behind Pete. He grabbed it and stepped on the other officer's wrist, forcing him to release his gun. Holding them at gunpoint, he ordered them into the bathroom and made them cuff themselves to the lavatory pipes and throw him the key.

"Fellows, I don't have time to play cops and robbers with you. Sorry." Those pipes wouldn't keep those officers in place long. Then the entire Riverton police force would be after him. He rushed out the door, slamming it behind him. Jumping into the Ford, he spun out of the parking lot on two wheels.

Moments later, Myra Claire drove up to the Shady Lawn and parked in front of the office. Harvey was checking out a somber, middle age couple who had been in town for a funeral. When he saw Myra Claire, he discreetly winked. The couple left and Harvey greeted Myra Claire warmly. "If you're looking for Pete, I heard him drive off in a hurry five minutes ago."

"I came to see you," she said. She told him she was leaving but wanted to thank him for arranging her accommodations at the college. "The campus is lovely and so quiet with all the students away for the summer."

"You're leaving?"

"Yes. What I came for has been accomplished. Frannie's going to be safe. She's on her way to her granny's in North Carolina where that pervert Wooten will never find her."

"That's good news," Harvey said beaming, "but Pete's going to be awful lonely without you."

Myra Claire said, "Well, you know what they say, 'Out of sight, out of mind.'"

"They also say, 'Absence makes the heart grow fonder.'"

Myra Claire forced a smile. "In this case, I'm sure it will be out of sight, out of mind."

Harvey frowned. "You two didn't have a tiff, did you?" He flexed his muscles. "Now if you need Harvey to bend some kinks out of Turner, just let me know."

"You men!" Myra Claire spewed. "You think violence is the solution to every problem."

"Uh oh," Harvey winced.

Myra Claire blushed for her unexpected burst of passion. "Sorry, Harvey. You didn't deserve that. Pete and I did have a sort of break up. No, not really a break up because there was never really a connection to break. Just a misunderstanding on my part."

"Not so," Harvey said. "He cares for you. Maybe he just doesn't know it yet."

"Maybe he did." Myra Claire said. "Like any summer romance, it's over."

At that moment the two detectives burst in the door, with handcuffs dangling from their wrists.

Looking surprised to see them again, Harvey said, "What brings you back?"

The spokesman said, "Pete Turner. We want him. You know where he is?"

"I heard him leave five minutes ago. Sounded like he was in a hurry. You just missed him."

"No, we didn't miss him. He's not only under arrest for kidnapping, but for assaulting two police officers."

"You? What did he do?"

"That's not important. If Turner comes back here, notify the police immediately."

"You said kidnapping. Who is it he's supposed to have kidnapped?" Myra Claire asked, pursing her lips and giving the officers a look that said, "You don't know what you're talking about."

"An eleven year old child."

"If you mean Frannie, Frances Gregg, she's on a bus to North Carolina," Myra Claire said, hoping this was a logical explanation for their misinformation.

"You know the girl?" the officer asked.

"Yes. Yes, I do."

"Sometime early this morning her stepmother heard her talking to Turner outside her bedroom window. Later, when she went to wake her, the girl was gone."

"Pete Turner is not your kidnapper," Myra Claire said with growing alarm. "You're looking for the wrong man. Pete has been trying to protect Frannie."

"That's right," Harvey said. "This Orville Wooten has abducted the girl twice and would have had his way with her but for Pete."

Myra Claire explained, "Wooten frequently stays at his sister's house next door to the Gregg's apartment. He lives in a trailer off Burris Road."

"If she was abducted twice, why hasn't Turner notified the police?" the lead detective asked, looking skeptical.

"I can't answer for Pete, but you need to be going after Wooten! Now! Poor Frannie! You've got to find her! Wooten has her!" Myra Claire was shaking and pale. The officers continued to stand where they were and to scrutinize her. She thought, *Pete has big business in Pennsylvania. I'm sure it has to do with his intention to harm his uncle, but he cares about Frannie. If those officers tried to arrest him for abducting her, then he knows she's missing and he's on his way to find her.*

"And Turner, you know where he is?" the officer asked.

Myra Claire huffed. She was about to say, "I can help you. I think I know where Wooten's taken her," but their skepticism of Pete's innocence cautioned her to be silent. It seemed they were more interested in catching Pete than saving Frannie. "He's not who you want. Pete did not kidnap anybody."

The officer handed her his card and gave one to Harvey. Giving Myra Claire a stern look he said, "If you hear from Turner, call us." They turned and stalked out.

Myra Claire's eyes were wide with fury and fear. She turned to Harvey, "I think I know where Frannie might be. Pete's gone after her. I'm sure of it. I'll never tell those idiots! Not until Pete can prove Wooten is the one they should be arresting. If you're a praying man, pray now!" She started out the door.

"Myra Claire, where are you going?"

"To find a pedophile."

"Not alone. I'm coming with you."

"I'll be careful. Someone needs to be here in case Pete calls."

"It's too dangerous for you to go alone. I'm coming."

Myra Claire bit her lip. "Quick, give me a piece of paper and a pen."

Harvey opened a drawer and slapped a pen and sheet of paper on the counter. "What are you thinking?"

Myra Claire said, "Let me go alone to see what I can find out. It will take me twenty or thirty minutes to get there. If you don't hear from me within the hour, send the police." She scribbled directions to Wooten's trailer and the cabin. She looked up at Harvey. "You'll need to listen carefully. Burris is a narrow, unpaved road that turns off of Highway 58. The sign is bent and you can easily miss it. Wooten's trailer is about a mile and a half down Burris and hidden in the woods about 200 feet from the road. The woods are mostly pine so if you watch for it, you can just see it through the trees. There are no other trailers or houses close by. Go past the trailer. About a mile after you pass it, Burris comes to a dead end. About 100 feet before the road ends there's a truck path on the right. You have to know it's there to find it. The entrance is hidden by branches and thick bushes. It's like looking for a needle in a hay stack. It's the way to the cabin where Wooten may have Frannie. There's a secondary path that leads to nowhere except to double back on itself. Stay on the main path. It winds deeper and deeper into the woods and eventually takes you to the cabin. It had to be the Holy Spirit that showed us the way the other day because He knew we'd need to get there now." She slid the paper toward Harvey. "You think you've got that?" Myra Claire was already backing out the door as Harvey nodded.

Looking around to make sure the officers had left, she cranked up the Buick and sped to the highway. She convinced herself that because Pete had rescued Frannie before, he'd have everything under control by the time she got there. Yet she had to know both of them were okay. How could she leave and go home without that confirmation.

The sun was out. Pete put on his dark glasses. His foot on the gas pedal took on a mind of its own, pushing to get away from Riverton and headed north before the entire Riverton police force would be looking for him. Then he forced himself to hold back. He couldn't afford to get stopped for speeding. Fearful, frustrating, confusing thoughts swirled through his mind like a raging river at flood stage.

He'd been a fugitive before, but then he was running from himself. If only Frannie could have been on that bus to North Carolina. Now he *had* to deliver the blood money. Finally, he was on his way to obtain the justice that the law had denied Mary Kate–and now this! All these years he had thought of nothing else but making Farley pay. It was what he lived for. He couldn't turn away now. The man said have the money in the well by midnight or the deal's off. These people were pro's. They meant what they said. They'd decide he was unstable, a bad risk. There would be no second chance. Not with them.

Not with Angel. Angel had befriended him, but after this, he too would consider Pete a bad risk. It might take ten years to find the right connection to take out his uncle. In the meantime, Farley would go free. He would build his speedway on the Turner land, and Mary Kate would still go unavenged. Pete slammed his fist against the steering wheel. Why was it Frannie always upset his plans?

The picture of the blonde child at the construction site rose up before him. He knew Frannie would be next if someone didn't get to her in time, and the police would never find her. The truck path to the cabin was so obscured, he and Myra Claire wouldn't have discovered it if they had not lucked out and seen Wooten emerging from the hidden road. How many children had there been before the blonde child? Surely Frannie would be next. It was too late to help the blonde child, too late to help Mary Kate, but maybe not too late to save Frannie. The truth was Mary Kate was gone and she was never coming back. Frannie might still be alive...

Wooten knew Pete and Myra Claire had discovered the cabin. He'd come upon them red handed, but Myra Claire was gone. He didn't need to worry about her. The note said Wooten had shown up while she was packing the car, and Marvin kept watch to make sure he didn't return. She should be safely on her way home.

The one thing Pete had going for him that might make the difference between Frannie's life and death was the element of surprise. Wooten believed Pete to be safely behind bars. That was Pete's trump card, and he had his gun. He surmised that Wooten didn't own a gun. He hadn't seen any at the trailer or the cabin. He remembered Wooten's expert aim with the knife when he chopped the copperhead in two. Apparently he didn't like guns or wasn't as good a marksman with a gun as he was with the knife. He would surprise Wooten and get Frannie. Then he'd turn the dirty creep over to the police...if there was still time... if it wasn't already too late. Pete hit the brakes, maneuvered a bootleg turn, and headed in the direction of Rougemont and Burris Road.

He hoped his daddy could forgive him if there was any chance he was watching. Pete hadn't believed in a heaven or a hell, although Myra Claire and Frannie, and now his brother Robert seemed so sure. Pete had heard his daddy tell his mother once when she was pestering him to go to church with her that he'd accepted Jesus as a young man. Then he said, "I'm through with religion. Don't talk to me about going to church." His daddy was an honest man, a good person. Wasn't that what counted? *And I'm neither. I have lived to have my uncle killed, to see him pay. Somehow now I wonder what was the point of it all, just a lot of loneliness and emptiness. Will doing away with Farley change that? Will it put the same light in my eyes that I see in Myra Claire and Frannie's. And, yes, even my brother Robert has it.*

Pete didn't know how to pray, but he knew how to bargain. "If You're listening, I know I'm not in any good standing with You, but I'll make a deal. Don't let anything happen to Frannie. Don't let that dirty pervert hurt her in any way, and I promise to forget about Farley." Pete caught his breath, shocked by his own words. He plunged ahead. "You save Frannie's life, and I'll give you his, even though You must know he doesn't deserve it. He can have the farm, build his speedway. I'm tired of the whole mess. Just let her live. That's all I'll ever ask of You." Pete felt a lump swell up in his throat. Then he felt this strange feeling like warm honey being poured over him. It was the most exhilarating feeling he'd ever experienced. It was like he could fly. It was even better than the high he got spinning around the race track. He cleared his throat and shot a glance toward the sky. "I'll take that as a 'yes,'" he said as he turned onto Burris Road.

Chapter Fifty-one

In the dark cramped space, Frannie realized she was gagged and bound hand and foot in the back of a moving vehicle. Still in her shorty pajamas, she was pinned in by rough boxes and tools. The rubber mat beneath her was gritty, cold, and hard. She remembered Pete tapping at her window… but it wasn't Pete. It was Wooten…with a knife. *Where is he taking me?* Her heart began to race. She could barely make her tongue form words of a prayer, but she managed to mutter inarticulate syllables the way her granny taught her to pray. The spirit helps when you don't know how to form your thoughts. That's what her granny said. It's a secret prayer that only God understands. Gradually, as she prayed, her confidence returned. God was faithful. By the time the motion ceased, she had stopped shaking. *Mr. Pete will come for me. God will send him. I know it.*

Wooten opened the back of the paneled truck and dragged Frannie out by her ankles, then dumped her on the ground. He untied her legs. She was smelling his cigarettes and his sickening cologne. That brought back the awful night in the tall grass behind the old gas station when she bit his ear, when she had run through the dark, run through prickly bushes, stumbled over old tires and broken concrete…when Mr. Pete had rescued her. Now she was in a different place. Would Mr. Pete even be able to find her? Roughly Wooten pulled her to her feet and pushed her toward the door of a small cabin.

Inside, he threw her down on the cool ground and tied her to a pole. He ripped the tape from her mouth, thinking he might learn something, like how much her parents knew and whether they had been talking to the police. He said, "Now, don't you go bitting again. I'd for sure have to kill you then set you on fire. If you just wanted to be friends, but you don't." He lit a cigarette and smoked a few minutes. "I gotta think about what I'm going do with you." He blew smoke through his nose into the air. "If you just wanted to be friends, I could let you live, but not you. You're ornery and hard to get along with."

Frannie prayed again, quietly in the spirit to push back the fear rising up in her throat, wanting to suffocate her.

Seeing her lips moving and her soft audible sounds, Wooten asked, "What'd you say? Speak up so's I can hear you."

"Not meaning to be impolite, but I'm not talking to you."

Wooten squinted as if he didn't hear her just right.

"I'm praying," Frannie said.

"Stop it," he ordered. He reached for the tape he'd pulled from her mouth. It lay on the ground. He made a half-hearted attempt to stick it back over her mouth, but it failed to hold, hanging by a corner from her chin.

"What's the matter?" Frannie said. "You afraid?"

"I ain't afraid of nothing," he said.

"Are you afraid of dying?" Frannie asked.

"I told you, I ain't afraid of nothing. And I'm not the one's going to die. It's just spooky, you praying. Nobody listening." He pulled the tape dangling from her chin and looked at it. "What's there to be afraid of?" he asked, looking away and smoking his cigarette.

"If you ask Jesus in your heart, God will forgive you for trying to hurt little kids. Then you can go to heaven. You don't want to go to hell; it's a terrible place. It's hot and dark and everybody there is screaming because they missed their chance to go to heaven when Jesus made it so easy. Just believe and ask. It's what the Bible says.

Wooten laughed. "Ain't no hell."

"Yes, there is."

"You ever seen it?"

"The Bible says so."

"Never read it."

Frannie said, "If there's no heaven and no hell, you won't lose anything by asking Jesus to save you, but what if there is? Just what if you're wrong?"

"I give you a simple choice to be friends and all I get is you preaching to me. I knew I was going to have to kill you."

"You can't kill me," Frannie said with a matter-of-fact forward thrust of her chin. "God won't let you."

"No god ever stopped me before."

"Let me go," Frannie said. "You don't have to be bad."

"Didn't I tell you I ain't bad, no worse than lot of other people? And I ain't no hypercritic like you Jesus freaks."

Frannie countered, "My granny says we are all imperfect, a work in progress, but God loves us. That's why He sent Jesus to take the punishment we deserve. He'll forgive you. He helps us to be a better person that we can be on our own."

Wooten spat on the ground. "Ain't nobody ever loved me, and I done just fine on my own."

Frannie slumped her shoulders and sighed with exasperation. "I warn you. Mr. Pete will find me. He's got a gun. He might shoot you, and then you'll go to hell." She frowned. "It will be too late," she said emphatically.

"Turner?" Wooten laughed and took a long draw from his cigarette. "He ain't coming for nobody."

"Yes he will," Frannie said.

"Now you ain't so smart as you think you are. Turner ain't coming for nobody because he's in jail. Yep, he's locked up in that Carterville jail. He's not coming for nobody."

"No. Mr. Pete's in Riverton."

"He ain't in Riverton no more. Not anymore. He's a bootlegger. He's locked up for carrying moonshine in his car. The cops got him. Caught him red handed with moonshine and locked him up." Wooten pulled the last draw on his cigarette, and with a satisfied smile, ground out the butt with the toe of his boot, the same boot Frannie recognized from the night he first attacked her.

"Mr. Pete is *not* in jail. He was in the backyard tonight when I pelted you with chinaberries."

Wooten's boot halted its motion. "What's it you're saying?" Wooten eyed Frannie curiously. "You lying girl."

Fire flashed in her brown eyes. "I don't lie!" Then she gasped, remembering a whole string of lies or half-truths she'd told in just one week. "Jesus, I know you forgive me and I'm sorry. Please help to never tell another lie."

"There you go praying again," he said, but now he wasn't looking at Frannie. He was looking toward the door and muttering to himself. "So Turner's not in jail. Back in the yard was he? Laughing at me when that brat threw those berries." He scratched the stubble on his chin and frowned. "So Turner'll come looking for the brat."

Fannie watched him pace about, talking to himself.

"What's he want with her anyway? That's a question. Will he come alone, or will he bring cops? How come he ain't gone to them before now? If he had, they'd have been knocking on my door asking me questions. That's a curious thing, that he ain't talked to them already. He's a bootlegger and I reckon bootleggers keep away from the cops, or maybe he's planning to keep this little morsel for himself. Yeah. He'll come alone. If he was going to the cops, he'd of done it before now."

He walked over to a pile of junk and debris in a corner of the cabin. Picking through it he found a roll of silver tape and a teddy bear. He turned back to Frannie. "I just wanted to be friends, but no, you wouldn't do right. Even now I was a willing to give you one more chance after you let that Turner fellow be your friend instead of me. But you had to go preaching to me." He brought the bear to Frannie and threw it down at her feet.

"That's the bear Mr. Pete won for me at the carnival. Where did you get it?"

"Found it in Turner's car when I planted the moonshine. Thought it might come in handy." Wooten rubbed his chin again. "Well, well, Turner must of talked his way out of that jail, probably bribed that sheriff. Well, I got a new plan that'll kill two with one stone and put all the blame on him. Wooten threw his head back and gave a weird, menacing laugh. He began to untie Frannie from the post.

"What are you going to do with my bear?"

He pulled her to her feet. "I'm sure I can think of something.'"

"Where are you taking me?"

"Damnation but you ask a bunch of questions, but I can fix that." He stuffed a cloth in her mouth and taped it up with fresh tape.

He pushed her out the door and around to the back where he'd parked the work truck. He re-tied her feet and lifted her into the back. Again Frannie recoiled at his closeness, his body sweat mixed with the musky cologne and tobacco.

Staring up at the dark sky, he pondered how long before Turner would find out the girl was missing. "I got no way of knowing, but sure as shootin' he'll be here. It's not daylight yet, though it won't be long. I gotta to work fast." He opened the back and pushed her in before closing the doors with a bang. To himself he muttered. "Lot a trouble this brat. Lot a trouble."

As soon as Frannie was disposed of in the rear of the truck, Wooten jumped in and drove to the trailer to get some tools. It rattled and bumped along the wheel ruts, jostling Frannie about. Tears wet her cheeks as every part of her small, cold body felt bruised. She couldn't even sob with the cloth stuffed in her mouth.

At his trailer, Wooten hurried to the flatbed truck. From it he grabbed a cardboard box filled with trash from one of his plumbing jobs. He emptied the box and filled it with several items he found in the truck bed, including a shovel, a small pulley wheel, and some netting. He counted off his list on his fingers, trying to recall everything he needed. "That Turner may be taller than me and stronger, but I got my bag of tricks." Breathing heavily, Wooten went inside the trailer and brought out a knapsack, a hammer, a handful of nails and several feet of flexible, medium wire. He threw these in the floorboard of the paneled truck. Frannie could hear and feel the banging, and her heart raced as she wondered what Wooten was doing, and if all this effort and noise had anything to do with her.

When he was sure he had everything he came for, with Frannie bouncing painfully in the back, he sped back to the cabin.

At the cabin he tossed all the items on the work table. He hustled back outside, and with the shovel, began digging and scraping away dirt from the front door until he uncovered a four by four sheet of plywood. He tugged away the plywood, exposing a pit over five feet deep. He walked around and surveyed it. "Dug this hole when that hobo was thinking to squat in my cabin. Figured if he broke a leg, he'd be warned to stay away. When he fell in, he sprained his ankle real bad. I come back to check my trap and found him. That ankle was swollen twice its size so he couldn't climb out. I didn't show any mercy when I yanked him out. Flashed my knife at him and told him 'Don't come around her again.' He ran off like his pants were on fire and I've not seen him anymore." Wooten looked around, studying the woods behind him. "Now maybe Turner will sprain his ankle, or break a leg, but what's a little pain for Turner? Before long he won't ever feel anything again."

Once the pit was uncovered, Wooten began to criss-cross pine branches over the opening, forming a net. Then he camouflaged it with smaller pine boughs and next some pine straw. "When Turner stumbles into the hole, then that will tell me he's here. Wooten looked up at the sky. "The sun's about to come up."

He went inside the cabin and began stuffing the items from the box into the knapsack. When he had all the items he needed, he hoisted the knapsack onto his shoulder and climbed onto the table, and from there onto the crude center beam that ran the length of the cabin. He edged his way to the end of it nearest the door and a crossbeam where he could balance himself and open the knapsack. He installed the pulley close to the ceiling. Once it was secure, he threaded the wire through it. Then he made his way back to the table to get the empty box and crawled back to where the pulley wire dangled. He attached an end of the wire to the bottom side of the box at the middle and balanced the box on the beam. Then he jumped to the ground and tested his booby trap, pulling on the free end of the wire. The box tilted so that when filled, its contents would spill out. This he'd done within ten minutes. Frannie's chinaberry barrage had given him the idea, only he believed his was better.

Pete was a mile from Burris Road when he saw what appeared to be a highway patrol car approaching from the opposite direction. As it came closer, he could see the black and white markings and the light on top. "It's cops alright." He cringed and sucked in his breath. They'd be looking for his '40 Ford. What had that cop said back at the motel, "You're disgusting and weird, Turner." He'd never convince them otherwise until he could prove the pedophile was Wooten. Even that didn't seem important now. He had to get to Frannie.

The cop was almost upon him. He watched, holding his breath, expecting to see the patrol car swerve around behind him. Pete bit his nail. He'd just have to play like a bootlegger and outrun him.

He breathed a sigh of relief when the patrol car sped by him. Apparently, they weren't looking for him yet.

In another mile, he turned into Burris. Wary of meeting Wooten on the road, he strained to hear the approach of another vehicle above the sound of his own motor, doubtful he could pull into the trees before Wooten saw him. However, he neither saw nor heard any sign of another vehicle. He still counted on surprising Wooten. That way apprehending him would be quick and uncomplicated.

Once he passed the trailer, he searched for the obscure opening where the wheel ruts led to the cabin. He missed it the first time. Frustrated he was going to be too late, he turned around. On the second try, he found the hidden path. He drove as close to the cabin as he dared, then pulled the Ford into the trees and out of sight. He jumped from the car and ran on foot in the direction of the cabin.

Satisfied his equipment would work, Wooten hurried outside to fill the knapsack with the heaviest and sharpest rocks he could find. When his bag was full, he shouldered it and went back to the table and up onto the beam to the pulley. Straddling the beam, he emptied the rocks into the box. Then he jumped down to the ground. To accomplish the final step in the set up, he needed to attach the dangling end of the wire to the inside top of the door. "Turner's smarter than that hobo. If he somehow manages to figure out about the hole, this will get him when he steps inside the cabin. He'll be looking for the kid when he pushes the door open. The wire attached to the door will tip the box and dump the rocks on top of him. That will disorient him until I can net him and knock him unconscious."

He hurried to the table and grabbed the hammer, but where were the nails? Impatiently, he searched the pocket of the knapsack where he remembered putting them. Instead, he found a small hole in one corner. "The nails must have fallen out," he muttered. As he started out to search the ground for them, he thought of one finishing touch. He picked the brat's stuffed bear from the floor and placed it on the ground just in front of the covered trap, so that the bear would be the first thing Turner would see when he approached the cabin. He would go for the bear, fall in the hole, and if that didn't sprain an ankle or cripple him somehow, the rock slide would catch him off guard when he entered the doorway. That should muddle him just long enough. Wooten rubbed his chin stubbles and smirked. *By the time I whack him, he won't know what hit him!*

Chapter Fifty-two

Pete spotted the cabin through the trees. It was impossible to move without snapping twigs, but since Wooten believed he was in jail, Pete hoped he wouldn't notice. Wooten would be thinking snapping twigs and rustling leaves were the normal sounds made by the woodland animals. Nevertheless, despite his impatience to get to Frannie, he tried to make as little noise as possible.

Cautiously Wooten stepped outside and looked about. His eyes roamed the surrounding trees. Satisfied Turner hadn't shown up yet, he began searching for nails that might have spilled from his knapsack. Then, the pop of a twig alerted him. He ducked behind the cabin and listened. Probably just a squirrel, but maybe not. Another pop and another. Had his company arrived? Unmistakably, he heard footsteps.

Pete edged closer to where the sunlight shone down on the grey cabin like a search beam coming through the opening in the trees. He considered what must be the awful, dirty secrets those rough walls and boarded up windows concealed. "Time to expose those secrets," Pete breathed. He wondered if he'd find the key in the crook of the tree branch and Frannie imprisoned inside. Was she even here? If Wooten was inside, he hadn't thought ahead about what he'd do next. Was Frannie even alive? He had to believe he and the Man Upstairs had made a deal. There was that feeling of warm honey. It had been so real, so exhilarating. He knew he didn't imagine it.

While he was contemplating a plan, keeping in the cover of the trees, he crept around to the back of the cabin. Nothing there but Wooten's paneled work truck. At the same time, Wooten crept to the side corner. Pete breathed in the silence with a sense of a foreboding quiet. Wooten's work demanded a shroud of silence for his evil purposes.

Sticking close to the side of the cabin, Pete pulled out his gun. He knew he was physically stronger than his adversary; that's why he had to depend on disguises and tricks, but Wooten was clever. For once, with the element of surprise, Pete believed he had the upper hand.

He moved around the side toward the front and immediately the brown bear lying on the ground caught his eye. "Frannie's bear. I know that's hers, the one we got at the carnival. He's still got the blue bow around his neck. That must mean she's been here." He moved around close enough to see the door. There was no padlock. He inched closer, ready to kick the door and rush inside. Would Frannie be tied down on the table, prepared for Wooten's butchery? He had to make himself believe she was alive. Suspense mixed with dread was choking him.

Yet, something about that bear lying there bothered him.

He ran one hand through his hair. The bear had been in his car. He remembered when he threw it there after the cop saw it in his room. Frannie didn't have it because she didn't want her parents to know she'd been to the carnival with Pete. Had she taken it from his car after Bill and Diane found out? She hadn't mentioned taking it, but Pete didn't remember seeing the bear lately. She must have taken it without telling him, but that wasn't like Frannie, or maybe she forgot to mention it. Still, it bothered him. It was too obvious, like a lure…and then it occurred to Pete, *He's expecting me!*

It hit him like a punch in the stomach. Frannie had told Wooten that Pete wasn't in jail. He knew it as well as he knew his name because she hadn't learned to keep anything to herself. So, now he had to try to figure what scheme Wooten had devised for him. It had something to do with that bear, but what? He clutched the gun tighter. His one ace in the hole was gone. Stepping back in the cover of the woods, he decided to look around, maybe find some clue while he was pondering what to do. Yet, time was of the essence. He had to think fast.

Wooten observed Pete's every move, like watching an actor play a scene. "Damnation. He is so close. What's he waiting on? Go for the bear, dummy." As Pete edged back into the trees, Wooten wondered if Turner was leaving or what.

Pete began a quick search in the woods around the cabin, trying to find some helpful clue as to what Wooten was up to and to come up with a plan. He knew that if Wooten got him trapped, there was no one coming to help him. He should have called the cops. It was foolhardy to tackle this alone. If only Frannie hadn't spilled the beans, but he knew she had.

He found nothing. He slipped around the back to the work truck, unaware Frannie was imprisoned in the back. Frannie had managed to dislodge one side of the tape covering her mouth by rubbing it against her shoulder. She tried to pray softly.

Pete opened the door on the driver's side. He didn't know what he expected to find, but it wasn't there. Frannie heard the sound of the door opening. "It's him," she whispered. "What's he going to do next?" Her heart raced. "What will happen to me now?" She kept very still, hardly breathing.

There was an inside partition separating the front of the truck from the back where Wooten kept tools and supplies. Pete crept around to the back. Frannie heard the footsteps coming around. She swallowed, hardly able to breath, dreading what Wooten had in mind to do next. Pete's hand was on the handle to open the back when he felt a sharp pain.

He bent over to see a knife blade protruding near the back of his knee bend. The pain was excruciating. He stifled a cry. Tears flooded his eyes and rolled down his face. He'd seen in the navy that injuries to the knee could make grown men cry and now he knew why. The air moved over him. He perceived the danger and instinctively pivoted on his good leg. There was a swooshing sound. He looked up to see a stout stick of wood coming down toward him. With arms extended he shielded his head as Wooten swung again. Pete's gun flew from his hand. Despite his pain, Pete scrambled to his feet to wrest the club from Wooten, but his adversary was quick and wiry. He jumped back out of Pete's reach.

There wasn't time for Pete to retrieve his gun before Wooten swung again, aiming for his wounded knee. Pete grabbed onto the piece of wood, attempting to wrench it away. They struggled. Pete anchored himself with his good leg, attempting to use the club as a brace to push Wooten to the ground, but like a cat, Wooten managed to stay on his feet. They moved as one person in a strange dance toward the front of the cabin, each man moving forward one step and backward two, neither letting go of the stick of wood. Then Pete noticed Wooten suddenly to lose concentration as he tried to glance behind him. Pete used the moment to jerk the wood from Wooten's grip. He realized Wooten wanted to avoid the space in front of the cabin. There had to be some kind of trap set. He swung at Wooten, but Wooten ducked and moved out of the way. The dance resumed, both of them trying to grab the wood and club the other, but Pete was staggering, hardly able to keep his focus. He took a deep breath. With his jaw set, he wrested control of the weapon and slammed it into Wooten's shoulder. Wooten stumbled backward, grabbing his shoulder and spewing curses.

Pete dropped to the ground. The knife in his leg was driving him to distraction. He reached down and pulled the knife out, wincing and groaning as blood gushed out in spurts. Before Pete could take aim with the knife, Wooten grabbed the stick and whacked the blade from Pete's hand. It went flying through the air and stuck in the trunk of a large tree.

Wooten swung the stick again. Pete ducked and kept limping backward out of his reach. Wooten pursued him. With each swing of the stick, Pete shielded himself with his arms as Wooten tried to edge him closer and closer to the hidden pit. Finally, Wooten got in a good swing that whacked Pete in the face. He crumpled to his knees. Wooten leaned close and raised the stick for one more whack, intending to knock Pete unconscious.

Pete saw blood pouring out from the gash in his leg. He felt he was done for. He didn't think he had the strength to stand; yet the thought of Frannie in a plastic trash bag, buried at the construction site, gave him one last surge of energy he didn't know he could muster. He stood to his feet and Wooten raised the club to strike again. Pete lunged forward and bear hugged Wooten, struggling to grab the arm holding the club while pushing Wooten backward toward the ground he was sure Wooten wanted to avoid. Suddenly Wooten screamed as his foot slipped. Pete gave a push and Wooten felt the ground give way under him.

Before Pete's astonished eyes, Wooten fell backward into the pit. By the time he could gather himself up, Pete had retrieved his gun and pointed it at Wooten.

He ordered Wooten out of the pit, watching as he hoisted himself up. Apparently, the wiry fellow hadn't broken any bones. "Now lie down on the ground and keep your hands over your head. If you move, I'll shoot."

Keeping an eye on Wooten, Pete stumbled over to pull the knife from the tree trunk. Painfully, he lowered himself to the ground and stripped off his plaid shirt. He used the knife to rip a long piece from the shirt to use as a tourniquet to wrap his leg. When he was done, he demanded, "Where's Frannie?"

"The kid's inside."

Pete took a breath. "Is she alive?"

"I haven't done anything to the br...the kid. She come of her own free will. Kid just wanted a little adventure."

Pete gave a weak laugh, trying to concentrate beyond the throbbing hurt in his shin. "Sure she did. Let's see what she has to say, and she better be okay. Now stand to your feet. You try anything funny, any sudden move and I'll love an excuse to shoot you." Pete waved the gun toward the door. "You first, and keep those hands high."

They stepped around the hole. Wooten pushed open the door, realizing his good fortune in not having gotten the opportunity to attach the wire to the box of rocks. He walked through and stood to one side. From the doorway, Pete scanned the dim room looking for Frannie. He took a step forward. As he crossed the threshold, Wooten simply reached one raised hand slightly higher and grabbed the dangling wire above the door. He gave a tug and stepped out of the way. Pete heard a strange rumble over his head. He looked up too late to prevent a rock slide from coming down on him.

While Pete was disoriented, Wooten grabbed the net he'd put near the door and threw it over him. Pete struggled to untangle himself, but Wooten grabbed a rock and slammed Pete in the head. Pete fell forward. Wooten dragged him to the work table where he bound his hands behind him and then tied him to the table leg. Next he bound his feet. "Now, Turner, you're ready to carry out my plan, and this time you're done for. No more get outa jail free cards for you."

430

Chapter Fifty-three

By now Myra Claire had memorized the landscape at the entrance to Burris Road and easily spotted the bent sign. She whipped the Buick into the turn. There was no other vehicle in sight. The way was clear. She pulled off into the trees where she and Pete had parked before, remembering how Wooten almost caught them in his trailer. Despite her tense nerves, she smiled at how they had jumped from the trailer without Wooten seeing them and had run back to the Ford like two thieves.

She hopped out of her car and dashed across the road to the cover of the pines and brush surrounding the trailer. She waited, hearing only the woodland silence. Taking a deep breath, she edged closer. "Lord, help!" she whispered. She could see the door of the trailer stood slightly ajar, as if someone had momentarily gone inside, or left in a hurry. With her heart pounding in her ears, she crept up the steps and pushed the door open another twelve inches. Creaking punctuated the eerie silence. She waited, ready to dash off before she was discovered. However, there was no other sound except the roaring in her ears. Holding the small pistol Harvey had given her, she stepped inside.

When Pete came to, the first thing he felt was the pain in his leg throbbing throughout his entire body. Then he remembered Wooten falling in the pit, the one meant for him; then, entering the cabin; the rock slide that knocked him down; the net that entangled him; then blackness. He was barely aware of the ache in his head compared to the throbbing in his leg. He was losing blood. The tight bandage he'd made from his plaid shirt was already soaked, but was probably saving his life. Saving it for what, he didn't know. In the darkened room, he realized he was bound to a leg of the work table.

"So, you had yourself a little nap, and now you got work to do."

Pete looked up to see that Wooten stood over him, holding the small kerosene lamp in one hand and Pete's gun in the other.

"What are you talking about and where's Frannie?" Pete said, struggling to compose his thoughts.

"I made a slight transfer, from my truck to the trunk of your Ford, your getaway car."

"You put Frannie in the trunk?" He strained forward, but was forced to yield to his restraints. "Get her out. She'll die of fright!"

"No, she's not dead." Wooten laughed. Then, with an evil smirk he said, "Let me remind you who's giving orders." He waved Pete's gun in his face. "We're about to take a drive."

"Where to? And what for?"

"That's more than you need to know just now. All you got to do is make sure you do what you're told if you don't want the kid hurt."

Wooten sat the lamp on the ground and cut the ropes binding Pete to the table leg.

"Now get up," Wooten ordered. He picked up the lamp and pointed toward the door.

Pete tried to stand. He bent over and grabbed the table to steady himself. What was Wooten planning? Whatever it was, he doubted it would bode well for Frannie or for him. Despite his wooziness, he knew he had to do something. If he could just think clearly, but there wasn't time for that. Impulsively, he lunged at Wooten. The lamp flew from Wooten's hand and spilled fire in a pile of trash heaped in one corner. Pete crumpled onto his knees. Wooten began cursing and dancing out the flames while keeping his eyes and the gun trained on Pete. "Could leave them here and let the fire take care of them. No. Would have to drag the brat in too before old James sees the smoke and calls for the fire trucks. Too risky."

When Wooten was satisfied he had stamped out the flames, he snarled, "Get on your feet." Pete noticed Wooten's hand, the one holding the gun, shook. He suspected Wooten didn't like guns, but he was still too weak to make another attempt to disarm him. Wooten shoved Pete out the door and toward the Ford parked behind the cabin. "Now, open the trunk."

Pete did. There lay Frannie gagged and bound. When she saw Pete, her eyes grew wide with surprise. She tried to say something, but with the gag all she could make were frustrated grunts.

Wooten chortled, "Just so you don't try anything else stupid," and closed the trunk. He directed Pete to the driver's side. "Get in."

Pete clinched his jaw, but having no other choice at the moment, he obeyed.

"Now, drive. I give directions."

"Not until you tell me where we're going."

"You do what I say, or the brat gets hurt."

Pete started up the Ford. Wooten ordered him to drive down the truck path and get onto Burris Road. "You can find that can't you?" Wooten said tauntingly.

As Pete pulled away from the cabin, he saw a piece of his shirt hanging on a bush. "How'd that get there?"

"Anyone comes around looking for the brat will see you snagged your shirt on those briars when you brought her here."

"What are you saying?" Pete demanded.

"You the one got the girl and brought her to this remote cabin to have your way with her. If the cops come asking me question, I can tell them I caught you snooping around my property a few days ago."

The Ford bumped along the ruts through the woods. When he pulled onto Burris, Wooten said, "No speeding and nothing funny or I put a bullet in your head."

What's he waiting for? Why not just kill us now? Pete wondered.

Inside the cabin, unimpeded by Wooten's hurried and distracted attempts to squash the flames in the pile of trash, one tiny spark smoldered and, in time would spark a flame. The flame would singe a piece of hemp rope close by and then burst into life, devouring scraps of straw and debris until the fire began to lick at the boards of the cabin.

Myra Claire crept through the trailer, wincing with each creaking step. She soon determined no one was there. Wooten had not hidden Frannie in the trailer. That left the cabin. For a moment she stood to collect her thoughts. There was a phone on the kitchen wall. Was this the time to call Harvey for back up? Maybe Pete had called and he had already rescued Frannie. She thought calling would be the sensible thing to do. She picked up the receiver and listened to the buzz tone a minute before hanging it up. She wouldn't call yet. If Harvey hadn't heard from Pete, she didn't want him notifying the police until Pete was clear of any suspicion. She'd told him if he didn't hear from her within the hour, he should bring the police. She had twenty minutes to check out the cabin. She walked back to the door.

Cautiously, she stepped outside and tuned her ears to the silence as her eyes scanned the landscape. Seeing nothing, she dashed through the trees and waited. Just as she was about to step into the road, she stopped herself. There was the hum of a motor. Ducking back out of sight, she watched a car approach from around the bend. It was Pete's Ford! She breathed a sigh of relief and raised her hand to flag him down, but as the car came closer, she saw there were two in the Ford.

Instinctively, she stepped back out of sight. Was it Pete with Frannie? As the car came within two feet of her, she recognized it was Pete driving, but the passenger was not Frannie. There was a glint from the sun, a flash of metal. It appeared to be... Why was a gun pointed toward Pete? She sucked in her breath, watching the Ford rumble past. Her eyes grew wide with questions. There were two in the Ford. Pete was driving, and...the passenger, pointing a gun at Pete's head, was Wooten! In retrospect she recognized his shape. It was Wooten pointing a gun at Pete! She was sure of it!

She stood momentarily watching the Ford disappear down the road and tried to digest what she'd just seen. Wooten had a gun pointed at Pete's head. He was forcing Pete to drive where? And where was Frannie? Myra Claire surmised that Wooten would not direct Pete toward town, but toward the mountains because she had no doubt he intended to kill him and dispose of his body.

She ran back to the trailer and called the Riverton Police Department. When the dispatcher put her through to the detective, Myra Claire quickly described the situation, informing him that the real pedophile had Pete at gunpoint in Pete's '40 black Ford coup. She explained that the two were headed down Burris Road, probably about to go west on Highway 58. The detective seemed reluctant to cooperate, especially when she had obviously known where Turner was headed when he left the motel and had withheld that information. Myra Claire's voice became shrill with exasperation and concern for Pete. "My father is a judge. Don't try to dismiss what I'm telling you or I'll have your badge," she threatened and slammed the phone down.

Then she called Harvey. "Pete's in trouble," she declared breathlessly. "He and Wooten just passed by in Pete's Ford and Wooten had a gun pointed at Pete. Frannie wasn't in the car. I've notified that detective that Pete and Wooten are probably headed west toward the mountains, and now I'm going to check out that cabin I told you about. Pray that I find Frannie and that she's alive. I'll let you know as soon as I find her." Before Harvey could reply, Myra Claire slammed down the phone and dashed out to her car.

On the way, she picked up the faint odor of smoke. As she turned into the truck path and drove deeper into the woods, an acrid haze floated in the air. However, she had to concentrate on her struggled to keep the Buick in the ruts. The several minutes it took to get to the cabin seemed to drag in slow motion. Upon reaching the cabin, she saw smoke seeping from under the door and from the cracks between the boarded windows. The cabin was on fire! Wooten was taking Pete somewhere at gun point, but Frannie wasn't with them. If Wooten held Pete at gunpoint, had he left Frannie in the cabin and set fire to it to cover his evil? Was this how he intended to silence her? Pete had proven to be a tenacious threat to him. Now Wooten intended to eliminate them both. There wasn't time to call for help. If Frannie was inside, Myra Claire had to get to her. Quickly she removed her blouse, doused it with water from a thermos she had with her, and covered her face and head. Then she burst through the door into the heat and smoke calling "Frannie! Frannie!"

After driving for twenty minutes, Pete could see they were leaving the Piedmont. They would soon be going up the mountain and the road would become a continuum of treacherous snake-like curves. There were numerous places in these mountains where a motorist's brakes often failed.

Pete began to get a picture of what Wooten was up to. He remembered Wooten tossing Frannie's bear on the ground near the tree line before they drove away from the cabin. What had he said? He had muttered something about the Ford being Pete's getaway car. The piece of cloth from Pete's shirt on the briar bush, his car tracks in the soft mud where Wooten had parked it behind the cabin, these were intended as circumstantial evidence to point to Pete as the pedophile!

Neither Pete nor Frannie would be alive to contradict that "evidence." His leg oozed blood and Pete felt his physical strength as well as his hope ebbing from him. Wooten had the gun, and the mountain loomed up ahead. They weren't into the curves yet. Pete calculated they had less than fifteen minutes. "But I thought we had a deal," Pete said. "I thought You agreed."

"What?" Wooten said.

"Nothing," Pete said, realizing he'd spoken out loud. He turned to Wooten. "I said you'll never get away with this. Whatever you're planning you won't get away with it."

"Just keep driving or the kid dies."

"You have no intention of letting either of us live. We know too much." Pete slammed his fist against the steering wheel and snarled, "You're a sicko, sick! You know that? You won't get away with your evil doings. The police are looking for this Ford right now."

"If they stop us, it's still a bootlegger's word against a law abiding citizen. Who's to say you didn't do it yourself. You can't prove anything. That's been your problem all along, hadn't it?" He grinned. "Once these brakes fail and you go over the side of the mountain like your daddy, well tut tut, there's not going to be anything left of you to be telling tales."

"So that's your scheme. And what about Frannie?"

"Oh, the brat. Since she's in the trunk where you put her, there won't be anything left of her either but maybe some charred bones. Just think, you'll go off in a burst of light, heat rippling through your bodies, but you probably won't know it." Wooten began to laugh hysterically, pressing the gun against Pete's temple.

Pete swallowed hard, fearing the gun might really go off. Hoping to distract him, he said, "So, how long have you been molesting little girls?"

Wooten turned toward Pete with narrowed eyes. "I just make friends. That's all."

Pete sneered. "Is that what you call what you did to that little blonde haired girl?

"How'd you know about her?" Wooten looked at Pete curiously.

"I saw you bury her at that construction site. How does a man sink so low that he can chop up a little child like a butchered animal and bury her under cement?" As soon as Pete said the words he grimaced. A sour taste came up into his mouth. He'd meant to hire a hit man to kill his uncle. He hadn't asked how it would be done nor would he have cared. If Farley had been tortured or butchered alive, Pete would have been happy to hear it. The more brutal, the better.

"So, you followed me." Wooten laughed. "She'll be covered over with concrete today. And you're never going to prove anything because you won't be around. I keep asking why you haven't talked to the cops. Maybe you had your own plans for the kid. Why you been hanging around her, taking her to the fair and all that? What business have you got in Riverton you don't want the cops snooping into?" When Pete ignored the question, Wooten said, "Your problem Turner is you stick your nose where it don't belong. You should have minded your own business and saved me all this trouble, but since you didn't you gotta pay."

"You haven't won yet. Maybe neither one of us is a very good person, but Frannie is innocent. She's never done anything to you. She doesn't deserve to be hurt."

"Bit my ear. All's I wanted was to be friends."

"Just let Frannie live."

"Can't do that," Wooten said. "Now shut up and keep driving."

Pete swallowed. "Show me what to do, not for me, but for Frannie."

"What?" Wooten demanded.

He'd spoken out loud again. He must be hallucinating. Despite the hopelessness of the situation and the disgust he felt for himself, he sensed that warm honey pour down over him again. It was the strangest sensation of peace that washed over him.

Even the throbbing pain from his wound seemed eased. Pete suddenly pressed the accelerator.

"Slow down," Wooten screamed. "I told you nothing funny. I'll kill you in a heartbeat."

"You're going to kill me anyway," Pete said, "but did you said slow down?" Pete hit the brake throwing Wooten forward so that he knocked his head against the dash. Then he hit the accelerator, flinging him backward. Holding the car in the road with one hand, Pete swung his fist into Wooten's face. Then, in one swift motion before his adversary could recover himself, Pete hit the brake, pulled the emergency handle, turned the wheel and slid the fishtailing Ford into a 180 degree bootleg turn, tossing Wooten about like a rag doll, first sideways into the door, then onto the floor. Wooten screamed curses and fired the gun. Too late to duck, Pete felt the bullet whiz by his ear. He hadn't been hit. The bullet must have missed his head by a hair's breath. Pete screeched the Ford to the side of the road and lunged for the gun. Wooten tried to stretch it beyond Pete's reach, but his wiriness did not help him in the confined space in the floorboard. With a surge of adrenalin, Pete threw himself onto Wooten, knocking the gun from his enemy's grip. It dropped on the seat. Wooten scrambled to grab it.

Wooten's hand grasped the metal handle of the gun. Pointing it at Pete, he ordered, "Get out of the car and get on the ground. Keep your hands over your head. You can join the brat in the trunk. The two of you oughta be real close back there." Wooten started up from the floor, but in the tight space, he banged his head against the dash again. In one second, Pete slammed his fist into the weasel face. He jerked Wooten's head back with one hand and snatched the gun with the other. Pete held Wooten's neck in a strangle hold. Then he slammed the handle of the gun into the back of Wooten's head, and further disoriented him.

Pete got out of the Ford and hobbled to the passenger side. Opening the door he dragged Wooten over the rough, stony ground to the back of the Ford. When he determined Wooten was conscious, he ordered him to stand to his feet.

Wooten got up, his expression now fearful. "What you going to do with me?" he whimpered.

"Now I'm giving the orders," Pete said with a snarl. "Open the trunk and carefully lift Frannie out." When Wooten complied, Pete said, "Now sit her there in that patch of grass." Wooten sat her down where Pete indicated. Then Pete put the gun to Wooten's head. "Get in the trunk." Wooten whimpered and climbed in. Pete slammed it shut. Then he went over to Frannie. Gently he pulled the tape from her mouth and removed the cloth.

For once, Frannie could barely speak. Her mouth was dry, but when she found her voice, she gasped, "Mr. Pete, I knew you'd come."

Pete said, "We'll get those ropes off soon."

"Okay," she said.

At the first service station he came to, Pete stopped and limped inside. The attendant was a skinny young man who looked like a gust of wind would blow him away, but his eyes were bright and direct. Pete said, "I need some gas and a knife to cut some rope."

The fellow reached in the pocket of his denim overalls and pulled out a pocket knife. "Will this do?"

With a nod, Pete took it and hobbled out to Frannie. The attendant followed him to fill the Ford with gas. Ignoring Wooten's panicked cries and banging on the trunk lid, Pete cut the ropes binding Frannie's wrists and ankles. He took the same rope and, opening the trunk, used it to bind Wooten's wrists and ankles. The attendant kept his eyes on the hose as if it were a common occurrence to see a child bound with ropes and a man hollering from inside the trunk. Pete followed him back inside the store. Laying a bill on the counter, he asked the attendant for a glass of water and a pack of peanut butter nabs. He took these to Frannie. It had been hours since she'd had food or water. She gulped the water down and asked for more. Pete made it back inside for a refill and while she sat in the Ford and drank the water, the skinny fellow said, "Looks like you got a bad leg there. You need to get that attended to." Pete's pants leg and tourniquet were soaked with blood. "Here let me look at that wound."

"I'd be grateful for some aspirin," Pete said.

He handed him a bottle of aspirin and another glass of water. While Pete swallowed a handful of the tablets, the attendant sat him down and cut off the blood soaked tourniquet and then ripped open the leg of his Levis to expose the wound. Pete winced at the slightest pressure. With his slender fingers, the man gently cleaned the wound with alcohol and bound it with gauze. "That's gonna require stitches. Better get to a doctor right away."

Pete thanked him. "Now I need to use your phone."

"If you're gonna call a doctor, I can get you his number."

"Thanks, but I have someone else to call first."

He pointed him to the phone on the wall at the rear of the store.

Pete dialed the Shady Lawn. He wanted to ask Harvey to call the Greggs and then the police to let them know Frannie was safe and the real pedophile was imprisoned in Pete's trunk. To Pete's chagrin, the old man answered. He told Pete that Harvey had gone.

"This is urgent. Can you tell me where I can reach him?"

"Don't know," the fellow muttered."

Pete sighed and ran his hand through his hair. He started to hang up when he heard the old fellow say, "Some cabin."

"What cabin?"

"How should I know? Cabin's all he said. That the girl was going to the cabin. He left to find her I reckon."

"What girl? Frannie?"

"No. Not her name."

Again Pete started to hang up.

"It was...Myra Claire," the man said.

"Myra Claire?"

"That's what I said."

Pete hung up, frustrated he wasn't able to talk to Harvey. The old man didn't make any sense. Why would Harvey go to find Myra Claire at Wooten's cabin when she left hours ago for home? Obviously, he didn't know what he was talking about.

Pete turned to the young man who'd been so accommodating and explained that the cries from his trunk came from a pedophile wanted by the Riverton police.

"I figured you'd made a citizen's arrest," he said.

"Yeah," Pete said with a nod and hurried outside. As he hobbled to the Ford, he pondered the old man's words. He told Frannie, "Apparently, Miss Myra Claire went to Wooten's cabin instead of going home. Somehow she must have heard you were missing. We can assume she went with the police. I guess we'll find out. Anyway, are you up to going for a ride?"

Frannie nodded.

"You're sure you're okay?"

Still munching her nabs, Frannie said, "Yes."

Pete was feeling weak in body, but in his spirit he'd could never remember feeling so elated. Realizing that with his strength and endurance greatly reduced from the throbbing knife wound, if Wooten had come up with any plan other than one that required a bootlegger's best talent, the outcome might have been very different. It gave Pete a sense of wonder to contemplate this. He remembered the deal he'd made with the Almighty, Who had certainly kept His end of the bargain. That amazed and humbled him. He had made a deal with the Almighty and got better than he deserved. The young attendant at the station had cleaned the wound and wrapped it good with a clean bandage. That had stopped the bleeding, although walking on the leg would cause it to bleed again. Even so, he was managing better than he would have thought. All the way to the cabin Pete imagined how good it would be to present Frannie safe and unharmed to Myra Claire and Harvey.

It took thirty minutes for them to reach Burris road. Driving past Wooten's trailer, he noticed the smelled of smoke. At the entrance to the truck path much of the foliage that had previously obscured it appeared mown down as if a large vehicle had ploughed through. Smoke drifted through the woods. "What's going on?" Pete said. The smell of smoke and wet wood grew stronger as they drove nearer the cabin. "Must have been a fire," Pete told Frannie. About that time a police officer approached and waved him back. Pete got out of the Ford and limped forward. "Where's the fire?" he asked.

"You need to turn back. It's a small cabin, but until the firemen get it completely out, it could spread."

Then Pete remembered the kerosene lamp and Wooten trying to stamp out the flames. And what about Myra Claire. Where was she?

Chapter Fifty-four

Pete backed the Ford down the truck path out to the road. "Where's Myra Claire?" Pete wondered aloud. "She probably left when she saw the smoke, or the cops turned her away like they did us. He pulled in behind Wooten's trailer. "Frannie, I haven't seen Myra Claire's car. She probably has left, but I want to go back to the fire." Knowing Frannie had never seen the trailer and had no frightening recollections, he said, "I hate to ask you to wait any longer. You've been through such an ordeal, but will you be okay here for about ten minutes? Will you be afraid? Wooten's safely in my trunk. He'll be with me, but if you don't want to wait here, I'll understand."

"I'm not afraid, Mr. Pete. I'll be okay."

"There's a TV inside. We can use his phone to call your daddy and Diane to let them know you're okay."

Pete went in the trailer ahead of the girl to make sure there's was nothing in there to upset her. He checked out the bathroom and advised her not to use it because it was dirty, but to go to the edge of the woods if she had to. Then he called the Greggs. Diane answered and Pete let Frannie talk to her to assure her she was well and that she'd be home in a little while. Pete expected Diane to call Bill to the phone to talk to his daughter, but she didn't.

After Pete was satisfied that Frannie was settled comfortably, he drove back to the cabin. Getting out of the Ford, one of the county officers again waved him away. "Didn't I already tell you to leave?"

"I'm looking for a friend, a young woman, but I guess she left when she saw the fire."

"You are the second man to come asking for her. We sent him away too."

"Another man came looking for her? What did he look like?"

From the officer's description Pete concluded the man was Harvey. So, Myra Claire came looking for Frannie and Harvey followed her. They saw the fire and left. Myra Claire's safe. He sighed with relief.

"Her Buick's over there." The officer pointed. "Bout two hundred feet back in the woods. Your friend was very brave. Apparently, she tried to rescue someone trapped inside."

"Her Buick? Still here? What do you mean she was brave?" Pete asked, his heart clinching in a knot.

"The man who was here looking for her ahead of you, he said she came to find a child that a pedophile had brought to this cabin."

Pete didn't try to explain about Frannie. He swallowed, "But where is she now? Are you saying she went in the burning cabin?"

Another officer called out, "Ed get him outa here. This is a possible crime scene."

"She did, but so far, no body has been recovered. Now, I have to ask you to leave. You heard the boss."

Pete groaned in agony. He closed his eyes and leaned against a tree, ignoring the officer's hand on his shoulder, encouraging him to go with Officer Jim. Myra Claire had assumed Frannie was in the cabin, and of course, when she saw the fire she went in to rescue her.

He had been so pumped up with a new kind of hope. He should have known better than to get carried away like that. Life never turned out that way. The good was always marred with the bad. In the good times, which were rare, you always waited for the other shoe to drop and it always did. Whoever said that good was supposed to triumph over evil lied. No! It's the good people like Mary Kate and Myra Claire who pay. *And I got Myra Claire into all this. Now she's dead.*

The officer put pressure on Pete's shoulder. "Which way is your car? I'm sorry for your loss, but you have to leave. Only authorized personnel can be here. If somebody died in the fire, there will be an investigation."

Pete turned to retrace his steps to the Ford. Without enthusiasm he said, "There's a man in my trunk, Orville Wooten, who's wanted by the Riverton police for abducting an eleven year old girl."

"In the trunk of your car?"

"That's right," Pete said with slumped shoulders. "Come and see." Limping, he led the officer to the Ford. "I can also prove he's a pedophile who's murdered at least one young girl. She's buried at a construction site."

Wooten, hearing voices began calling out, "Help!"

Pete opened the trunk to the sight of Wooten bound and angry as a snake.

"He did it!" Wooten screamed, leaning his head toward Pete. "He's the one burned my cabin and abducted the poor girl. Arrest him! Arrest him!"

Officer Ed glared at Wooten and said to Pete, "We can help you with this. We cooperate with the Riverton police. He called out, "Hey, Jim. Over here. How about getting this creep out of the man's trunk and take him to the jail." Glancing at Pete's leg he said, "Looks like you need to get to a doctor. We'll take care of Wooten from here. It will be our pleasure."

Officer Jim sauntered toward them.

Chapter Fifty-four

"He says his prisoner is a pedophile of interest to the Riverton police."

Wooten tried to protest his innocence, but Officer Jim released the cuffs hanging from his belt and snapped them on Wooten wrists. He pulled him from the trunk and pushed him toward a police vehicle.

In a matter of seconds, Wooten became a whimpering coward. Pete heard him crying his name. "Turner! Turner!" Pete looked around. He saw Officer Jim trying to force Wooten in the back of the police car, but Wooten was insisting on getting Pete's attention. "Turner," he called. "Let me talk to the kid. I gotta talk to her."

Pete scowled and walked toward the patrol car. "What? You want to tell her you're sorry?" Pete said with a sneer.

"I gotta talk to her. I gotta talk to her. I'm scared."

"Yeah," Pete said. "You ought to be scared. You know what inmates do to sickos like you in prison? After they castrate you, they'll hang you by your sorry neck. You won't be around long enough to ever bother her again."

"I'm scared. I'm scared," Wooten repeated. "I'm scared of hell. The kid told me about hell. I don't wanna to go to hell." He began to sob. "She said I could ask her God and He'd let me into heaven, but I ain't never talked to Him. I don't know how."

Astonished, Pete looked at Wooten. "You think the likes of you can go to heaven?"

Wooten shook his head emphatically. "The kid said so," and he continued to blubber.

Pete didn't know whether to laugh at the preposterous idea or to spit on Wooten in contempt, but then he remembered his own sins, and now added to all the others, he was responsible for Myra Claire's death. If he could have foreseen the price he would pay, if he could just go back to yesterday...The desire for revenge that drove him and so obsessed him seemed unimportant now. He looked at Wooten and felt ashamed for condemning him as disgusting as he was. He thought about

Frannie's big heart and he found himself saying in a soft and more conciliatory tone, "I'll tell her what you said. I'm sure she'll pray for you."

"You won't forget?" Wooten asked. "Tell her to talk to her God for me."

"I won't forget."

Still whimpering, Wooten allowed the officer to push him into the backseat of the patrol car. As Pete watched the car move away through the trees, he murmured, "Maybe she will pray for both of us."

The first officer, Ed, said to Pete, "Your name?"

"Turner. Pete Turner."

"What happened? How'd he end up in your trunk?"

Pete shook his head in weariness. "It's too complicated to explain right now."

"I can see you're hurt. We'll get your story later."

Pete watched the patrol car carrying Wooten pull away. He turned to the officer, "You said that her body hadn't been found. So, how do you know the woman actually went inside the cabin? If you've found no body, no remains."

"We have not found the child's remains."

"Of course you haven't," Pete said losing patience, "but what about Myra Claire?"

"You mean your brave friend who tried to rescue her? She was overcome by the smoke."

"That's what you assume since you haven't found her body," Pete said through clenched teeth. Pete looked ready to choke the officer.

"Not *her* body. The kid's. A caller reported the fire. Didn't give his name. That's how the firemen got here in time to rescue the woman before the whole structure went up in flames."

"Wait a minute," Pete said, grabbing the officer by the shoulder. "Myra Claire, the young woman who went in to rescue the child, do you mean you haven't found *her* body, or the child she tried to rescue?"

"So far we haven't found the body of the child she went in there to save. That brave young woman kept saying, 'Get Frannie. Get Frannie.'" He shook his head regretfully.

Pete clutched the officer's arm as if he feared he would escape and dash his flickering hope. "But Myra Claire, the brave one, she's alive? You say the firemen got to her in time?" "That's what I said. The firemen got to her in time. She was coughing and vomiting and saying, 'Get Frannie,' when they brought her out. She suffered smoke inhalation and some burns. The medics who took her away to the hospital say she'll survive, but it's really too bad about the kid."

Pete fell to his healthy knee. This time his groan was one of grateful relief. "There is a God," he whispered. "There is a God!"

The officer looked confused. Pete didn't take time to explain. Despite his injury he tried to run to the Ford.

An hour later, Pete and Frannie climbed the steps to the Gregg's apartment. Frannie expressed regret that they'd been unable to talk to Myra Claire at the hospital. She was sleeping and they were only able to leave flowers from the hospital gift shop.

At the top of the steps Diane opened the screen door and embraced Frannie. "I'm so sorry, Frances," she whispered. "I'm so sorry we didn't believe you."

"It's okay," the child said.

Shaking her head, Diane explained that Bill had sobbed and paced the floor all morning as soon as he realized his daughter was missing. "When Frances's grandmother called to find out why she wasn't on the bus, he wouldn't talk to her. He made me tell her we overslept and Frances missed the bus."

"But he knows she's safe now?"

Diane nodded.

"Where is he?"

"The doctor called in a sedative. He's resting."

Pete swallowed the words he wanted to say. The man was weak. Now he understood perfectly why Frannie couldn't tell him about Wooten abducting her. She wasn't protecting herself. She was trying to protect Bill from another breakdown.

Diane said, "He's worried that...he's afraid. He's wanting to know if..."

Pete sighed. "Nothing happened to Frannie, except maybe she's a little wiser. She's still innocent. Thank God. He protected her."

"Didn't I tell you, Mr. Pete?" Frannie smiled.

"You did Frannie. I wish I had your faith."

Frannie said, "You need to talk to my granny, Mr. Pete."

"Speaking of your grandmother," Diane said, "Bill thinks you should stay with her for a while, just as planned."

"You're thinking of putting her on the bus?" Pete asked.

"Bill's in no condition to drive her. I've got to take care of him."

"Of course you do," Pete said, raising an eyebrow. "I'll take her to her granny's."

"That would be a big help," Diane said. "Obviously Bill's in no condition to accept any more pressure right now."

I wonder what would happen if he weren't coddled, if he had to act like a man.

As if Diane read Pete's thoughts, she said, "The psychiatrists say that there are things from his childhood and he'll never be emotionally strong."

"My granny tells him he needs to believe the Gospel."

"Yes, your grandmother thinks that's the cure for every ill," Diane said, rolling her eyes.

"It seems it would be in everyone's best interest for me to take Frannie now. If you'll get her things, we'll get on the road."

"But your leg, Mr. Pete. You need to see the doctor."

"I have it bandaged. The bleeding's stopped. As long as I have some aspirin for pain, I can make it few more hours until I get you to Wilmington."

"Can I go in and kiss Daddy goodbye?"

"Be very quiet about it," Diane said.

Pete took her things to the Ford. He came back up the steps as Frannie hugged her stepmother. Then, wearing a big smile, as pleased as she could be to ride three hours with her special guardian angel, she followed Pete to the car. He closed her door and slid in on the driver's side.

Frannie said, "I won't get to tell Miss Myra Claire goodbye."

"She promised to see you before Christmas, didn't she? Myra Claire will keep her promise." Pete pulled onto Main Street, thinking to himself that he would come back to Riverton tomorrow and see her then, if she wanted to see him. They had not parted on friendly terms. What a stupid, blind jerk he'd been.

Chapter Fifty-five

It had been two days since Pete took Frannie to her grandma's. The sprightly old lady had appeared in her gingham apron at her cottage door with a welcoming smile and outstretched arms for her grandchild, while her piercing blue eyes gave Pete the once over. After Frannie explained all Pete had done, standing in for her real guardian angel, Granny invited him to stay for dinner. They shared bowls of her peas and beans cooked for hours with fat back and served with sweet cornbread. Pete understood why Frannie was so fond of the little lady with the grey bun and musical voice. The sense of warmth and acceptance reminded him again of warm honey flowing over him. He'd never expected to share that experience with anyone, but found himself opening up to Granny with all the details. She told him it was the Holy Spirit. She shared verses from her well-worn Bible about how Jesus died in Pete's place, redeeming him from every sin. Pete let her take his hand and lead him in the prayer of salvation. Afterward, he truly felt the burdens of a lifetime of anger and bitterness roll off his shoulders. The hours seemed to melt away in her presence, but at evening when she invited Pete to stay over, he told her he wanted to get back to Riverton and see Myra Claire at the hospital. He couldn't wait to tell her he was not the same Pete, but a new man in Christ.

He reached the hospital a few minutes before visiting hours ended at nine o'clock. When he got to Myra Claire's room, there was a different name on the door. Disconcerted, he pushed it open and looked in. Not Myra Claire, but a man occupied the bed. Pete drew back and hurried to the nurses' station to find out where they'd put his brave friend.

The duty nurse peered through her glasses at Pete and crisply informed him Miss Covington was released earlier in the day.

"Did she go home? Was she able to drive?" Pete asked with concern.

"Are you immediate family?"

"Well, no."

She folded her arms. "Well, I can tell you some of her family came for her."

Pete walked to the Ford, disappointed to have missed her. He drove non-stop to Wilkes County and with every mile he grew more convinced Myra Claire wouldn't want to see him, and he didn't blame her. With all she had figured out about him, why would she want to have anything to do with him?

He didn't go back to the Turner Farm. If not already the possession of Farley, it soon would be. Pete felt no bitterness or regret at the prospect of his uncle getting the land, and that convinced him something truly amazing had taken place in his heart. He savored this new sense of freedom, like walking on air. His life held the promise of new, good things. The only ripple was accepting the fact that he'd ended things badly with Myra Claire and missed any chance he might have had with her. From the very beginning, when he drove up to Judge Covington's house the first day he met her, he'd tried flirting in the most arrogant, insulting manner, not to forget his spouting off about law and justice. If it hadn't been for her compassionate heart for a little girl stalked by a pedophile, she would never have come to Riverton to help him. After all that had happened with his exposing her to danger and what might have been her tragic death in the fire, he couldn't expect to get the judge's approval to court her. It was best he forget Myra Claire. If he should run into her somewhere, she would be polite. She's was too classy to be rude regardless of how she felt about him. Looking back, there was a time Pete knew there had been a connection. He'd felt it, but he also knew he'd blown it.

He drove to the boarding house where Jennings lived. The landlady took him up some stairs to Jennings's room and knocked on the door. When Jennings opened it, his face expressed shock at seeing Pete standing in front of him. The landlady excused herself, and Jennings immediately plied Pete with questions. Finally Pete said, "Are you going to keep me standing here in the hall all night?"

Jennings showed Pete into his small apartment. It was fairly neat for a bachelor with a sofa, a television, and a single bed in one corner. On the wall were picture posters of local bootleggers like Millard Ashley, Willie Clay Call, and Junior Johnson, who had made a name for themselves at the local race tracks, then on to the larger ones. Pete smiled that there was no picture of Bennie Farnes. When Jennings resumed asking his questions, Pete said, "I need rest. We can talk tomorrow. I'll sleep on the floor. Just throw me a pillow if you have one."

Motioning to the couch, Jennings handed Pete a pillow and said, "There's something you'll want to know. Rumor has it that Farley is dying."

"What did you say?" Pete froze on the inside. Had the job been carried out anyway? He'd set the wheels in motion, although he'd never paid the blood money. Could Angel have advanced the blood money to the hit man after all?

"The word is that Farley is dying."

"What happened?"

"I don't know. I just heard it a few days ago from Charlie, but he didn't know no details."

Pete fell onto the couch. "Did I have something to do with it?"

"I don't know. Did you?"

"I wanted him dead. You knew that, but I didn't pay the blood money, because..." Pete swallowed. "I made a bargain with the Almighty, Farley's life for Frannie's."

"Who in the heck is Frannie."

"It's a long story. Let's just say Frannie was divine intervention. I didn't pay the blood money all because of her. I've become a Christian."

"You mean you got religion?" Jennings looked skeptical.

"It's not like that." Pete leaned back and closed his eyes. "We'll talk tomorrow. I didn't pay the blood money."

Jennings shook his head like he didn't believe what he'd just heard. "Like you said, "we can talk tomorrow."

Pete's last whisper was "I've been forgiven, but maybe I still have to pay for all the years I've hated Farley. Doesn't the Bible say you reap what you sow?"

It was the middle of the afternoon on Wednesday before Pete woke up feeling groggy and disoriented. He opened his eyes and slowly recalled sleeping on the couch where Jennings boarded. He checked his watch, seeing he'd slept more than twelve hours. Then he remembered the restless misery before he finally drifted into sleep. After that, fitful dreams tormented him. In a recurring scene, he saw Farley emerge from the door of the Turner farmhouse just as Pete remembered him on the day of Mary Kate's funeral. Many times in the past, Pete imagined himself shooting Farley and watching him fall dead and roll down the porch steps, but in this dream, a hit man hidden in a copse of trees was aiming a rifle at his uncle. With all Pete's strength he ran toward his uncle, trying desperately to reach him and shouting, "Down! Get down!" but Farley couldn't hear him over the sound of the rifle shot. Pete could only watch helplessly as red blood oozed from Farley's chest. Then he would wake up in a sweat, knowing he was as guilty as if he'd pulled the trigger himself.

He got off the couch. There was no sign of Jennings. He'd gone to work at the still. Pete found a coffee pot and brewed a strong cup. Then he called his brother. Robert insisted he come for dinner in the evening and meet his family. If Robert knew Pete had planned Farley's death, would he welcome him into his home? Pete didn't know how to tell Robert "no," so reluctantly he accepted. Besides, he might need his brother's services as a criminal defense attorney for solicitation of murder for hire.

By eight o'clock, the sun had gone down and the late August evening carried a hint of fall with the temperature dropping into the 60s. On the back screened porch Pete paced nervously, waiting for Robert to come out and join him. He'd met the family, played with five year old Bradley and seven year old Julia. Then he'd stuffed himself with Jessica's baked spaghetti and yeast rolls. Now Robert was helping get the children to bed and Pete dreaded what he was about to disclose to his brother.

In an attempt to appear relaxed, he sat down one more time in the cushioned wicker arm chair and took a drink of his coffee. Robert seemed genuinely happy about Pete's recent conversion. He'd found a moment to share that with Robert before dinner. He was eager to share it, but he wondered when he told his brother about his contact with the hit man, would Robert believe Pete's conversion was real, or an attempt to get sympathy? Pete knew something different had happened inside him, but he couldn't just expect to forget all the years he'd thought of nothing but how to get his revenge on his arrogant, prosperous uncle. It had galled him every moment of every day of the last ten years that Farley had escaped his crimes without even a slight tarnish to his reputation. Now, Pete realized he, not Farley, had been the one to suffer. He had been the one to drink of the poison cup of unforgiveness, and now it was too late. Farley was dying and Pete couldn't undo it. He deserved to be punished. Maybe it was wrong to even ask Robert to defend him.

He looked up as Robert moved his son's toy scooter out of the way with one hand and sat his coffee cup on a side table with the other.

Robert sat down in a cushioned seat and gave a contented sigh. "We finally got the children settled down and in bed. Bradley didn't want to go to bed. He wanted his uncle Pete to swing him up in the air again, but Jessica told him he'd worn you out for tonight."

Pete said, "You've done all right for yourself, Robert. This is a nice house and you have a beautiful family. That sure was a good meal Jessica fixed, the best spaghetti and yeast rolls. We didn't very often have spaghetti on the farm, and if we did, it was Franco American out of a can."

"If it weren't for the Lord, I would have lost it all," Robert said with misting eyes. He's done more for me than I could ever have done for myself, and now, little brother, you're a believer too. I'm thankful Frannie's grandmother led you to accept Jesus as your Lord and Savior. Now you need to get in a good Bible-believing church and learn what that means. You need to find a good church where you get good teaching and fellowship with mature Christians who can help you in your walk with the Lord, where you can be accountable. Why don't you come to New Zion with us?"

Pete cleared his throat, thinking church people would not want a felon in their midst. "I have somethings to settle first, something I have to tell you."

Robert gave Pete a puzzled look. "Okay. If it's about the farm, you haven't asked about the farm. I thought you would ask first thing if Farley had signed those papers."

Pete swallowed. He couldn't breathe. His hands shook so uncontrollably he dared not lift his coffee cup for fear he'd drop it as he waited for Robert's next words. "I know he's dying." Pete's words tumbled out with no more hope than a condemned man.

"So you've heard," Robert said with a frown. "That's why he was so long in Mexico. He went to get some treatment that's not approved in this country. You know, like some of those movie stars have done. However, it didn't work. He could die any time."

"Treatment?" Pete asked, confusion written all over his face.

"For the cancer," Robert said.

"Cancer?" Pete repeated, unsure his ears weren't playing tricks.

"Yes," Robert said, taking a sip from his cup.

Pete relaxed all over and quietly released a long breath. He hadn't killed his uncle! He had a habit of expecting bad, but now that he had a Savior, he met amazing grace every time he turned around. Once again he had received a blessing he didn't expect or deserve. Gratefulness filled him to overflowing. He wanted to shout, but instead he said with controlled emotion, "I have to see Farley before he dies. I want to tell him I forgive him. It's what I have to do."

"He's in a private room at Baptist Hospital in Winston. Since you're family, they'll let you see him briefly. He's not doing well."

Both of them sat quietly for a few minutes as they pondered the enormity of what lay in Farley's future. Then Robert broke the somber mood and said, "I ran into Myra Claire Covington downtown yesterday afternoon. She was helping the judge out of the car to take him for a routine doctor's appointment. She asked about you. I didn't know that you and she were friends."

"She asked about me?" Pete said, trying to sound matter-of-fact.

"Yeah." Robert said, tilting his head, expecting further explanation.

"Myra Claire came to Riverton," Pete said.

"You never mentioned her when you told me about saving that little girl from the pedophile. So how did you meet her?" "I met her in Charlie's before going to Riverton. I asked her to come. When I told you the Riverton story, I left out the part about Myra Claire."

"Tell me now, the part you left out," Robert said with a raised eyebrow.

Pete shared the entire story of the Riverton episode, sticking to the facts, but leaving out the intense feelings he had developed for Myra Claire and how he'd ruined any chance he would ever have with her. Pete ran his hand through his hair. "I had a lot of nerve to involve her in a dangerous situation like that. It was selfish. I was only thinking of how she could help me. Then she was in the fire. She could have died. It would have been my fault. I don't even like to think about it."

Robert shook his head in amazement. "I never realized you were so driven by hate for Farley. That explains why you left home and never contacted your family, why you didn't come to Momma's funeral. Thank God, He's rescued you from all that. As for Myra Claire, she's a grown woman and quite level headed. She made the decision to go to Riverton and get involved in helping that child. Little brother, when are you going to stop blaming yourself for situations outside your control?"

"When I stop causing hurt to people I care for because of my selfishness and negligence."

"Pete, Myra Claire came to Riverton of her own free will. She chose to go into that burning cabin after the girl. Stop letting the devil put you under condemnation. You've blamed yourself for Mary Kate's suffering all these years. Now you want to blame yourself for what happened to Myra Claire, but what good has it done you? Jesus paid the price for your guilt and failures. Accept what He did for you on the cross and receive His mercy and grace. He died to make you free. Enjoy the freedom and stop condemning yourself."

Pete sipped his tea and made no comment, trying to absorb what Robert had said. Would Myra Claire see it that way? Could he hope there was still a chance for a new beginning with her?

"Since Myra Claire asked about you, why not give her a call. You can at least be friends, and come to church. She'll be there."

"Maybe," Pete said. There was still something he had to do to truly put the past behind him and that was to see Farley. What a wonderful opportunity to be God's instrument to pull a man back from the brink of hell. He would share his testimony and see Farley saved. God's Son had died to set him free and now he had the amazing opportunity to share that good news with someone else.

Chapter Fifty-six

The usual lunch crowd and a few truck drivers passing down Highway 21 filled Charlie's Diner. Charlie perspired over the grill and Jimmy Garner wiped tables and worked the cash register. Pete sat at the counter drinking Charlie's popular sweet tea, almost a punch with the frozen lemonade he added to it. "Hud," four seats from Pete at the end of the counter, hunched over a newspaper and smoked and coughed. Chris Riley chomped down on a chopped barbecue sandwich, and lanky Johnny Purdue ambled in and took a seat beside him. He turned to Pete, "Ain't seen you at Billy Hinton's cow pasture since you beat Bennie Farnes at Hillsboro. Where you been racin'?"

"Nowhere," Pete said.

Sheriff Money and Deputy Lance Ward strolled in, taking the two of the four empty stools. When Charlie turned around to get burgers from the cooler, he saw the sheriff and whispered to Jimmy. "He's gonna want that barbecue with 'no fat.' I'm starting to feel bad about it. One of these days I've got to quit that joke before I kill him with a heart attack, but I reckon he'll complain if I don't make his barbecue the same."

"Hey, Sheriff," Johnny Purdue said. "What's the word on Bennie Farnes? We heard he shot some fellow over a woman, Judy Smith, won't it? She sure ain't no looker. Don't see why he'd fight over her. Was he drunk when he shot him?"

Jimmy, all ears, swiped the cloth over the counter, rubbing it enough to wear a hole in it.

"Now, John, you know I can't say nothing 'bout a case under investigation. He put his elbows on the counter. "Charlie, gimme that barbecue sandwich. No fat."

"Hud" looked up from his newspaper. "Farnes done it all right. I know the fellow he shot, Tom Willis, kin to my wife. He's in Baptist Hospital with a wound in his side, but he didn't hit no vital organs. He'll be okay, lucky for Bennie." He turned to Pete. "He's been sore ever since you beat him at the dirt track. Probably why he got so mad that he shot Willis."

"Awe, he's a hothead anyhow," Purdue allowed. "You ain't been at the tracks since you beat Farnes. Where you been racing Pete?"

"Nowhere," Pete said.

"We ain't seen you around. What you been up to?" Purdue said.

"Staying out of trouble," Pete said with a grin.

"You sure?" Money asked. "Not up there in them hills making moonshine, are you, boy?"

"No, I'm finished with the whiskey business," Pete said.

Money looked at Pete. Now you ain't lying, thinking you kin throw me off? Because I know you Turners. You been shiners since before you settled here and you always gonna be shiners, but we'll get you eventually, you and your uncle Jake."

"No, Sheriff. I can't speak for Uncle Jake, but I'm finished with it. I'm a Christian now."

The entire diner became a still frame from a silent movie. The only sound was the sizzle from the grill. The sheriff stared at Pete, quizzically, eyeball to eyeball. After a minute he said, "You telling us you got religion."

"Not religion. I've got Jesus."

Somebody cleared his throat.

The sheriff pondered Pete's statement then asked. "You gonna be crazy like your momma?"

"Depends on your definition of crazy," Pete said, "To be misguided like my momma in some of her doctrine is better than being lost and going to hell like I was. She still believed Jesus took her sins and died on the cross for her. She was saved and she's in heaven now."

At that declaration, all movement and sound resumed. Pete knew they'd all heard the Gospel before. It was old news, not good news to them. It just hadn't penetrated their hearts.

"So, what you gonna do, farm?"

"Not interested in farming," Pete said.

"That's right. You a college boy," Lance said. "You gonna try to be a lawyer like your brother?"

"No," Pete said. "I got some ideas. We'll see."

"So if you ain't been making moonshine and you ain't been racing, where you been keeping yourself?" Chris Riley said. "You been hiding from Bennie Farnes," he laughed, "because he was sure sore at you beating him. He might of shot you instead a Tom Willis if you'd been around."

Pete hesitated to say he'd been in Riverton. A few days ago it was essential, he believed, to keep his whereabouts a secret. He breathed a sigh as the sense of freedom rushed over him and brought tears to his eyes. No more need to keep secrets. He hadn't paid the blood money. Farley's dying was none of his doing. He thanked God for that! "Riverton. I've been in Riverton visiting a friend."

"Riverton," Riley echoed. "Ain't Riverton near the Dodd River?"

"Yeah," Sheriff Money said. "It's on the Dodd River."

"Ain't that where I read in the paper that they fished out that Italian's body?" Riley asked.

"That's the place," "Hud" said.

"What Italian?" Pete said.

Riley said, "Since you wasn't aroun'," you wouldn't know. If you'd a seen him, you'd a remembered, short, pudgy little Italian, drove aroun' in a big shiny Cadillac. He ate here at Charlie's a few times. I heard him say he come from New York. If you was here, you couldn't of helped but notice his fancy clothes. I reckon them shoes he wore was real alleygater."

Without looking up, Sheriff Money said, "He was here checking out the area for a client of his. Come to my office and told me so. Said he was in real estate and his client was thinking of starting a business here. Might have liked it so well in Wilkes, he would of settled here himself."

"Reckon he won't be coming now," Lance speculated.

"He sure wanted to meet your fine uncle," the sheriff said. "Too bad about the cancer."

"So, what happened to him, to the Italian?" Pete said.

"Guess you ain't read the papers," Purdue said. "He drowned somewheres near Riverton. The paper said authorities think he hit his head when he fell from a pier or dock. Not hard enough to kill him, but maybe he couldn't swim. Paper said they don't think foul play was involved, but guess they'll never know."

"Is that so?" Pete said rubbing his chin. Then he looked at his watch and stood up.

It was time Myra Claire stopped by to pick up barbecue for the judge. She came on Saturday now that she was back in school Charlie had told him. He put some money on the counter for his tea and walked back to the screened door. For a moment he stopped by the table where he remembered Wooten sitting with the little blonde girl. *I knew then she was afraid. You can smell evil, especially when you're as familiar with it as I was. Thank God Frannie didn't end up the same way.* It was strange to contemplate these events so fresh, yet a lifetime ago. He had a new life now and there was someone he hoped to share it with. He pushed open the screen and the bright sunlight reflected off the red hair that reminded him of tongues of fire, friendly fire, he hoped. The piercing green eyes flashed recognition and Myra smiled, "Pete?"

"I was waiting for you."

"You were?"

"That day you were cutting grass, I asked you to go to a movie. How about tonight?"

With a twinkle she pretended to think over the invitation. "I suppose I know you well enough to accept."

"I'll pick you up at seven."

Later that evening after the movie, which Pete hardly remembered because she let him hold her hand, they stopped by Charlie's Diner when they saw a light on. "He's in the back probably cooking a fresh ham for next week's barbecue," Pete said. They went in the back way and sure enough Charlie was taking a ham from the oven. Pete and Myra Claire sat down at the counter. Charlie left the door between the kitchen and the serving area open so he could hear, although Pete was completely focused on Myra Claire.

Pete related how he took Frannie to her granny's and how he prayed the prayer of salvation with the dear little lady. "I'm a new man. I feel new on the inside."

Myra Claire smiled and reached for his hand.

Charlie cleared his throat. "I'm getting ready to lock up."

"We're leaving. Go home Charlie. We just stopped in because your light was on and we wanted thank you."

"For what?" Charlie said.

"For being here, I guess," Pete said. "The first time I saw Myra Claire was here. She was coming in to get the judge's barbecue. If you didn't make the best barbecue in two counties, I might never have met her."

Charlie grinned. "I'm glad that's why you came by. The last time I had to patch you up."

Pete and Myra Claire stood up. Pete shook Charlie's hand and Myra Claire gave him a hug. Then Pete took Myra

Claire's hand and led her to the Ford. He drove to the judge's yellow house at the top of the hill and around the circle driveway, stopping near a lamppost that cast a circle of light over them. The porch light burned and one light shone in the living room window.

Pete turned to Myra Claire. "I went to see my uncle Farley. He's been released from the hospital. He wants to die at home. It was strange, almost eerie. James Connolly, his faithful caretaker came out to let me inside when I announced myself through the intercom. Farley said he plans to leave him a substantial part of his accumulated wealth. The rest he will leave to his siblings. He thinks his good works and the good name he leaves behind will matter somehow in the larger scheme of things." Pete spoke with emotion, "I wanted him dead. Little did I know even then that he was dying. To think how near I came to hiring someone to kill a dead man." Pete shook his head. "I could have gone to prison."

"Why did you go to see him?"

"To share my testimony. I told him I had forgiven him for hurting Mary Kate and for whatever part he had in her death, whether direct or indirect. I'll always believe he had her killed and made it look like suicide. He didn't deny it. In fact, I am sure he wanted me to think so. At the time there was only a sham investigation by Money's father-in-law."

"What happened when you shared your testimony? Was there any sign of repentance?"

"It was shocking to see this once tall, imposing statue of a man reduced to a skeleton. His skin was wrinkled and yellow, just a thin covering over bone. His eyes were sunken in the sockets. His yellowed teeth appeared prominent in a face so skeletal it was macabre. Death is evil, even though people try to glorify it."

Myra Claire said, "Death, according to the Bible, is the last enemy to be put under foot."

Pete said, "Farley may have lost his health but not his arrogance. He laughed at me though he could hardly draw a breath. How does a man face death without Jesus? Yet, I would have. Now I don't understand how in his condition he could sneer at my testimony. I thought I would lead him in a prayer of salvation, but he wanted no part of it. I think despite his sneering and arrogance, he's furious at God for the cancer. I tried to tell him God didn't put the cancer on him, that God is good. When I said that, he told me to get out. I thought I would see him gasp his last breath then he was so angry."

Myra took Pete's hand. "You did your part. You're not responsible for his response."

"I know. I'm beginning to understand God's free gift of grace. It's so amazing that we don't, *can't* earn it. All we can do is receive it and enjoy it! Even a creep like Wooten is made in God's image. When I last saw him, when the officers were trying to put him in the patrol car, he called for me. Said he needed to talk to Frannie."

"To Frannie?"

"Yeah. Said he was afraid of hell. That Frannie!" Pete shook his head. "Witnessing to him, worrying about his salvation, the man who was abducting her with every intention of killing her. He said to tell her to talk to her God for him."

"Did you?"

"Honestly, I forgot to mention it to her."

"Frannie has already laid the foundation. If he truly wants to accept Jesus, I'll drive to Riverton to see him."

"I'll go with you," Pete said.

Myra Claire nodded her approval.

Pete's eyes smiled. He'd never known such freedom and approval as he felt from his heavenly Father, not even from his earthly father who in Pete's eyes was still the man he most admired. "So, the farm is mine," he said, "and I want you to know I'm finished with the whiskey business."

"What will you do? The whiskey business is really all you know."

"Well, Pete said, nervously tapping the steering wheel. "I thought the Turner land would be a great place for a Christian retreat and summer kids' camp, but like you said, all I really know is the whiskey business."

"You would need a helper," she said.

"Yeah, a wife."

"Did you have someone in mind?" Myra Claire asked.

"You bet I do," he said with a crooked grin. He took a deep breath. "If she was okay with it, I was thinking of seeing the judge tomorrow to get his permission to ask for her hand."

"The judge is inside. He's still awake."

"Is that like a "yes," he said, reaching for her.

Myra Claire's eyes glistened with tears. "You are a changed man, Pete. I knew the old Pete, and the transformation is amazing, amazing grace."

Acknowledgments

B efore I ever imagined I would write a novel, my pastor, Stan Grant, told a story in one of his sermons that made a lasting impression on me. When I decided to write *The Poison Cup*, I knew from the start that I would draw my theme from his true account of how a man's unforgiveness nearly destroyed him.

I owe a big debt of gratitude to Greg Smith of Agile Writers. It was my association with him and his Agile Writers method that gave me the impetus to begin.

I happily acknowledge and thank my husband, Spencer. Without his support I would never have believed in myself. Once I decided that my story would be set in the moonshine country of the Appalachian foothills near where he grew up, he proved to be a rich source of information. A few of my minor characters I drew from people he knew. Some humorous comments made by my character, Charlie Ross, were inspired by words reputed to have been spoken by my father-in-law, Floyd Davis, Sr., and the Crossroads Diner was a picture of *Davis Esso Lunch*, a place where I often watched Mr. Davis at the grill. However, all characters were a work of fiction.

Other sources of my research for the setting and the moonshiners were Jack Henderson, a former sheriff in the area at the time of the story, and Ronnie Hanes who had relatives that were bootleggers.

Ed Beck, who raced the dirt tracks in those times, told me mesmerizing stories. He and his wife, Beverly, took Spencer and me to a dirt track race in Potomac, Maryland so that I could experience the noise and get into the spirit of the actual event!

Gail Strother spent many hours editing the manuscript and marking my overabundance of em dashes.

My son, Bret, also edited the manuscript. When my talented daughter-in-law, Becky, designed the cover, he watched their four children.

I sincerely appreciate the interest and encouragement along the way from my good friends Gail Strother, Elizabeth Huffman, Betty Van Sickle, and Carol Smithson. Thanks. It meant a lot.

Last, but certainly not least, I thank those at Xulon Press who turned my manuscript into a book. Thank you Michelle Gill for selling me on Xulon; Thank you, Jennifer Kasper, my project coordinator, for your patience. It has been a pleasure to work with you.

CPSIA information can be obtained
at www.ICGtesting.com
Printed in the USA
LVOW08s1003301117

558025LV00009B/304/P